The Shrieking Pit

By Arthur J. Rees

Originally published in 1918

The Shrieking Pit

Published by Intrepid Ink, LLC

Intrepid Ink, LLC provides full publishing services to authors of fiction and non-fiction books, eBooks and websites. From editing to formatting, to publishing, to marketing, Intrepid Ink gets your creative works into the hands of the people who want to read them.
Find out more at www.IntrepidInk.com.

ISBN 10: 0-9843857-9-7
ISBN 13: 978-0-9843857-9-9

Printed in the United States of America

FOREWORD

The Norfolk coast was still a remote place at the start of the twentieth century. Bordering on the North Sea, it was exposed to violent storms and consisted mostly of marshland and isolated villages, with a rustic population speaking a language only vaguely recognizable as English.

It is a region with a long and checkered history. It's marshes have served as a refuge for rebels and criminals from Norman times, while its wild and lightly peopled coast as served as a favorite route for smugglers, spies, and would be invaders. Farther back in time, prehistoric peoples lived off the sea and mined the deposits of flint such as the pit that gives this novel it's name.

All this provides a suitably atmospheric backdrop for Arthur J. Rees's tale of murder and deception. It is set in the year 1916, with World War I looming in the distance and occasionally intruding much closer to home with Zeppelin raids and German naval forays along the coast.

As the war turned into a stalemate in France, shell-shock became all too common wit front line soldiers. Known as "battle fatigue" during World War II and now called PTSD or "Post Traumatic Stress Disorder" it is the inevitable result of solders fighting too long under horrific conditions while watching their friends and comrades die all around them.

While it has probably been around as long as there has been war, it was only with World War I that it was treated as an actual medical condition and not just cowardice or a defect of character. Still, there was a stigma attached to it, particularly by people who had not had firsthand experience with war. The medical and psychiatric establishments were not unified in their opinion of shell-shock, nor were the upper levels of the military who saw it draining away men just when they were needed the most. It is not surprising then the young James Ronald Penreath should feel a certain degree of guilt that he has been invalided out of the army with shell-shock.

In The Shrieking Pit, Rees raises some interesting questions about the validity and accuracy of the medical diagnosis of psychiatric disorders. He also makes some observations about the police and the courts and their willingness to accept the fact that a mistake has been made. I think these points add some extra dimensions to what is already a good story, which I hope you will enjoy.

About the Author
Arthur J. Rees (Arthur John) 1872-1942, was born in Australia worked as a newspaper man before moving to England in his twenties. He wrote numerous mystery novels starting with The Merry Marauders in 1913. Other works include The Hand in the Dark (1920) and The Moon Rock (1922). His last book, The Single Clue was published in 1940 shortly before his death. He collaborated with John R. Watson on two novels, The Hampstead Mystery (1916), and The Mystery of the Downs (1928).

Greg Fowlkes
Editor-In-Chief
Resurrected Press

To My Sisters in Australia, Annie and Frances

The sea beats in at Blakeney–
Beats wild and waste at Blakeney;
O'er ruined quay and cobbled street,
O'er broken masts of fisher fleet,
Which go no more to sea.

The bitter pools at ebb-tide lie,
In barren sands at Blakeney;
Green, grey and green the marshes creep,
To where the grey north waters leap
By dead and silent Blakeney.

And Time is dead at Blakeney–
In old, forgotten Blakeney;
What care they for Time's Scythe or Glass;
Who do not feel the hours pass,
Who sleep in sea-worn Blakeney?

By the old grey church in Blakeney,
By quenched turret light in Blakeney,
They slumber deep, they do not know,
If Life's told tale is Death and Woe;
Through all eternity.

But Love still lives at Blakeney,
'Tis graven deep at Blakeney;
Of Love which seeks beyond the grave,
Of Love's sad faith which fain would save–
The headstones tell the story.

Grave-grasses grow at Blakeney
Sea pansies, sedge, and rosemary;
Frail fronds thrust forth in dim dank air,
A message from those lying there:
Wan leaves of memory.

I send you this from Blakeney—
From distant, dreaming Blakeney;
Love and Remembrance: These are sure;
Though Death is strong they shall endure,
Till all things cease to be.

A. J. R.

PREFACE

As the scenes of this story are laid in a part of Norfolk which will be readily identified by many Norfolk people, it is perhaps well to state that all the personages are fictitious, and that the Norfolk police officials who appear in the book have no existence outside these pages.

They and the other characters are drawn entirely from imagination.

To East Anglian readers I offer my apologies for any faults there may be in reproducing the Norfolk dialect. My excuse is the fascination the language produced on myself, and that it is as essential to the scene of the story as the marshes and the sea. Though I have found it impossible to transliterate the pronunciation into the ordinary English alphabet, I hope I have been able to convey enough of the characteristic speech of the native to enable those familiar with it to put it for themselves into the accents of their own people. To those who are not familiar with the dialect, I can only say, "Go and study this relic of old English in that remote part of the country where the story is laid, where the ghosts of a ruined past mingle with the primitive survivors of to-day, who walk very near the unseen."

A. J. R.
LONDON

1

Colwyn had never seen anything quite so eccentric in a public room as the behaviour of the young man breakfasting alone at the alcove table in the bay embrasure, and he became so absorbed in watching him that he permitted his own meal to grow cold, impatiently waving away the waiter who sought with obtrusive obsequiousness to recall his wandering attention by thrusting the menu card before him. To outward seeming the occupant of the alcove table was a good-looking young man, whose clear blue eyes, tanned skin and well-knit frame indicated the truly national product of common sense, cold water, and out-of-door pursuits; of a wholesomely English if not markedly intellectual type, pleasant to look at, and unmistakably of good birth and breeding. When a young man of this description, your fellow guest at a fashionable seaside hotel, who had been in the habit of giving you a courteous nod on his morning journey across the archipelago of snowy-topped tables under the convoy of the head waiter to his own table, comes in to breakfast with shaking hands, flushed face, and passes your table with unseeing eyes, you would probably conclude that he was under the influence of liquor, and in your English way you would severely blame him, not so much for the moral turpitude involved in his excess as for the bad taste, which prompted him to show himself in public in such a condition. If, on reaching his place, the young man's conduct took the additional extravagant form of picking up a table-knife and sticking it into the table in front of him, you would probably enlarge your previous conclusion by admitting the hypotheses of drugs or dementia to account for such remarkable behaviour.

All these things were done by the young man at the alcove table in the breakfast room of the Grand Hotel, Durrington, on an October morning in the year 1916; but Colwyn, who was only half an Englishman, and, moreover, had an original mind, did not attribute them to drink, morphia, or madness. Colwyn flattered himself that he knew the outward signs of these diseases too well to be deceived into thinking that the splendid specimen of young physical manhood at the far table was the victim of any of them. His own impression was that it was a case of shell-shock. It was true that, apart from the doubtful evidence of a bronzed skin and upright frame, there was nothing about him to suggest that he had been a soldier: no service lapel or regimental badge in his grey Norfolk jacket. But an Englishman of his class would be hardly likely to wear either once he had left the Army. It was almost certain that he must have seen service in the war, and by no means improbable that he had been bowled over by shell-shock, like many thousands more of equally splendid specimens of young manhood. Any other conclusion to account for the strange condition of a young man like him seemed unworthy and repellent.

"It *must* be shell-shock, and a very bad case–probably supposed to be cured, and sent up here to recuperate," thought Colwyn. "I'll keep an eye on him."

As Colwyn resumed his breakfast it occurred to him that some of the other guests might have been alarmed by the young man's behaviour, and he cast his eyes round the room to see if anybody else had noticed him.

There were about thirty guests in the big breakfast apartment, which had been built to accommodate five times the number–a charming, luxuriously furnished place, with massive white pillars supporting a frescoed ceiling, and lighted by numerous bay windows opening on to the North Sea, which was sparkling brightly in a brilliant October sunshine. The thirty people comprised the whole of the hotel visitors, for in the year 1916 holiday seekers preferred some safer resort than a part of the Norfolk coast which lay in the track of enemy airships seeking a way to London.

Two nights before a Zeppelin had dropped a couple of bombs on the Durrington front, and the majority of hotel visitors had departed by the next morning's train, disregarding the proprietor's assurance that the affair was a pure accident, a German oversight which was not likely to happen again. Off the nervous ones went, and left the big hotel, the long curved seafront, the miles of yellow sand, the high green headlands, the best golf-links in the East of England, and all the other attractions mentioned in the hotel advertisements, to a handful of people, who were too nerve-proof, lazy, fatalistic, or indifferent to bother about Zeppelins.

These thirty guests, scattered far and wide over the spacious isolation of the breakfast-room, in twos and threes, and little groups, seemed, with one exception, too engrossed in the solemn British rite of beginning the day well with a good breakfast to bother their heads about the conduct of the young man at the alcove table. They were, for the most part, characteristic war-time holiday-makers: the men, obviously above military age, in Norfolk tweeds or golf suits; two young officers at a table by the window, and—as indifference to Zeppelins is not confined to the sterner sex—a sprinkling of ladies, plump and matronly, or of the masculine walking type, with two charmingly pretty girls and a gay young war widow to leaven the mass.

The exception was a tall and portly gentleman with a slightly bald head, glossy brown beard, gold-rimmed eye-glasses perilously balanced on a prominent nose, and an important manner. He was breakfasting alone at a table not far from Colwyn's, and Colwyn noticed that he kept glancing at the alcove table where the young man sat. As Colwyn looked in his direction their eyes met, and the portly gentleman nodded portentously in the direction of the alcove table, as an indication that he also had been watching the curious behaviour of the occupant. A moment afterwards he got up and walked across to the pillar against which Colwyn's table was placed.

"Will you permit me to take a seat at your table?" he remarked urbanely. "I am afraid we are going to have trouble over there directly," he added, sinking his voice as he nodded in the direction of the distant alcove table. "We may have to act promptly. Nobody else seems to have noticed anything. We can watch him from behind this pillar without his seeing us."

Colwyn nodded in return with a quick comprehension of all the other's speech implied, and pushed a chair towards his visitor, who sat down and resumed his watch of the young man at the alcove table. Colwyn bestowed a swift glance on his companion which took in everything. The tall man in glasses looked too human for a lawyer, too intelligent for a schoolmaster, and too well-dressed for an ordinary medical man. Colwyn, versed in judging men swiftly from externals, noting the urbane, somewhat pompous face, the authoritative, professional pose, the well-shaped, plump white hands, and the general air of well-being and prosperity which exuded from the whole man, placed him as a successful practitioner in the more lucrative path of medicine—probably a fashionable Harley Street specialist.

Colwyn returned to his scrutiny of the young man at the alcove table, and he and his companion studied him intently for some time in silence. But the young man, for the moment, was comparatively quiet, gazing moodily through the open window over the waters of the North Sea, an untasted sole in front of him, and an impassive waiter pouring out his coffee as though the spectacle of a young man sticking a knife into the table-cloth was a commonplace occurrence at the Grand Hotel, and all in the day's doings. When the waiter had finished pouring out the coffee and noiselessly departed, the young man tasted it with an indifferent air, pushed it from him, and resumed his former occupation of staring out of the window.

"He seems quiet enough now," observed Colwyn, turning to his companion. "What do you think is the matter with him—shell-shock?"

"I would not care to hazard a definite opinion on so cursory an observation," returned the other, in a dry, reticent, ultra-professional manner. "But I will go so far as to say that I do not think it is a case of shell-shock. If it is what I suspect, that first attack was the precursor of another, possibly a worse attack. Ha! it is commencing. Look at his thumb—that is the danger signal!"

Colwyn looked across the room again. The young man was still sitting in the same posture, with his gaze bent on the open sea. His left hand was extended rigidly on the table in front of him, with the thumb, extended at right angles, oscillating rapidly in a peculiar manner.

"This attack may pass away like the other, but if he looks round at anybody, and makes the slightest move, we must secure him immediately," said Colwyn's companion, speaking in a whisper.

He had barely finished speaking when the young man turned his head from the open window and fixed his blue eyes vacantly on the table nearest him, where an elderly clergyman, a golfing friend, and their wives, were breakfasting together. With a swift movement the young man got up, and started to walk towards this table.

Colwyn, who was watching every movement of the young man closely, could not determine, then or afterwards, whether he meditated an attack on the occupants of the next table, or merely intended to leave the breakfast room. The clergyman's table was directly in front of the alcove and in a line with the pair of swinging glass doors which were the only exit from the breakfast-room. But Colwyn's companion did not wait for the matter to be put to the test. At the first movement of the young man he sprang to his feet and, without waiting to see whether Colwyn was following him, raced across the room and caught the young man by the arm while he was yet some feet away from the clergyman's table. The young man struggled desperately in his grasp for some moments, then suddenly collapsed and fell inert in the other's arms. Colwyn walked over to the spot in time to see his portly companion lay the young man down on the carpet and bend over to loosen his collar.

The young man lay apparently unconscious on the floor, breathing stertorously, with convulsed features and closed eyes. After the lapse of some minutes he opened his eyes, glanced listlessly at the circle of frightened people who had gathered around him, and feebly endeavoured to sit up. Colwyn's companion, who was bending over him feeling his heart, helped him to a sitting posture, and then, glancing at the faces crowded around, exclaimed in a sharp voice:

"He wants air. Please move back there a little."

"Certainly, Sir Henry." It was a stout man in a check golfing suit who spoke. "But the ladies are very anxious to know if it is anything serious."

"No, no. He will be quite all right directly. Just fall back, and give him more air. Here, you!"–This to one of the gaping waiters–"just slip across to the office and find out the number of this gentleman's room."

The waiter hurried away and speedily returned with the proprietor of the hotel, a little man in check trousers and a frock coat, with a bald head and an anxious, yet resigned eye which was obviously prepared for the worst. His demeanour was that of a man who, already overloaded by misfortune, was bracing his sinews to bear the last straw. As he approached the group near the alcove table he smoothed his harassed features into an expression of solicitude, and, addressing himself to the man who was supporting the young man on the floor, said, in a voice intended to be sympathetic,

"I thought I had better come myself, Sir Henry. I could not understand from Antoine what you wanted or what had happened. Antoine said something about somebody dying in the breakfast-room—"

"Nothing of the sort!" snapped the gentleman addressed as Sir Henry, shifting his posture a little so as to enable the young man to lean against his shoulder. "Haven't you eyes in your head, Willsden? Cannot you see for yourself that this gentleman has merely had a fainting fit?"

"I'm delighted to hear it, Sir Henry," replied the hotel proprietor. But his face expressed no visible gratification. To a man who had had his hotel emptied by a Zeppelin raid the difference between a single guest fainting instead of dying was merely infinitesimal.

"Who is this gentleman, and what's the number of his room?" continued Sir Henry. "He will be better lying quietly on his bed."

"His name is Ronald, and his room is No. 32–on the first floor, Sir Henry."

"Very good. I'll take him up there at once."

"Shall I help you, Sir Henry? Perhaps he could be carried up. One of the waiters could take his feet, or perhaps it would be better to have two."

"There's not the slightest necessity. He'll be able to walk in a minute–with a little assistance. Ah, that's better!" The abrupt manner in which Sir Henry addressed the hotel proprietor insensibly softened itself into the best bedside manner when he spoke to the patient on the carpet, who, from a sitting posture, was now endeavouring to struggle to his feet. "You think you can get up, eh? Well, it won't do you any harm. That's the way!" Sir Henry assisted the young man to rise, and supported him with his arm. "Now, the next thing is to get him to his room. No, no, not you, Willsden–you're too small. Where's that gentleman I was sitting with a few minutes ago? Ah, thank you"–as Colwyn stepped forward and took the other arm–"now, let us take him gently upstairs."

The young man allowed himself to be led away without resistance. He walked, or rather stumbled, along between his guides like a man in a dream. Colwyn noticed that his eyes were half-closed, and that his head sagged slightly from side to side as he was led along. A waiter held open the glass doors which led into the lounge, and a palpitating chambermaid, hastily summoned from the upper regions, tripped ahead up the broad carpeted stairs and along the passage to show the way to the young man's bedroom.

2

Sir Henry dismissed the chambermaid at the door, and Colwyn and he lifted the young man on to the bed. He lay like a man in a stupor, breathing heavily, his face flushed, his eyes nearly closed. Sir Henry drew up the blind, and by the additional light examined him thoroughly, listening closely to the action of his heart, and examining the pupils of his eyes by rolling back the upper lid with some small instrument he took from his pocket.

"He'll do now," he said, after loosening the patient's clothes for his greater comfort. "He'll come to in about five minutes, and may be all right again shortly afterwards. But there are certain peculiar features about this case which are new in my experience, and rather alarm me. Certainly the young man ought not to be left to himself. His friends should be sent for. Do you know anything about him? Is he staying at the hotel alone? I only arrived here last night."

"I believe he is staying at the hotel alone. He has been here for a fortnight or more, and I have never seen him speak to anybody, though I have exchanged nods with him every morning. His principal recreation seems to lie in taking long solitary walks along the coast. He has been in the habit of going out every day, and not returning until dinner is half over. Perhaps the hotel proprietor knows who his friends are."

"Would you be so kind as to step downstairs and inquire? I do not wish to leave him, but his friends should be telegraphed to at once and asked to come and take charge of him."

"Certainly. And I'll send the telegram while I am down there."

But Colwyn returned in a few moments to say that the hotel proprietor knew nothing of his guest. He had never stayed in the house before, and he had booked his room by a trunk call from London. On arrival he had filled in the registration paper in the name of James Ronald, but had left blank the spaces for his private and business addresses. He looked such a gentleman that the proprietor had not ventured to draw his attention to the omissions.

"Another instance of how hotels neglect to comply with the requirements of the Defence of the Realm Act!" exclaimed Sir Henry. "Really, it is very awkward. I hardly know, in the circumstances, how to act. Speaking as a medical man, I say that he should not be left alone, but if he orders us out of his room when he recovers his senses what are we to do? Can you suggest anything?" He shot a keen glance at his companion.

"I should be in a better position to answer you if I knew what you consider him to be really suffering from. I was under the impression it was a bad case of shell-shock, but your remarks suggest that it is something worse. May I ask, as you are a medical man, what you consider the nature of his illness?"

Sir Henry bestowed another searching glance on the speaker. He noted, for the first time, the keen alertness and intellectuality of the other's face. It was a fine strong face, with a pair of luminous grey eyes, a likeable long nose, and clean-shaven, humorous mouth—a man to trust and depend upon.

"I hardly know what to do," said Sir Henry, after a lengthy pause, which he had evidently devoted to considering the wisdom of acceding to his companion's request. "This gentleman has not consulted me professionally, and I hardly feel justified in confiding my hurried and imperfect diagnosis of his case, without his knowledge, to a perfect stranger. On the other hand, there are reasons why somebody should know, if we are to help him in his weak state. Perhaps, sir, if you told me your name—"

"Certainly: my name is Colwyn–Grant Colwyn."

"You are the famous American detective of that name?"

"You are good enough to say so."

"Why not? Who has not heard of you, and your skill in the unraveling of crime? There are many people on both sides of the Atlantic who regard you as a public benefactor. But I am surprised. You do not at all resemble my idea of Colwyn."

"Why not?"

"You do not talk like an American, for one thing."

"You forget I have been over here long enough to learn the language. Besides, I am half English."

Sir Henry laughed good-humouredly.

"That's a fair answer, Mr. Colwyn. Of course, your being Colwyn alters the question. I have no hesitation in confiding in you. I am Sir Henry Durwood–no doubt you have heard of me. Naturally, I have to be careful."

Colwyn looked at his companion with renewed interest. Who had not heard of Sir Henry Durwood, the nerve specialist whose skill had made his name a household word amongst the most exclusive women in England, and, incidentally, won him a knighthood? There were professional detractors who hinted that Sir Henry had climbed into the heaven of Harley Street and fat fees by the ladder of social influence which a wealthy, well-born wife had provided, with no qualifications of his own except "the best bedside manner in England" and a thorough knowledge of the weaknesses of the feminine temperament. But his admirers–and they were legion–declared that Sir Henry Durwood was the only man in London who really understood how to treat the complex nervous system of the present generation. These thoughts ran through Colwyn's mind as he murmured that the opinion of such an eminent specialist as Sir Henry

Durwood on the case before them must naturally outweigh his own.

"You are very good to say so." Sir Henry spoke as though the tribute were no more than his due. "In my opinion, the symptoms of this young man point to epilepsy, and his behaviour downstairs was due to a seizure from which he is slowly recovering."

"Epilepsy! Haut or petit mal?"

"The lesser form—petit mal, in my opinion."

"But are his symptoms consistent with the form of epilepsy known as petit mal, Sir Henry? I thought in that lesser form of the disease the victim merely suffered from slight seizures of transient unconsciousness, without convulsions, regaining control of himself after losing himself, to speak broadly, for a few seconds or so."

"Ah, I see you know something of the disease. That simplifies matters. The layman's mind is usually at sea when it comes to discussing a complicated affection of the nervous system like epilepsy. You are more or less right in your definition of petit mal. But that is the simple form, without complications. In this case there are complications, in my opinion. I should say that this young man's attack was combined with the form of epilepsy known as *furor epilepticus.*"

"I am afraid you are getting beyond my depth, Sir Henry. What is *furor epilepticus?*"

"It is a term applied to the violence sometimes displayed by the patient during an attack of petit mal. The manifestation is extreme violence—usually much greater than in violent anger, as a rule."

"I believe there are cases on record of epileptics having committed the most violent outrages against those nearest and dearest to them. Is that what you mean by *furor epilepticus?*"

"Yes; but that attacks are generally directed towards strangers—rarely towards loved ones, though there have been such cases."

"I begin to understand. When we were at the breakfast table your professional eye diagnosed this young man's symptoms—his nervous tremors, his excitability, and the extravagant action with the knife—as premonitory symptoms of an attack of *furor epilepticus*, in which the sufferer would be liable to a dangerous outburst of violence?"

"Exactly. The minor symptoms suggested petit mal, but the act of sticking the knife into the table pointed strongly to the complication of *furor epilepticus*. That was why I went over to your table to have your assistance in case of trouble."

"You feared he would attack one of the guests?"

"Yes, epileptics are extremely dangerous in that condition, and will commit murder if they are in possession of a weapon. There have been cases in which they have succeeded in killing the victims of their fury."

"Without being conscious of it?"

"Without being conscious of it then or afterwards. After the patient recovers from one of these attacks his mind is generally a complete blank, but occasionally he will have a troubled or confused sense of something having happened to him—like a man awakened from a bad dream, which he cannot recall. This young man may come to his senses without remembering anything which occurred downstairs, or he may be vaguely alarmed, and ask a number of questions. In either case, it will be some time—from half an hour to several hours—before his mind begins to work normally again."

"Do you think it was his intention, when he got up from his table, to attack the group at the table nearest him—that elderly clergyman and his party?"

"I think it highly probable that he would have attacked the first person within his reach—that is why I wanted to prevent him."

"But he didn't carry the knife with him from his table."

"My dear sir"–Sir Henry's voice conveyed the proper amount of professional superiority–"you speak as though you thought a victim of *furor epilepticus* was a rational being. He is nothing of the kind. While the attack lasts he is an uncontrollable maniac, not responsible for his actions in the slightest degree."

"But, if he is capable of conceiving the idea of attacking his fellow creatures, surely he is capable of picking up a knife for the purpose, particularly when he has just previously had one in his hand?" urged Colwyn. "I have no intention of setting up my opinion against yours, Sir Henry, but there are certain aspects of this young man's illness which are not altogether consistent with my own experience of epileptics. As a criminologist, I have given some study to the effect of epilepsy and other nervous diseases on the criminal temperament. For instance, this young man did not give the usual cry of an epileptic when he sprang up from the table. And if it is merely an attack of petit mal, why is he so long in recovering consciousness?"

"The so-called epileptic cry is not invariably present, and petit mal is sometimes the half-way house to haut mal," responded Sir Henry. "I have said that this case presents several unusual features, but, in my opinion, there is nothing absolutely inconsistent with epilepsy, combined with *furor epilepticus*. And here is one symptom rarely found in any fit except an epileptic seizure." The specialist pointed to a faint fleck of foam which showed beneath the young man's brown moustache.

Colwyn bent over him and wiped his lips with his handkerchief. As he did so the young man's eyes unclosed. He regarded Colwyn languidly for a moment or two, and then sat upright on the bed.

"Who are you?" he exclaimed.

"It's quite all right, Mr. Ronald," said the specialist, in his most soothing bedside manner. "Just take things easily. You have been ill, but you are almost yourself again. Let me feel your pulse–ha, very good indeed! We will have you on your legs in no time."

The young man verified the truth of the latter prediction by springing off his bed and regarding his visitors keenly. There was now, at all events, no lack of sanity and intelligence in his gaze.

"What has happened? How did I get here?"

"You fainted, and we brought you up to your room," interposed Colwyn tactfully, before Sir Henry could speak.

"Awfully kind of you. I remember now. I felt a bit seedy as I went downstairs, but I thought it would pass off. I don't remember much more about it. I hope I didn't make too much of an ass of myself before the others, going off like a girl in that way. You must have had no end of a bother in dragging me upstairs–very good of you to take the trouble." He smiled faintly, and produced a cigarette case.

"How do you feel now?" asked Sir Henry Durwood solemnly, disregarding the proffered case.

"A bit as though I'd been kicked on the top of the head by a horse, but it'll soon pass off. Fact is, I got a touch of sun when I was out there"–he waved his hand vaguely towards the East–"and it gives me a bit of trouble at times. But I'll be all right directly. I'm sorry to have given you so much trouble."

He proffered this explanation with an easy courtesy, accompanied by a slight deprecating smile which admirably conveyed the regret of a well-bred man for having given trouble to strangers. It was difficult to reconcile his self-control with his previous extravagance downstairs. But to Colwyn it was apparent that his composure was simulated, the effort of a sensitive man who had betrayed a weakness to strangers, for the fingers which held a cigarette trembled slightly, and there were troubled shadows in the depths of the dark blue eyes. Colwyn admired the young man's pluck–he would wish to behave the same way himself in similar circumstances, he felt–and he realised that the best service he and Sir Henry Durwood could render their fellow guest was to leave him alone.

But Sir Henry was far from regarding the matter in the same light. As a doctor he was more at home in other people's bedrooms than his own, for rumour whispered that Lady Durwood was so jealous of her husband's professional privileges as a fashionable ladies' physician that she was in the habit of administering strong doses of matrimonial truths to him every night at home. Sir Henry settled himself in his chair, adjusted his eye-glasses more firmly on his nose and regarded the young man standing by the mantelpiece with a bland professional smile, slightly dashed by the recollection that he was not receiving a fee for his visit.

"You have made a good recovery, but you'll need care," he said. "Speaking as a professional man–I am Sir Henry Durwood–I think it would be better for you if you had somebody with you who understood your case. With your–er–complaint, it is very desirable that you should not be left to the mercy of strangers. I would advise, strongly advise you, to communicate with your friends. I shall be only too happy to do so on your behalf if you will give me their address. In the meantime–until they arrive–my advice to you is to rest."

A look of annoyance flashed through the young man's eyes. He evidently resented the specialist's advice; indeed, his glance plainly revealed that he regarded it as a piece of gratuitous impertinence. He answered coldly:

"Many thanks, Sir Henry, but I think I shall be able to look after myself."

"That is not an uncommon feature of your complaint," said the specialist. An oracular shake of the head conveyed more than the words.

"What do you imagine my complaint, as you term it, to be?" asked the young man curtly.

Colwyn wondered whether even a fashionable physician, used to the freedom with which fashionable ladies discussed their ailments, would have the courage to tell a stranger that he regarded him as an epileptic. The matter was not put to the test–perhaps fortunately–for at that moment there was a sharp tap at the door, which opened to admit a chambermaid who seemed the last word in frills and smartness.

"If you please, Sir Henry," said the girl, with a sidelong glance at the tall handsome young man by the mantelpiece, "Lady Durwood would be obliged if you would go to her room at once."

It speaks well for Sir Henry Durwood that the physician was instantly merged in the husband. "Tell Lady Durwood I will come at once," he said. "You'll excuse me," he added, with a courtly bow to his patient. "Perhaps–if you wish–you might care to see me later."

"Many thanks, Sir Henry, but there will be no need." He bowed gravely to the specialist, but smiled cordially and held out his hand to Colwyn, as the latter prepared to follow Sir Henry out of the room. "I hope to see you later," he said.

But when Colwyn, after a day spent on the golf-links, went into the dining-room for dinner that evening, the young man's place was vacant. After the meal Colwyn went to the office to inquire if Mr. Ronald was still unwell, and learnt, to his surprise, that he had departed from the hotel an hour or so after his illness.

3

Lunch was over the following day, and the majority of the hotel guests were assembled in the lounge, some sitting round a log fire which roared and crackled in the old-fashioned fireplace, others wandering backwards and forwards to the hotel entrance to cast a weather eye on the black and threatening sky.

During the night there had been one of those violent changes in the weather with which the denizens of the British Isles are not altogether unfamiliar; a heavy storm had come shrieking down the North Sea, and though the rain had ceased about eleven o'clock the wind had blown hard all through the night, bringing with it from the Arctic a driving sleet and the first touch of bitter, icy, winter cold.

The ladies of the hotel, who the previous day had paraded the front in light summer frocks, sat shivering round the fire in furs; and the men walked up and down in little groups discussing the weather and the war. The golfers stood apart debating, after their wont, the possibility of trying a round in spite of the weather. The elderly clergyman was prepared to risk it if he could find a partner, and, with the aid of an umbrella held upside down, was demonstrating to an attentive circle the possibility of going round the most open course in England in the teeth of the fiercest gale that ever blew, provided that a brassy was used instead of a driver.

"I don't see how you could drive a ball with either to-day," said one of the doubtful ones. "You'd be driving right against the wind for the first four holes, and when you have the wind behind you at the bend in the cliff by the fifth, the force of the gale would probably carry your

ball half a mile out to sea. These links here are supposed
to be the most exposed in England."

"My dear sir, you surely do not call this a gale,"
retorted the clergyman. "I have played some of my best
games in a stronger wind than this. And as for this being
the most exposed course in England–well, let me ask you
one question: have you ever played over the Worthing
course with a strong northeast gale–a gale, mind you, not
a wind–sweeping over the Downs?"

"Can't say I have," grunted the previous speaker, a
tall cadaverous man, wrapped from head to foot in a great
grey ulster, and wearing woollen gloves. "In fact, I've
never been on the Worthing course."

"I thought not." The clergyman's face showed a
golfer's satisfaction at having tripped a fellow player.
"The Worthing course is the most difficult course in
England, all up hill and down dale, and full of pitfalls for
those who don't know its peculiarities. I had a very
remarkable experience there, last year, with the crack
local player–his handicap was plus two. We played a
round in a gale with the wind whistling over the high
downs at the rate of seventy or eighty miles an hour. My
partner didn't want to play at first because of the
weather, but I persuaded him to go round, and I beat him
by two up and four to play solely by relying on the brassy
and midiron. He stuck to the driver, and lost in
consequence. I'll just show you how the game went.
Suppose the first hole to be just beyond the hall door
there, and you drive off from here. Now, imagine that
umbrella stand–would you mind moving away a little
from it, sir? Thank you–to be a group of fir trees fully a
hundred yards to the right of the fairway. Well, I got a
shot 160 yards up the fairway with a low straight ball
which never lifted more than a yard from the green, but
my opponent, instead of sticking to the brassy, as I did,
preferred to use his big driver, and what do you think
happened to him? The wind took his ball clean over the
fir trees."

The story was interrupted by the sudden entrance from outside of a young officer who had been taking a turn on the front. He strode hurriedly into the lounge, with a look of excitement on his good-humoured boyish face, and accosted the golfers, who happened to be nearest the door.

"I say, you fellows, what do you think has happened? You remember that chap who fainted yesterday morning? Well, he's wanted for committing a murder!"

The piece of news created the sensation that its imparter had counted upon. "A murder!" was echoed from different parts of the lounge in varying degrees of horror, amazement and dread, and the majority of the guests came eagerly crowding round to hear the details.

"Yes, a murder!" repeated the young officer, with relish. "And, what's more, he committed it after he left here yesterday. He walked across to some inn a few miles from here along the coast, put up there for the night, and in the middle of the night stabbed some old chap who was staying there."

There was a lengthy pause while the hotel guests digested this startling information, and endeavoured to register anew their previous faint impressions of the young man of the alcove table in the new light of his personality as an alleged murderer. The pause was followed by an excited hum of conversation and eager questions, the ladies all talking at once.

"What a providential escape we have all had!" exclaimed the clergyman's wife, her fresh comely face turning pale.

"That's just what I said myself, madam, when I heard the news," replied the young officer.

"I presume this murderous young ruffian has been secured?" asked the clergyman, who had turned even paler than his wife. "The police, I hope, have him under arrest."

The young officer shook his head.

"He's shown them a clean pair of heels. He may be heading back this way, for all I know. There will be a hue and cry over the whole of Norfolk for him by to-night, but murderers are usually very crafty, and difficult to catch. I bet they won't catch him before he murders somebody else."

The men looked at one another gravely, and some of the ladies gave vent to cries of alarm, and clung to their husband's arms. The clergyman turned angrily on the man who had brought the news.

"What do you mean, sir, by blurting out a piece of news like this before a number of ladies?" he said sternly. "It was imprudent and foolish in the last degree. You have alarmed them exceedingly."

"Oh, that's all tosh!" replied the other rudely. "They were bound to hear of it sooner or later; why, everybody on the front is talking about it. I thought you'd be awfully bucked to hear the news, seeing that you were sitting at the next table to him yesterday morning."

"Who gave you this information?" asked Colwyn, who had just come down stairs wearing a motor coat and cap, and paused on his way to the door on hearing the loud voices of the excited group round the young officer.

"One of the fishermen on the front. The police constable at the place where the murder was committed– a little village with some outlandish name–came over here to report the news. This is the nearest police station to the spot, it seems."

"But is he quite certain that the man who is supposed to have committed the murder is the young man who fainted yesterday morning?" asked Sir Henry Durwood, who had joined the group. "Has he been positively identified?"

"The fisherman tells me that there's no doubt it's him–the description's identical. He cleared out before the murder was discovered. There's a rare hue and cry all along the coast. They are organizing search parties.

There's one going out from here this afternoon. I'm going with it."

Colwyn left the group of hotel guests, and went to the front door. Sir Henry Durwood, after a moment's hesitation, followed him. The detective was standing in the hotel porch, thoughtfully smoking a cigar, and looking out over the raging sea. He nodded cordially to the specialist.

"What do you think of this story?" asked Sir Henry.

"I was just about to walk down to the police station to make some inquiries," responded Colwyn. "It is impossible to tell from that man's story how much is truth and how much mere gossip."

"I'm afraid it's true enough," replied Sir Henry Durwood. "You'll remember I warned him yesterday to send for his friends. A man in his condition of health should not have been permitted to wander about the country unattended. He has probably had another attack of *furor epilepticus*, and killed somebody while under its influence. Dear, dear, what a dreadful thing! It may be said that I should have taken a firmer hand with him yesterday, but what more could I have done? It's a very awkward situation—very. I hope you'll remember, Mr. Colwyn, that I did all that was humanly possible for a professional man to do—in fact, I went beyond the bounds of professional decorum, in tendering advice to a perfect stranger. And you will also remember that what I told you about his condition was in the strictest confidence. I should like very much to accompany you to the police station, if you have no objection—I feel strongly interested in the case."

"I shall be glad if you will come," replied the detective.

Colwyn turned down the short street to the front, where a footpath protected by a hand rail had been made along the edge of the cliff for the benefit of jaded London visitors who wanted to get the best value for their money in the bracing Norfolk air. At the present moment that air, shrieking across the North Sea with almost hurricane force, was too bracing for weak nerves on the exposed path, and it was real hard work to force a way, even with the help of the handrail, against the wind, to say nothing of the spray which was flung up in clouds from the thundering masses of yellow waves dashing at the foot of the cliffs below. Sir Henry Durwood, at any rate, was very glad when his companion turned away from the cliffs into one of the narrow tortuous streets running off the front into High Street.

Colwyn paused in front of a stone building, half way up the street, which displayed the words, "County Police," on a board outside. Knots of people were standing about in the road–fishermen in jerseys and sea boots, some women, and a sprinkling of children–brought together by the news of murder, but kept from encroaching on the sacred domain of law and order by a massive red-faced country policeman, who stood at the gate in an awkward pose of official dignity, staring straight in front of him, ignoring the eager questions which were showered on him by the crowd. The group of people nearest the gate fell back a little as they approached, and the policeman on duty looked at them inquiringly.

Colwyn asked him the name of the officer in charge of the district, and received the reply that it was Superintendent Galloway. The policeman looked somewhat doubtful when Colwyn asked him to take in his card with the request for an interview. He compromised between his determination to do the right thing and his desire not to offend two well-dressed gentlemen by taking Colwyn into his confidence.

"Well, you see, sir, it's like this," he said, sinking his voice so that his remarks should not be heard by the surrounding rabble. "I don't like to interrupt Superintendent Galloway unless it's very important. The chief constable is with him."

"Do you mean Mr. Cromering, from Norwich?" asked Colwyn.

The policeman nodded.

"He came over here by the morning train," he explained.

"Very good. I know Mr. Cromering well. Will you please take this card to the chief constable and say that I should be glad of the favour of a short interview? This is a piece of luck," he added to Sir Henry, as the constable took the card and disappeared into the building. "We shall now be able to find out all we want to know."

The police constable came hastening back, and with a very respectful air informed them that Mr. Cromering would be only too happy to see Mr. Colwyn. He led them forthwith into the building, down a passage, knocked at a door, and without waiting for a response, ushered them into a large room and quietly withdrew.

There were two officials in the room. One, in uniform, a heavily built stout man with sandy hair and a red freckled face, sat at a large roll-top desk writing at the dictation of the other, who wore civilian clothes. The second official was small and elderly, of dry and meagre appearance, with a thin pale face, and sunken blue eyes beneath gold-rimmed spectacles. This gentleman left off dictating as Colwyn and Sir Henry Durwood entered, and advanced to greet the detective with a look which might have been mistaken for gratitude in a less important personage.

Mr. Cromering's gratitude to Colwyn was not due to any assistance he had received from the detective in the elucidation of baffling crime mysteries. It arose from an entirely different cause. Wolfe is supposed to have said that he would sooner have been remembered as the author of Gray's "Elegy in a Country Churchyard" than as the conqueror of Quebec. Mr. Cromering would sooner have been the editor of the *English Review* than the chief constable of Norfolk. His tastes were bookish; Nature had intended him for the librarian of a circulating library: the safe pilot of middle class ladies through the ocean of new fiction which overwhelms the British Isles twice a year. His particular hobby was paleontology. He was the author of *The Jurassic Deposits of Norfolk*, with Some Remarks on the Kimeridge Clay–an exhaustive study of the geological formation of the county and the remains of prehistoric reptiles, fishes, mollusca and crustacea which had been discovered therein. This work, which had taken six years to prepare, had almost been lost to the world through the carelessness of the Postal Department, which had allowed the manuscript to go astray while in transit from Norfolk to the London publishers.

The distracted author had stirred up the postal authorities at London and Norwich, and had ultimately received a courteous communication from the Postmaster General to the effect that all efforts to trace the missing packet had failed. A friend of Mr. Cromering's suggested that he should invoke the aid of the famous detective Colwyn, who had a name for solving mysteries which baffled the police. Mr. Cromering took the advice and wrote to Colwyn, offering to mention his name in a preface to *The Jurassic Deposits* if he succeeded in recovering the missing manuscript. Colwyn, by dint of bringing to bear a little more intelligence and energy than the postal officials had displayed, ran the manuscript to earth in three days, and forwarded it to the owner with a courteous note declining the honour of the offered preface as too great a reward for such a small service.

"Very happy to meet you, Mr. Colwyn," said the chief constable, as he came forward with extended hand. "I've long wanted to thank you personally for your kindness—your great kindness to me last year. Although I feel I can never repay it, I'm glad to have the opportunity of expressing it."

"I'm afraid you are over-estimating a very small service," said Colwyn, with a smile.

"Very small?" The chief constable's emphasis of the words suggested that his pride as an author had been hurt. "If you had not recovered the manuscript, a work of considerable interest to students of British paleontology would have been lost. I must show you a letter I have just received from Sir Thomas Potter, of the British Museum, agreeing with my conclusions about the fossil remains of Ichthyosaurus, Plesiosaurus, and Mosasaurs, discovered last year at Roslyn Hole. It is very gratifying to me; very gratifying. But what can I do for you, Mr. Colwyn?"

"First let me introduce to you Sir Henry Durwood," said Colwyn.

"Durwood? Did you say Durwood?" said the little man, eagerly advancing upon the specialist with outstretched hand. "I'm delighted to meet one of our topmost men of science. Your illuminating work on Elephas Meridionalis is a classic."

"I'm afraid you're confusing Sir Henry with a different Durwood," said the detective, coming to the rescue. "Sir Henry Durwood is the distinguished specialist of Harley Street, and not the paleontologist of that name. We have called to make some inquiries about the murder which was committed somewhere near here last night."

"The ruling passion, Mr. Colwyn, the ruling passion! Personally I should be only too glad of your assistance in the case in question, but I'm afraid there's no deep mystery to unravel–it's not worth your while. It would be like cracking a nut with a steam hammer for you to devote your brains to this case. All the indications point strongly to one man."

"A young man who was staying at the *Grand* till yesterday?" inquired the detective.

The chief constable nodded.

"We're looking for a young man who's been staying at the *Grand* for some weeks past under the name of Ronald. He's a stranger to the district, and nobody seems to know anything about him. Perhaps you gentlemen can tell me something about him."

"Very little, I'm afraid," replied Colwyn. "I've seen him at meal times, and nodded to him, but never spoken to him till yesterday, when he had a fainting fit at breakfast. Sir Henry Durwood and I helped him to his bedroom, and exchanged a few remarks with him on his recovery."

"Yes, I've been told of that illness," said Mr. Cromering, meditating. "Did he do or say anything while you were with him that would throw any light on the subsequent tragic events of the night, for which he is now under suspicion?"

Colwyn related what had happened at breakfast and afterwards. Mr. Cromering listened attentively, and turning to Sir Henry Durwood asked him if he had seen Ronald before the previous day.

"I saw him yesterday for the first time at the breakfast table," replied Sir Henry Durwood. "I arrived only the previous night. He was taken ill at breakfast. Mr. Colwyn and I assisted him to his room and left him there. I know nothing whatever about him."

"What was the nature of his illness?" inquired the chief constable.

"It had some of the symptoms of a seizure," replied Sir Henry guardedly. "I begged him, when he recovered, not to leave his room. I even offered to communicate with his friends, by telephone, if he would give me their address, but he refused."

"It is a pity he did not take your advice," responded the chief constable. "He appears to have left the hotel shortly after his illness, and walked along the coast to a little hamlet called Flegne, about ten miles from here. He reached there in the evening, and put up at the village inn, the *Golden Anchor*, for the night. He left early in the morning, before anybody was up. Shortly afterwards the body of Mr. Roger Glenthorpe, an elderly archeologist, who had been staying at the inn for some time past making researches into the fossil remains common to that part of Norfolk, was found in a pit near the house. The tracks of boot-prints from near the inn to the mouth of the pit, and back again, indicate that Mr. Glenthorpe was murdered in his bedroom at the inn, and his body afterwards carried by the murderer to the pit in which it was found."

"In order to conceal the crime?" said Colwyn.

"Precisely. Two men employed by Mr. Glenthorpe saw the footprints earlier in the morning, and when it was discovered that Mr. Glenthorpe was missing, one of them was lowered into the pit by a rope and found the body at the bottom. The pit forms a portion of a number of so-called hut circles, or prehistoric shelters of the early Briton, which are not uncommon in this part of Norfolk."

"And you have strong grounds for believing that this young man Ronald, who was staying at the *Grand* till yesterday, is the murderer?"

"The very strongest. He slept in the room next to the murdered man's, and disappeared hurriedly in the early morning from the inn some time before the body was discovered. It is his boot-tracks which led to and from the pit where the body was found. A considerable sum of money has been stolen from the deceased, and we have ascertained that Ronald was in desperate straits for money. Another point against Ronald is that Mr. Glenthorpe was stabbed, and a knife which was used by Ronald at the dinner table that night is missing. It is believed that the murder was committed with this knife. But if you feel interested in the case, Mr. Colwyn, you had better hear the report of Police Constable Queensmead."

The chief constable touched a bell, and directed the policeman who answered it to bring in Constable Queensmead.

The policeman who appeared in answer to this summons was a thickset sturdy Norfolk man, with an intelligent face and shrewd dark eyes. On the chief constable informing him that he was to give the gentlemen the details of the *Golden Anchor* murder, he produced a notebook from his tunic, and commenced the story with official precision.

Ronald had arrived at the inn before dark on the previous evening, and had asked for a bed for the night. A little later Mr. Glenthorpe, the murdered man, who had been staying at the inn for some time past, had come in for his dinner, and was so pleased to meet a gentleman in that rough and lonely place that he had asked Ronald to dine with him. The dinner was served in an upstairs sitting-room, and during the course of the meal Mr. Glenthorpe talked freely of his scientific researches in the district, and informed his guest that he had that day been to Heathfield to draw £300 to purchase a piece of land containing some valuable fossil remains which he intended to excavate. The two gentlemen sat talking after dinner till between ten and eleven, and then retired to rest in adjoining rooms, in a wing of the inn occupied by nobody else. In the morning Ronald departed before anybody, except the servant, was up, refusing to wait for his boots to be cleaned. The servant, who had had the boots in her hands, had noticed that one of the boots had a circular rubber heel on it, but not the other. Ronald gave her a pound to pay for his bed, and the note was one of the first Treasury issue, as were the notes which Mr. Glenthorpe had drawn from the bank at Heathfield the day before. The men who had seen the footprints to the pit earlier in the morning, informed Queensmead of their discovery on learning that Mr. Glenthorpe had disappeared. Queensmead examined the footprints, and, with the assistance of the men, recovered the body. Queensmead telephoned a description of Ronald to the police stations along the coast, then mounted his bicycle and caught the train at Leyland in order to report the matter to the district headquarters at Durrington.

"I suppose there is no doubt that the young man who stayed at the inn is identical with Ronald," said the detective, when the constable had finished his story. "Do the descriptions tally in every respect?"

"Read the particulars you have prepared for the hand-bills, Queensmead," said the chief constable.

The constable produced a paper from his pocket and read: "Description of wanted man: About 28 years of age, five feet nine or ten inches high, fair complexion rather sunburnt, blue eyes, straight nose, fair hair, tooth-brush moustache, clean-cut features, well-shaped hands and feet, white, even teeth. Was attired in grey Norfolk or sporting lounge jacket, knickerbockers and stockings to match, with soft grey hat of same material. Wore a gold signet-ring on little finger of left hand. Distinguishing marks, a small star-shaped scar on left cheek, slightly drags left foot in walking. Manner superior, evidently a gentleman."

"That is conclusive enough," said Colwyn. "It tallies in every respect. The scar is an unmistakable mark. I noticed it the first time I saw Ronald."

"I noticed it also," said Sir Henry Durwood.

"It seems a clear case to me," said the chief constable. "I have signed a warrant for Ronald's arrest, and Superintendent Galloway has notified all the local stations along the coast to have the district searched. We think it very possible that Ronald is in hiding somewhere in the marshes. We have also notified the district railway stations to be on the lookout for anybody answering his description, in case he tries to escape by rail."

"It seems a strange case," remarked the detective thoughtfully. "Why should a young man of Ronald's type leave his hotel and go across to this remote inn, and commit this brutal murder?"

"He was very short of money. We have ascertained that he had been requested to leave the hotel here because he could not pay his bill. He has paid nothing since he has been here, and owed more than £30. The proprietor told him yesterday morning, as he was going in to breakfast, that he must leave the hotel at once if he could not pay his bill. He went away shortly after the scene in the breakfast room which was witnessed by you gentlemen, and left his luggage behind him. I suspect the proprietor would not allow him to take his luggage until he had discharged his bill."

"It strikes me as a remarkable case, nevertheless," said Colwyn. "I should like to look into it a little further, with your permission."

"Certainly," replied the chief constable courteously. "Superintendent Galloway will be in charge of the case. I suggested that he should ask for a man to be sent down from Scotland Yard, but he does not think it necessary. I feel sure that he will be delighted to have the assistance of such a celebrated detective as yourself. When are you starting for Flegne, Galloway?"

"In half an hour," replied the superintendent. "I shall have to walk from Leyland–five miles or more. The train does not go beyond there."

"Then I will drive you over in my car," said the detective.

"In that case perhaps you'll permit me to accompany you," said the chief constable. "I should very much like to observe your methods."

"And I too," said Sir Henry Durwood.

4

The road to Flegne skirted the settled and prosperous cliff uplands, thence ran through the sea marshes which stretched along that part of the Norfolk coast as far as the eye could reach until they were merged and lost to view in the cold northern mists.

The road, after leaving the uplands, descended in a sinuous curve towards the sea, but the party in the motor car were stopped on their way down by a young mounted officer, who, on learning of their destination, told them they would have to make an inland detour for some miles, as the military authorities had closed that part of the coast to ordinary traffic.

As they turned away from the coast, the chief constable informed Colwyn that the prohibited area was full of troops guarding a little bay called Leyland Hoop, where the water was so deep that hostile transports might anchor close inshore, and where, according to ancient local tradition,

"He who would Old England win,
Must at the Leyland Hoop begin."

After traversing a mile or so of open country, and passing through one or two scattered villages, they turned back to the coast again on the other side of a high green headland which marked the end of the prohibited area, and, crossing the bridge of a shallow muddy river, found themselves in the area of the marshes.

It was a region of swamps and stagnant dykes, of tussock land and wet flats, with scarcely a stir of life in any part of it, and nothing to take the eye except a stone cottage here and there.

The marshes stretched from the road to the sea, nearly a mile away. Man had almost given up the task of attempting to wrest a living from this inhospitable region. The boat channels which threaded the ooze were choked with weed and covered with green slime from long disuse, the little stone quays were thick with moss, the rotting planks of a broken fishing boat were foul with the encrustations of long years, the stone cottages by the roadside seemed deserted. Here and there the marshes had encroached upon the far side of the road, creeping half a mile or more farther inland, destroying the wholesome earth like rust corroding steel, and stretching slimy tentacles towards the farmlands on the rise.

Humanity had retreated from the inroads of the sea only after a stubborn fight. The ruins of an Augustinian priory, a crumbling fragment of a Norman tower, the mouldering remnant of a castellated hall, showed how prolonged had been the struggle with the elements of Nature before Man had acknowledged his defeat and retreated, leaving hostages behind him. And–significant indication of the bitterness of the fight–it was to be noted that, while the builders of a bygone generation had built to face the sea, the handful of their successors who still kept up the losing fight had built their beach-stone cottages with sturdy stone backs to the road, for the greater protection of the inmates from the fierce winter gales which swept across the marshes from the North Sea.

The car had travelled some miles through this desolate region when the chief constable directed Colwyn's attention to a spire rising from the flats a mile or so away, and said it was the church of Flegne-next-sea. Colwyn increased his speed a little, and in a few minutes the car had reached the outskirts of the little hamlet, which consisted of a straggling row of beach-stone cottages, a few gaunt farm-houses on the rise, and a cruciform church standing back from the village on a little hill, with high turret or beacon lights which had warned the North Sea mariners of a former generation of the dangers of that treacherous coast.

In times past Flegne-next-sea–pronounced "Fly" by the natives, "Fleen" by etymologists, and "Flegney" by the rare intrusive Cockney–had doubtless been a prosperous little port, but the encroaching sea had long since killed its trade, scattered its inhabitants, and reduced it to a spectre of human habitation compelled to keep the scene of its former activities after life had departed. Half the stone cottages were untenanted, with broken windows, flapping doors, and gardens overgrown with rank marsh weeds. The road through the village had fallen into disrepair, and oozed beneath the weight of the car, a few boards thrown higgledy-piggledy across in places representing the local effort to preserve the roadway from the invading marshes. The little canal quay–a wooden one–was a tangle of rotting boards and loose piles, and the stagnant green water of the shallow canal was abandoned to a few grey geese, which honked angrily at the passing car. There was no sign of life in the village street, and no sound except the autumn wind moaning across the marshes and the boom of the distant sea against the breakwater.

"There's the inn–straight in front," said Police-Constable Queensmead, pointing to it.

The *Golden Anchor* inn must have been built in the days of Sir Cloudesley Shovel, for nothing remained of the maritime prosperity which had originally bestowed the name upon the building. It was of rough stone, coloured a dirty white, with two queer circular windows high up in the wall on one side, the other side resting on a little, round-shouldered hill. It was built facing away from the sea like the beach-stone cottages, from which it was separated by a patch of common. From the rear of the inn the marshes stretched in unbroken monotony to the line of leaping white sea dashing sullenly against the breakwater wall, and ran for miles north and south in a desolate uniformity, still and grey as the sky above, devoid of life except for a few migrant birds feeding in the salt creeks or winging their way seaward in strong, silent flight. The rays of the afternoon sun, momentarily piercing the thick clouds, fell on the white wall and round glazed windows of the inn, giving it a sinister resemblance to a dead face.

Colwyn brought his car to a standstill on the edge of the saturated strip of common.

"We shall have to walk across," he said.

"Nobody will run off with the car," said Galloway, scrambling down from his seat.

"The murderer brought the body from the back of the house across this green, and carried it up that rise in front of the inn," said Queensmead. "You cannot see the pit from here, but it is close to that little wood on the summit. The footprints do not show in the grass, but they are very plain in the clay a little farther on, and lead straight to the pit."

"How deep is the pit?" asked Colwyn.

"About thirty feet. It was not an easy matter to bring up the body."

"We will examine the pit and the footprints later," said Mr. Cromering. "Let us go inside first."

Picking their way across the common to the front of the inn, they encountered a little group of men conversing underneath the rusty old anchor signboard which dangled from a stout stanchion above the front door of the inn. Some men, wearing sea-boots and jerseys, others in labouring garb, splashed with clay and mud, were standing about. They ceased their conversation as the party from the motor-car appeared around the corner, and, moving a respectful distance away, watched them covertly.

The front door of the inn was closed. Superintendent Galloway tapped at it sharply, and after the lapse of a moment or two the door was opened, and a man appeared on the threshold. Seeing the police uniforms he stepped outside as if to make more room for the party to enter the narrow passage from which he had emerged. Colwyn noticed that he was so tall that he had to stoop in the old-fashioned doorway as he came out.

Seen at close quarters, this man was a strange specimen of humanity. He was well over six feet in height, and so cadaverous, thin and gaunt that he might well have been mistaken for the presiding genius of the marshes who had stricken that part of the Norfolk coast with aridity and barrenness. But there was no lack of strength in his frame as he advanced briskly towards his visitors. His face was not the least remarkable part of him. It was ridiculously small and narrow for so big a frame, with a great curved beak of a nose, and small bright eyes set close together. Those eyes were at the present moment glancing with bird-like swiftness from one to the other of his visitors.

"You are the innkeeper–the landlord of this place?" asked Mr. Cromering.

"At your service, sir. Won't you go inside?" His voice was the best part of him; soft and gentle, with a cultivated accent which suggested that the speaker had known a different environment at some time or other.

"Show us into a private room," said Mr. Cromering.

The innkeeper escorted the party along the passage, and took them into a room with a low ceiling and sanded floor, smelling of tobacco, explaining, as he placed chairs, that it was the bar parlour, but they would be quiet and free from interruption in it, because he had closed the inn that day in anticipation of the police visit.

"Quite right–very proper," said the chief constable.

"Will you and the other gentlemen take any refreshment, after your journey?" suggested the innkeeper. "I'm afraid the resources of the inn are small, but there is some excellent old brandy."

He stretched out an arm towards the bell rope behind him. Colwyn noticed that his hand was long and thin and yellow–a skeleton claw covered with parchment.

"Never mind the brandy just now," said Mr. Cromering, taking on himself to refuse on behalf of his companions the proffered refreshment. "We have much to do and it will be time enough for refreshments afterwards. We will view the body first, and make inquiries after. Where is the body, Benson?"

"Upstairs, sir."

"Take us to the room."

The innkeeper led the way upstairs along a dark and narrow passage. When he reached a door near the end, he opened it and stood aside for them to enter.

"This is the room," he said, in a low voice. It was Colwyn's keen eye that noted the key in the door. "What is that key doing in the door, on the outside?" he asked. "How long has it been there?"

"The maid found it there this morning, sir, when she went up with Mr. Glenthorpe's hot water. That made her suspect something must be wrong, because Mr. Glenthorpe was in the habit of locking his door of a night and placing the key under his pillow. So, after knocking and getting no answer, she opened the door, and found the room empty."

"The door was not locked, though the key was in the door?"

"No, sir, and everything in the room was just as usual. Nothing had been disturbed."

"And was that bedroom window open when you found the room empty?" asked Superintendent Galloway, pointing to it through the open doorway.

"Yes, sir–just as you see it now. I gave orders that nothing was to be touched."

"Ronald slept in this room," said Queensmead, indicating the door of the adjoining bedroom.

"We will look at that later," said Galloway.

The interior of the room they entered was surprisingly light and cheerful and spacious, having nothing in common with those low gloomy vaults, crammed with clumsy furniture and moth-eaten stuffed animals, which generally pass muster as bedrooms in English country inns. Instead of the small circular windows of the south side, there was a large modern two-paned window in a line with the door, opening on to the other side of the house. The bottom pane was up, and the window opened as wide as possible. A very modern touch, unusual in a remote country inn, was a rose coloured gas globe suspended from the ceiling, in the middle of the room. The furniture belonged to a past period, but it was handsome and well-kept—a Spanish mahogany wardrobe, chest of drawers and washstand with chairs to match. Modern articles, such as a small writing-desk near the window, some library books, a fountain pen, a reading-lamp by the bedside, and an attaché case, suggested the personal possessions and modern tastes of the last occupant. A comfortable carpet covered the floor, and some faded oil-paintings adorned the walls.

The bed—a large wooden one, but not a fourposter—stood on the left-hand side of the room from the entrance, with the head against the wall nearest the outside passage, and the foot partly in line with the open window, which was about eight feet away from it. The door when pushed back swung just clear of a small bedroom table beside the bed, on which the reading lamp stood, with a book beside it. The other side of the bed was close to the wall which divided the room from the next bedroom, so that there was a large clear space on the outside, between the bed and the door. The gas fitting, which was suspended from the ceiling in this open space, hung rather low, the bottom of the globe being not more than six feet from the floor. The globe was cracked, and the incandescent burner was broken.

The murdered man had been laid in the middle of the bed, and covered with a sheet. Superintendent Galloway quietly drew the sheet away, revealing the massive white head and clear-cut death mask of a man of sixty or sixty-five; a fine powerful face, benign in expression, with a chin and mouth of marked character and individuality. But the distorted contour of the half-open mouth, and the almost piteous expression of the unclosed sightless eyes, seemed to beseech the assistance of those who now bent over him, revealing only too clearly that death had come suddenly and unexpectedly.

"He was a great archeologist—one of the greatest in England," said Mr. Cromering gently, with something of a tremor in his voice, as he gazed down at the dead man's face. "To think that such a man should have been struck down by an assassin's blow. What a loss!"

"Let us see how he was murdered," said the more practical Galloway, who was standing beside his superior officer. He drew off the covering sheet as he spoke, and dropped it lightly on the floor.

The body thus revealed was that of a slightly built man of medium height. It was clad in a flannel sleeping suit, spattered with mud and clay, and oozing with water. The arms were inclining outwards from the body, and the legs were doubled up. There were a few spots of blood on the left breast, and immediately beneath, almost on the left side, just visible in the stripe of the pyjama jacket, was the blow which had caused death—a small orifice like a knife cut, just over the heart.

"It is a very small wound to have killed so strong a man," said Mr. Cromering. "There is hardly any blood."

Sir Henry examined the wound closely. "The blow was struck with great force, and penetrated the heart. The weapon used—a small, thin, steel instrument—and internal bleeding, account for the small external flow."

"What do you mean by a thin, steel instrument?" asked Superintendent Galloway. "Would an ordinary table-knife answer that description?"

"Certainly. In fact, the nature of the wound strongly suggests that it was made by a round-headed, flat-bladed weapon, such as an ordinary table or dinner knife. The thrust was made horizontally,–that is, across the ribs and between them, instead of perpendicularly, which is the usual method of stabbing. Apparently the murderer realised that his knife was too broad for the purpose, and turned it the other way, so as to make sure of penetrating the ribs and reaching the heart."

"Does not that suggest a rather unusual knowledge of human anatomy on the murderer's part?" asked Mr. Cromering.

"I do not think so. Anybody can tell how far apart the human ribs are by feeling them."

"It is easy to see, Sir Henry, that the wound was made by a thin-bladed knife, but why do you think it was also round-headed?" asked Superintendent Galloway. "Might it not have been a sharp-pointed one?"

"Or even a dagger?" suggested Mr. Cromering.

"Certainly not a dagger. The ordinary dagger would have made a wider perforation with a corresponding increase in the blood-flow. My theory of a round-headed knife is based on the circumstance of a portion of the deceased's pyjama jacket having been carried into the wound. A sharp-pointed knife would have made a clean cut through the jacket."

"I see," said Superintendent Galloway, with a sharp nod.

"Therefore, we may assume, in the case before us,"– Sir Henry Durwood waved a fat white hand in the direction of the corpse as though he were delivering an anatomical lecture before a class of medical students– "that the victim was killed with a flat, round knife with a round edge, held sideways. Furthermore, the position of the wound reveals that the blow was too much on the left side to pierce the centre of the heart directly, but was a slanting blow, delivered with such force that it has probably pierced the heart on the *right* side, causing instant death."

"The weapon, then, entered the body in a lateral direction, that is, from left to right?" asked Colwyn, who had been closely following the specialist's remarks.

"That is what I meant to convey," responded Sir Henry, in his most professional manner. "The blade entered on the left side, and travelled towards the centre of the body."

"From the nature of the wound would you say that the knife entered almost parallel with the ribs, though slanting slightly downwards, in order to pierce the heart on the right side?"

"That would be the general direction, though it is impossible to ascertain, without a postmortem examination, the exact spot where the heart was pierced."

"But the wound slants in such a way as to prove that the blow was struck from left to right?" persisted Colwyn.

"Undoubtedly," responded Sir Henry.

5

During the latter part of the conversation Superintendent Galloway walked to the open window, and looked out. He turned round swiftly, with a look of unusual animation on his heavy features, and exclaimed: "The murderer entered through the window."

The others went over to the window. The inn on that side had been built into a small hill of beehive shape, which had been partly levelled to make way for the foundations. Seen from outside, the inn, with its back to the sea and a corner of its front entering the hillside, bore a remote resemblance to some nakedly ugly animal with its nose burrowed into the earth. Part of the bar was actually underground, and the windows of the rooms immediately above looked out on the hillside. The window of Mr. Glenthorpe's room, which was above the bar parlour, was not more than four or five feet away from the round-shouldered side of the hill. From that point the hill fell away rapidly, and the first-story windows at the back, where the house rose from the flat edge of the marsh, were about fifteen feet from the ground. The space between the inn wall and the beehive curve of the hill, which was very narrow under Mr. Glenthorpe's window, but widened as the hill fell away, was covered with a russet-coloured clay, which contrasted vividly with the sombre grey and drab tints of the marshes.

"It was an easy matter to get in this window," said Superintendent Galloway. "And here's the proof that the murderer came in this way." He stooped and picked up something from the floor, close to the window, and held it out in the palm of his hand for the inspection of his companions. It was a small piece of red clay, like the russet-coloured clay outside the window.

"Here is another clue," said Colwyn, pointing to a fragment of black material adhering to a nail near the bottom of the window.

"Ronald ripped something he was wearing while getting through the window," said Galloway, detaching the fragment, which he and Colwyn examined closely.

"Have you noticed that?" said Colwyn, pointing to a pool of water which had collected near the open window, between the edge of the carpet and the skirting board.

"Yes," replied Galloway. "It was raining heavily last night."

With eyes sharpened by his discoveries, Galloway made a careful search of the carpet, and found several more crumbs of red clay between the window and the bed. Near the bed he detected some splashes of candle-grease, which he detached from the carpet with his pocket-knife. He also picked up the stump of a burnt wooden match, and the broken unlighted rink head of another. After showing these things to his companions he placed them carefully in an empty match-box, which he put in his pocket.

"Somebody has bumped against this gas globe pretty hard," said Colwyn. "The glass is broken and the incandescent burner smashed."

He bent down to examine the white fragments of the burner which were scattered about the carpet, and as he did so he noticed another broken wooden match, and two more splashes of candle-grease directly beneath the gas-jet. He removed the candle-grease carefully, and showed it to Galloway.

"More candle-grease!" the latter said. "Well, that's not likely to prove anything except that Ronald was careless with his light. I suppose the wind caused the candle to gutter. I would willingly exchange the candle-grease for some finger-prints. There's not a sign of finger-prints anywhere. Ronald must have worn gloves. Now, let us have a look at Ronald's room. I want to see if he could get out of his own window on to the hillside. His window is higher from the ground than this window. The hill falls away very sharply."

The bedroom Ronald had occupied was small and narrow, and its meagre furniture was in striking contrast with the comfortable appointments of the room they had just left. It contained a single bed, a chest of drawers, a washstand, and a wardrobe. The latter, a cumbrous article of furniture, stood between the bed and the wall, against the side nearest to Mr. Glenthorpe's room.

Galloway strode across to the window, which was open, and looked out. The hillside fell away so rapidly that the bottom of the window was quite eight feet from the ground outside.

"Not much of a drop for an athletic young fellow like Ronald," said Galloway to Colwyn, who had joined him.

"The window is very much smaller than the one in Mr. Glenthorpe's bedroom," said Colwyn.

"But large enough for a man to get through. Look here! I can get my head and shoulders through, and where the head and shoulders go the rest of the body will follow. Ronald got through it last night and into the next room by the other window. There can be no doubt that that was how the murder was committed."

Galloway left the window, and examined the bedroom carefully. He turned down the bed-clothes, and scrutinised the sheets and pillows.

"I thought he might have left some blood-stains on the linen, after carrying the body downstairs," he explained. "But he hasn't."

"Sir Henry says the bleeding was largely internal," remarked Mr. Cromering. "That would account for the absence of any tell-tale marks on the bed-clothes."

"He was too clever to wash his hands when he came back," grumbled Galloway, turning to the washstand and examining the towels. "He's a cool customer."

"I notice that the candle in the candlestick is a wax one," said Colwyn.

"And burnt more than half-way down," commented Galloway, glancing at it.

"You attach no significance to the fact that the candle is a wax one?" questioned the detective.

"No, do you?" replied Galloway, with a puzzled glance.

Colwyn did not reply to the question. He was looking attentively at the large wardrobe by the side of the bed.

"That's a strange place to put a wardrobe," he said. "It would be difficult to get out of bed without barking one's shins against it."

"It was probably put there to hide the falling wall-paper,–the place is going to rack and ruin," said Galloway, pointing to the top of the wardrobe, where the faded wall-paper, mildewed and wet with damp, was hanging in festoons. "Now, Queensmead, lead the way outside. I've seen all I want to see in this room."

"Would you like to see the room where Ronald and Mr. Glenthorpe dined?" suggested the constable. "It's on this floor, on the other side of Mr. Glenthorpe's bedroom."

"We can see that later. I want to examine outside before it gets dark." They left the room. The innkeeper was waiting patiently in the passage, standing motionless at the head of the staircase, with his head inclining forward, like a marsh heron fishing in a dyke. He hastened towards them.

"I noticed a reading-lamp by Mr. Glenthorpe's bedside, Mr. Benson," said Colwyn. "Did he use that as well as the gas?"

"He rarely used the gas, sir, though it was put into the room at his request. He found the reading-lamp suited his sight better."

"Did he use candles? I saw no candlestick in the room." "He never used candles, sir—only the reading-lamp."

"When was the gas-globe smashed? Last night?"

"It must have been, sir. Ann says it was quite all right yesterday."

"I've got my own idea how that was done," said Galloway, who had been an attentive listener to the innkeeper's replies to Colwyn's questions. "Show the way downstairs to the back door, Mr. Benson."

The innkeeper preceded them down the stairs and along the passage to another one, which terminated in a latched door, which he opened.

"How was this door fastened last night?" asked Galloway.

"By this bolt at the top," said the innkeeper, pointing to it. "There is no key—only this catch."

"Is this the only back outlet from the inn?" asked Colwyn.

"Yes, sir."

At Galloway's suggestion they first went to the side of the inn, in order to examine the ground beneath the windows. The fence enclosing the yard had fallen into disrepair, and had many gaps in it. There were no footprints visible in the red clay of the natural passage-way between the inn wall and the hill, either beneath the window of Ronald's room or Mr. Glenthorpe's window.

"The absence of footprints means nothing," said Galloway. "Ronald may have climbed from one room to the other in his stocking feet, and then put on his boots to remove the body. Even if he wore his boots he might have left no marks, if he walked lightly."

"I am not so sure of that," said Colwyn. "But what do you make of this?"

He pointed to an impression in the red earth underneath Mr. Glenthorpe's window—a line so faint as to be barely noticeable, running outward from the wall for about eighteen inches, with another line about the same length running at right angles from it. Superintendent Galloway examined these two lines closely and then shook his head as though to intimate he could make nothing of them.

"What do you think they are?" said Mr. Cromering, turning to Colwyn. "I think they may have been made by a box," was the reply.

"You are not suggesting that the murderer threw a box out of the window?" exclaimed Superintendent Galloway, staring at the detective. "Look how straight the line from the wall is! A box would have fallen crookedly."

"I do not suggest anything of the kind. If it was a box, it is more likely it was placed outside the window."

"For what purpose?"

"To help the murderer climb into the room."

"He didn't need it," replied Galloway. "It's an easy matter to get through this window from the ground. I can do it myself." He placed his hands on the sill, sprang on to the window ledge, and dropped back again. "I attach no importance to these lines. They are so faint that they might have been made months ago. There is nothing to be seen here, so we may as well go and look at the footprints. Show us where the marks of the footsteps commence, Queensmead."

The constable led the way to the other side of the house and across the green. The grass terminated a little distance from the inn in a clay bank bordering a wide tract of bare and sterile land, which extended almost to the summit of the rise. Clearly defined in the clay and the black soft earth were two sets of footprints, one going towards the rise, and the other returning. The outgoing footsteps were deeply and distinctly outlined from heel to toe. The right foot plainly showed the circular mark of a rubber heel, which was missing in the other, though a sharp indentation showed the mark of the spike to which the rubber had been fastened.

"The footprints lead straight to the mouth of the pit where the body was thrown," said Queensmead.

"What a clue!" exclaimed Superintendent Galloway, his eyes sparkling with excitement. "You are quite certain the inn servant can swear that these marks were made by Ronald's boots, Queensmead?"

"There's no doubt on that point, sir," replied the constable. "She had the boots in her hands this morning, just before Ronald put them on, and she distinctly noticed that there was a rubber heel on the right boot, but not on the other."

"It seems a strange thing for a young man of Ronald's position to have rubber heels affixed to his boots," remarked Mr. Cromering. "I was under the impression that they were an economical device of the working classes. But perhaps he found them useful to save his feet from jarring."

"We shall find them useful to hang him," responded Galloway curtly. "Let us proceed to the pit, gentlemen. May I ask you to keep clear of the footprints? I do not want them obliterated before I can take plaster casts."

They followed the footsteps up the rise. Near the summit they disappeared in a growth of nettles, but reappeared on the other side, skirting a number of bowl-shaped depressions clustered in groups along the brow of the rise. These were the hut circles–the pit dwellings of the early Britons, shallow excavations from six to eight feet deep, all running into one another, and choked with a rank growth of weeds. Between them and a little wood which covered the rest of the summit was an open space, with a hole gaping nakedly in the bare earth.

"That's the pit where the body was thrown," said Queensmead, walking to the brink.

The pit descended straight as a mining shaft until the sides disappeared in the interior gloom. It was impossible to guess at its depth because of the tangled creepers which lined its sides and obscured the view, but Mr. Cromering, speaking from his extensive knowledge of Norfolk geology, said it was fully thirty feet deep. He added that there was considerable difference of opinion among antiquaries to account for its greater depth. Some believed the pit was simply a larger specimen of the adjoining hut circles, running into a natural underground passage which had previously existed. But the more generally accepted theory was that the hut circles marked the site of a prehistoric village, and the deeper pit had been the quarry from which the Neolithic men had obtained the flints of which they made their implements. These flints were imbedded in the chalk a long way from the surface, and to obtain them the cave men burrowed deeply into the clay, and then excavated horizontal galleries into the chalk. Several of the red-deer antler picks which they used for the purpose had been discovered when the pit was first explored twenty-five years ago.

"Mr. Glenthorpe was very much interested in the prehistoric and late Stone Age remains which are to be found in abundance along the Norfolk coast," he added. "He has enriched the national museums with a valuable collection of prehistoric man's implements and utensils, which he recovered in various parts of Norfolk. For some time past he had been carrying out explorations in this district in order to add to the collection. It is sad to think that he met his death while thus employed, and that his murdered body was thrown in the very pit which was, as it were, the centre of his explorations and the object of his keenest scientific curiosity."

"Did you ever see clearer footprints?" exclaimed the more practical-minded Galloway. "Look how deep they are near the edge of the pit, where the murderer braced himself to throw the body off his back into the hole. See! there is a spot of blood on the edge."

It was as he had said. The footprints were clear and distinct to the brink of the pit, but fainter as they turned away, showing that the man who had carried the body had stepped more lightly and easily after relieving himself of his terrible burden.

"I must take plaster casts of those prints before it rains," said Galloway. "They are far too valuable a piece of evidence to be lost. They form the final link in the case against Ronald."

"You regard the case as conclusive, then?" said Colwyn.

"Of course I do. It is now a simple matter to reconstruct the crime from beginning to end. Ronald got through Mr. Glenthorpe's window last night in the dark. As the catch has not been forced, he either found it unlocked or opened it with a knife. After getting into the room he walked towards the foot of the bed. He listened to make sure that Mr. Glenthorpe was asleep, and then struck the match I picked up near the foot of the bed, lit the candle he was carrying, put it on the table beside the bed, and stabbed the sleeping man. Having secured the money, he unlocked the door, carried the corpse out on his shoulder, closed the door behind him but did not lock it, then took the body downstairs, let himself out of the back door, carried it up here and cast it into the pit. That's how the murder was committed."

"I agree with you that the murderer entered through the window," said Colwyn. "But why did he do so? It strikes me as important to clear that up. If Ronald is the murderer, why did he take the trouble to enter the room from the outside when he slept in the next room?"

"Surely you have not forgotten that the door was locked from inside? Benson says Mr. Glenthorpe was in the habit of locking his door and sleeping with the key under the pillow. Ronald no doubt first tried to enter the room by the door, but, finding it locked, climbed out of his window, and got into the room through the other window. He dared not break open the door for fear of disturbing the inmate or alarming the house."

"Then how do you account for the key being found in the outside of Mr. Glenthorpe's door this morning?"

"Quite easily. During the struggle or in the victim's death convulsions the bed-clothes were disarranged, and Ronald saw the key beneath the pillow. Or he may have searched for it, as he knew he would need it before he could open the door and remove the body. It was easy for him to climb through the window to commit the murder, but he couldn't remove the body that way. After finding the key he unlocked the door, and put the key in the outside, intending to lock the door and remove the key as he left the room, so as to defer the discovery that Mr. Glenthorpe was missing until as long after his own departure in the morning as possible. He may have found it a difficult matter to stoop and lock the door and withdraw the key while he was encumbered with the corpse, so left it in the door till he returned from the pit. When he returned he was so exhausted with carrying the body several hundred yards, mostly uphill, that he forgot all about the key. That is my theory to account for the key being in the outside of the door."

"It's an ingenious one, at all events," commented Colwyn. "But would such a careful deliberate murderer overlook the key when he returned?"

"Nothing more likely," said the confident superintendent. "It's in trifles like this that murderers give themselves away. The notorious Deeming, who murdered several wives, and disposed of their bodies by burying them under hearthstones and covering them with cement, would probably never have been caught if he had not taken away with him a canary which belonged to the last woman he murdered. It was a clue that couldn't be missed—like the silk skein in Fair Rosamond's Bower."

"Here's another point: why did not Ronald, having disposed of the body, disappear at once, instead of waiting for the morning?"

"Because if his room had been found empty in the morning, as well as that of Mr. Glenthorpe's, the double disappearance would have aroused instant suspicion and search. Ronald gauged the moment of his departure very cleverly, in my opinion. On the one hand, he wanted to get away before the discovery of Mr. Glenthorpe's empty bedroom; and, on the other hand, he wished to stay at the inn long enough to suggest that he had no reason for flight, but was merely compelled to make an early departure. The trouble and risk he took to conceal the body outside prove conclusively that he thought the pit a sufficiently safe hiding-place to retard discovery of the crime for a considerable time, and he probably thought that even when it was discovered that Mr. Glenthorpe was missing his absence would not, at first, arouse suspicions that he had met with foul play.

"It was not as though Mr. Glenthorpe was living at home with relatives who would have immediately raised a hue and cry. He was a lonely old man living in an inn amongst strangers, who were not likely to be interested in his goings and comings. That suggests another alternative theory to account for the key in the door: Ronald may have left it in the door to convey the impression that Mr. Glenthorpe had gone out for an early walk. That belief would at least gain Ronald a few hours to make good his escape from this part of the country and get away by train before any suspicions were aroused. The fact that none of Mr. Glenthorpe's clothes were missing was not likely to be discovered in an inn until suspicion was aroused. Ronald laid his plans well, but how was he to know that in his path to the pit he walked over soil as plastic and impressionable as wax?"

"But in spite of that you assume he knew exactly where this pit was situated?"

"Nothing more likely. It is well-known to archeologists. Ronald may well have heard of it while staying at Durrington, or he may have known of it personally through some previous visit to this part of the world. And there is also evidence that Mr. Glenthorpe told him of the hut circles and the pit during dinner last night."

"Just one more doubt, Superintendent. How do you account for the cracked gas globe and the broken incandescent mantle?"

"Ronald probably knocked his head against it as he approached the bed," said Galloway promptly.

"Hardly. Ronald's height, according to the description, is five feet ten inches. That happens to be also my height, and I can pass under the gas globe without touching it."

"Then it was broken when Ronald was carrying the corpse downstairs," replied Galloway, after a moment's reflection. "He carried the corpse on his shoulders and part of the body would be above his head."

"Superintendent Galloway has an answer for everything," said Colwyn with a smile, to Mr. Cromering. "He is persuasive if not always convincing."

"The case seems clear enough to me," said the chief constable thoughtfully. "Come, gentlemen, let us return to the inn. We have a number of things to do, and not much time to do them in."

6

The inn, seen in the grey evening of a grey day, had a stark and sinister aspect, an atmosphere of mystery and secretiveness, an air of solitary aloofness in the dreary marshes, standing half shrouded in the night mists which were sluggishly crawling across the oozing flats from the sea. It was not a place where people could be happy—this battered abode of a past age on the edge of the North Sea, with the bitter waters of the marshes lapping its foundations, and the cold winds for ever wailing round its gaunt white walls.

The portion buried in the hillside, with only the tops of the windows peering above, suggested the hidden holes and burrowing byways of a dead and gone generation of smugglers who had used the inn in the heyday of Norfolk's sea prosperity. It may have been a thought of the possibilities of the inn as a hiding place which prompted Mr. Cromering to exclaim, after gazing at it attentively for some seconds:

"We had better go through this place from the bottom."

As they approached the inn a stout short man, who was looking out from the low and narrow doorway, retreated into the interior, and immediately afterwards the long figure of the innkeeper emerged as though he had been awaiting the return of the party, and had posted somebody to watch for them.

The innkeeper showed no surprise on receiving Mr. Cromering's instruction to show them over the inn. Walking before them he led them along a side passage opposite the bar, opening doors as he went, and drawing aside for them to enter and look at the rooms thus revealed.

It was a strange rambling old place inside, full of nooks and crannies, and unexpected odd corners and apertures, short galleries and stone passages winding everywhere and leading nowhere; the downstairs rooms on different levels, with stone steps into them, and queer slits of windows pierced high up in the thick walls. On the ground floor a central passage divided the inn into two portions. On the one side were several rooms, some empty and destitute of furniture, others barely furnished and empty, and a big gloomy kitchen in which a stout countrywoman, who shook and bobbed at the sight of the visitors, was washing greens at a dirty deal table. Off the kitchen were two small rooms, poorly furnished as servants' bedrooms, and the windows of these looked out on the marshes at the back of the house. On the other side of the centre passage was the bar, which was subterranean at the far end, with the cellar adjoining tunnelled into the hillside. In the recesses of the cellar the short stout man they had seen at the doorway was, by the light of a tallow candle, affixing a spigot to one of the barrels which stood against the earthen wall. Behind the bar was a small bar parlour, and behind that two more rooms, the house on that side finishing in a low and narrow gallery running parallel with the outside wall.

The staircase upstairs opened into a stone passage, running from the front of the inn to the back. On the left-hand side of the passage, going from the head of the stairs to the back of the house, were four rooms. The first was a small, comfortably furnished sitting room, where Mr. Glenthorpe and his guest had dined the previous night. The bed chamber of the murdered man adjoined this room. Next came the room in which Ronald had slept, and then an empty lumber room. There were four bedrooms on the other side, all unfurnished, except one at the far end of the passage, the lumber-room. The innkeeper explained that the murdered man had been the sole occupant of that wing of the house until the previous night, when Mr. Ronald had occupied the room next to him. At this end of the passage another and narrower passage ran at right angles from it along the back of the house, with several rooms opening off it on one side only. The first of these rooms was empty; the next room contained a small iron bedstead, a chair, and a table, and the innkeeper said that it was his bedroom. At the next door he paused, and turning to Mr. Cromering hesitatingly remarked:

"This is my mother's room, sir. She is an invalid."

"We will not disturb your mother, we will merely glance into the room," said the kindly chief constable.

"It is not that, sir. She is—" He broke off abruptly, and knocked at the door.

After a few moments' pause there was the sound of somebody within turning a key in the lock, then the door was opened by a young girl, who, at the sight of the visitors, walked hurriedly across to a bedstead at the far end of the room, on which something grey was moving, and stood in front of it as though she would guard the occupant of the bed from the intruding eyes of strangers.

"It's all right, Peggy," said the innkeeper. "We shall not be here long. My daughter is afraid you will disturb her grandmother," he said turning to the gentlemen. "My mother is—" A motion of his finger towards his forehead completed the sentence more significantly than words.

The figure on the bed in the corner was in the shadow, but they could make it out to be that of an old and shrivelled woman in a grey flannel nightdress, who was sitting up in bed, swinging backward and forward, holding some object in her arms, clasped tightly to her breast, while her small dark eyes, deepset under furrowed brows, gazed at the visitors with the unmeaning stare of an animal.

But Colwyn's eyes were drawn to the girl at the bedside. She was beautiful, of a type sufficiently rare to attract attention anywhere. Her delicate profile and dainty grace shone in the shadow of the sordid room like an exquisite picture. He was aware of a skin of transparent whiteness, a wistful sensitive mouth, a pair of wonderful eyes with the green-grey colour of the sea in their depths, and a crown of red-gold hair. She was poorly, almost shabbily, dressed, but the crude cheap garbing of a country dressmaker was unable to mar the graceful outlines of her slim young figure. But it was the impassivity of the face and detachment of attitude which chained Colwyn's attention and stimulated his intellectual curiosity. The human face is usually an index to the owner's character, but this girl's face was a mask which revealed nothing. The features might have been marble for anything they displayed, as she stood by the bedside regarding with grave inscrutable eyes the group of men in the doorway. There was something pathetic in the contrast between her grace and beauty and stillness and the uncouth gestures and meaningless stare of the old woman in the bed behind her.

The old woman, moving from side to side with the unhappy restlessness which characterises the insane, dropped over the side of the bed the object she had been nursing in her arms, and looked at the girl with the dumb entreaty of an animal. The girl stooped down by the side of the bed, picked up the fallen article, and restored it to the mad woman. It was a doll.

Mr. Cromering, who saw the action and the article, flushed like a man who had seen something which should be kept secret, and turned to leave the room. The others followed, and immediately afterwards they heard the door closed after them, and the key turned in the lock.

Superintendent Galloway, who had more of the inquiring turn of mind of the police official than the chief constable, asked the innkeeper several questions about his mother and her condition. The innkeeper said her insanity was the outcome of an accident which had happened two years before. She was sitting dozing by the kitchen fire when a large boiler of water overturned, scalding her terribly, and the shock and pain had sent her mad. She had never left the bedroom since, and had gradually become reduced to a condition of imbecility, alternated by occasional outbursts of violence.

"Is she ever allowed out of the room?" asked Superintendent Galloway quickly, as though a sudden thought had struck him.

"Never, sir; she never tries to get out of bed except when she's violent. She will sit there for hours, playing with a doll, but when she has her paroxysms she runs round and round the room, crying out as you heard her just now, and throwing the things about. Did you notice, sir, that there was no glassware in the room? She has tried to injure herself with glass and crockery in her violent fits."

"How often does she have paroxysms of violent madness?" asked the chief constable.

"Not often, sir; usually about the turn of the moon, or when there is a gale at sea."

"There was a gale at sea last night," said Colwyn. "Did your mother have an attack then?"

"Peggy said when she came downstairs last night she thought there were signs of an attack coming on, but when I looked in on Mother as I was going to bed, shortly before eleven, she seemed quiet enough, so I locked her door and went to bed."

"Do you mean to say that you leave this poor mad woman in her bedroom all night alone?" asked the chief constable.

"It's the best thing to be done, sir," replied the innkeeper, with an apologetic air. "We tried having somebody to sleep with her, but it only made her worse, and the doctor who saw her last year said it wasn't necessary. Peggy is with her a lot in the daytime, and often until she goes to bed. So she's really not left alone very much, because Ann goes into her room as soon as she gets up in the morning–about six o'clock."

"And is your mother always secured in her room—is the door always locked?" asked Superintendent Galloway.

"Yes, sir: the door is always locked inside or outside, and when I go to bed at night I take the key into my room and hang it on a nail. Ann comes in and gets it in the morning."

"You did that last night, as usual?"

"Yes, sir. Mother was quiet—just as you saw her now. She is quiet most of the time."

"God help her, poor soul!" exclaimed the chief constable. "Where does this passage lead to, Benson?" he asked, as if to change the conversation, pointing to a gloomy gallery running off the passage in which they were standing.

"It leads to two rooms looking out over the end of the inn, sir," replied the innkeeper. "They are the only two rooms you haven't seen."

"Who occupies this room?" asked Superintendent Galloway, opening the door of the first, and disclosing a small, plainly furnished bedroom.

"My daughter, sir."

"The next one is empty and unfurnished, like many of the others," observed the chief constable. "This place seems too big for you, Benson. Were all these rooms destitute of furniture when you took over the inn?"

"Not all, sir, but the inn being too big for me I sold the furniture for what it would fetch. It was no use to me."

"Why don't you take a smaller place?" asked Superintendent Galloway, abruptly. "You'll never do any good on this part of the coast—it's played out, and there's no population."

"I'm well aware of that, sir, but it's difficult for a man like me to make a shift once he gets into a place. There's Mother for one thing."

"She ought to be placed in a lunatic asylum," said the superintendent, looking sternly at the innkeeper.

"It's a hard thing, sir, to put your own mother away. Besides, begging your pardon, she's hardly bad enough for a lunatic asylum."

"Let us go downstairs, Galloway, if we have seen the whole of the inn," said the chief constable, breaking into this colloquy. "Time is really getting on."

They went downstairs again to the small room they had been shown into when they first entered the inn, Mr. Cromering after despatching the innkeeper for refreshments for the party glanced once more at his watch, and remarked to Colwyn that he was afraid he would have to ask him to drive him in his car back to Durrington without delay.

"Galloway will stay here for the inquest to-morrow," he added. "But I must get back to Norwich to-night."

"It is not necessary to go back to Durrington, to get to Norwich," said Colwyn; "there's a train passes through Heathfield on the branch line, at 5.40." He consulted his own watch as he spoke. "It's now just four o'clock. Heathfield cannot be more than six miles away across country. I can run you over there in twenty minutes. That would give you an hour or so more here. I am speaking for myself as well as you," he added, with a smile. "I should like to know a little more about this case."

"But I shall be taking you out of your way, and delaying the return of you and Sir Henry to Durrington."

"I should like to return here and stay until after the inquest. Perhaps Sir Henry would not mind returning to Durrington from Heathfield. He will be able to catch the Durrington train at Cottenden, and get back to his hotel in time for dinner. Would you mind, Sir Henry?"

"Not in the least," replied Sir Henry politely.

"Then I think I might stay a little longer," said the chief constable. "What's the road like to Heathfield, Galloway? You know something about this part of the country."

"Very bad," replied the superintendent uncompromisingly, who had his own reasons for wanting to get rid of his superior officer and the detective.

"It will be all right in daylight, and I'll risk it coming back," said the detective cheerfully.

He spoke with the resolute air of one used to making prompt decisions, and Mr. Cromering yielded with the feeble smile of a man who was rather glad to be released of the task of making up his own mind. The entrance of the innkeeper with refreshments put an end to the discussion. He thrust upon the police officials present the responsibility of breaking the licensed hours in which liquor might be drunk in war time by serving them with sherry, old brandy, and biscuits.

The chief constable made himself a party to this breach of the law by helping himself to a glass of sherry. The wine was excellent and dry, and he poured himself out another. The result of this stimulant was directly apparent in the firm tones with which he announced his intention of examining those inmates of the inn who could throw any light on the murder of the previous night. He directed Superintendent Galloway to sit beside him and take notes of the information thus elicited for the use of the coroner the following day.

"I think it would be as well to begin with the story of the innkeeper," he added. "Please pull that bell-rope, Galloway."

7

The innkeeper answered the bell in person, and was ordered by the chief constable to take a seat and tell everything he knew about the previous night's events, without equivocation or reserve. He took a chair at the table, his bright bird's glance wandering from one to the other of the faces opposite him as he smoothed with one claw-like hand the thatch of iron-grey hair which hung down over his forehead almost to his eyes.

"Where shall I begin?" he asked. "You had better start by telling us how this young man Ronald came to your house yesterday afternoon, and then give us an account of the subsequent events, so far as you know them," said the chief constable.

"I was down near the breakwater yesterday evening, setting some eel-lines in the canal, when he arrived," commenced the innkeeper. "When I came in, Charles—that's the waiter—told me there was a young gentleman in the bar parlour waiting to see me. I went into the parlour, and saw the young man sitting near the door. He looked very tired and weary, and said he wished to stay at the inn for the night."

"How was he dressed?" asked Superintendent Galloway, looking up from his note-book.

"In a grey Norfolk suit, with knickerbockers, and a soft felt hat."

"Had you ever seen him before?"

"No, sir. He was a complete stranger to me. I could see he was a gentleman. I told him I could not take him in, as the inn was only a poor rough place, with no accommodation for gentlefolk at the best of times, let alone war-time. The young gentleman said he was very tired and would sleep anywhere, and was not particular about food. He told me he had lost his way on the marshes, and a fisherman had directed him to the inn."

"Did he say where he had come from?" asked the chief constable.

"No, sir, and I didn't think to ask him. I might have done so, but Mr. Glenthorpe walked into the parlour just then, carrying some partridges in his hand. He didn't see the young gentleman at first–he was sitting in the corner behind the door–but told me to have one of the partridges cooked for his dinner. They had just been given to him, he said, by the farmer whose land he was going to excavate next week. As he turned to go out he saw the young gentleman sitting in the corner, and he said, in his hearty way: 'Good evening, sir; it is not often that we have any society in these parts.' The young gentleman told him what he had told me–how he had wandered away from Durrington and got lost, and had come to the inn in the hopes of getting a bed for the night. 'Glad to see a civilised human being in these parts,' said Mr. Glenthorpe. 'I hope you'll give me the pleasure of your company at dinner. Benson, tell Ann to cook another partridge.' 'I don't know whether the innkeeper will allow me that pleasure,' replied the young gentleman. 'He says he cannot put me up for the night.' 'Of course he'll put you up,' said Mr. Glenthorpe. 'Not even a Norfolk innkeeper would turn you out on to the North Sea marshes at this time of year.' That settled the question, because I couldn't afford to offend Mr. Glenthorpe, and besides, his providing the dinner helped me out of a difficulty. So I went out to give orders about the dinner, leaving Mr. Glenthorpe and him sitting together talking."

"Did you get him to fill in a registration form?" asked Superintendent Galloway.

"I forgot to ask him, sir," replied the innkeeper.

"That is gross and inexcusable carelessness on your part, Benson," said Galloway sternly. "I shall have to report it."

"I do not understand much about these things, sir," replied the innkeeper apologetically. "It is so rarely that we have a visitor to the place."

"The authorities will hold you responsible. You are supposed to know the law, and help to carry it out. What's the use of devising regulations for the security of the country if they are not carried out? You innkeepers and hotel-keepers are really very careless. Go on with your story, Benson."

"He and Mr. Glenthorpe had dinner together in the little upstairs sitting room which Mr. Glenthorpe kept for his own private use. He did his writing in it, and the flints and fossils he discovered in his excavations were stored in the cupboards. His meals were always taken up there, and last night he ordered the dinner to be taken up there as usual, and the table to be laid for two. Charles waited at table, but I was up there twice—first time with some sherry, and the second time was about an hour afterwards, when the gentlemen had finished dinner. I took up a bottle of some old brandy that the inn used to be famous for—it's the same that you gentlemen have been drinking. When I knocked at the door with the brandy it was Mr. Glenthorpe who called 'Come in!' He was standing in front of the fire, with a fossil in his hand, and he was telling the young man about how he came to discover it. I put the brandy on the table and left the room.

"That was the last time I saw him alive. Charles came down with the dinner things about half-past nine, and said he was not wanted upstairs any more. Charles went to bed shortly afterwards—he sleeps in one of the two rooms off the kitchen. I went to my own bedroom before ten, after first telling Ann, the servant, who was doing some ironing in the kitchen, to turn off the gas at the meter if the gentlemen retired before she finished, but not to bother if they were still sitting up. It had been decided that the young gentleman should occupy the bedroom next to Mr. Glenthorpe, and Ann was a bit late with her ordinary work because it had taken her some time to get his room ready. The room had not been occupied for some time, and she'd had to air the bed-clothes and make the bed afresh.

"The next morning I was a bit late getting down—there's nothing to open the inn for in the mornings—and Ann told me as soon as I got down that the young gentleman had left nearly an hour before. She had taken him up an early cup of tea at seven o'clock, and he opened the door to her knock, and took it from her. He was fully dressed, except for his boots, which he had in his hand, and he asked her to clean them, as he wanted to leave at once. She was walking away with the boots, when he called her back and took them from her, saying that it didn't matter about cleaning them, as he was in a hurry. When she gave him the boots he put a note into her hand, and said that was to pay for his bill.

"It was the key in the outside of Mr. Glenthorpe's room which led to us finding out that he was not in the room. As I told you upstairs, sir, he used to always lock his door when he went to bed and put the key under the pillow. Ann noticed the key in the outside of the door when she went up with his breakfast tray—he never took early morning tea but he always breakfasted in his room. That would be about eight o'clock. She thought it strange to see the key in the door, and as she could get no answer to her knock she tried the door, found it unlocked and the room empty. She came downstairs and told me. I thought at first that Mr. Glenthorpe might have got up early to go and look at his excavations, but I went up to his room and saw the signs of a struggle and blood-stains on the bed-clothes, and I knew that something must have happened to him. I went into the village and told Constable Queensmead. He came to the inn, and made a search inside and outside and found the footprints leading to the pit on the rise. One of Mr. Glenthorpe's men who had been down the pit for flints was lowered by a rope, and brought up the body."

The innkeeper took a leather wallet from his pocket and produced from it a Treasury £1 note. "This is the note the young gentleman left behind with Ann to pay his bill," he explained, pushing it across the table to the chief constable.

"I would draw your attention, sir, to the fact that this Treasury note is one of the first issue–printed in black on white paper," remarked Superintendent Galloway to his superior officer. "Constable Queensmead has ascertained that the £300 which Mr. Glenthorpe drew out of the bank yesterday was all in £1 notes of the first issue. That money is missing from the dead man's effects."

The chief constable looked thoughtfully at the note through his glasses, and then passed it to Colwyn, who examined it closely, and took a note of the number, and held it up to the light to see the watermark.

"Did you or the servant find any weapon in Mr. Glenthorpe's room?" asked the chief constable.

"No, sir."

"You have missed a knife though, have you not?" asked Superintendent Galloway.

"Yes, sir."

"What sort of a knife?"

"A table-knife."

"Was it one of the knives sent up to the sitting-room last night?"

"Yes, sir. At least Charles says so. He has charge of the cutlery."

"Then Charles had better tell us about it," interposed the chief constable. "You say you went to bed before ten o'clock, Benson. Did you hear anything in the night?"

"No, sir, I fell asleep almost immediately. My room is a good distance from Mr. Glenthorpe's room."

"I do not think we have any more questions to ask you, Benson."

"Pardon the curiosity of a medical man, Mr. Cromering," remarked Sir Henry, "but would it be possible to ask the innkeeper whether he noticed anything peculiar about Mr. Ronald's demeanour, when he arrived at the inn, or when he saw him at dinner subsequently?"

"You hear that question, Benson?" said the chief constable. "Did you notice anything strange about Mr. Ronald's conduct when first he came to the inn or at any time?"

"I cannot say I did, sir. I thought he looked very tired when he first came into the inn, and his eyes were heavy as though with want of sleep."

"He seemed quite sane and rational?"

"Quite, sir."

"Did you notice any symptoms of mental disturbance or irritability about him at any time?" struck in Sir Henry Durwood.

"No, sir. He was a little bit angry at first when I said I couldn't take him in, but he struck me as quite cool and collected."

Sir Henry looked a little disappointed at this reply. He asked no more questions, but entered a note in a small note-book which he took from his waistcoat pocket. Mr. Cromering intimated to the innkeeper that he had finished questioning him, and would like to examine the waiter, Charles.

"If you wouldn't mind pulling the bell-rope behind you, sir," hinted the innkeeper.

In response to a pull at the old-fashioned bell-rope, the stout country servant, who had been washing greens in the kitchen, entered the room.

"Where is Charles, Ann?" asked the innkeeper.

"He's in the kitchen," replied the woman nervously.

"Then tell him he is wanted here immediately."

"You run your inn in a queer sort of way, Benson," remarked Superintendent Galloway, in his loud voice, as the woman went away on her errand. "Why couldn't

Charles have answered the bell himself, if he is in the kitchen? What does he wait on, if not the bar parlour?"

"Charles is stone deaf, sir," replied the innkeeper.

8

The man who entered the room was of sufficiently remarkable appearance to have attracted attention anywhere. He was short, but so fat that he looked less than his actual height, which was barely five feet. His ponderous head, which was covered with short stiff black hair, like a brush, seemed to merge into his body without any neck, and two black eyes glittered like diamond points in the white expanse of his hairless face. As he advanced towards the table these eyes roved quickly from one to the other of the faces on the other side of the table. He was in every way a remarkable contrast to his employer, and a painter in search of a subject might have been tempted to take the pair as models for a picture of Don Quixote and Sancho Panza.

"Take that chair and answer my questions," said Mr. Cromering, addressing the waiter in a very loud voice. "Oh, I forgot," he added, to the innkeeper. "How do you manage to communicate with him if he is stone deaf?"

"Quite easily, sir. Charles understands the lip language—he reads your lips while you speak. It is not even necessary to raise your voice, so long as you pronounce each word distinctly."

"Sit down, Charles—do you understand me?" said the chief constable doubtfully. By way of helping the waiter to comprehend he pointed to the chair the innkeeper had vacated.

The waiter crossed the room and took the chair. Like so many fat men, his movements were quick, agile, and noiseless, but as he came forward it was noticeable that his right arm was deformed, and much shorter than the other.

The chief constable eyed the strange figure before him in some perplexity, and the fat white-faced deaf man confronted him stolidly, with his black twinkling eyes fixed on his face. His gaze, which was directed to the mouth and did not reach the eyes, was so disconcerting to Mr. Cromering that he cleared his throat with several nervous "hems" before commencing his examination:

"Your name is—?"

"Charles Lynn, sir."

The reply was delivered in a whispered voice, the not infrequent result of prolonged deafness, complete isolation from the rest of humanity causing the gradual loss of sound values in the afflicted person; but the whisper, coming from such a mountain of flesh, conveyed the impression that the speaker's voice was half-strangled in layers of fat, and with difficulty gasped a way to the air. Mr. Cromering looked hard at the waiter as though suspecting him of some trick, but Charles' eyes were fixed on the mouth of his interrogator, awaiting his next question.

"I understand that you waited on the two gentlemen in the upstairs sitting-room last night"–Mr. Cromering still spoke in such an unnecessarily loud voice that he grew red in the face with the exertion–"the gentleman who was murdered, and the young man Ronald, who came to the inn last night. Do you understand me?"

"Yes, sir. I waited on the gentlemen, sir."

"Very well. I want you to tell us all that took place between these gentlemen while you were in the room. You were there all through the dinner, I suppose?"

"Yes, sir, but I didn't follow all of the conversation because of my infirmity." He touched his ears as he spoke. "I gathered some remarks of Mr. Glenthorpe's, because he told me to stand opposite him and watch his lips for orders, but I didn't get much of what the young gentleman said, because I was standing behind his chair most of the time so as to see Mr. Glenthorpe's lips better."

"Well, tell us all you did gather of the conversation, and everything you saw."

"I beg your pardon, sir"–the interruption came from Superintendent Galloway–"but would it not be advisable to get from the waiter first something of what passed between him and Ronald when Ronald came to the inn last night? The waiter was the first to see him, Benson says."

"Quite right. I had forgotten. Tell us, Charles, what passed when Ronald first came to the inn in the afternoon."

"It was between five and six o'clock, sir, when the young gentleman came to the front door and asked for the landlord. I told him he was out, but would be back shortly. The young gentleman said he was very tired, as he had walked a long distance and lost his way in the marshes, and would I show him into a private room and send him some refreshments. I took him into the bar parlour–this room, sir–and brought him refreshments. He seemed very tired–hardly able to lift one leg after the other."

"Did he look ill–or strange?"

"I didn't notice anything strange about him, sir, but he dropped into a chair as though he was exhausted, and told me to send the landlord to him as soon as he came in. I left him sitting there, and when Mr. Benson returned I told him, and he went in to him. I didn't see the young gentleman again until I waited on him and Mr. Glenthorpe at dinner in the upstairs sitting-room."

"Very good. Tell us what happened there."

"I laid the table, and took up the dinner at half-past seven. Those were Mr. Glenthorpe's orders. When I went up the first time the table was covered with flints and fossils, which Mr. Glenthorpe was showing the young gentleman, and I helped Mr. Glenthorpe put these back into the cupboards, and then I laid the table. When I took up the dinner the gentlemen sat down to it, and Mr.

Glenthorpe rang for Mr. Benson, and told him to bring up some sherry. When the sherry came up Mr. Glenthorpe told the young gentleman that it was a special wine sent down by his London wine merchants, and he asked Mr. Ronald what he thought of it. Mr. Ronald said he thought it was an excellent dry wine. The gentlemen didn't talk much during dinner, though Mr. Glenthorpe was a little upset about the partridges. He said they had been cooked too dry. He asked the young gentleman what he thought of them, but I don't know what he replied, for I was not watching his lips.

"Mr. Glenthorpe quite recovered himself by the time coffee was served, and was talking a lot about his researches in the neighbourhood. It was very learned talk, but it seemed to interest Mr. Ronald, for he asked a number of questions. Mr. Glenthorpe seemed very pleased with his interest, and told him about a valuable discovery made in a field near what he called the hut circles. He said he had bought the field off the farmer for £300, and was going to commence his excavations immediately. As the farmer refused to take a cheque for the land he had been over to the bank at Heathfield for the money, and had brought it back with him so as to pay it over in the morning and take possession of the field. Mr. Glenthorpe complained that the bank had made him take all the money in Treasury notes, and he took them out of his pocket and showed them to the young gentleman, saying how bulky they were, and pointing out that they were all of the first issue."

"And what did Ronald say to that?"

If the chief constable's question covered a trap, the waiter seemed unconscious of it.

"I wasn't looking at him, sir, and did not hear his reply. After putting the money back in his pocket, Mr. Glenthorpe told me to go downstairs and tell Mr. Benson to bring up some of the old brandy. Mr. Benson came back with me, and Mr. Glenthorpe took the bottle from him and filled the glasses himself, telling the young gentleman that the brandy was the best in England, a relic of the old smuggling days, but far too good for scoundrels who had never paid the King's revenue one half-penny. Then when Mr. Benson had left the room he began to talk about the field again, and how anxious he was to start the excavations. That was about all I heard, sir, for shortly afterwards Mr. Glenthorpe told me to clear away the things, which took me several trips downstairs, because, not having the full use of my right hand, I have to use a small tray. It was not till this morning, when I was cleaning the cutlery, that I noticed that one of the knives I had taken upstairs the night before was missing. I think that is all, sir."

The silence which followed, broken only by the rapid travelling of Superintendent Galloway's pen across the paper, revealed how intently the fat man's auditors had followed his whispered recital of the events before the murder. It was Superintendent Galloway who, putting down his fountain pen, asked the waiter to describe the knife he had missed.

"It was a small, white-handled knife, sir—not one of the dinner knives, but one of the smaller ones."

"Are you sure it was one of the knives you took upstairs last night?"

"Quite sure, sir. We are very short of good cutlery, and I picked out this knife to put by the young gentleman's plate because it was a very good one. It and the carving-knife are the only two knives we have in that particular white-handled pattern."

"Was this knife sharp?"

"Very sharp, with a rather thin blade. I keep all my cutlery in good order, sir."

"You seem to have heard a lot that passed last night in spite of your deafness," said Superintendent Galloway, in the blustering manner he had found very useful in browbeating rural witnesses in the police courts. "Is it customary for waiters to listen to everything that is said when they are waiting at table?"

"I did not hear everything, sir," rejoined the waiter, and his soft whisper was in striking contrast to the superintendent's hectoring tones. "I explained to the other gentleman that I heard very little the young gentleman said, because I wasn't watching his lips. It was principally Mr. Glenthorpe's part of the conversation I have related. I followed almost everything he said because I was watching his lips closely the whole of the time."

"Why?" snapped Superintendent Galloway.

"It was Mr. Glenthorpe's strict instructions that I was to watch his lips closely every time I waited on him, because of my infirmity. He disliked very much being waited on by a deaf waiter when first he came to the inn. He said he didn't want to have to bellow out when he wanted anything. But when he found that I could understand lip language, and could follow what he was saying by watching his lips, he allowed me to wait on him, but he gave me strict instructions never to take my eyes off him when I was waiting on him, because he disliked having to repeat an order."

At the request of Sir Henry, Superintendent Galloway asked the waiter if he had noticed anything peculiar in the actions of the murdered man's guest during the dinner. The waiter replied that he had not noticed the young gentleman particularly. So far as his observation went the young gentleman had acted just like an ordinary young gentleman, and he had noticed nothing strange or eccentric about him.

Mr. Cromering decided to occupy the remaining time at his disposal by questioning Ann. The stout servant was brought from the kitchen in a state of trepidation, and, after curtsying awkwardly to the assembled gentlemen, flopped heavily into a chair, covered her face with her apron, and burst into sobs. Her story—which was extracted from her with much difficulty—bore out the innkeeper's account of her early morning interview with Ronald. She said the poor young gentleman had opened the door when she knocked with his tea. He was fully dressed, with his boots in his hand, and he said he wouldn't wait for any breakfast, though she had offered to cook him some fresh fish the master had caught the day before. He asked her to clean his boots, but as she was carrying them away he called her back and said he would wear them as they were. They were all covered with mud—a regular mask of mud. She wanted to rub the mud off, but he said that didn't matter: he was in a hurry to get away. While she had them in her hands she turned them up and looked at the bottoms, intending to put them to the kitchen fire to dry them if the soles were wet, and it was then she noticed that there was a circular rubber heel on one which was missing on the other—only the iron peg being left. She took particular notice of the peg, because she intended to hammer it down in the kitchen, thinking it must be very uncomfortable to walk on, but the young gentleman didn't give her the chance—he just took the boots from her and walked into his room, shutting the door behind him.

Thus far Ann proceeded, between convulsive sobs and jelly-like tremors of her fat frame. By dint of further questioning, it was elicited from her that during this colloquy at the bedroom door the young gentleman had put a pound note into her hand, and told her to give it to her master in payment of his bill. "It won't be so much as that, sir," she had said. "What about the change?"

"Oh, damn the change!" the young gentleman had said, very impatient-like, and then he had said, "Here's something for yourself," and put five shillings into her hand.

"Did the young gentleman seem at all excited during the time you saw him?" asked the chief constable, anticipating the inevitable question from Sir Henry.

"I don't know what you mean by excited, sir. He seemed rarely impatient to be gone, though anybody might be excited at having to walk across them nasty marshes in the morning mist without a bite to stay the stomach. I only hope he didn't catch a chill, the poor young man."

Further questions on this point only brought forth another shower of tears, and a sobbing asseveration that she hadn't taken particular notice of the young gentleman, who was a kind, liberal-hearted gentleman, no matter what some folk might think. It was evident that the tip of five shillings had won her heart.

The chief constable waited for the storm to subside before he was able to extract the information that Ann hadn't seen the young gentleman leave the house. He had gone when she took up Mr. Glenthorpe's breakfast nearly an hour later, and made the discovery that the key of Mr. Glenthorpe's room was in the outside of the door, and his room empty. The young gentleman could easily have left the inn without being seen, for she and Charles were in the kitchen, and nobody else was downstairs at the time.

It was in response to Colwyn's whispered suggestion that the chief constable asked Ann if she had turned off the gas at the meter the previous night. Yes, she had, she said. She heard the gentlemen leave the sitting-room upstairs and say good-night to each other as they went to their bedrooms, and she turned off the gas at the meter underneath the stair five minutes afterwards, when she had finished her ironing, and went to bed herself. That would be about half-past ten.

Mr. Cromering, who did not understand the purport of the question, was satisfied with the answer, and allowed the servant to retire. But Colwyn, as he went out to the front to get the motor ready for the journey to Heathfield, was of a different opinion.

"Ann may have turned off the gas as she said," he thought, "but it was turned on again during the night.

Did Ann know this, and keep it back, or was it turned on and off again without her knowledge?"

9

"Everything fits in beautifully," said Superintendent Galloway confidently. "I never knew a clearer case. All that remains for me to do is to lay my hands on this chap Ronald, and an intelligent jury will see to the rest."

The police official and the detective had dined together in the small bar parlour on Colwyn's return from driving Mr. Cromering and Sir Henry Durwood to Heathfield Station. The superintendent had done more than justice to the meal, and a subsequent glass of the smugglers' brandy had so mellowed the milk of human kindness in his composition that he felt inclined for a little friendly conversation with his companion.

"You are very confident," said Colwyn.

"Of course I am confident. I have reason to be so. Everything I have seen to-day supports my original theory about this crime."

"And what is your theory as to the manner in which this crime was committed? I have gathered a general idea of the line you are taking by listening to your conversation this afternoon, but I should like you to state your theory in precise terms. It is an interesting case, with some peculiar points about it which a frank discussion might help to elucidate."

Superintendent Galloway looked suspiciously at Colwyn out of his small hard grey eyes. His official mind scented an attempt to trap him, and his Norfolk prudence prompted him to get what he could from the detective but to give nothing away in return.

"I see you're suspicious of me, Galloway," continued Colwyn with a smile. "You've heard of city detectives and their ways, and you're thinking to yourself that a Norfolk man is more than a match for any of them."

This sally was so akin to what was passing in the superintendent's mind that a grim smile momentarily relaxed his rugged features.

"My thoughts are my own, I suppose," he said.

"Not when you've just given them away," replied Colwyn, in a bantering tone. "My dear Galloway, your ingenuous countenance is a mirror to your mind, in which he who runs may read. But you are quite wrong in suspecting me. I have no ulterior motive. My only interest in this crime–or in any crime–is to solve it. Anybody can have the credit, as far as I am concerned. Newspaper notoriety is nothing to me."

"You've managed to get a good deal of it without looking for it, then," retorted the superintendent cannily. "It was only the other day I was reading a long article in one of the London newspapers about you, praising you for tracking the criminals in the Treasury Bonds case. The police were not mentioned."

"Fame–or notoriety–sometimes comes to those who seek it least," replied the detective genially. "I assure you that article came unasked. I'm a stranger to the political art of keeping sweet with the journalists–it was a statesman, you know, who summed up gratitude as a lively sense of favours to come. Now, in this case, let us play fair, actuated by the one desire to see that justice is done. This case does not strike me as quite such a simple affair as it seems to you. You approach it with a preconceived theory to which you are determined to adhere. Your theory is plausible and convincing–to some extent–but that is all the more reason why you should examine and test every link in the chain. You cannot solve difficult points by ignoring them and, to my mind, there are some difficult and perplexing features about this case which do not altogether fit in with your theory."

"If my mind is an open book to you perhaps you'll tell me what my theory is," responded Superintendent Galloway, sourly.

"Yes; that's a fair challenge." The detective pushed back his chair, and stood with his back against the mantelpiece, with a cigar in his mouth. "Your theory in this case is that chance and opportunity have made the crime and the criminal. Chance brings this young man Ronald to this lonely Norfolk inn, and sees to it that he is allowed to remain when the landlord wants to turn him away. Chance throws him into the society of a man of culture and education, who is only too glad of the opportunity of relieving the tedium of his surroundings in this rough uncultivated place by passing a few hours in the companionship of a man of his own rank of life. Chance contrives that this gentleman shall have in his possession a large sum of money which he shows to Ronald, who is greatly in need of money. Opportunity suggests the murder, provides the weapon, and gives Ronald the next room to his intended victim in a wing of the inn occupied by nobody else.

"Your theory as to how the murder was actually committed strikes me as possible enough—up to a certain point. You think that Ronald, after waiting until everybody in the inn is likely to be asleep, steals out of his own room to the room of his victim. He finds the door locked. Chance, however, has thoughtfully provided him with a window opening on to a hillside, which enables him to climb out of his own window and into the window of the next room. He gets in, murders Mr. Glenthorpe, secures his money, and, finding the key of his bedroom under the pillow, carries the body of his victim downstairs, and outside, casting it into a deep hole some distance from the house, in the hope of preventing or retarding discovery of the crime. Through an oversight he forgets the key in the door, which he had placed in the outside before carrying off the body, intending when he returned to lock the door and carry the key away with him.

"Next morning you have the highly suspicious circumstance of the young man's hurried departure, his refusal to have his boots cleaned, the incident of the £1 note, and the unshakable fact that the footprints leading to and from the pit where the body was discovered had been made by his boots.

"As a further contributory link in the chain of evidence against Ronald, you intend to use the fact that he was turned out of the Grand Hotel, Durrington, the previous day because he couldn't pay his hotel bill, because this fact, combined with the fact that Mr. Glenthorpe showed him the money he had drawn from the bank at Heathfield, supplies a strong motive for the crime. In this connection you intend to try to establish that the Treasury note which Ronald left to pay his inn bill was one of those in Mr. Glenthorpe's possession, because it happens to be one of the First Treasury issue, printed in black and white, and all Mr. Glenthorpe's notes were of that issue, according to the murdered man's own statement. That, I take it, is the police theory of this case."

"It is," said Superintendent Galloway. "You've put it a bit more fancifully than I should, but it comes to the same thing. But what do you make out of the incident at the Grand Hotel, Durrington, yesterday morning? You were there, and saw it all. Does it seem strange to you that Ronald should have come straight to this inn and committed a murder after making that scene at the hotel? Do you think it suggests that Ronald has, well–impulses of violence, let us say?" Superintendent Galloway poured himself out another glass of old brandy and sipped it deliberately, watching the detective cautiously between the sips.

Colwyn was silent for a moment. He was quick to comprehend the double-barrelled motive which underlay the superintendent's question, and he had no intention of letting the police officer pump him for his own ends.

"Sir Henry Durwood would be better able to answer that question than I," he said.

"I asked him when we were driving over here this afternoon, but he shut up like an oyster—you know what these professional men are, with their stiff-and-starched ideas of etiquette," grumbled the superintendent.

A flicker of amusement showed in Colwyn's eyes. Really the superintendent was easily drawn, for an East Anglian countryman. "After all, it is only Sir Henry Durwood's opinion that Ronald intended violence at the *Grand*," he said. "Sir Henry did not give him the opportunity to carry out his intention—if he had such an intention."

"Exactly my opinion," exclaimed Superintendent Galloway, eagerly rising to the fly. "I have ascertained that Ronald's behaviour during the time he was staying at the hotel was that of an ordinary sane Englishman. The proprietor says he was quite a gentleman, with nothing eccentric or peculiar about him, and the servants say the same. They are the best judges, after all. And nobody noticed anything peculiar about him at the breakfast table except yourself and Sir Henry—and what happened? Nothing, except that he was a bit excited—and no wonder, after the young man had just been ordered to leave the hotel. Then Sir Henry grabbed hold of him and he fainted—or pretended to faint; it may have been all part of his game. Sir Henry may have thought he intended to do something or other, but no British judge would admit that as evidence for the defence. This chap Ronald is as sane as you or me, and a deep, cunning cold-blooded scoundrel to boot. If the defence try to put up a plea of insanity they'll find themselves in the wrong box. There's not a jury in the world that wouldn't hang him on the evidence against him."

This time Colwyn could not forbear smiling at the guileless way in which Superintendent Galloway had revealed the thoughts which had been passing through his mind. But his amusement was momentary, and it was in a grave, earnest tone that he replied:

"The hotel incident is a puzzling one, but I agree with you that it doesn't enter into the police case against Ronald. It is your duty to deal with the facts of the case, and if you think that Ronald committed this murder—"

"If I think that Ronald committed this murder!" Superintendent Galloway's interruption was both amazed and indignant. "I'm as certain he committed the murder as if I saw him do it with my own eyes. Did you, or anybody else, ever see a clearer case?"

"It is because the circumstantial evidence against him is so strong that I speak as I do," continued Colwyn, in the same earnest tones. "Innocent men have been hanged in England before now on circumstantial evidence. It is for that very reason that we should guard ourselves against the tendency to accept the circumstantial evidence against him as proof of his guilt, instead of examining all the facts with an open mind. We are the investigators of the circumstances: it is not for us to prejudge. That is the worst of circumstantial evidence: it tends to prejudgment, and sometimes to the ignoring of circumstances and facts which might tell in favour of the suspect, if they were examined with a more impartial eye. It is for these reasons that I am always careful to suspend judgment in cases of circumstantial evidence, and examine carefully even the smallest trifles which might tell in favour of the man to whom circumstantial evidence points.

"Have you discovered anything, since you have been at the inn, which shakes the theory that Ronald is the murderer?"

"I have come to the conclusion that the case is much more complex and puzzling than was at first supposed."

"I should like to know what makes you think that," returned Superintendent Galloway. "Up to the present I have seen nothing to shake my conviction that Ronald is the guilty man. What have you discovered that makes you think otherwise?"

"I do not go as far as that—yet. But I have come across certain things which, to my mind, need elucidation before it is possible to pronounce definitely on Ronald's guilt or innocence. To take them consecutively, let me repeat that I cannot reconcile Ronald's excitable conduct at the Durrington hotel with his supposed actions at the inn. In the former case he behaved like a man who, whether insane or merely excited, had not the slightest fear of the consequences. At this inn he acted like a crafty cautious scoundrel who had weighed the consequences of his acts beforehand, and took every possible precaution to save his own skin. You see nothing inconsistent in this—"

"I do not," interjected the superintendent firmly.

"Quite so. Then, the next point that perplexes me is why Ronald took the trouble to carry the body of his victim to the pit and throw it in."

"For the motive of concealment, and to retard discovery. But for the footprints it would probably have given him several days—perhaps weeks—in which to make good his escape."

"Did he not run a bigger risk of discovery by carrying the body downstairs in an occupied house, and across several hundred yards of open land close to the village?"

"Not in a remote spot like this. They keep early hours in this part of the country. I guarantee if you walked through the village now you wouldn't see a soul stirring."

"Ronald was not likely to know that. Next, how did Ronald, a stranger to the place, know the locality of this pit so accurately as to be able to walk straight to it?"

"Easily. He might have approached the inn from that side, and passed it on his way. And nothing is more likely than Mr. Glenthorpe would tell him about the pit in the course of his conversation about the excavations. There is also the possibility that Ronald knew of the existence of the pit from a previous visit to this part of the country."

"My next point is that Ronald was put to sleep in what he imagined was an upstairs bedroom. How did he discover that his bedroom, and the bedroom of Mr. Glenthorpe's adjoining, opened on to a hillside which enabled him to get out of one bedroom and into the other?"

"Again, Mr. Glenthorpe probably told him–he seems to have been a garrulous old chap, according to all accounts. Or Ronald may have looked out of his window when he was retiring, and seen it for himself. I always look out of a bedroom window, and particularly if it is a strange bedroom, before getting into bed."

"These are matters of opinion, and, though your explanations are possible ones, I do not agree with you. We are looking at this case from entirely different points of view. You believe that Ronald committed the murder, and you are allowing that belief to colour everything connected with the case. I am looking at this murder as a mystery which has not yet been solved, and, without excluding the possibility that Ronald is the murderer, I am not going, because of the circumstantial evidence against him, to accept his guilt as a foregone conclusion until I have carefully examined and tested all the facts for and against that theory.

"The one outstanding probability is that Mr. Glenthorpe was murdered for his money. Now, excluding for the time being the circumstantial evidence against Ronald–though without losing sight of it–the next point that arises is was he murdered by somebody in the inn or by somebody from outside–say, for example, one of the villagers employed on his excavation works. The waiter's story of the missing knife suggests the former theory, but I do not regard that evidence as incontrovertible. The knife might have been stolen from the kitchen by a man who had been drinking at the bar; indeed, until we have recovered the weapon it is not even established that this was the knife with which the murder was committed. It might have been some other knife. We must not take the waiter's story for granted until we have recovered the knife, and not necessarily then. But that story, as it stands, inclines to support the theory that the murder was committed by somebody in the inn. On the other hand, the theory of an outside murderer lends itself to a very plausible reconstruction of the crime. Suppose, for example, the murder had been committed by one of Mr. Glenthorpe's workmen, actuated by the dual motives of revenge and robbery, or by either motive. Apparently the whole village knew of Mr. Glenthorpe's intention to draw this money which was in his possession when he was murdered—he seems to have been a man who talked very freely of his private affairs—and the amount, £300, would be a fortune to an agricultural labourer or a fisherman. Such a man would know all about the bedroom windows on that side of the inn opening on to the hillside, and would naturally choose that means of entry to commit the crime. And, if he were a labourer in Mr. Glenthorpe's employ, the thought of concealing the body by casting it into the pit would probably occur to him."

"I do not think there is much in that theory," said Superintendent Galloway thoughtfully. "Still, it is worth putting to the test. I'll inquire in the morning if any of the villagers are suspicious characters, or whether any of Glenthorpe's men had a grudge against him."

"Now let us leave theories and speculations and come to facts. Our investigations of the murdered man's room this afternoon gave us several clues, not the least important of which is that we are enabled to fix the actual time of the murder with some degree of accuracy. It is always useful, in a case of murder, to be able to establish the approximate time at which it was committed. In this case, the murder was certainly committed between the hours of 11 p.m. and 11.30 p.m., and, in all probability, not much before half-past eleven."

"How do you fix it so accurately as that?" asked the police officer, looking keenly at the detective.

"According to Ann, the gentlemen went to their rooms about half-past ten, and she turned off the gas downstairs shortly afterwards, and went to bed herself. When we examined the room this afternoon, we found patches of red mud of the same colour and consistency of the soil outside the window leading from the window to the bedside, and a pool—a small isolated pool—of water near the open window. There were, as you recollect, no footprints outside the window. On the other hand, the footprints from the inn to the pit are clear and distinct. Rain commenced to fall last night shortly before eleven, but it did not fall heavily until eleven o'clock. From then till half-past eleven it was a regular downpour, when it ceased, and it has not rained since. Now, the patches of red mud in the bedroom, and the obliteration of footprints outside the window, prove that the murderer entered the room during the storm, but the footprints leading to the pit prove that the body was not removed from the room until the rain had completely ceased, otherwise they would have been obliterated also, or partly obliterated. These facts make it clear that the murder was committed between eleven and half-past, but the pool of water near the window enables us to fix the time more accurately still, and say that he entered the room during the time the rain was at its heaviest—that is, between ten minutes past and half-past eleven."

"I'm hanged if I see how you fix it so definitely," said the superintendent, who had been following the other's deductions with interest. "The pool of water may have collected at any time, once the window was open."

"My dear Galloway, you are working on the rule-of-thumb deduction that the rain blew in the open window and formed the pool. As a matter of fact, it did nothing of the kind. The wind was blowing the other way, and *away* from that side of the house. Furthermore, the hill on that side of the inn acts as a natural barrier against rain and weather."

"Then how the deuce do you account for the water in the room?"

"Surely you have not forgotten the piece of black material we found sticking on the nail outside the window?"

"I have not forgotten it, but I do not see how you connect it with the pool of water."

"Because it is a piece of umbrella silk. The murderer was carrying an umbrella–and an open umbrella–have you the piece of silk? If so, let us look at it."

The superintendent produced the square inch of silk from his waistcoat pocket, and examined it closely: "Of course it's umbrella silk," he exclaimed, slapping his leg. "Funny I didn't recognise it at the time."

"Perhaps I wouldn't have recognised it myself, but for the fact that a piece of umbrella silk formed an important clue in a recent case I was engaged upon," replied the detective. "Experience counts for a lot–sometimes. See, this piece of silk is hemmed on the edge–pretty conclusive proof that the murderer was carrying the umbrella open, to shield him from the rain, and that it caught on the nail outside the window, tearing off the edge. He closed it as he got inside the window, and placed it near the window-sill, and the rain dripped off it and formed the pool of water. The size of the pool, and the fact that the murderer carried an open umbrella to shield him, prove pretty conclusively that he made his entrance into the room during the time the rain was falling heaviest–which was between 11.10 p.m. and 11.30.

"We now come to what is the most important discovery of all–the pieces of candle-grease we found in the murdered man's bedroom. They help to establish two curious facts, the least important of which is that somebody tried to light the gas in Mr. Glenthorpe's room last night, and, failing to do so, went downstairs and turned on the gas at the meter."

"What if they did?" grunted Superintendent Galloway, pouring out another glass of brandy. He was secretly annoyed at having overlooked the clue of the umbrella silk, and was human enough to be angry with the detective for opening his eyes to the fact. "I don't see how you're going to prove it, and, even if you did, it doesn't matter a dump one way or the other."

"We'll let that point go," rejoined Colwyn curtly. "Your attitude in shutting your eyes to facts hardly encourages me to proceed, but I'll try. Would you mind showing me those bits of candle-grease you picked up in the bedroom?"

Superintendent Galloway produced a metal match-box from his pocket, emptied some pieces of candle-grease, a burnt wooden match and a broken matchhead from it, and sat back eyeing the detective with a supercilious smile. Colwyn, after examining them closely, brought from his own pocket an envelope, and shook several more pieces of candle-grease on the table.

"Look at these pieces of candle-grease side by side," he said. "Yours were picked up alongside the bed; I found mine underneath the gas burner."

Superintendent Galloway glanced at the pieces of candle-grease with the same supercilious smile. "I see them," he said. "They are pieces of candle-grease. What of them?"

"Do you not see that they are different kinds of candle-grease? The pieces you picked up alongside the bed are tallow; mine, picked up from underneath the gas-globe, are wax."

The Superintendent had not noticed the difference in the candle-grease, but he thought it beneath his dignity to examine them again. "The murderer may have had two candles," he said oracularly. "Anyway, what does it matter? They're both candle-grease."

Colwyn swept his fragments back into his pocket with a quick impatient gesture. "Both candle-grease, as you say," he returned sharply. "We do not seem to be making much progress in our investigations, so let us discontinue them. Good-night."

10

Colwyn went to bed, but not to sleep. Hour after hour he lay awake, staring into the darkness, endeavouring to put together the facts he had discovered during the afternoon's investigations at the inn. But they resembled those irritating odd-shaped pieces of a puzzle which refuse to fit into the remainder no matter which way they are turned. Try as he would, he could not fit his clues into harmony with the police theory of the murder.

On the other hand, he could not, nor did he attempt, to shut his eyes to the strong case against Ronald, for he fully realised that there was much to be explained in the young man's actions before any alternative theory to that held by the police could be sustained. But so far he did not see his way to an alternative theory. He sought vainly for a foundation on which to build his clues and discoveries; for some overlooked trifle which would help him to read aright the true order and significance of the jumbled assortment of events in this strange case.

In the first place, was Ronald's explanation, about losing his way and wandering to the inn by chance, the true one? The police accepted it without question, but was it likely that a man who was in the habit of taking long walks about the coast would lose his way easily? As against that doubt, there were the statements of the innkeeper and the deaf waiter that they had never seen Ronald before. If Ronald were not guilty, why had he departed so hurriedly from the inn that morning? And if he were not the murderer what was the explanation of the damning evidence of the footprints leading to the pit in which the body of the murdered man had been flung? If the discovery of the two kinds of candle-grease in Mr. Glenthorpe's bedroom indicated that two persons were in the room on the night of the murder, who were those two persons, and what did they both go there for?

He reflected that his only tangible reason, so far, for not accepting the police theory was based on the belief that two people had been in the murdered man's room, and that belief rested on the discovery of a spot of candle-grease which in itself was merely presumptive, but not conclusive evidence. It was necessary to establish beyond doubt the supposition that two people had been in the room before he could presume to draw inferences from it. And, if he succeeded in establishing that supposition, might not Ronald have been one of the two persons, and the actual murderer? What was the significance of the broken incandescent burner, the turned-on gas, and the faint mark under the window?

These questions revolved in Colwyn's head in a circle, always bringing him back to his starting point that the solution of the case did not lie on the surface, and that the police theory could not be made to fit in with his own discoveries. The latter were in themselves internal evidence that the whole truth had not yet been brought to light.

Gradually the line of the circle grew nebulous, and Colwyn was fast falling asleep through sheer weariness, when a slight sharp sound, like that made by turning a key in a lock, brought him back to wide-eyed wakefulness. He sat up in bed, listening with strained ears, feeling for the box of matches at his bedside. He found them, and endeavoured to strike a light. But the matches were war matches, and one after another broke off in his hand against the side of the box. He tried holding the next close to the head, but the head flew off. With a muttered malediction on British manufacturers, Colwyn struck several more in rapid succession before he succeeded in lighting the candle at his bedside. He got quietly out of bed, and, leaving the candle on the table, opened his door noiselessly and looked out into the passage.

He had been put to sleep in a small bedroom in the deserted upstairs wing where the murder had been committed. His room was opposite the lumber room, which was three doors away from the room in which the body of the dead man lay. When the question of accommodation for Superintendent Galloway and himself had been discussed, the former had chosen to have a bed made up in the bar parlour downstairs as more comfortable and snug than any of the bedrooms upstairs, but Colwyn had consented to sleep in the deserted wing. The innkeeper, who had lighted him upstairs, had apologised for the humble room and scanty furniture, but Colwyn had laughingly accepted the shortcomings of the room as a point of no importance, and had stood at his door for some moments watching a queer effect in shadows caused by the innkeeper's candle throwing gigantic wavering outlines of his gaunt retreating figure on the bare stone wall as he went down the side passage to his own bedroom.

Colwyn, looking out into the passage, could hear or see nothing to account for the sound that had startled him into wakefulness. The candle by his bedside gave a feeble glimmer which did not reach to the door, and the passage was as dark and silent as the interior of a vault. The stillness and blackness seemed to float into the bedroom like a cloud. But he was certain he had not been mistaken. A door had been unlocked somewhere in the darkness, and it had been unlocked by human hands. Who had come to that deserted wing of the inn in the small hours, and on what business? He decided to explore the passage and find out.

He left the door of his room partly open while he donned a few articles of clothing, and pulled a pair of slippers on his feet. He glanced at his watch, and noted with surprise that it wanted but a few minutes to three o'clock. He extinguished his candle and, taking his electric torch, crept silently into the passage.

He recalled the arrangements of the rooms as he had observed them the previous afternoon. There were three more bedrooms adjoining his, all empty. On the other side of the passage was the lumber room opposite, next came the room in which Ronald slept, then the dead man's room, and finally the sitting-room he had occupied. The door of the sitting-room opened not very far from the head of the stairs.

Colwyn first examined the bedrooms on his side of the passage, stepping as noiselessly as a cat, opening and shutting each door without a sound, and scrutinising the interiors by the light of his torch. They were empty and deserted, as he had seen them the previous afternoon. On reaching the end of the passage he glanced over the head of the staircase, but there was no light glimmering in the square well of darkness and no sound in the lower part of the house to suggest that anybody was stirring downstairs. He turned away, and made his way back along the passage, trying the doors on the other side with equal precaution as he went. The first three doors—the sitting-room, the murdered man's bedroom, and Ronald's bedroom—were locked, as he had seen them locked the previous afternoon by Superintendent Galloway, who had carried the keys away with him until after the inquest on the body.

The lumber room at the other end of the passage had not been locked, and the door stood ajar. Colwyn entered it, and by the glancing light of the torch looked over the heavy furniture, mouldering linen, and stiffly upended bedpoles and curtain rods which nearly filled the room. The clock of a bygone generation stood on the mantelpiece, and the black winding hole in its white face seemed to leer at him like an evil eye as the light of the torch fell on it. But nobody had been in the room. The dust which encrusted the furniture and the floor had not been disturbed for months.

Colwyn returned, puzzled, to his own room. Could he have been mistaken? Was it possible that the sound he had heard had been caused by the door of the lumber room swinging to? No! the sound had been too clear and distinct to admit the possibility of mistake, and it had been made by the grating of a key in a lock, not by a swinging door. He stood in the darkness by his open door, listening intently. Several minutes passed in profound silence, and then there came a scraping, spluttering sound. Somebody not far away had struck a match. Looking cautiously out into the passage, he saw, to his utter amazement, a gleam of light appear beneath the door in which the dead man lay. The next moment the gleam moved up the line of the door sideways, cutting into the darkness outside like a knife. The gleam became broader until the whole door was revealed. Somebody inside was opening it. Even as he looked a hand stole forth from the aperture through which the light streamed, and rested on the jamb outside.

Colwyn was a man of strong nerves, but that sudden manifestation of light and a human hand from a sealed death chamber momentarily unbalanced his common sense, and caused it to swing like a pendulum towards the supernatural. He would not have been surprised if the light and the hand had been followed by the apparition of the murdered man on the threshold, demanding vengeance on his murderer. The feeling passed immediately, and with the return of reason the detective stepped back into his room, closed his door quietly, and watched through a knife's edge slit for the visitor to the death chamber to appear.

The door of the dead man's room opened gently, and the face of the innkeeper's daughter peered forth into the darkness, her impassive face, behind which everything was hid, showing like a beautiful waxen mask against the light of the candle she held in her hand. Her clear gaze rested on Colwyn's door, and it seemed to him for a moment as though their glances met through the slit, then her eyes swept along the passage from one end to the other. As if satisfied by the scrutiny that she had nothing to fear, she stepped forth from the death chamber, closed and locked the door behind her, withdrew the key, walked swiftly along the passage to the head of the stairs, and descended them.

Colwyn opened his door and followed her. He paused outside to pick up the boots which he had placed there to be cleaned, and carrying them in his hand, ran quickly to the head of the stairs. Looking over the landing, he saw the girl reach the bottom of the stairs and turn down the passage towards the back door, still carrying the lighted candle in her hand.

When Colwyn reached the bottom, the girl and the light had disappeared. But a swift gust of wind in the passage revealed to him that she had gone out by the back door, and closed it after her. He followed along the passage till he felt the latch of the back door in his hand. The door yielded to the lifting of the latch, and he found himself in the open air.

It was a grey northern night, with a bitter wind driving the sea mist in billows over the marshes, and a waning half moon shining fitfully through the dingy clouds which scudded across a lead-coloured sky. By the light of the moon he saw the figure of the girl, already some distance from the house, swiftly making her way along the reedy canal path which threaded the oozing marshes.

Colwyn was not a stranger to marshlands. He had waded knee-deep from dawn to dusk through Irish bogs after wild geese; he had followed the migratory seafowl of Finland, Russia and Serbia into their Scottish breeding haunts, and he had once tried to keep pace with the sweep of the Bore over the Solway Marshes, but he had never undertaken a task so difficult as following this girl across a Norfolk marshland. The path she trod so unhesitatingly was narrow, and slippery, with the canal on one side and the marshes on the other. In keeping clear of the canal Colwyn frequently found himself slipping into the marshes. His feet and legs speedily became wet and caked with ooze, and once he nearly lost one of his boots, which he had pulled on hurriedly outside the inn, and left unlaced. But the girl walked straight on with a swift and even gait, treading the narrow path across the morass as securely as though she had been on the high road. Colwyn soon realised that the path they were following was taking them straight across the marshes to the sea. The surging of the waves against the breakwater sounded increasingly loud on his ears, and after a while he saw the breakwater itself rise momentarily out of the darkness like a yellow wall, only to disappear again. But presently it was visible once more, looming out in increasing clearness, with a ghostly glimmering of the grey waters of the North Sea heaving turbulently outside.

As they neared the breakwater the path became drier and firmer, and the light of the moon, falling through a ragged rift in the scurrying clouds, showed a line of sand banks and strips of tussock-land emerging from the marshes as the marshes approached the sea.

The girl kept on with the same resolute pace, until she reached a spot where the canal found its outlet to the sea. There she turned aside and skirted the breakwater wall for a little distance, as if searching for something. The next moment she was scaling the breakwater wall. Colwyn was too far away to intercept her, or reach her if she slipped. He stopped and watched her climb to the top of the wall, and stand there, like a creature of the sea, with the spray leaping hungrily at her slight figure. He saw her take something from the bosom of her dress and cast it into the wild waste of seething waters in front of her. Having done this she turned to descend the breakwater. Colwyn had barely time to leave the path, and take refuge in the shadow of the wall, before she reached the path again and set out to retrace her steps across the lonely marshes.

11

Colwyn waited on the marshes until the coming of the dawn revealed the breakwater and the sea crashing against it. A brief scrutiny of the white waste of waters, raging endlessly against the barrier, convinced him of the futility of attempting to discover what the innkeeper's daughter had thrown from the breakwater wall an hour before. The sea would retain her secret.

The sea mist hung heavily over the marshes as Colwyn cautiously picked his way back along the slippery canal path. Sooner than he expected, the inn appeared from the grey mist like a sheeted ghost. Colwyn stood for a few moments regarding the place attentively. There was something weird and sinister about this lonely inn on the edge of the marshes. Strange things must have happened there in the past, but the lawless secrets of a bygone generation of smugglers had been safely kept by the old inn. The cold morning light imparted the semblance of a leer to the circular windows high up in the white wall, as though they defied the world to discover the secret of the death of Roger Glenthorpe.

There was no sign of life about the inn as Colwyn approached it. The back door yielded to his pull on the latch, and he gained his room unobserved; apparently all the inmates were still wrapped in slumber. Colwyn spent half an hour or so in making some sort of a toilet. He had brought a suit-case with him in the car, so he changed his wet clothes, shaved himself in cold water, washed, and brushed his hair. He looked at his watch, and found that it was after six o'clock. He wondered if the girl Peggy was sleeping after her night's adventure.

A swishing noise, somewhere in the lower regions, broke the profound stillness of the house. Somebody was washing the floor, somewhere. Colwyn opened his door and went downstairs. Ann, the stout servant, was washing the passage. She was on her hands and knees, with her back towards the staircase, swabbing vigorously, and did not see the detective descending the stairs.

"Good morning, Ann," said Colwyn, pleasantly.

She turned her head quickly, with a start, and Colwyn could have sworn that the quick glance she gave him was one of fear. But she merely said, "Good morning, sir," and went on with her work, while the detective stood looking at her. She finished the passage in a few minutes and got awkwardly to her feet, wiping her red hands on her coarse apron.

"You and I are the only early risers in the house, it seems, Ann," said Colwyn, still regarding her attentively.

"If you please, sir, Charles is up, and gone out to the canal to see if there are any fish for breakfast on the master's night lines."

"Fresh fish for breakfast! Well, that's a very good thing," replied the detective, reflecting it was just as well that he had got in before Charles went out. "What time does Mr. Benson come down?"

"About half-past seven, sir, as a general rule, but sometimes he has his breakfast in bed."

"That's not a bad idea at times, Ann. But I see you are impatient to get on with your work. Would you mind if I went into the kitchen and talked to you while you are preparing breakfast?"

Again there was a gleam of fear in the woman's eyes as she looked quickly at the detective, but her voice was self-possessed as she replied:

"Very well, sir," and turned down the passage which led to the kitchen.

"What time was it when you turned off the gas the night before last?" asked Colwyn, when the kitchen was reached. "You told us yesterday that it was about half-past ten, but you did not seem very sure of the exact time. Can you not fix it accurately? Try and think."

The look the woman gave Colwyn this time was undoubtedly one of relief.

"Well, sir," she said, "I usually turn off the gas at ten o'clock, but, to tell you the truth, I was a little bit late that night."

"A little bit late, eh? That means you forgot all about it."

"I did forget about it, and that's the truth. The master told me not to turn off the meter until the gentlemen in the parlour upstairs had gone to bed. Charles told me when he came down from the upstairs parlour with the last of the dinner things that the gentlemen were still sitting in front of the fire talking, but some time after Charles had come down and gone to bed I heard them moving about upstairs, as though they were going to their rooms."

"What time was that?" asked the detective.

"Just half-past ten. I happened to glance at the kitchen clock at the time. Charles, who had been told that he wouldn't be wanted upstairs again, had gone to bed quite half an hour before, but I didn't go until I had folded some clothes which I had airing in front of the kitchen fire. When I did get to bed, and was just falling off to sleep, I suddenly remembered that I had forgotten to turn off the gas at the meter. I got out of bed again, lit my candle, and went up the passage to the meter, which is just under the foot of the stairs, turned off the gas, and went back to bed."

"Did you notice the time then?"

"The kitchen clock was just chiming eleven as I got back to my bed."

"You are sure it was not twelve?"

"Quite sure, sir."

"Did you hear any sound upstairs?"

"No, sir. It was as quiet as the dead."

"Was it raining at that time?"

"It started to rain heavens hard just as I got back to bed, but before that the wind was moaning round the house, as it do moan in these parts, and I knew we was in for a storm. I was glad enough to get back to my warm bed."

"You might have seen something, if you had been a little later. The staircase is the only way the body could have been brought down from *there*." The detective pointed to the room above where the dead man lay.

The woman trembled violently. "It's God's mercy I didn't see something," she said, and her voice fell to a husky whisper. "I should 'a' died wi' fright if I had seen *it* being brought downstairs. All day long I've been thanking God I didn't see anything."

"Do nobody else but you and Charles sleep downstairs?"

"Nobody, sir. I sleep in a small room off the kitchen, but Charles sleeps in one of the rooms in the passage which leads off the kitchen, the first room, not far from my own. But that'd been no help to me if I'd seen anything. I might have screamed the house down before Charles would have heard me, he being stone deaf."

"Quite true, Ann. And now is that all you have to tell me about the gas?"

The woman seemed to have some difficulty in replying, but finally she stammered out in an embarrassed voice, plucking at her apron the while:

"Yes, sir."

"Look at me, Ann, and tell me the truth. Come now, it will be better for everybody."

The countrywoman looked at the detective with whitening face, and there was something in his penetrating gaze that kept her frightened eyes fixed on his.

"Please, sir—"

"Yes, Ann, go on," prompted the detective encouragingly.

But the woman didn't go on; there crept into her face instead an obstinate look, her mouth closed tightly, and her hands ceased twitching.

"I've told you everything, sir," she said quietly.

"You've not told me you found the meter turned on when you got up next morning," replied the detective sternly.

The woman's fat face turned haggard with anxiety, and then she began to cry softly with her apron to her eyes.

"Why did you not tell us this, Ann?"

"If you please, sir, I thought that the master mightn't like it if he knew. He's very particular about having the gas turned off at night, and he might have thought I had forgotten it."

Colwyn gave her another searching look.

"Even if that were true, Ann, you have no right to keep back anything that may tend to shield the guilty, or injure the innocent."

"I didn't think it mattered, sir."

"You still say that you heard nothing after you went to bed?"

"No, sir. I fell asleep as soon as I got into bed."

"So you said before, but you did not tell us the whole truth yesterday, you know, and I do not know whether to believe you now."

"Hush, sir, there's somebody coming down the passage."

Colwyn strolled into the passage and encountered Superintendent Galloway coming towards the kitchen. He stared at the detective and exclaimed:

"Hello, you're up early."

"Yes; I found it difficult to sleep, so I came downstairs."

"I hope you've not been making love to Ann," said Galloway, who had his own sense of humour. "I'm looking for this infernal waiter, Charles. He is never about when he's wanted. Charles! Charles!"

Superintendent Galloway's shouts brought Ann hurrying from the kitchen, and she explained to him, as she had explained to Colwyn, that Charles had gone on to the marshes to look for fish.

"Send him to my room as soon as he comes in; I've other fish for him to fry," grumbled the superintendent. "A queer household this," he said to Colwyn, as they walked along the passage. "Ah, here is Charles, fish and all."

The fat waiter was hurrying in with a string of fish in his hand, and he came towards them in response to Superintendent Galloway's commanding gesture. The superintendent told him to go out and intercept Constable Queensmead before he went out with his search party, and bring him to the inn. Charles nodded an indication that he understood the instruction, and turned away to execute it.

"I want Queensmead to get a dozen of the village blockheads together for a jury," he said to Colwyn. "The coroner sent me word before we left Durrington yesterday that he'd be over this morning, but he did not say what time, and I forgot to ask him. He's the man to kick up a devil of a shindy if he came and found we were not ready for him."

Queensmead speedily appeared in response to the summons, listened quietly to Superintendent Galloway's laconic command to catch a jury and catch them quick, and went back to the village to secure twelve good men and true.

Colwyn and Galloway meanwhile breakfasted together in the bar parlour, on some of the fish which Charles had brought in. As nothing followed the fish Superintendent Galloway, who was an excellent trencherman, rang the bell and ordered the waiter to bring some eggs and bacon. The waiter hesitated a moment, and then said that he believed they were out of bacon. There were some eggs, if they would do.

"Bring me a couple, boiled, as quick as you like," said the superintendent. "This is a queer kind of inn," he grumbled to Colwyn. "They don't give you enough to eat."

"I think they're a little short themselves," replied Colwyn.

"By Jove, I believe you're right!" said the superintendent, staring hard at the edibles on the table before him. "There's not much here–a piece of butter no bigger than a walnut, a spoonful of jam, and tea as weak as water. Come to think of it, they gave us nothing but some of Glenthorpe's left over game for dinner last night. You're right, they are *hard up.*"

Superintendent Galloway looked at Colwyn with as much animation on his heavy features as though he had lighted on some new and important discovery. Colwyn, who had finished his breakfast and was not particularly interested in the conversation, strolled out with the intention of smoking a cigar outside the front door. In the passage he encountered Ann, bearing a tray with two cups and saucers, a pot of tea and some bread and butter which she proceeded to carry upstairs. Colwyn wondered for whom the breakfast was intended. There were three people upstairs–the father, his daughter, and the poor mad woman, and the breakfast was laid for two. The appearance of the innkeeper descending the stairs, answered the question. Colwyn accosted him as he came down.

"You're a late riser, Benson."

"Yes, sir, it's a bit difficult to handle Mother in the morning: the only way to keep her quiet is for me to stay with her until Peggy is ready to go to her and give her her breakfast. Mother is quiet enough with Peggy and me, but nobody else can do anything with her, and sometimes nobody can do anything with her except my daughter. She spends a lot of time with her, sir."

The innkeeper looked more like a bird than ever as he proffered this explanation, standing at the foot of the stairs dressed as he had been the previous night, with his bright bird's eyes peering from beneath his shock of iron-grey hair at the man in front of him. Colwyn noticed that his hair had been recently wet, and plastered straight down so that it hung like a ridge over his forehead–just as it had been the previous night. Colwyn wondered why the man wore his hair like that. Did he always affect that eccentric style of hairdressing, or had he adopted it to alter his personal appearance–to disguise himself, or to conceal something?

"It's no life for a young girl," said the detective, in answer to the innkeeper's last remark.

"I know that, sir. But what am I to do? I cannot afford to keep a nurse. Peggy never complains. She's used to it. But if you'll excuse me, sir. I must go and get the room ready for the inquest."

"What room is it going to be held in?"

"Superintendent Galloway told me to put a table and some chairs into the last empty room off the passage leading into the kitchen. It's the biggest room in the house, and there are plenty of chairs in the lumber room upstairs."

"It should do excellently for the purpose, I should think," said Colwyn.

A few moments later he saw the innkeeper and the waiter carrying chairs from the lumber room downstairs into the empty room, where Ann dusted them. Then they carried in a small table from another room. Superintendent Galloway, with inky fingers and a red face, and a sheaf of foolscap papers in his hand, came bustling out of the bar parlour to superintend the arrangements. When the chairs had been placed to his liking he ordered the innkeeper to bring him a glass of ale. While he was drinking it Constable Queensmead entered the front door with a file of shambling, rough-looking villagers trailing behind him, and announced to his superior officer that the men were intended to form a jury. Superintendent Galloway seemed quite satisfied with their appearance, and remarked to Colwyn that he didn't care how soon the coroner arrived—now he had the jury and witnesses ready for him.

"How many witnesses do you propose to call?" said Colwyn.

"Five: Queensmead, Benson, the waiter, and the two men who found the footprints leading to the pit and who recovered the body and brought it here. That's enough for a committal. The coroner will no doubt bring a doctor from Heathfield to certify the cause of death. I've got all the statements ready. I took Benson's and the waiter's yesterday. The waiter's evidence is the principal thing, of course. Do you remember suggesting to me last night the possibility of this murder having been committed by one of Mr. Glenthorpe's workmen with a grudge against him? Well, it's a very strange thing, but Queensmead was telling me this morning that one of Mr. Glenthorpe's workmen had a grudge against him. He's a chap named Hyson, the local ne'er-do-well, who was almost starving when Mr. Glenthorpe came to the district. Glenthorpe was warned against employing him, but the fellow got round him with a piteous tale, and he put him on. He proved to be just as ungrateful as the average British workman, and caused the old gentleman a lot of trouble. He seems to have been a bit of a sea lawyer, and tried to disaffect the other workmen by talking to them about socialism, and the rights of labour, and that sort of rubbish. When I heard this I had the chap brought to the inn and cross-questioned him a bit, but I am certain that he had nothing to do with the murder. He's a weak, spineless sort of chap, full of argument and fond of beer—that's his character in the village—and the last man in the world to commit a murder like this. I flatter myself," added Superintendent Galloway in a tone of mingled self-complacency and pride, "that I know a murderer when I see one."

"Have you made any inquiries about umbrellas?" asked Colwyn.

"Yes. Apparently Ronald did not bring an umbrella with him, though it's cost me some trouble to establish that fact. It is astonishing how unobservant people are about such things as umbrellas, sticks, and handbags. Most people remember faces and clothes with some accuracy, but cannot recall whether a person carried an umbrella or walking-stick. Charles is not sure whether Ronald carried an umbrella, Benson thinks he did not, and Ann is sure he didn't. The balance of evidence being on the negative side, I assume that Ronald did not bring an umbrella to the inn, because it was more likely to have been noticed if he had. I next inquired about the umbrellas in the house. At first I was told there were only two—a cumbrous, Robinson Crusoe sort of affair, kept in the kitchen and used by the servant, and a smaller one, belonging to Benson's daughter. I have examined both. The covering of the girl's umbrella is complete. Ann's is rent in several places, but the covering is blue, whereas the piece of umbrella covering we found adhering to Mr. Glenthorpe's window is black. While I was questioning Ann she suddenly remembered that there was another umbrella in that lumber-room upstairs. We went upstairs to look for it, but we couldn't find it, though Ann says she saw it there a day or two before the murder. I think we may assume that Ronald took it."

"But Ronald was a stranger to the place. How would he know the umbrella was in the lumber-room?" said Colwyn, who had followed Galloway's narrative with close attention.

"The door of the lumber-room stands ajar. Ronald probably looked in from curiosity, and saw the umbrella."

The easy assurance with which Superintendent Galloway dismissed or got over difficulties which interfered with his own theory did not commend itself to Colwyn, but he did not pursue the point further.

"Is the umbrella still missing?" he asked.

"Yes. It seems that even a murderer cannot be trusted to return an umbrella." Superintendent Galloway laughed shortly at his grim joke and walked away to supervise the preparations for the inquest.

The coroner presently arrived from Heathfield in a small runabout motor-car which he drove himself, with a tall man sitting beside him, and a short pursy young man in the back seat nursing a portable typewriter and an attaché case on his knees. Toiling in the rear, some distance behind the car, was a figure on a bicycle, which subsequently turned out to be the reporter of the Heathfield local paper, who had come over with instructions from one of the London agencies to send a twenty line report of the inquest for the London press. In peace times "specials" would probably have been despatched from the metropolis to "do a display story," and interview some of the persons concerned, but the war had discounted by seventy-five per cent the value of murders as newspaper "copy."

The coroner, a short, stout, commonplace little man, jumped out of the car as soon as it stopped, and bustled into the inn with an air of fussy official importance, leaving his companions to follow.

"Good day, Galloway," he exclaimed, as that officer came forward to greet him. "I hope you've got everything ready."

"Everything's ready, Mr. Edgehill. Do you intend to commence before lunch?"

"Of course I do. Are you aware that it is war-time? How many witnesses have you?"

"Five, sir. Their statements have all been taken."

"Then I shall go straight through—it seems a simple case—merely a matter of form, from what I have heard of it. I have another inquest at Downside at four o'clock.

Where's the body? Upstairs? Doctor"–this to the tall thin man who had sat beside him in the run-about–"will you go upstairs with Queensmead and make your examination? Where's the jury? Pendy"–this to the young man with the typewriter and attaché case–"get everything ready and swear in the jury. Galloway will show you the room. What's that? Oh, that's quite all right"–this in reply to some murmured apology on the part of Superintendent Galloway for the mental incapacity of the jury–"we ought to be glad to get juries at all–in war-time."

Colwyn had feared that the result of the inquest was a foregone conclusion the moment he saw the coroner alighting from his motor-car outside the inn. Ten minutes later, when the little man had commenced his investigations, he realised that the proceedings were merely a formal compliance with the law, and in no sense of the word an inquiry.

Mr. Edgehill, the coroner, was one of those people who seized upon the war as a pretext for the exercise of their natural proclivity to interfere in other people's affairs. He took the opportunity that every inquest gave him to lecture the British public on their duties and responsibilities in war-time. The body on which he was sitting formed his text, the jury was his congregation, and the newspaper reporters the vehicles by which his admonitions were conveyed to the nation. Mr. Edgehill saw a shirker in every suicide, national improvidence in a corpse with empty pockets, and had even been able to discover a declining war *morale* in death by misadventure. He thanked God for air raids and food queues because they brought the war home to civilians, and he was never tired of asserting that he lived on half the voluntary rations scale, did harder work, felt ten years younger, and a hundred times more virtuous, in consequence.

If he did not actually insert the last clause his look implied a superior virtue to his fellow creatures, and was meekly accepted as such. He never held an inquest without introducing some remarks upon uninterned aliens, the military age, Ireland and conscription, soldiers' wives and drinking, the prevalence of bigamy, and other popular war-time topics. In short, Mr. Edgehill, like many other people, had used the war to emerge from a chrysalis existence as a local bore into a butterfly career as a public nuisance. In that capacity he was still good "copy" in some of the London newspapers, and was even occasionally referred to in leading articles as a fine example of the sturdy country spirit which Londoners would do well to emulate.

Before commencing his inquiry into the death of Mr. Glenthorpe, the coroner indignantly expressed his surprise that a small hamlet like Flegne could produce so many able-bodied men to serve on a jury in war-time. But after ascertaining that all the members of the jury were over military age, with the exception of one man who was afflicted with heart disease, he suffered the inquest to proceed.

The evidence of the innkeeper and the waiter was a repetition of the story they had told to the chief constable on the preceding day. Constable Queensmead, in his composed way, gave an account of his preliminary investigations into the crime, and the finding of the body.

The only additional evidence brought forward was given by two of the men who had been in the late Mr. Glenthorpe's employ. These men, Herward and Duney, had found the track of the footprints in the clay near the pit on going to work the previous morning. After the discovery that Mr. Glenthorpe was missing from the inn, Herward had been let down into the pit by a rope, and had brought up the body. Both these men told their story with a wealth of unlettered detail, and Duney, who was one of the aboriginals of the district, added his personal opinion that t'oud ma'aster mun 'a' been very dead afore the chap got him in the pit, else he would 'a' dinged one of the chap's eyes in, t'oud ma'aster not bein' a man to be taken anywhere against his will. However, the chap that carried him must 'a' been powerful strong, because Herward told him his own arms were begunnin' ter ache good tidily just a-howdin' him up to the rope when they wor being a-hawled out the pit.

The coroner, in his summing up, dwelt upon the strong circumstantial evidence against Ronald, and the folly of the deceased in withdrawing a large sum of money from the bank for the purpose of carrying out scientific research in war-time. "Had he invested that money in war bonds he would have probably been alive to-day," said Mr. Edgehill gravely. The jury had no hesitation in returning a verdict of wilful murder against James Ronald.

The coroner, the doctor, the clerk carrying the typewriter and the attaché case, and Superintendent Galloway departed in the runabout motor-car shortly afterwards. Before evening a mortuary van, with two men, appeared from Heathfield and removed the body of the murdered man.

12

If the inmates of the inn felt any surprise at Colwyn's remaining after the inquest, they did not betray it. That evening Ann nervously intercepted him to ask if he would have a partridge for his dinner, and Colwyn, remembering the shortness of the inn larder, replied that a partridge would do very well. Later on Charles served it in the bar parlour, and waited with his black eyes fixed on Colwyn's lips, sometimes anticipating his orders before they were uttered. He brought a bottle of claret from the inn cellar, assuring Colwyn in his soft whisper that he would find the wine excellent, and Colwyn, after sampling it, found no reason for disagreeing with the waiter's judgment.

At the conclusion of the meal Colwyn sent for the innkeeper, and asked him a number of questions about the district and its inhabitants. The innkeeper intimated that Flegne was a poor place at the best of times, but the war had made it worse, and the poorer folk–the villagers who lived in the beach-stone cottages–were sometimes hard-pressed to keep body and soul together. They did what they could, eking out their scanty earnings by eel-fishing on the marshes, and occasionally snaring a few wild fowl. Mr. Glenthorpe's researches in the district had been a godsend because of the employment he had given, which had brought a little ready money into the place.

It was obvious to Colwyn's alert intelligence that the innkeeper did not care to talk about his dead guest. There was no visible reluctance–indeed, it would have been hard to trace the sign of any particular emotion on his queer, bird-like face–but his replies were slow in coming when questioned about Mr. Glenthorpe, and he made several attempts to turn the conversation in another direction. When he had finished a glass of wine Colwyn offered him, he got up from the table with the remark that it was time for him to return to the bar.

"I will go with you," said Colwyn. "It will help to pass away an hour."

There were about a dozen men in the bar—agricultural labourers and fishermen—clustered in groups of twos and threes in front of the counter, or sitting on stools by the wall, drinking ale by the light of a smoky oil lamp which hung from the rafters. The fat deaf waiter was in the earthy recess behind the counter, drawing ale into stone mugs.

A loud voice which had been holding forth ceased suddenly as Colwyn entered. The inmates of the bar regarded him questioningly, and some resentfully, as though they considered his presence an intrusion. But Colwyn was accustomed to making himself at home in all sorts of company. He walked across the bar, called for some whisky, and, while it was being served, addressed a friendly remark to the nearest group to him. One of the men, a white-bearded, keen-eyed Norfolk man, answered his question civilly enough. He had asked about wild fowl shooting in the neighbourhood, and the old man had been a water bailiff on the Broads in his younger days. The question of sport will draw most men together. One after another of the villagers joined in the conversation, and were soon as much at home with Colwyn as though they had known him from boyhood. Some of them were going eel-fishing that night, and Colwyn violated the provisions of the "no treating" order to give them a glass of whisky to keep out the cold of the marshes. The rest of the tap room he regaled with ale.

From these Norfolk fishermen Colwyn learnt many of the secrets of the wild and many cunning methods of capturing its creatures, but the real object of his visit to the bar—to discover whether any of the frequenters of the *Golden Anchor* had ever seen Ronald in the district before the evening of the murder—remained unsatisfied. He was a stranger to "theer" parts, the men said, in response to questions on the subject.

But "theer" parts were limited to a mile or so of the marshland in which they spent their narrow, lonely lives. Their conversation revealed that they seldom went outside that narrow domain. Durrington, which was little more than ten miles away, was only a name to them. Many of them had not been as far as Leyland for months. They spent their days catching eels in the marsh canals, or in setting lobster and crab traps outside the breakwater. The agricultural labourers tilled the same patch of ground year after year. They had no recreations except an occasional night at the inn; their existence was a lifelong struggle with Nature for a bare subsistence. Most of them had been born in the beach-stone cottages where their fathers had been born before them, and most of them would die, as their fathers had died, in the little damp bedrooms where they had first seen the light, passing away, as their fathers had passed away, listening to the sound of the North Sea restlessly beating against the breakwater. That sound was never out of their ears while they lived, and it was the dirge to which they died. Such was their life, but they knew no other, and wished no other.

Colwyn was early astir the following morning, and after breakfast went out. His purpose was to try to discover something which would throw light on Ronald's appearance at Flegne. With that object he scoured the country for some miles in the direction of Heathfield, for he deemed the possibility of Ronald having come by that route worth inquiring into. But his time was wasted; none of his inquiries brought to light anything to suggest that Ronald had ever been in the district before.

When he returned to the village the day was more than half spent. As he entered the inn, he encountered Charles, who stopped when he saw him.

"There are two men in the bar asking to see you, sir," he said, in his soft whisper. "Duney and Backlos are their names. They say they saw you in the bar last night, and they would like to speak to you privately, if you have no objection."

"Show them into the bar parlour," the detective said. "And, Charles, you might ask Ann to let me have a little lunch when they are gone."

Colwyn proceeded to the bar parlour. A moment or two afterwards the waiter ushered in two men and withdrew, closing the door after him.

In response to Colwyn's request, his two visitors seated themselves awkwardly, but they seemed to have considerable difficulty in stating the object of their visit. Duney, one of the men who had helped to recover Mr. Glenthorpe's body from the pit, was a short, thickset, hairy-faced man, with round surprised eyes, which he kept intently fixed upon the detective's face, as though seeking inspiration for speech from that source. The other man, Backlos, was a tall, hawk-featured man with a sweeping black moustache, who needed only gaudy habiliments to make him the ideal pirate king of the comic opera stage. It was he who spoke first.

"If you please, ma'aster, we uns come to you thinkin' as you might gi' us a bit o' advice."

"About somefin' we seed last night," explained Mr. Duney, finding his own voice at the sound of his companion's.

"I thowt 'ow 'twas agreed 'tween us I wor to tell the gentleman, bor?" growled the pirate king, turning a pair of dusky eyes on his companion. "Yow allus have a way o' overdoin' things, you know, Dick."

"Right, bor, right," replied Mr. Duney. "Yow oughter know I only wanted to help yow out, Billy."

"I dawn't want onny helpin' out," replied the pirate. "It's loike this 'ere, ma'aster," he continued, turning again to Colwyn. "Arter Dick and I left the *Anchor* las' night, we thowt we'd be walkin' a spell. We wor a talkin' o' th' murder at th' time, and wonderin' what we wor to do fur another job o' work, things bein' moighty bad heerabouts, when, as we neared top o' th' rise, we heered the rummiest kind o' noise a man ever heerd, comin' from that theer wood by th' pits. Dick says to me, in a skeered kind of voice, 'That's fair a rum un,' says he. There wornt much mune at th' time, but we could see things clar enough, and thow we looked around us we couldn't see a livin' thing a movin' either nigh th' woods nor on th' ma'shes. While we looked we seed a big harnsee rise out o' th' woods and go a flappin' away across th' ma'shes. Then all of a suddint we saw somefin' come a-wamblin' outer the shadder o' the wood, and run along by th' edge of ut. We couldn't make out a' furst what it moight be, thow for sure we got a rare fright. For my part, I thowt it might a' been ole Black Shuck, thow th' night didn't seem windy enough for un."

"Stop a bit," said Colwyn. "What do you mean by Black Shuck? Oh, I remember. It's a Norfolk tradition or ghost story, isn't it? Black Shuck is supposed to be a big black dog, with one eye in the middle of the head, who runs without sound and howls louder than the wind. Whoever meets him is sure to die before the year is out."

"That's him," said Mr. Backlos, affirming, with a grave nod of his head, his own profound belief in the canine apparition in question. "My grandfeyther seen un once not a hundred yards from the very spot were we wor standin' last night, and, sure enough, he died afore three months wor out. Dick and I couldn't tell what it wor we see creepin' out o' th' shadder o' th' wood, an' to tell yow th' trewth, ma'aster, we didn't care to look agen. I asked Dick if he didn't think it wor Black Shuck. 'Naw daywt,' says Dick, 'if it ain't somefin' worse.' 'What do'st a' mean, bor?' says I. 'Well,' says Dick slowly like, 'it might be the sperrit from th' pit, for 'twas in no mortal man to holler out like that cry we just heered.' Wornt those yower words, bor?"

Mr. Duney, thus appealed to, nodded portentously, as though to indicate that his words were well justified.

"Never mind the spirit from the pit," said Colwyn. "Go on with your story."

"Well, ma'aster, just as we wor walkin' away from th' wood as fast as ever we could, th' mune come out from behind th' shadder of a cloud, and threw a light right ower th' wood. We just happened to give a glance round ahind us at th' time, to see if we wor bein' follered, and, by its light, we saw a man a creepin' back into th' wood."

"A man? Are you sure it was a man?"

"There's no manner o' doubt about that, ma'aster. We both saw it once, and we didn't wait to look again. We run as hard as we could pelt to Dick's cottage by the ma'shes, and got inside and stood listenin' to heer if we were bein' follered. Dick says to me, says 'e, 'S'posen it wor the chap who murdered owd Mr. Glenthorpe at the *Anchor*?' I thowt as much meself, but a' tried to laugh it off, and says to Dick, 'What for should it be him? He's far enough away by this time, for we s'arched the place round fur miles, and we took in that theer wood where we just see un.' 'We never s'arched th' wood,' says Dick, 'leastways, not proper, an' it's a rare hidin' place for un.' 'So it be, to be sure,' says I. 'If he sees that there light we'll be browt out from heer dead men,' says Dick. 'So we will, for sartin,' says I. 'Let's put out th' light, so th' bloody-minded murderer won't ha' narthin' to go by if he ain't seen it yet.' So we put out th' light and stayed theer till th' mornin', when we went out to work, and then when I seed Dick later we thowt we'd come and tell you all about it, seein' as yower a gentleman, and in consiquence a man of larnin', and might p'rhaps tell us what we'd better do."

"You have certainly done the proper thing in disclosing what you have seen," said the detective, after a thoughtful pause. "But why have you come to me in the matter? It seems to me that the proper course to pursue would be to lay your information before Constable Queensmead."

The two men exchanged a glance of conscious embarrassment. Then Mr. Backlos, with the air of a man who had made up his mind to take the bull by the horns, blurted out:

"It's like this, ma'aster. We be in a bit o' a fix about that. Yow see, last night we were out arter conies, and thow I can swar we were out in th' open and not lookin' for conies on annybody's land, cos Dick an' I have already bin fined ten bob for snarin' conies on Farmer Cranley's land, an' if we went to Queensmead he moight think we'd been a snarin' there again. So Dick says to me, says he, 'Why not see the chap wot came into th' *Anchor* bar last night? Annybody can see wi' half an eye that he's a real swell, for didn't he stand treat all round–an' wot he says we'll go by, and 'e won't treat us dirty, whatever he says, though, mind ye, bor, there's narthin' to gi' away. So let's go to thissun, an' tell un all about it.'"

"I also tol' yow, Billy, that if thar be a reward out for this chap wot killed Mr. Glenthorpe, thissun 'ud tell us how to get it without sharin' wi' Queensmead, who does narthin' but take th' bread owt o' ower mouths, he bein' so sharp about th' conies. For if this chap in th' woods is the one wot killed owd Mr. Glenthorpe, we have a right to th' money for cotchin' un. Didn't I say that, Billy?"

"Yow did, bor, yow did; them wor yower vaery words," acquiesced Mr. Backlos.

"I think you had better leave the matter in my hands," said Colwyn, with difficulty repressing a smile at this exceedingly Norfolk explanation. "And now, you had better have a drink, for I am sure you must be dry after all that talk."

The men, after drinking Colwyn's health in two mugs of ale, departed with placid countenances, and Colwyn was left to meditate over the news they had imparted. The result of his meditations was that he presently went forth in search of Police Constable Queensmead.

The constable lived in the village street—in a beach-stone cottage which was in slightly better repair than its neighbours, and much better kept. There were white curtains in the windows, and in the garden a few late stocks and hardy climbing roses were making a brave effort to bloom in depressing surroundings. It was Queensmead who answered the door to the detective's knock, and he led the way inside to his little office when he saw who his visitor was.

"I do not think these chaps saw anything except what their own fears created," he said, after Colwyn had told him as much of the two men's story as he saw fit to impart. "I searched the wood thoroughly the day after the murder. Ronald was not there then."

"He may have come back since."

Queensmead's dark eyes lingered thoughtfully on the detective's face, as though seeking to gather the meaning underlying his words.

"Why should he do such a foolish thing, sir?" he asked.

"It is not always easy to account for a man's actions."

"It is hard to account for a man wanted by the police running his head into a noose."

"Ronald may not know he is wanted by the police."

"Why, of course he must know. If he doesn't—" Queensmead broke off suddenly and looked at the detective queerly, as if suddenly realising all that the remark implied. "You must have some strange ideas about this case," he added slowly.

"I have, but we won't go into them now," said the detective, with a slight smile. He appreciated the fact that the other was, to use an American colloquialism, "quick on the uptake."

"Your immediate duty is clear."

"You mean I should search the wood again?" said Queensmead, with the same quick comprehension as before. "Very well. Will you come with me?"

Colwyn nodded, and Queensmead, without more ado, took a revolver and a pair of handcuffs from a cupboard, slipped them into his pockets, and announced that he was ready. He opened the door for his visitor to precede him, and they set forth.

The hut circles on the rise looked more desolate than ever in the waning afternoon light. The excavations commenced by Mr. Glenthorpe had been abandoned, and a spade left sticking in the upturned earth had rusted in the damp air. The track of the footprints to the pit in which the body had been flung still showed distinctly in the clay, and the splash of blood gleamed dully on the edge of the hole. On the other side of the pit the trees of the wood stood in stunted outline against a lowering black sky.

The two men entered the wood silently. The trees were of great age, the trunks thick and gnarled, with low twisted boughs, running and interlacing in every direction. So thickly were they intertwined that it was twilight in the sombre depths of the wood, although the fierce winds from the North Sea had already stripped the upper branches of leaves. The ground was covered with a rank and rotting undergrowth, from which tiny spirals of vapour, like gnomes' fires, floated upwards. The silence was absolute; even the birds of the coast seemed to shun the place, which looked as if it had been untrodden since the days when the beast men of the Stone Age prowled through its dim recesses to the hut circles on the rise.

Colwyn and Queensmead searched the wood and the matted undergrowth as they progressed, closely scrutinising the ferny hollows, looking up into the trees, examining the thickets and clumps of shrubs. They had reached the centre of the wood, and were picking their way through a rank growth of nettles which covered the decayed bracken, when Colwyn experienced a mental perception as tangible as a cold hand placed upon the brow of a sleeper. He had the swift feeling that there was somebody else besides themselves in the solitude of the wood—somebody who was watching them. He looked

around him intently, and his eyes fell upon a screen of
interlaced branches which grew on the other side of the
dip they were traversing. Without any conscious effort on
his own part, his eyes travelled to the thickest part of the
obstruction, and encountered another pair of eyes gazing
at him steadily from the depths of the leafy screen. That
gaze held his own for a moment, and then vanished. He
looked again, but the screen was now unbroken, and not
the rustle of a leaf betrayed the person who was
concealed within.

Colwyn touched Queensmead's arm.

"There is somebody hiding in those bushes ahead of
us," he whispered.

Queensmead's eyes ran swiftly along the clump of
bushes ahead, and he raised his revolver.

"Come out, or I'll fire!" he cried.

His sharp command shattered the heavy silence like
the crack of a firearm. The next moment the figure of a
man broke from the twisted branches and walked down
the slope towards them. It was Ronald.

"Put   up   your   hands,   Ronald,"   commanded
Queensmead   sternly,   poising   the   revolver   at   the
advancing man. "Put them up, or I'll fire."

"Fire if you like."

The words fell from Ronald's lips wearily, but he did
not put up his hands. His clothes were torn and stained,
his face gaunt and lined, and in his tired eyes was the
look of a man who had lived in the solitudes with no other
companion but despair. Queensmead stepped forward
and with a swift gesture snapped the handcuffs on his
wrist.

"I arrest you for the murder of Roger Glenthorpe," he
said.

"I could have got away from you if I had wanted," said
the young man wearily. "But what was the use? I'm glad
it is over."

"I warn you, Ronald, that any statement you now make may be used against you on your trial," broke in Queensmead harshly.

"My good fellow, I know all about that." The sudden note of imperiousness in his manner reminded Colwyn of the way in which he had snubbed Sir Henry Durwood in his bedroom at the Durrington hotel three mornings before. But it was in his previous indifferent tone that the young man added: "Have either of you a spirit flask?"

Police Constable Queensmead eyed his captive with the critical eye of an officer of justice upon whom devolved the responsibility of bringing his man fit and well to trial. Ronald's face had gone haggard and white, and he lurched a little in his walk. Then he stood still, and regarded the two men weakly.

"I'm about done up," he admitted.

"We'd better take him to the inn and get him some brandy," said Queensmead. "Take his other arm, will you?"

They returned slowly with Ronald between them. He did not ask where they were taking him, but stumbled along on their supporting arms like a man in a dream, with his eyes fixed on the ground. When clear of the wood, Queensmead led his prisoner past the pit where Mr. Glenthorpe's body had been cast, but Ronald did not even glance at the yawning hole alongside of him. It was when they were descending the slope towards the inn that Colwyn noticed a change in his indifferent demeanour. He raised his head and surveyed the inn with sombre eyes, and then his glance travelled swiftly to his pinioned hands. For a moment his frame stiffened slightly, as though he were about to resist being taken farther. But if that were his intention the mood passed. The next moment he was walking along with his previous indifference.

When they reached the inn Queensmead asked Colwyn in a whisper to keep an eye on the prisoner while he went inside and got the brandy. As soon as he had gone Colwyn turned to Ronald and earnestly said:

"You may not know me, apart from our chance meeting at Durrington, but I am anxious to help you, if you are innocent."

"I have heard of you. You are Colwyn, the private detective."

"That makes it easier then, for you will know that I have no object in this case except to bring the truth to light. If you have anything to say that will help me to do that I beg of you to do so. You may safely trust me."

"I know that, Mr. Colwyn, but I have nothing to say." Ronald spoke wearily–almost indifferently.

"Nothing?" Astonishment and disappointment were mingled in the detective's voice.

"Nothing."

Before anything more could be said Queensmead reappeared from the inn with some brandy in a glass. Ronald raised it to his lips with his manacled hands, then turned away in response to an imperative gesture from Queensmead. Colwyn stood where he was for a moment, watching them, then turned to enter the inn. As he did so, his eyes fell upon the white face of Peggy, framed in the gathering gloom of the passage, staring with frightened eyes at the retreating forms of the village constable and his prisoner. She slipped out of the door and took a few hurried steps in their direction. But when she reached the strip of green which bordered the side of the inn she stopped with a despairing gesture, as though realising the futility of her effort, and turned to retrace her steps. Colwyn advanced rapidly towards her.

"I want to speak to you," he said curtly.

She stood still, but there was a prescient flash in her eyes as she looked at him.

"You were in the dead man's room last night," he said. "What were you doing there?"

"I do not know that it is any business of yours," she replied, in a low tone.

"I do not think you had better adopt that attitude," he said quietly. "You know you had no right to go into that room. I do not wish to threaten you, but you had better tell me the truth."

She stood silent for a moment, as though weighing his words. Then she said:

"I will tell you why I went there, not because I am afraid of anything you can do, but because I am not afraid of the truth. I went there because of a promise I made to Mr. Glenthorpe. He was very kind and good to me—when he was alive. Only two days before he met his death he asked me, if anything happened to him at any time, to go to his bedroom and remove a packet I would find in a little secret drawer in his writing table, and destroy it without opening it. He showed me where the packet was, and how to open the drawer. After he was dead I thought of my promise, and tried several times to slip into the room and get the packet, but there was always somebody about. So I went in last night, after everybody was in bed, because I thought the police might find the packet in searching his desk, and I should have been very unhappy if I had not been able to keep my promise."

"How did you get into the room? The door was locked, and Superintendent Galloway had the key."

"He left it on the mantelpiece downstairs. I saw it there earlier in the evening, and when he was out of the room I slipped in and took it, and put the key of my own room in its place. I replaced it next morning."

"What did you do with the packet you removed?"

"I took it across the marshes and threw it into the sea," she replied, looking steadily into his face.

"Why did you go to that trouble? Why did you not burn it?"

"I had no fire, and I dared not keep it till the morning. Besides, there were rings and things in the packet—his dead wife's jewellery. He told me so."

He looked at her keenly. She had told him the truth about her visit to the breakwater, but how much of the rest of her story was true?

"So that is your explanation?" he said.

"Yes."

"I am sorry to say that I find it difficult to believe. If you are deceiving me you are very foolish."

"I have told you the truth, Mr. Colwyn," she said, and, turning away, returned to the inn.

13

Ronald's strange silence after his arrest decided Colwyn to relinquish his investigations and return to Durrington. His tacit admissions, coupled with the damaging evidence against him, enforced conviction in the young man's guilt in spite of the detective's previous belief to the contrary. In assisting Queensmead in his search Colwyn had cherished the hope that Ronald, if captured, would declare his innocence and gladly respond to his overture of help. But, instead of doing so, Ronald had taken up an attitude which was suspicious in the highest degree, and one which caused the detective to falter in his belief that the Glenthorpe murder case was a much deeper mystery than the police imagined. Ronald's attitude, by its accordance with the facts previously known or believed about the case, belittled the detective's own discoveries, and caused him to come to the conclusion that it was hardly worth while to go farther into it.

Nevertheless, it was in a perplexed and puzzled state of mind that he returned to Durrington, and his perplexity was not lessened by a piece of information given to him at luncheon by Sir Henry. The specialist started up from his seat as soon as he saw the detective, and made his way across to his table.

"My dear fellow," he burst out, "I have the most amazing piece of news. Who do you think this chap Ronald turns out to be? None other than James Ronald Penreath, only son of Sir James Penreath—Penreath of Twelvetrees—one of the oldest families in England, dating back before the Conquest! Not very much money, but very good blood—none better in England, in fact. The family seat is in Berkshire, and the family take their name from a village near Reading, where a battle was fought in 800 odd between the Danes and Saxons under Ethelwulf. You won't get a much older ancestry than *that*. Sir James married the daughter of Sir William Shirley, the member for Carbury, Cheshire—her family was not so good as his, but an honourable county family, nevertheless. This young man is their only child. A nice disgrace he's brought on the family name, the foolish fellow!"

"Who told you this?" asked Colwyn.

"Superintendent Galloway told me last night. The description of the young man was published in the London press in order to assist his capture, and it appears it was seen by the young lady to whom he is affianced, Miss Constance Willoughby, who is at present in London, engaged in war work. I have never met Miss Willoughby, but her aunt, Mrs. Hugh Brewer, with whom she is living at Lancaster Gate, is well-known to me. She is an immensely wealthy woman, who devotes her life to public works, and moves in the most exclusive philanthropic circles. The young lady was terribly distressed at the similarity of details in the description of the wanted man and that of her betrothed, particularly the scar on the cheek. Although she could not believe they referred to Mr. Penreath, she deemed it advisable to communicate with the Penreath family solicitor, Mr. Oakham, of Oakham and Pendules.

"Mr. Oakham called up Superintendent Galloway on the trunk line yesterday, to make inquiries, and shortly afterwards the news came through of Ronald's arrest. Superintendent Galloway was rather perturbed at learning that the arrested man resembled the description of the heir of one of the oldest baronetcies in England, and sought me to ask my advice. As he rather vulgarly put it, he was scared at having flushed such high game, and he thought, in view of my professional connection with some of the highest families in the land, that I might be able to give him information which would save him from the possibility of making a mistake–if such a possibility existed."

"Superintendent Galloway did not seem much worried by any such fears the last time I saw him," said Colwyn. "His one idea then was to catch Ronald and hang him as speedily as possible."

"The case wears another aspect now," replied Sir Henry gravely, oblivious of the irony in the detective's tones. "To arrest a nobody named Ronald is one thing, but to arrest the son of Penreath of Twelvetrees is quite a different matter. The police–quite rightly, in my opinion– wish to guard against the slightest possibility of mistake."

"There is no certainty that Ronald is the son of Sir James Penreath," said Colwyn thoughtfully. "Printed descriptions of people are very misleading."

"Exactly my contention," replied Sir Henry eagerly. "I told Galloway that the best way to settle the point was to let the young lady see the prisoner. The police are acting on the suggestion. Mr. Oakham is coming down with Miss Willoughby and her aunt from London by the afternoon train. They will go straight to Heathfield, where they will see Ronald before his removal to Norwich gaol. Superintendent Galloway is driving over from here in a taxicab to meet them at the station and escort them to the lock-up, and I am going with him. It is a frightful ordeal for two highly-strung ladies to have to undergo, and my professional skill may be needed to help them through with it. I shall suggest that they return here with me afterwards, and stay for the night at the hotel, instead of returning to London immediately. The night's rest will serve to recuperate their systems after the worry and excitement."

"No doubt," said Colwyn, who began to see how Sir Henry Durwood had built up such a flourishing practice as a ladies' specialist.

Sir Henry, having imparted his information, promised to acquaint him with the result of the afternoon's interview, and bustled out of the breakfast room in response to the imperious signalling of his wife's eye.

It was after dinner that evening, in the lounge, that Sir Henry again approached Colwyn, smoking a cigar, which represented the amount of a medical man's fee in certain London suburbs. But as Sir Henry counted his fees in guineas, and not in half-crowns, he could afford to be luxurious in his smoking. He took a seat beside the detective and, turning upon him his professionally portentous "all is over" face, remarked:

"There is no mistake. Ronald is Sir James Penreath's son."

"Miss Willoughby identified him, then?"

"It was a case of mutual identification. Mr. Penreath, to give him his proper name, was brought under escort into the room where we were seated. He started back at the sight of Miss Willoughby–I suppose he had no idea whom he was going to see–and said, 'Why, Constance!' The poor girl looked up at him and exclaimed, 'Oh, James, how could you?' and burst into a flood of tears. It was a very painful scene."

"I have no doubt it was–for all concerned," was Colwyn's dry comment. "Why did Miss Willoughby greet her betrothed husband in that way, as though she were convinced of his guilt? What does she know about the case?"

"Superintendent Galloway prepared her mind for the worst during the ride from the station to the gaol. She asked him a number of questions, and he told her that there was no doubt that the man she was going to see was the man who had murdered Mr. Glenthorpe."

"I suspected as much. But what else transpired during the interview? How did Penreath receive Miss Willoughby's remark?"

"Most peculiarly. He seemed about to speak, then checked himself with a half smile, looked down on the ground, and said no more. Superintendent Galloway signed to the policemen to remove him, and we withdrew. The interview did not last more than a minute or so."

"Miss Willoughby did not see him alone, then?"

"No. Galloway told her that she would not be permitted to see him alone."

"And nothing more was said on either side while Penreath was in the room?"

"Nothing. Penreath's attitude struck me as that of a man who did not wish to speak. He appeared self-conscious and confused, like a man with a secret to hide."

"Perhaps his silence was due to pride. After Miss Willoughby's tactless remark he may have thought there was no use saying anything when his sweetheart believed him guilty." Colwyn spoke without conviction; the memory of Penreath's demeanour to him after his arrest was too fresh in his mind.

"You wrong Miss Willoughby. She is only too anxious to catch at any straw of hope. When she learnt that you had been making some investigations into the case she expressed an anxiety to see you. She and her aunt yielded to my advice, and returned here to spend the night at the hotel before going back to London. As they did not feel inclined to face the ordeal of public scrutiny after the events of the day they are dining in private, and they have asked me to take you to their room when you are at liberty. Mr. Oakham has gone to Norwich, where he will stay for some days to prepare the defence of this unhappy young man, but he is coming here in the morning to see the ladies before they depart for London. He asked me to tell you that he would like to see you also."

"I shall be glad to see him, and Miss Willoughby as well. Have the ladies asked you your opinion of the case?"

"Naturally they did. I gave them the best comfort I could by hinting that in my opinion Mr. Penreath is not in a state of mind at present in which he can be held responsible for his actions. I did not say anything about epilepsy–the word is not a pleasant one to use before ladies."

"Did you tell them this in front of Galloway?"

"Certainly not. A professional man in my position cannot be too careful. I am glad now that I was so circumspect about this matter in my dealings with the police–very glad indeed. It was my duty to tell Mr. Oakham, and I did so. He was interested in what I told him–exceedingly so, and was anxious to know if I had given my opinion of Penreath's condition to anybody else. I mentioned that I had told you–in confidence."

"And it was then, no doubt, that Mr. Oakham said he would like to see me. I fancy I gather his drift. And now shall we visit Miss Willoughby?"

"Yes, I should say the ladies will be expecting us," said Sir Henry, looking at a fat watch with jewelled hands which registered golden minutes for him in Harley Street. He beckoned a waiter, and asked him to conduct them to Mrs. Brewer's sitting-room. The waiter led them along a corridor on the first floor, tapped deferentially, opened the door noiselessly in response to a feminine injunction to "come in," waited for the gentlemen to enter, and then closed the door behind them.

Two ladies rose to greet them. One was small and overdressed, with fluffy hair and China blue eyes. She carried some knitting in her hand, and a pet dog under her arm. Colwyn had no difficulty in identifying her with the frequent photographs of Mrs. Brewer which appeared in Society and illustrated papers. She belonged to a class of women who took advantage of the war to advertise themselves by philanthropic benefactions and war work, but she was able to distance most of her competitors for newspaper notoriety by reason of her wealth. Her niece, Miss Constance Willoughby, was of a different type. She was tall and graceful, with dark eyes and level brows. A straight nose and a firm chin indicated that their possessor was not lacking in a will of her own. Her manner was self-possessed and assured–a trifle too much so for a sensitive girl in the circumstances, Colwyn thought. Then he remembered having read in some paper that Miss Willoughby was one of the leaders of the new feminist movement which believed that the war had brought about the complete emancipation of English woman-hood, and with it the right to possess and display those qualities of character which hitherto were supposed to be peculiarly masculine. It was perhaps owing to her advocacy of these claims that Miss Willoughby felt herself called upon to display self-possession and self-control at a trying time. Colwyn, appraising her with his clear eye as Sir Henry introduced him, found himself speculating as to the reasons which had caused Penreath and her to fall in love with one another.

"Please sit down, Mr. Colwyn," said Mrs. Brewer, resuming a comfortable arm-chair in front of the fire, and adjusting the Pekingese on her lap. "I am so grateful to you for coming to see us in this unconventional way. I have been so anxious to see you! Everybody has heard of you, Mr. Colwyn—you're so famous. It was only the other day that I was reading a long article about you in some paper or other. I forget the name of the paper, but I remember that it said a lot of flattering things about you and your discoveries in crime. It said—Oh, you naughty, naughty Jellicoe." This to the dog, which had become entangled in the skein of wool on her lap, and was making frantic efforts to free itself. "Bad little doggie, you've ruined this sock, and some poor soldier will have to go with bare feet because you've been naughty! Are you a judge of Pekingese, Mr. Colwyn? Don't you think Jellicoe a dear?"

"Do you mean Sir John Jellicoe, Mrs. Brewer?"

"Of course not! I mean my Pekingese. I've named him after our great gallant commander, because it is through him we are all able to sleep safe and sound in our beds these dreadful nights."

"Sir John Jellicoe ought to feel flattered," said Colwyn gravely.

"Yes, I really think he should," replied Mrs. Brewer innocently. "Jellicoe is not a pretty name for a dog, but I think we should all be patriotic just now. But tell me what you think of this dreadful case, Mr. Colwyn. I am so frightfully distressed about it that I really don't know what to do. How could Mr. Penreath do such a shocking thing? Why didn't he go back to the front, if he had to kill somebody, instead of hiding away from everybody and murdering this poor old man in this wild spot? Such a disgrace to us all!"

"Mr. Penreath has been in the Army, then?" asked Colwyn.

"Of course. Didn't you know? He was in Mesopotamia, but was sent to the West Front recently, where he won the D.S.O. for an act of great gallantry under heavy fire, but was shortly afterwards invalided out of the Army. It was in all the papers at the time."

"You forget, my dear lady, that Mr. Penreath did not disclose his full name while he was staying here," interposed Sir Henry solemnly. "I myself was in complete ignorance of his identity until last night."

"Why, of course—you told me this afternoon. My poor head! Whatever induced Mr. Penreath to do such a thing as to conceal his name? So common and vulgar! What motive could he have? What do you think his motive was, Mr. Colwyn?"

"I think, Aunt Florence, as your nerves are bad, that you had better permit me to talk to Mr. Colwyn," said Miss Willoughby, speaking for the first time. "Otherwise we shall get into a worse tangle than the Pekingese."

"I am sure I shall be only too relieved if you will talk to Mr. Colwyn," rejoined the elder woman. "My head is really not equal to the task—my nerves are so frightfully unstrung."

Mrs. Brewer returned to the task of untangling the dog from the knitting wool, and the girl faced the detective earnestly.

"Mr. Colwyn," she said, "I understand you have been investigating this terrible affair. Will you tell me what you think of it? Do you believe that Mr. Penreath is guilty? You need not fear to be frank with me."

"I will not hesitate to be so. I shall be pleased to give you my conclusions about this case—so far as I have formed any—but I should be greatly obliged if you would answer a few questions first. That might help me to clear up one or two points on which I am at present in doubt, and make my statement to you clearer."

"Ask me any questions you wish."

"Thank you. In the first place, how long is it since Mr. Penreath returned from the front, invalided out of the Army?"

"About two months ago."

"Was he wounded?"

"No. I understand that he broke down through shell-shock, and the doctors said that it would be some time before he completely recovered. I do not know the details. Mr. Penreath was very sensitive and reticent about the matter, and so I forbore questioning him."

Colwyn nodded sympathetically.

"I understand. Have you noticed much difference in his demeanour since he returned from the front?"

"That question is a little difficult to answer," said the girl, hesitating.

"I can quite understand how you feel about it. My motive in asking the question is to see if we can ascertain why Penreath came to Norfolk under a concealed name, and then wandered over to this place, Flegne, in an almost penniless condition, when he had plenty of friends who would have supplied his needs, and, I should say, had money of his own in the bank, for it is quite certain that he would be in receipt of an allowance from his father. He acted most unusually for a young man of his standing and position, and I am wondering if shell-shock left him in that restless, unsettled, reckless condition which is one of its worst effects."

"I have seen so little of him since he returned from the front that it is difficult for me to answer you," said the girl, after a pause. "He went down to Berkshire to his father's place on his return, and stayed there a month. Then he came to London, and we met several times, but rarely alone. I am very deeply engaged in war work, and was unable to give him much of my time. When I did see him he struck me as rather moody and distrait, but I put that down to his illness, and the fact that he must naturally feel unhappy at his forced inaction. My friends paid him much attention and sent him many invitations—in fact, they would have made quite a fuss of him if he had let them—and, of course, he had friends of his own, but he didn't seem to want to go anywhere, and he told me once or twice that he wished people would let him alone. I pointed out to him that he had his duty to do in Society as well as at the front, but he said he disliked Society, particularly in war-time. About three weeks ago he told me one night at a dance that he was sick of London, and thought he would be better for a change of air. He was looking rather pale, and I agreed he would be the better for a change. I asked him where he intended going, and he said he thought he would try the east coast—he didn't say what part. He left me with the intention of going away the next day. That was the last I saw of him—until to-day."

"You got no letter from him?"

"I did not hear from him—nor of him—until I saw his description published in the London newspapers as that of a criminal wanted by the police."

Miss Willoughby uttered the last sentence in some bitterness, with a sparkle of resentment in her eyes. It was apparent that she considered she had been badly treated by her lover, and that his arrest had hardened, instead of softening, her feelings of resentment.

"I am much obliged to you for answering my questions, Miss Willoughby," said the detective. "As I told you before, they are not dictated by curiosity, but in the hope of eliciting some information which would throw light on this puzzling case."

"A puzzling case! You consider it a puzzling case, Mr. Colwyn?" She glanced at him with a more eager and girlish expression than he had yet seen on her face. "I understood from the police officer that there was no room for doubt in the matter. Sir Henry Durwood shares the police view." She turned a swift questioning glance in the specialist's direction.

Sir Henry caught the glance, and felt it incumbent upon himself to utter a solemn commonplace.

"I beg of you not to raise false hopes in Miss Willoughby's breast, Mr. Colwyn," he said.

"I have no intention of doing so," returned the detective. "On the other hand, I protest against everybody condemning Penreath until it is certain he is guilty. And now, Miss Willoughby, I will tell you what I have discovered."

He entered upon a brief account of his investigations at the inn, with the exception that he omitted the visit of Peggy to the murdered man's chamber and her subsequent explanation. Miss Willoughby listened attentively, and, when he had concluded, remarked:

"Do you think the wax and tallow candle-grease dropped in the room suggests the presence of two persons?"

"I feel sure that it does."

"And who do you think the other was?"

"It is not yet proved that Penreath was one of them."

She flushed under the implied reproof, and hurriedly added:

"Have you acquainted the police with your discoveries, Mr. Colwyn?"

"I have, and I am bound to say that they attach very little importance to them."

"Do you propose to go any further with your investigations?"

"I would prefer not to answer that question until I have seen Mr. Oakham to-morrow."

14

When Colwyn went in to lunch the following day after a walk on the front, he found Sir Henry awaiting him in the lounge with a visitor whose identity the detective guessed before Sir Henry introduced him. "This is Mr. Oakham," said Sir Henry. "I have told him of your investigation into this painful case which has brought him to Norfolk."

"An investigation in which you helped," said Colwyn, with a smile.

"I am afraid it would be stretching the fable of the mouse and the lion to suggest that I was able to help such a renowned criminal investigator as yourself," returned Sir Henry waggishly. "When Mr. Oakham learnt that you had been investigating this case he expressed a strong desire to see you."

"I am returning to London by the afternoon express, Mr. Colwyn," said the solicitor. "I should be glad if you could spare me a little of your time before I go."

"Certainly," replied Colwyn, courteously. "It had better be at once, had it not? You have not very much time at your disposal."

"If it does not inconvenience you," replied Mr. Oakham politely. "But your lunch—"

"That can wait," said the detective. "I feel deeply interested in this case of young Penreath."

"Mr. Oakham saw him this morning before coming over," said Sir Henry. "He is quite mad, and refuses to say anything. Therefore, we have come to the conclusion——" "Really, Sir Henry, you shouldn't have said that." Mr. Oakham's tone was both shocked and expostulatory.

"Why not?" retorted Sir Henry innocently. "Mr. Colwyn knows all about it–I told him myself. I thought you wanted him to help you?"

"I am aware of that, but, my dear sir, this is an extremely delicate and difficult business. As Mr. Penreath's professional adviser, I must beg of you to exercise more reticence."

"Then I had better go and have my lunch while you two have a chat," said Sir Henry urbanely, "or I shall only be putting my foot in it again. Mr. Oakham, I shall see you before you go." Sir Henry moved off in the direction of the luncheon room.

"Perhaps you will come to my sitting-room," said Colwyn to Mr. Oakham. "We can talk quietly there."

"Thank you," responded Mr. Oakham, and he went with the detective upstairs.

Mr. Oakham, of Oakham and Pendules, Temple Gardens, was a little white-haired man of seventy, attired in the sombre black of the Victorian era, with a polished reticent manner befitting the senior partner of a firm of solicitors owning the most aristocratic practice in England; a firm so eminently respectable that they never rendered a bill of costs to a client until he was dead, when the amount of legal expenses incurred during his lifetime was treated as a charge upon the family estate, and deducted from the moneys accruing to the next heir, who, in his turn, was allowed to run his allotted course without a bill from Oakham and Pendules. They were a discreet and dignified firm, as ancient as some of the names whose family secrets were locked away in their office deed boxes, and were reputed to know more of the inner history of the gentry in Burke's Peerage than all the rest of the legal profession put together.

The arrest of the only son of Sir James Penreath, of Twelvetrees, Berks, on a charge of murder, had shocked Mr. Oakham deeply. Divorces had come his way in plenty, though he remembered the day when they were considered scandalous in good families. But the modern generation had changed all that, and Mr. Oakham had since listened to so many stories of marital wrongs, and had assisted in obtaining so many orders for restitution of conjugal rights, that he had come to regard divorce as fashionable enough to be respectable. He was intimately versed in most human failings and follies, and a past master in preventing their consequences coming to light.

Financial embarrassments he was well used to–they might almost be said to be his forte–for many of his clients had more lineage than money, but the crime of murder was a thing outside his professional experience.

The upper classes of the present generation had, in this respect at least, improved on the morals of their freebooting ancestors, and murder had gone so completely out of fashion among the aristocracy that Mr. Oakham had never been called upon to prepare the defence of a client charged with killing a fellow creature. Mr. Oakham regarded murder as an ungentlemanly crime. He believed that no gentleman would commit murder unless he were mad. Since his arrival in Norfolk he had come to the conclusion that young Penreath was not only mad, but that he had committed the murder with which he stood charged. Sir Henry Durwood had been responsible for the first opinion, and the police had helped him to form the second. Two interviews he had had with his client since his arrest had strengthened and deepened both convictions.

It was in this frame of mind that Mr. Oakham seated himself in the detective's sitting room. He accepted a cigar from Colwyn's case, and looked amiably at his companion, who waited for him to speak. The interview had been of the solicitor's seeking, and it was for him to disclose his object in doing so.

"This is a very unfortunate case, Mr. Colwyn," the solicitor remarked.

"Yes; it seems so," replied Colwyn.

"I am afraid there is not the slightest doubt that this unhappy young man has committed this murder."

"You have arrived at that conclusion?"

"It is impossible to arrive at any other conclusion, in view of the evidence."

"It is purely circumstantial. I thought that perhaps Penreath would have some statement to make which would throw a different light on the case."

"I will be frank with you, Mr. Colwyn," said the solicitor. "You are acquainted with all the facts of the case, and I hope you will be able to help us. Penreath's attitude is a very strange one. Apparently he does not apprehend the grave position in which he stands. I am forced to the conclusion that he is suffering from an unhappy aberration of the intellect, which has led to his committing this crime. His conduct since coming to Norfolk has not been that of a sane man. He has hidden himself away from his friends, and stayed here under a false name. I understand that he behaved in an eccentric and violent way in the breakfast room of this hotel on the morning of the day he left for the place where the murder was subsequently committed."

"You have learnt this from Sir Henry, I presume?"

"Yes. Sir Henry has conveyed to me his opinion, based on his observation of Mr. Penreath's eccentricity at the breakfast table the last morning of his stay here, that Mr. Penreath is an epileptic, liable to attacks of *furor epilepticus*–a phase of the disease which sometimes leads to outbreaks of terrible violence. He thought it advisable that I should know this at once, in view of what has happened since. Sir Henry informed me that he confided a similar opinion to you, as you were present at the time, and assisted him to convey Penreath upstairs. May I ask what opinion you formed of his behaviour at the breakfast table, Mr. Colwyn?"

"I thought he was excited–nothing more."

"But the violence, Mr. Colwyn! Sir Henry Durwood says Penreath was about to commit a violent assault on the people at the next table when he interfered."

"The violence was not apparent–to me," returned the detective, who did not feel called upon to disclose his secret belief that Sir Henry had acted hastily. "Apart from the excitement he displayed on this particular morning, Penreath seemed to me a normal and average young Englishman of his class. I certainly saw no signs of insanity about him. It occurred to me at the time that his excitement might be the outcome of shell-shock. We had had an air raid two nights before, and some shell-shock cases are badly affected by air raids. I have since been informed that Penreath was invalided out of the Army recently, suffering from shell-shock."

"In Sir Henry's opinion the shell-shock has aggravated a tendency to the disease."

"Has Penreath ever shown any previous signs of epilepsy?"

"Not so far as I am aware, but his mother developed the disease in later years, and ultimately died from it. Her illness was a source of great worry and anxiety to Sir James. And epilepsy is hereditary."

"Pathologists differ on that point. I know something of the disease, and I doubt whether Penreath is an epileptic. He showed none of the symptoms which I have always associated with epilepsy."

"An eminent specialist like Sir Henry is hardly likely to be mistaken. The fact that Penreath seemed a sane and collected individual to your eye proves nothing. Epileptic attacks are intermittent, and the sufferer may appear quite sane between the attacks. Epilepsy is a remarkable disease. A latent tendency to it may exist for years without those nearest and dearest to the sufferer suspecting it, so Sir Henry says. Penreath's case is a very strange and sad one."

"It is a strange case in very way," said Colwyn earnestly. "Why should a young man like Penreath go over to this remote Norfolk village, where he had not been before, and murder an old man whom he had never seen previously? The police theory that this murder was committed for the sake of £300 which the victim had drawn out of the bank that day seems incredible to me, in the case of a young man like Penreath."

"The only way of accounting for the whole unhappy business is on Sir Henry's hypothesis that Penreath is mad. In acute epileptic mania there are cases in which there is a seeming calmness of conduct, and these are the most dangerous of all. The patient walks about like a man in a dream, impelled by a force which he cannot resist, and does all sorts of things without conscious purpose. He will take long walks to places he has never been, will steal money or valuables, and commit murder or suicide with apparent coolness and cunning. Sir Henry describes this as automatic action, and he says that it is a notable characteristic of the form of epileptic mania from which Penreath is suffering. You will observe that these symptoms fit in with all the facts of the case against Penreath. The facts, unfortunately, are so clear that there is no gainsaying them."

"It seems so now," said Colwyn thoughtfully. "Yet, when I was investigating the facts at the time, I came across several points which seemed to suggest the possibility of an alternative theory to the police theory."

"I should like to know what those points are."

"I will tell you."

The detective proceeded to set forth the result of his visit to the inn, and the solicitor listened to him with close attention. When he had finished Mr. Oakham remarked:

"I am afraid there is not much in these points, Mr. Colwyn. Your suggestion that there were two persons in the murdered man's room is interesting, but you have no evidence to support it. The girl's explanation of her visit to the room is probably the true one. Far be it from me, as Penreath's legal adviser, to throw away the slightest straw of hope, but your conjectures–for, to my mind, they are nothing more–are nothing against the array of facts and suspicious circumstances which have been collected by the police. And even if the police case were less strong, there is another grave fact which we cannot overlook."

"You mean that Penreath refuses to say anything?" said Colwyn.

"He appears to be somewhat indifferent to the outcome," returned the lawyer guardedly.

"It is his silence which baffles me," said Colwyn. "I saw him alone after his arrest, and told him I was willing to help him if he could tell me anything which would assist me to establish his innocence–if he were innocent. He replied that he had nothing to say."

"What you tell me deepens my conviction that Penreath does not realise the position in which he is placed, and cannot be held accountable for his actions."

"Is it your intention to plead mental incapacity at the trial?"

"Sir Henry Durwood has offered to give evidence that, in his opinion, Penreath is not responsible for his actions. The Penreath family is under a debt of gratitude to Sir Henry. I consider it little short of providential that Sir Henry was staying here at the time." Like most lawyers, Mr. Oakham had a firm belief in the interposition of Providence–particularly in the affairs of the families of the great. "And that is the reason for my coming over here to see you this morning, Mr. Colwyn. You were present at the breakfast table scene–you witnessed this young man's eccentricity and violence. The Penreath family is already under a debt of gratitude to you–will you increase the obligation? In other words, will you give evidence in support of the defence at the trial?"

"You want me to assist you in convincing the jury that Penreath is a criminal lunatic," said Colwyn. "That is

what your defence amounts to. It is a grave
responsibility. Doctors and specialists are sometimes
mistaken, you know."

"I am afraid there is very little doubt in this case.
Here is a young man of birth and breeding, who hides
from his friends under an assumed name, behaves in
public in an eccentric manner, is turned out of his hotel,
goes to a remote inn, and disappears before anybody is
up. The body of a gentleman who occupied the room next
to him is subsequently discovered in a pit close by, and
the footprints leading to the pit are those of our young
friend. The young man is subsequently arrested close to
the place where the body was thrown, and not then, or
since, has he offered his friends any explanation of his
actions. In the circumstances, therefore, I shall avail
myself of Sir Henry's evidence. In my own mind—from my
own observation and conversation with Penreath—I am
convinced that he cannot be held responsible for his
actions. In view of the tremendously strong case against
him, in view of his peculiar attitude to you—and others—in
the face of accusation, and in view of his previous
eccentric behaviour, I shall take the only possible course
to save the son of Penreath of Twelvetrees from the
gallows. I had hoped, Mr. Colwyn, that you, who
witnessed the scene at this hotel, and subsequently
helped Sir Henry Durwood convey this unhappy young
man upstairs, would see your way clear to support Sir
Henry's expert opinion that this young man is insane.
Your reputation and renown would carry weight with the
jury."

"I am sorry, but I am afraid you must do without me,"
replied Colwyn. "In view of Penreath's silence I can come
to no other conclusion, though against my better
judgment, than that he is guilty, but I cannot take upon
myself the responsibility of declaring that he is insane. In
spite of Sir Henry Durwood's opinion, I cannot believe
that he is, or was. It will be a difficult defence to establish
in the case of Penreath. If you wish the jury to say that

Penreath is the victim of what French writers call *epilepsie larvée,* in which an outbreak of brutal or homicidal violence takes the place of an epileptic fit, with a similar break in the continuity of consciousness, you will first have to convince the judge that Penreath's preceding fits were so slight as to permit the possibility of their being overlooked, and you will also have to establish beyond doubt that the break in his consciousness existed from the time of the scene in the hotel breakfast-room until the time the murder was committed. The test of that state is the unintelligent character of some of the acts of the sufferer. In my opinion, a defence of insanity is not likely to be successful. Personally, I shall go no further in the case, but I cannot give up my original opinion that the whole of the facts in this case have not been brought to light. Probably they never will be—now."

15

Although no hint of the defence was supposed to
transpire, the magic words "No precedent" were
whispered about in legal circles as the day for Penreath's
trial approached, and invested the case with more than
ordinary interest in professional eyes. Editors of London
legal journals endeavoured to extract something definite
from Mr. Oakham when he returned to London to brief
counsel and prepare the defence, but the lunches they
lavished on him in pursuit of information might have
been spent with equal profit on the Sphinx.

The editors had to content themselves with sending
shorthand writers to Norwich to report the case fully for
the benefit of their circle of readers, whose appetite for a
legal quibble was never satiated by repetition.

On the other hand, the case aroused but languid
interest in the breasts of the ordinary public. The
newspapers had not given the story of the murder much
prominence in their columns, because murders were only
good copy in war-time in the slack season between
military offensives, and, moreover, this particular case
lacked the essentials of what modern editors call, in
American journalese jargon, "a good feature story." In
other words, it was not sufficiently sensational or
immoral to appeal to the palates of newspaper readers. It
lacked the spectacular elements of a filmed drama; there
was no woman in the case or unwritten law.

It was true that the revelation of the identity of the
accused man had aroused a passing interest in the case,
bringing it up from paragraph value on the back page to a
"two-heading item" on the "splash" page, but that interest
soon died away, for, after all, the son of a Berkshire
baronet was small beer in war's levelling days, when

peers worked in overalls in munition factories, and
personages of even more exalted rank sold pennyworths
of ham in East-end communal kitchens.

Nevertheless, because of the perennial interest which
attaches to all murder trials, the Norwich Assizes Court
was filled with spectators on the dull drizzling November
day when the case was heard, and the fact that the
accused was young and good-looking and of gentle birth
probably accounted for the sprinkling of well-dressed
women amongst the audience. The younger ones eyed
him with sympathy as he was brought into the dock: his
good looks, his blue eyes, his air of breeding, his well-cut
clothes, appealed to their sensibilities, and if they had
been given the opportunity they would have acquitted
him without the formality of a trial as far "too nice a boy"
to have committed murder.

To the array of legal talent assembled together by the
golden wand of Costs the figure of the accused man had
no personal significance but the actual facts at issue
entered as little into their minds as into the pitying
hearts of the female spectators. The accused had no
individual existence so far as they were concerned: he
was merely a pawn in the great legal game, of which the
lawyers were the players and the judge the referee, and
the side which won the pawn won the game. As this
particular game represented an attack on the sacred
tradition of Precedent, both sides had secured the
strongest professional intellects possible to contest the
match, and the lesser legal fry of Norwich had gathered
together to witness the struggle, and pick up what points
they could.

The leader for the prosecution was Sir Herbert
Templewood, K.C., M.P., a political barrister, with a
Society wife, a polished manner, and a deadly gift of
cross-examination. With him was Mr. Grover Braecroft, a
dour Scotch lawyer of fifty-five, who was currently
believed to know the law from A to Z, and really had an
intimate acquaintance with those five letters which made

up the magic word Costs. Apart from this valuable knowledge, he was a cunning and crafty lawyer, picked in the present case to supply the brains to Sir Herbert Templewood's brilliance, and do the jackal work which the lion disdained. The pair were supported by a Crown Solicitor well versed in precedents–a little prim figure of a man who sat with so many volumes of judicial decisions and reports of test cases piled in front of him that only the upper portion of his grey head was visible above the books.

The defence relied mainly upon Mr. Reginald Middleheath, the eminent criminal counsel, who depended as much upon his portly imposing stage presence to bluff juries into an acquittal as upon his legal attainments, which were also considerable. Mr. Middleheath's cardinal article of legal faith was that all juries were fools, and should be treated as such, because if they once got the idea into their heads that they knew something about the case they were trying they were bound to convict in order to sustain their reputation for intelligence. One of Mr. Middleheath's favourite tricks for disabusing a jury of the belief that they possessed any common sense was, before addressing them, to stare each juryman in the face for half a minute or so in turn with his piercing penetrative eyes, accompanying the look with a pitying contemptuous smile, the gaze and the smile implying that counsel for the opposite side may have flattered them into believing that their intelligences were fit to try such an intricate case, but they couldn't deceive *him*.

Having robbed the jury of their self-esteem by this means, Mr. Middleheath would proceed to put them on good terms with themselves again by insinuating in persuasive tones that the case was one calculated to perplex the most astute legal brain. He would frankly confess that it had perplexed him at first, but as he had mastered its intricacies the jury were welcome to his

laboriously acquired knowledge in order to help them in
arriving at a right decision. Mr. Middleheath's junior was
Mr. Garden Greyson, a thin ascetic looking lawyer whose
knowledge of medical jurisprudence had brought him his
brief in the case. Mr. Oakham sat beside Mr. Greyson
with various big books in front of him.

The judge was Mr. Justice Redington, whose presence
on the bench was always considered a strengthening
factor in the Crown case. Judges differ as much as
ordinary human beings, and are as human in their
peculiarities as the juries they direct and the prisoners
they try. There are good-tempered and bad-tempered
judges, harsh and tender judges, learned and foolish
judges, there are even judges with an eye to self-
advertisement, and a few wise ones. Mr. Justice
Redington belonged to that class of judges who, while
endeavouring to hold the balance fairly between the
Crown and the defence, see to it that the accused does not
get overweight from the scales of justice. Such judges
take advantage of their judicial office by cross-examining
witnesses for the defence after the Crown Prosecutor has
finished with them, in the effort to bring to light some
damaging fact or contradiction which the previous
examination has failed to elicit. In other respects, Mr.
Justice Redington was a very fair judge, and he worked
as industriously as any newspaper reporter, taking
extensive notes of all his cases with a gold fountain pen,
which he filled himself from one of the court inkstands
whenever it ran dry. In appearance he was a florid and
pleasant looking man, and his hobby off the bench was
farming his own land and breeding prize cattle.

There were the usual preliminaries, equivalent to the
clearing of the course or the placing of the pieces, which
bored the regular habitués of the court but whetted the
appetites of the more unsophisticated spectators. First
there was the lengthy process of empanelling a jury, with
the inevitable accompaniment of challenges and
objections, until the most unintelligent looking dozen of

the panel finally found themselves in the jury box. Then the Clerk of Arraigns gabbled over the charges: wilful murder of Roger Glenthorpe on 26th October, 1916, and feloniously stealing from the said Roger Glenthorpe the sum of £300 on the same date. To these charges the accused man pleaded "Not guilty" in a low voice. The jury were directed on the first indictment only, and Sir Herbert Templewood got up to address the jury.

Sir Herbert knew very little about the case, but his junior was well informed; and what Mr. Braecroft didn't know he got from the Crown Solicitor, who sat behind the barristers' table, ready to lean forward at the slightest indication and supply any points which were required. Under this system of spoon-feeding Sir Herbert ambled comfortably along, reserving his showy paces for the cross-examination of witnesses for the defence.

Sir Herbert commenced by describing the case as a straightforward one which would offer no difficulty to an intelligent jury. It was true that it rested on circumstantial evidence, but that evidence was of the strongest nature, and pointed so clearly in the one direction, that the jury could come to no other conclusion than that the prisoner at the bar had committed the murder with which he stood charged.

With this preamble, the Crown Prosecutor proceeded to put together the chain of circumstantial evidence against the accused with the deliberate logic of the legal brain, piecing together incidents, interpreting clues, probing motives, and fashioning together the whole tremendous apparatus of circumstantial evidence with the intent air of a man building an unbreakable cage for a wild beast. As Colwyn had anticipated, the incident at the Durrington hotel had been dropped from the Crown case. That part of the presentment was confined to the statement that Penreath had registered at the hotel under a wrong name, and had left without paying his bill. The first fact suggested that the accused had something to hide, the second established a motive for the subsequent murder.

Sir Herbert Templewood concluded his address in less than an hour, and proceeded to call evidence for the prosecution. There were nine witnesses: that strangely assorted pair, the innkeeper and Charles, the deaf waiter, Ann, the servant, the two men who had recovered Mr. Glenthorpe's body from the pit, the Heathfield doctor, who testified as to the cause of death, Superintendent Galloway, who gave the court the result of the joint investigations of the chief constable and himself at the inn, Police-Constable Queensmead, who described the arrest and Inspector Fredericks, of Norwich, who was in charge of the Norwich station when the accused was taken there from Flegne. In order to save another witness being called, Counsel for the defence admitted that accused had registered at the Grand Hotel, Durrington, under a wrong name, and left without paying his bill.

Mr. Middleheath cross-examined none of the witnesses for the prosecution except the last one, and his forensic restraint was placed on record by the depositions clerk in the exact words of the unvarying formula between bench and bar. "Do you ask anything, Mr. Middleheath?" Mr. Justice Redington would ask, with punctilious politeness, when the Crown Prosecutor sat down after examining a witness. To which Mr. Middleheath would reply, in tones of equal courtesy: "I ask nothing, my lord." Counsel's cross-examination of Inspector Fredericks consisted of two questions, intended to throw light on the accused's state of mind after his arrest. Inspector Fredericks declared that he was, in his opinion, quite calm and rational.

Mr. Middleheath's opening address to the jury for the defence was brief, and, to sharp legal ears, vague and unconvincing. Although he pointed out that the evidence was purely circumstantial, and that in the absence of direct testimony the accused was entitled to the benefit of any reasonable doubt, he did not attempt to controvert the statements of the Crown witnesses, or suggest that the Crown had not established its case. His address, combined with the fact that he had not cross-examined any of the Crown witnesses, suggested to the listening lawyers that he had either a very strong defence or none at all. The point was left in suspense for the time being by Mr. Justice Redington suggesting that, in view of the lateness of the hour, Counsel should defer calling evidence for the defence until the following day. As a judicial suggestion is a command, the court was adjourned accordingly, the judge first warning the jury not to try to come to any conclusion, or form an opinion as to what their verdict should be, until they had heard the evidence for the prisoner.

When the case was continued the next day, the first witness called for the defence was Dr. Robert Greydon, an elderly country practitioner with the precise professional manner of a past medical generation, who stated that he practised at Twelvetrees, Berkshire, and was the family doctor of the Penreath family. In reply to Mr. Middleheath he stated that he had frequently attended the late Lady Penreath, the mother of the accused, for fits or seizures from which she suffered periodically, and that the London specialist who had been called into consultation on one occasion had agreed with him that the seizures were epileptic.

"I want to give every latitude to the defence," said Sir Herbert Templewood, rising in dignified protest, "but I am afraid I cannot permit this conversation to go in. My learned friend must call the London specialist if he wants to get it in."

"I will waive the point as my learned friend objects," said Mr. Middleheath, satisfied that he had "got it in" the jury's ears, "and content myself with asking Dr. Greydon whether, from his own knowledge, Lady Penreath suffered from epilepsy."

"Undoubtedly," replied the witness.

"One moment," said the judge, looking up from his notes. "Where is this evidence tending, Mr. Middleheath?"

"My lord," replied Mr. Middleheath solemnly, "I wish the court to know all the facts on which we rely."

The judge bowed his head and waved his gold fountain-pen as an indication that the examination might proceed. The witness said that Lady Penreath was undoubtedly an epileptic, and suffered from attacks extending over twenty years, commencing when her only son was five years old, and continuing till her death ten years ago. For some years the attacks were slight, without convulsions, but ultimately the grand mal became well developed, and several attacks in rapid succession ultimately caused her death. In the witness's opinion epilepsy was an hereditary disease, frequently transmitted to the offspring, if either or both parents suffered from it.

"Have you ever seen any signs of epilepsy in Lady Penreath's son–the prisoner at the bar?" asked Sir Herbert, who began to divine the direction of the defence.

"Never," replied the witness.

"Was he under your care in his infancy and boyhood? I mean were you called in to attend to his youthful ailments?"

"Yes, until he went to school."

"And was he a normal and healthy boy?"

"Quite."

"Did you see him when he returned home recently?" asked Mr. Middleheath, rising to re-examine.

"Yes."

"You are aware he was discharged from the Army suffering from shell-shock?"

"Yes."

"And did you notice a marked change in him?"

"Very marked indeed. He struck me as odd and forgetful at times, and sometimes he seemed momentarily to lose touch with his surroundings. He used to be very bright and good-tempered, but he returned from the war irritable and moody, and very silent, disliking, above all things, to be questioned about his experiences at the front. He used to be the very soul of courtesy, but when he returned from the front he refused to attend a 'welcome home' at the village church and hear the vicar read a congratulatory address."

"I hope you are not going to advance the latter incident as a proof of *non compos mentis*, Mr. Middleheath," said the judge facetiously.

In the ripples of mirth which this judicial sally aroused, the little doctor was permitted to leave the box, and depart for his native obscurity of Twelvetrees. He had served his purpose, so far as Mr. Middleheath was concerned, and Sir Herbert Templewood was too good a sportsman to waste skilful flies on such a small fish, which would do no honour to his bag if hooked.

Sir Herbert Templewood and every lawyer in court were by now aware that the defence were unable to meet the Crown case, but were going to fight for a verdict of insanity. The legal fraternity realised the difficulties of that defence in a case of murder. It would be necessary not only to convince the jury that the accused did not know the difference between right and wrong, but to convince the judge, in the finer legal interpretation of criminal insanity, that the accused did not know the nature of the act he was charged with committing, in the sense that he was unable to distinguish whether it was right or wrong at the moment of committing it. The law, which assumes that a man is sane and responsible for his acts, throws upon the defence the onus of proving otherwise, and proving it up to the hilt, before it permits an accused person to escape the responsibility of his acts. Such a defence usually resolves itself into a battle between medical experts and the counsel engaged, the Crown endeavouring to upset the medical evidence for the defence with medical evidence in rebuttal.

The lawyers in court settled back with a new enjoyment at the prospect of the legal and medical hair-splitting and quibbling which invariably accompanies an encounter of this kind, and Crown Counsel and solicitors displayed sudden activity. Sir Herbert Templewood and Mr. Braecroft held a whispered consultation, and then Mr. Braecroft passed a note to the Crown Solicitor, who hurried from the court and presently returned carrying a formidable pile of dusty volumes, which he placed in front of junior counsel. The most uninterested person in court seemed the man in the dock, who sat looking into a vacancy with a bored expression on his handsome face, as if he were indifferent to the fight on which his existence depended.

The next witness was Miss Constance Willoughby, who gave her testimony in low clear tones, and with perfect self-possession. It was observed by the feminine element in court that she did not look at her lover in the dock, but kept her eyes steadily fixed on Mr. Middleheath. Her story was a straightforward and simple one. She had become engaged to Mr. Penreath shortly before the war, and had seen him several times since he was invalided out of the Army. The last occasion was a month ago, when he called at her aunt's house at Lancaster Gate. She had noticed a great change in him since his return from the front. He was moody and depressed. She did not question him about his illness, as she thought he was out of spirits because he had been invalided out of the Army, and did not want to talk about it. He told her he intended to go away for a change until he got right again—he had not made up his mind where, but he thought somewhere on the East Coast, where it was cool and bracing, would suit him best—and he would write to her as soon as he got settled anywhere. She did not see him again, and did not hear from him or know anything of his movements till she read his description in a London paper as that of a man wanted by the Norfolk police for murder. Her aunt, who showed her the paper, communicated with the Penreaths' solicitor, Mr. Oakham. The following day she and her aunt were taken to Heathfield and identified the accused.

"Your aunt took action to allay your anxiety, I understand?" said Mr. Heathfield, whose watchful eye had noted the unfavourable effect of this statement on the jury.

The witness bowed.

"Yes," she replied. "I was terribly anxious, as I had not heard from Mr. Penreath since he went away. Anything was better than the suspense."

"You say accused was moody and depressed when you saw him?" asked Sir Herbert Templewood.

"Yes."

"May I take it that there was nothing terrifying in his behaviour–nothing to indicate that he was not in his right mind?"

"No," replied the witness slowly. "He did not frighten me, but I was concerned about him. He certainly looked ill, and I thought he seemed a little strange."

"As though he had something on his mind?" suggested Sir Herbert.

"Yes," assented the witness.

"Were you aware that the accused, when he went to see you at your aunt's home before he departed for Norfolk, was very short of money?"

"I was not. If I had known—"

"You would have helped him–is that what you were going to say?" asked Mr. Middleheath, as Sir Herbert resumed his seat without pursuing the point.

"My aunt would have helped Mr. Penreath if she had known he was in monetary difficulties."

"Thank you." Mr. Middleheath sat down, pulling his gown over his shoulders.

The witness was leaving the stand when the sharp authoritative voice of the judge stopped her.

"Wait a minute, please, I want to get this a little clearer. You said you were aware that the accused was discharged from the Army suffering from shell-shock. Did he tell you so himself?"

"No, my lord. I was informed so."

"Really, Mr. Middleheath—"

The judge's glance at Counsel for the Defence was so judicial that it brought Mr. Middleheath hurriedly to his feet again.

"My lord," he explained, "I intend to prove in due course that the prisoner was invalided out of the Army suffering from shell-shock."

"Very well." The judge motioned to the witness that she was at liberty to leave the box.

The appearance of Sir Henry Durwood in the box as the next witness indicated to Crown Counsel that the principal card for the defence was about to be played. Lawyers conduct defences as some people play bridge— they keep the biggest trump to the last. Sir Henry represented the highest trump in Mr. Middleheath's hand, and if he could not score with him the game was lost.

Sir Henry seemed not unconscious of his importance to the case as he stepped into the stand and bowed to the judge with bland professional equality. His evidence-in-chief was short, but to the point, and amounted to a recapitulation of the statement he had made to Colwyn in Penreath's bedroom on the morning of the episode in the breakfast-room of the Grand Hotel, Durrington. Sir Henry related the events of that morning for the benefit of the jury, and in sonorous tones expressed his professional opinion that the accused's strange behaviour on that occasion was the result of an attack of epilepsy— petit mal, combined with *furor epilepticus*.

The witness defined epilepsy as a disease of the nervous system, marked by attacks of unconsciousness, with or without convulsions. The loss of consciousness with severe convulsive seizures was known as grand mal, the transient loss of consciousness without convulsive seizures was called petit mal. Attacks of petit mal might come on at any time, and were usually accompanied by a feeling of faintness and vertigo. The general symptoms were sudden jerkings of the limbs, sudden tremors, giddiness and unconsciousness. The eyes became fixed, the face slightly pale, sometimes very red, and there was frequently some almost automatic action. In grand mal there was always warning of an attack, in petit mal there was no warning as a rule, but sometimes there was premonitory giddiness and restlessness. *Furor epilepticus* was a medical term applied to the violence displayed during attacks of petit mal, a violence which was much greater than extreme anger, and under its influence the subject was capable of committing the most violent outrages, even murder, without being conscious of the act.

"There is no doubt in your mind that the accused man had an attack of petit mal in the breakfast-room of the Durrington hotel the morning before the murder?" asked Mr. Middleheath.

"None whatever. All the symptoms pointed to it. He was sitting at the breakfast table when he suddenly ceased eating, and his eyes grew fixed. The knife which he held in his hand was dropped, but as the attack increased he picked it up again and thrust it into the table in front of him—a purely automatic action, in my opinion. When he sprang up from the table a little while afterwards he was under the influence of the epileptic fury, and would have made a violent attack on the people sitting at the next table if I had not seized him. Unconsciousness then supervened, and, with the aid of another of the hotel guests, I carried him to his room. It was there I noticed foam on his lips. When he returned to consciousness he had no recollection of what had occurred, which is consistent with an epileptic seizure. I saw that his condition was dangerous, and urged him to send for his friends, but he refused to do so."

"It would have been better if he had followed your advice. You say it is consistent with epilepsy for him to have no recollection of what occurred during this seizure in the hotel breakfast room. What would a man's condition of mind be if, during an attack of petit mal, he committed an act of violence, say murder, for example?"

"The mind is generally a complete blank. Sometimes there is a confused sense of something, but the patient has no recollection of what has occurred, in my experience."

"In this case the prisoner is charged with murder. Could he have committed this offence during another attack of *furor epilepticus* and recollect nothing about it afterwards? Is that consistent?"

"Yes, quite consistent," replied the witness.

"Is epilepsy an hereditary disease?"

"Yes."

"And if both parents, or one of them, suffered from epilepsy, would there be a great risk of the children suffering from it?"

"Every risk in the case of both persons being affected; some probability in the case of one."

"What do you think would be the effect of shell-shock on a person born of one epileptic parent?"

"It would probably aggravate a tendency to epilepsy, by lowering the general health."

"Thank you, Sir Henry."

Mr. Middleheath resumed his seat, and Sir Herbert Templewood got up to cross-examine.

16

Sir Herbert Templewood did not believe the evidence of the specialist, and he did not think the witness believed it himself. Sir Herbert did not think any the worse of the witness on that account. It was one of the recognised rules of the game to allow witnesses to stretch a point or two in favour of the defence where the social honour of highly respectable families was involved. Sir Herbert saw in the present defence the fact that the hand of his venerable friend, Mr. Oakham, had not lost its cunning. Mr. Oakham was a very respectable solicitor, acting for a very respectable client, and he had called a very respectable Harley Street specialist–who, by a most fortuitous circumstance, had been staying at the same hotel as the accused shortly before the murder was committed–to convince the jury that the young man was insane, and that his form of insanity was epilepsy, a disease which had prolonged lucid intervals.

A truly ingenious and eminently respectable defence, and one which, in his heart of hearts, perhaps, Sir Herbert might not have been sorry to see succeed, for he knew Sir James Penreath of Twelvetrees, and was sorry to see his son in such a position. But he had his duty to perform, and that duty was to discredit in the eyes of the jury the evidence of the witness in the box, because juries were prone to look upon specialists as men to whom all things had been revealed, and return a verdict accordingly.

Sir Herbert made one mistake in his analysis of the defence. Sir Henry, at least, believed in his own evidence and took himself very seriously as a specialist. Like most stupid men who have got somewhere in life, Sir Henry became self-assertive under the least semblance of contradiction, and he grew violent and red-faced under cross-examination. He would not hear of the possibility of a mistake in his diagnosis of the accused's symptoms, but insisted that the accused, when he saw him at the Durrington hotel, was suffering from an epileptic seizure, combined with *furor epilepticus*, and was in a state of mind which made him a menace to his fellow creatures. It was true he qualified his statements with the words "so far as my observation goes," but the qualification was given in a manner which suggested to the jury that five minutes of Sir Henry Durwood's observation were worth a month's of a dozen ordinary medical men.

Sir Henry's vehement insistence on his infallibility struck Sir Herbert as a flagrant violation of the rules of the game. He did not accept the protestations as genuine; he thought Sir Henry was overdoing his part, and playing to the gallery. He grew nettled in his turn, and, with a sudden access of vigour in his tone, said:

"You told my learned friend that it is quite consistent with the prisoner's malady that he could have committed the crime with which he stands charged, and remember nothing about it afterwards. Is that a fact?"

"Certainly."

"In that case, will you kindly explain how the prisoner came to leave the inn hurriedly, before anybody was up, the morning after the murder was committed? Why should he run away if he had no recollection of his act?"

"I must object to my learned friend describing the accused's departure from the inn as 'running away,'" said Mr. Middleheath, with a bland smile of protest. "It is highly improper, as nobody knows better than the Crown Prosecutor, and calculated to convey an altogether erroneous impression on the minds of the jury. There is not the slightest evidence to support such a statement. The evidence is that he saw the servant and paid his bill before departure. That is not running away."

"Very well, I will say hastened away," replied Sir Herbert impatiently. "Why should the accused hasten away from the inn if he retained no recollection of the events of the night?"

"He may have had a hazy recollection," replied Sir Henry. "Not of the act itself, but of strange events happening to him in the night–something like a bad dream, but more vivid. He may have found something unusual–such as wet clothes or muddy boots–for which he could not account. Then he would begin to wonder, and then perhaps there would come a hazy recollection of some trivial detail. Then, as he came to himself, he would begin to grow alarmed, and his impulse, as his normal mind returned to him, would be to leave the place where he was as soon as he could. This restlessness is a characteristic of epilepsy. In my opinion, it was this vague alarm, on finding himself in a position for which he could not account, which was the cause of the accused leaving the Durrington hotel. His last recollection, as he told me at the time, was entering the breakfast-room; he came to his senses in his bedroom, with strangers in the room."

"Does not recollection return completely in attacks of petit mal?"

"Sometimes it does; sometimes not. I remember a case in my student days where an epileptic violently assaulted a man in the street–almost murdered him in fact–then assaulted a man who tried to detain him, ran away, and remembered nothing about it afterwards."

"Is it consistent with petit mal, combined with *furor epilepticus*, for a man to commit murder, conceal the body of his victim, and remember nothing about it afterwards?"

"Quite consistent, though the probability is, as I said before, for him to have some hazy recollection when he came to his senses, which would lead to his leaving that place as quickly as he could."

"Would it be consistent with petit mal for a man to take a weapon away beforehand, and then, during a sudden fit of petit mal, use it upon the unfortunate victim?"

"If he took the weapon for another purpose, it is quite possible that he might use it afterwards."

"I should like to have that a little clearer," said the judge, interposing. "Do you mean to get the weapon for another, possibly quite innocent purpose, and then use it for an act of violence?"

"Yes, my lord," replied Sir Henry. "That is quite consistent with an attack of petit mal."

"When a man has periodical attacks of petit mal, would it not be possible, by observation of him between the attacks, or when he was suffering from the attacks, to tell whether he had a tendency to them?"

"No, only in a very few and exceptional cases."

"In your opinion epilepsy is an hereditary disease?"

"Undoubtedly."

"Are you aware that certain eminent French specialists, including Marie, are of the opinion that hereditary influences play a very small part in epilepsy?"

"That may be." Sir Henry dismissed the views of the French specialists with a condescending wave of his fat white hand.

"That does not alter your own opinion?"

"Certainly not."

"And do you say that because this man's mother suffered from epilepsy the chances are that he is suffering from it?"

"Pardon me, I said nothing of the kind. I think the chances are that he would have a highly organised nervous system, and would probably suffer from some nervous disease. In the case of the prisoner, I should say that shell-shock increased his predisposition to epilepsy."

"Do you suggest that shell-shock leads to epilepsy?"

"In general, no; in this particular case, possibly. A man may have shell-shock, and injury to the brain, which is not necessarily epileptic."

"It is possible for shell-shock alone to lead to a
subsequent attack of insanity?" asked the judge.

"It is possible–certainly."

"How often do these attacks of petit mal occur?" asked
Sir Herbert.

"They vary considerably according to the patient–
sometimes once a week, sometimes monthly, and there
have been cases in which the attacks are separated by
months."

"Are not two attacks in twenty-four hours
unprecedented?"

"Unusual, but not unprecedented. The excitement of
going from one place to another, and walking miles to get
there, would be a predisposing factor. Prisoner would
have been suffering from the effects of the first attack
when he left the Durrington hotel, and the excitement of
the change and the fatigue of walking all day would have
been very prejudicial to him, and account for the second
and more violent attack."

"How long do the after effects last–of an attack of
petit mal, I mean."

"It depends on the violence of the attack. Sometimes
as long as five or six hours. The recovery is generally
attended with general lassitude."

"There is no evidence to show that the prisoner
displayed any symptoms of epilepsy before the attack
which you witnessed at the Durrington hotel. Is it not
unusual for a person to reach the age of twenty-eight or
thereabouts without showing any previous signs of a
disease like epilepsy?"

"There must be a first attack–that goes without
saying," interposed the judge testily.

That concluded the cross-examination. Mr.
Middleheath, in re-examination, asked Sir Henry
whether foam at the lips was a distinguishing mark of
epilepsy.

"It generally indicates an epileptic tendency," replied Sir Henry Durwood.

At the conclusion of Sir Henry Durwood's evidence Mr. Middleheath called an official from the War Office to prove formally that Lieutenant James Penreath had been discharged from His Majesty's forces suffering from shell-shock.

"I understand that, prior to the illness which terminated his military career, Lieutenant Penreath had won a reputation as an exceedingly gallant soldier, and had been awarded the D.S.O," said Mr. Middleheath.

"That is so," replied the witness.

"Is that the case?" asked the judge.

"That, my lord, is the case," replied Mr. Middleheath.

Sir Herbert Templewood, on behalf of the Crown, proceeded to call rebutting medical evidence to support the Crown contention that the accused was sane and aware of the nature of his acts. The first witness was Dr. Henry Manton, of Heathfield, who said he saw the accused when he was brought into the station from Flegne by Police Constable Queensmead. He seemed perfectly rational, though disinclined to talk.

"Did you find any symptom upon him which pointed to his having recently suffered from epilepsy of any kind?" asked Sir Herbert.

"No."

"Do you agree with Sir Henry Durwood that between attacks of epilepsy the patient would exhibit no signs of the disease?" asked Mr. Middleheath.

"What do you mean by between the attacks?"

"I mean when he had completely recovered from one fit and before the next came on," explained counsel.

"I quite agree with that," replied the witness.

"How long does it usually take for a man to recover from an attack of epilepsy?"

"It depends on the severity of the attack."

"Well, take an attack serious enough to cause a man to commit murder."

"It may take hours—five or six hours. He would certainly be drowsy and heavy for three or four hours afterwards."

"But not longer—he would not show symptoms for thirty-six hours?"

"Certainly not."

"Then, may I take it from you, doctor, that after the five or six hours recovery after a bad attack an epileptic might show no signs of the disease—not even to medical eyes—till the next attack?"

"I should say so," replied the witness. "But I am not an authority on mental diseases."

"Thank you."

The next witness was Dr. Gilbert Horbury, who described himself as medical officer of His Majesty's prison, Norwich, and formerly medical officer of the London detention prison. In reply to Sir Herbert Templewood, he said he had had much experience in cases of insanity and alleged insanity. He had had the accused in the present case under observation since the time he had been brought to the gaol. He was very taciturn, but he was quiet and gentlemanly in his behaviour. His temperature and pulse were normal, but he slept badly, and twice he complained of pains in the head. Witness attributed the pains in the head to the effect of shell-shock. He had seen no signs which suggested, to his mind, that prisoner was an epileptic. In reply to a direct question by Sir Herbert Templewood, he expressed his deliberate professional opinion that the accused was not suffering from epilepsy in any form. Epilepsy did not start off with a bad attack ending in violence—or murder. There were premonitory symptoms and slight attacks extending over a considerable period, which must have manifested themselves, particularly in the case of a man who had been through an arduous military campaign. His illness might have had a bad effect on the brain, but if it had led to mental disease he would have expected it to show itself before.

From this point of view the witness, a dour, grey figure of a man, refused to be driven by cross-examination. His many professional years within the sordid atmosphere of gaol walls had taught him that most criminals were malingerers by instinct, and that pretended insanity was the commonest form of their imposition to evade the consequence of their misdeeds. The number of false cases which had passed through his hands had led him to the very human conclusion that all such defences were merely efforts to defraud the law, and, as a zealous officer of the law, he took a righteous satisfaction in discomfiting them, particularly when–as in the present instance–the defence was used to shield an accused of some social standing. For Dr. Horbury's political tendencies were levelling and iconoclastic, and he had a deep contempt for caste, titles, and monarchs.

He was too sophisticated as a witness to walk into Mr. Middleheath's trap and contradict Sir Henry's evidence directly, but he contrived to convey the impression that his own observation of accused, covering a period of nine days, was a better guide for the jury in arriving at a conclusion as to the accused's state of mind than Sir Henry's opinion, formed after a single and limited opportunity of diagnosing the case. He also managed to infer, in a gentlemanly professional way, that Sir Henry Durwood was deservedly eminent in the medical world as a nerve specialist, rather than as a mental specialist, whereas witness's own experience in mental cases had been very wide. He talked learnedly of the difficulty of diagnosing epilepsy except after prolonged observation, and cited lengthily from big books, which a court constable brought into court one by one, on symptoms, reflex causes, auras, grand mal, petit mal, Jacksonian epilepsy, and the like.

The only admission of any value that Mr. Middleheath could extract from Dr. Horbury was a statement that while he had seen no symptoms in the prisoner to suggest that he was an epileptic, epileptics did not, as a rule, show symptoms of the disease between the attack. "Therefore, assuming the fact that Penreath is subject to epilepsy, you would not necessarily expect to find any symptoms of the disease during the time he was awaiting trial?" asked Mr. Middleheath, eagerly following up the opening.

"Possibly nothing that one could swear to," rejoined the witness, in an exceedingly dry tone.

Mr. Middleheath essayed no more questions, but got the witness out of the box as quickly as possible, trusting to his own address to remove the effect of the evidence on the mind of the jury. At the outset of that address he pointed out that the case for the Crown rested upon purely circumstantial evidence, and that nobody had seen the prisoner commit the murder with which he was charged. The main portion of his remarks was directed to convincing the jury that the prisoner was the unhappy victim of epileptic attacks, in which he was not responsible for his actions. He scouted the theory of motive, as put forward by the Crown. It was not fair to suggest that the Treasury note which the accused paid to the servant at the inn was necessarily part of the dead man's money which had disappeared on the night of the murder and had not since been recovered. The fact that the accused had been turned out of the Grand Hotel, for not paying his hotel bill, was put forward by the Crown to show that he was in a penniless condition, but that assumption went too far. It might well be that a man in the accused's social standing would have a pound or two in his pocket, although he might not be able to meet an hotel bill of £30.

"Can you conceive this young man, this gallant soldier, this heir to an old and honourable name, with everything in life to look forward to, committing an atrocious murder for £300?" continued Mr. Middleheath.

"The traditions of his name and race, his upbringing, his recent gallant career as a soldier, alike forbid the sordid possibility. Moreover, he had no need to commit a crime to obtain money. His father, his friends, or the woman who was to be his wife, would have instantly supplied him with the money he needed, if they had known he was in want. To a young man in his station of life £300 is a comparatively small sum. Is it likely that he would have committed murder to obtain it?"

"On the other hand, the prisoner's actions, since returning to England, strongly suggest that his mind has been giving way for some time past. He was invalided from the Army suffering from shell-shock, with the result that his constitution became weakened, and the fatal taint of inherited epilepsy, which was in his blood, began to manifest itself. His family doctor and his fiancée have told you that his behaviour was strange before he left for Norfolk; since coming to Norfolk it has been unmistakably that of a man who is no longer sane. Was it the conduct of a sane man to conceal his whereabouts from his friends, and stay at an hotel without money till he was turned out, when he might have had plenty of money, or at all events saved himself the humiliation of being turned out of the hotel, at the cost of a telegram? And why did he subsequently go miles across country to a remote and wretched inn, where he had never been before, and beg for a bed for the night? Were these the acts of a sane man?"

In his peroration Mr. Middleheath laid particular emphasis on the evidence of Sir Henry Durwood, whose name was known throughout England as one of the most eminent specialists of his day. Sir Henry Durwood, Mr. Middleheath pointed out, had seen the prisoner in a fit at the Durrington hotel, and he emphatically declared that the accused was an epileptic, with homicidal tendencies. Such an opinion, coming from such a quarter, was, to Mr. Middleheath's mind, incontrovertible proof of the prisoner's insanity, and he did not see how the jury could go behind it in coming to a decision.

Sir Herbert Templewood's address consisted of a dry marshalling of the facts for and against the theory of insanity. Sir Herbert contended that the defence had failed to establish their contention that the accused man was not in his right mind. He impressed upon the jury the decided opinion of Dr. Horbury, who, as doctor of the metropolitan receiving gaol, had probably a wider experience of epilepsy and insanity than any specialist in the world. Dr. Horbury, after nine days close observation of the accused, had come to the conclusion that he was perfectly sane and responsible for his actions.

The general opinion among the bunch of legal wigs which gathered together at the barristers' table as Sir Herbert Templewood resumed his seat was that the issue had been very closely fought on both sides, and that the verdict would depend largely upon the way the judge summed up.

His lordship commenced his summing up by informing the jury that in the first place they must be satisfied that the prisoner was the person who killed Mr. Glenthorpe. He did not think they would have much difficulty on that head, because, although the evidence was purely circumstantial, it pointed strongly to the accused, and the defence had not seriously contested the charge. Therefore, if they were satisfied that the accused did, in fact, cause the death of Mr. Glenthorpe, the only question that remained for them to decide was the state of the prisoner's mind at the time. If they were satisfied that he was not insane at the time, they must find him guilty of murder. If, however, they came to the conclusion that he was insane at the time he committed the act, they would return a verdict that he was guilty of the act charged against him, but that he was insane at the time.

His lordship painstakingly defined the difference between sanity and insanity in the eyes of the law, but though his precise and legal definition called forth appreciative glances from the lawyers below him, it is doubtful whether the jury were much wiser for the explanation. After reviewing the evidence for the prosecution at considerable length, his lordship then proceeded, with judicial impartiality, to state the case for the defence. The case for the prisoner, he said, was that he had been strange or eccentric ever since he returned from the front suffering from shell-shock, that his eccentricity deepened into homicidal insanity, and that he committed the act of which he stood charged while suffering under an attack of epilepsy, which produced a state of mind that led the sufferer to commit an act of violence without understanding what he was doing. In view of the nature of this defence the jury were bound to look into the prisoner's family and hereditary history, and into his own acts before the murder, before coming to a conclusion as to his state of mind.

The defence, he thought, had proved sufficient to enable the jury to draw the conclusion that Lady Penreath, the mother of the prisoner, was an epileptic. The assertion that the prisoner was an epileptic rested upon the evidence of Sir Henry Durwood, for the evidence of Miss Willoughby and the family doctor went no further than to suggest a slight strangeness or departure from the prisoner's usual demeanour. Sir Henry Durwood, by reason of his professional standing, was entitled to be received with respect, but he had himself admitted that he had had no previous opportunity of diagnosing the case of accused, and that it was difficult to form an exact opinion in a disease like epilepsy. Dr. Horbury, on the other hand, had declared that the prisoner showed nothing symptomatic of epilepsy while awaiting remand. In Dr. Horbury's opinion, he was not an epileptic. Therefore the case resolved itself into a direct conflict of medical testimony, and it was for the jury to decide, and form a conclusion as to the man's state of mind in conjunction with the other evidence.

"The contention for the defence," continued his lordship, leaning forward and punctuating his words with sharp taps of his fountain pen on the desk in front of him, "is this: 'Look at this case fairly and clearly, and you are bound to come to the conclusion that this man is not in a sound frame of mind.' The prosecution, on the other hand, say, 'The facts of this case do not point to insanity at all, but to deliberate murder for gain.' The defence urge further, 'You have got to look at the probabilities. No man in prisoner's position, a gentleman by birth and upbringing, the heir of an old and proud name, with a hitherto unblemished reputation, and the prospects of a long and not inconspicuous career in front of him, would in his senses have murdered this old man.' That is a matter for you to consider, because we do know that brutal crimes are committed by the most unlikely persons. But the prosecution also allege motive, and you must consider the question of motive. It is suggested, and it is for you to consider whether rightly or wrongly suggested, that there was a motive in killing this man, because the prisoner was absolutely penniless and wanted to get money."

"Gentlemen, you will first apply your minds to considering all the evidence, and you will next consider whether you are satisfied that the prisoner knew the difference between right and wrong so far as the act with which he is charged is concerned. You must decide whether he knew the nature and quality of the act, and whether he knew the difference between that act being right, and that act being wrong. I have already pointed out to you that the law presumes him to be of sane mind, and able to distinguish between right and wrong, and it is for him to satisfy you, if he is to escape responsibility for this act, that he could not tell whether it was right or wrong. If you are satisfied of that, you ought to say that he is guilty of the act alleged, but insane at the time it was committed. If you are not satisfied on that point,

then it is your duty to find him guilty of murder.
Gentlemen, you will kindly retire and consider your
verdict."

The jury retired, and there ensued a period of tension,
which the lawyers employed in discussing the
technicalities of the case and the probabilities of an
acquittal. Mr. Oakham thought an acquittal was a
certainty, but Mr. Middleheath, with a deeper knowledge
of the ways of provincial juries, declared that the defence
would have stood a better chance of success before a
London jury, because Londoners had more imagination
than other Englishmen.

"You never can tell how a d—d muddle-headed
country jury will decide a highly technical case like this,"
said the K.C. peevishly. "I've lost stronger cases than this
before a Norfolk jury. Norfolk men are clannish, and
Horbury's evidence carried weight. He is a Norfolk man,
though he has been in London. One never knows, of
course. If the jury remain out over an hour I think we will
pull it off."

But the jury returned into court after an absence of
forty minutes. The judge, who was waiting in his private
room, was informed, and he entered the court and
resumed his seat. The jury answered to their names, and
then the Clerk of Arraigns, in a sing-song voice, said:

"Gentlemen, have you agreed upon your verdict? Do
you find the prisoner guilty or not guilty of wilful
murder?"

"Guilty!" answered the foreman, in a loud, clear voice.

"You say that he is guilty of murder, and that is the
verdict of you all?"

"That is the verdict of us all," was the response.

"James Ronald Penreath," continued the clerk,
turning to the accused man, and speaking in the same
sing-song tones of one who repeated a formula by rote,
"you stand convicted of the crime of wilful murder. Have
you anything to say for yourself why the Court should not
give you judgment of death according to law?" The man

in the dock, who had turned very pale, merely shook his head.

The judge, with expressionless face and in an expressionless voice, pronounced sentence of death.

17

Colwyn returned to Durrington in a perplexed and dissatisfied frame of mind. The trial, which he had attended and followed closely, had failed to convince him that all the facts concerning the death of Roger Glenthorpe had been brought to light. Really, the trial had not been a trial at all, but merely a battle of lawyers about the state of Penreath's mind.

If Penreath was really sane–and Colwyn, who had watched him closely during the trial, believed that he was–the Crown theory of the murder by no means accounted for all the amazing facts of the case.

Should he have done more? Colwyn asked himself this question again and again. But that query always led to another one–*Could* he have done more? In his mental probings the detective could rarely get away from the point–and when he did get away from it he always returned to it–that Penreath, by his dogged silence, had been largely responsible for his own conviction. If a man, charged with murder, refused to account for actions which pointed to him as the murderer, how could anybody help him? Silence, in certain circumstances, was the strongest presumptive proof of guilt. A man was the best judge of his own actions and, if he refused to speak when his own life might pay the forfeit for silence, he must have the strongest possible reason for holding his tongue. What other reason could Penreath have except the consciousness of guilt, and the hope of escaping the consequences through a loop-hole of the law?

Colwyn, however, was unable to accept this line of argument as conclusive, so he tried to put the case out of his mind. But the unsolved points of the mystery–the points that he himself had discovered during his visit to the inn—kept returning to his mind at all sorts of odd times, in the night, and during his walks. And each recurrence was accompanied by the consciousness that he had not done his best in the case, but had allowed the silence of the accused man to influence his judgment and slacken his efforts to unravel the clues he had originally discovered. Thus he travelled back to his starting-point, that the conviction of Penreath had not solved the mystery of the murder of Roger Glenthorpe.

The hotel and its guests bored him. The season was over, and the few people who remained were elderly and commonplace, prone to overeating, and to falling asleep round the lounge fire after dinner. The only topics of conversation were the weather, the war, and food. Sometimes the elderly clergyman, who still lingered, though the other golfers had gone, sought to turn the conversation to golf, but nobody listened to him except his wife, who sat opposite to him in the warmest part of the lounge placidly knitting socks for the War Comforts Fund. The Flegne murder and its result were not discussed; by tacit mutual understanding the guests never referred to the unpleasant fact that they had lived for some weeks under the same roof with a man who had since been declared a murderer by the laws of his country.

Colwyn decided to return to London, although the month he had allowed himself for a holiday was not completed. He was restless and uneasy and bored, and he thought that immersion in work would help him to forget the Glenthorpe case. He came to this decision at breakfast one morning. Within an hour he had paid his bill, received the polite regrets of the proprietor at his departure, and was motoring leisurely southward along the cliff road towards its junction with the main London road.

Important consequences frequently spring from trifling incidents. Colwyn, turning his car to the side of the road to avoid a flock of sheep, punctured a tyre on a sharp jagged piece of rock concealed in the loose sand at the side of the road. He had not a spare tyre on the car, and the shepherd informed him that the nearest town where he could hope to get the tyre replaced was Faircroft, but even that was doubtful, because Faircroft was a small town without a garage, and the one tradesman who did motor-car repairs was, just as likely as not, without the right kind of tyres, or equally likely to have none at all. As he had left Durrington barely three miles behind Colwyn decided to return there, to have the car repaired, and defer his departure till the following day.

He reached Durrington with a deflated tyre, took the car to the garage, and then went back to the hotel. It wanted nearly an hour to lunch-time, and on his way in he paused at the office window to inform the clerk that he had returned, and would stay till the following day. The proprietor was in the office, checking some figures. The latter looked up as Colwyn informed the lady clerk of his altered plans, and informed him that a young lady had been at the hotel inquiring for him shortly after his departure.

"What was her name?" asked the detective, in some surprise.

"She didn't give her name. She seemed very disappointed when she learnt that you had departed for London, and went away at once."

"What was she like?"

The proprietor and the lady clerk described her at the same time. In the former's eyes the visitor had appeared pretty and young with golden hair and a very clear complexion. The lady clerk, without the least departure from the standard of courtesy imposed upon her by her position, managed to indicate that the impression made upon her feminine mind was that of a white-faced girl with red hair. From both descriptions Colwyn had no difficulty in identifying the visitor as Peggy.

Why had she come to Durrington to see him? Obviously the visit was connected with the murder at the inn. Colwyn recalled his last conversation with her on the marshes the day after he had seen her come out of the dead man's room.

He hurried out in the hope of finding her. She had probably come by train from Leyland, and would go back the same way. Colwyn looked at his watch. It was a quarter past twelve, and there was no train back to Leyland till half-past one–so much Colwyn remembered from his study of the local time-table. Therefore, unless she had walked back to Flegne she should not be difficult to find–probably she was somewhere on the cliffs, or near the sea. Somehow, Peggy seemed to belong to the sea and Nature. It was difficult to picture her in a conventional setting.

It was by the sea that he found her, sitting in one of the shelters on the parade, with her hands clasped in her lap, looking listlessly at a fisher-boat putting out from the yellow sands below. She glanced round at the sound of his footsteps, and, seeing who it was, came out from the shelter and advanced to meet him.

"They told me at the hotel somebody had been asking for me, and I guessed it was you. You wanted to see me?"

"Yes." She did not express any surprise at his return, as another girl would, but stood with her hands still clasped in front of her, and a look of entreaty in her eyes. Colwyn noticed that her face had grown thinner, and that in the depths of her glance there lurked a troubled shadow.

"Shall we walk a little and you can tell me what you wish to say?"

"It is very kind of you."

He turned away from the front and towards the cliffs, judging that the girl would feel more disposed to talk freely away from human habitation and people. They went on for some distance in silence, the girl walking with a light quick step, looking straight in front of her, as though immersed in thought.

They reached a part of the cliffs where a low wall divided the foreland from an old churchyard which was fast crumbling into the sea. Peggy paused with her hand on the wall, and looked seaward. The sun, piercing a rift in the dark clouds, lighted the sullen grey waters with patches of gold. Colwyn, in the hope of inducing his companion to talk, pointed out the beautiful effect of the light and shadow on the sea.

"I hate the sea! I have never looked at it since the war started without seeing the many, many dead sailor boys at the bottom, staring up with their dead eyes through the weight of waters for a God of Justice in the heavens, and looking in vain." She turned her eyes from the sea, and looked at him passionately. "You do not care about the sea, either. You are only trying to put me at my ease—to help me say what I want to say. It is kind of you, but it is not necessary. I feel I can trust you—I must trust you. I am only a girl and there is nobody else in the world I dare trust. It is about—*him*. Have you seen him? Have you spoken to him? Did he speak about me?"

"I saw him only at the trial," replied Colwyn, with his ready comprehension. "I had no opportunity of speaking to him alone."

"I read about the trial in the paper," she went on. "They said that he was mad in order to try and save him, but he is not mad—he was too good and kind to be mad. Oh, why did he kill Mr. Glenthorpe? Will they kill him for that? You are clever, can you not save him? I have come to beg you to save him. Ever since they took him away I have seen his eyes wherever I go, looking at me reproachfully, as though calling upon me to save him. Last night, while I was in my grandmother's room, I thought I saw him standing there, and heard his voice, just as he used to speak. And in the night I woke up and thought I heard him whisper, 'Peggy, it is better to tell the truth.' This morning I could endure it no longer, and I came across to find you."

"You have known him before, then?"

"Yes." The girl met Colwyn's grave glance with clear, unafraid eyes. "I did not tell you before, not because I was afraid to trust you, for I liked you from the first, but I was afraid that if I told you all you would think him guilty, and not try to help him. And when you spoke to me on the marshes that day you believed he might be innocent."

"How do you know that?"

"I heard you say so to that police officer– Superintendent Galloway–after dinner the first night you were at Flegne. I was passing the bar parlour when you and he were talking about the murder, and I heard you say that you thought somebody else might have done it. The day after, when you saw me on the marshes, I was frightened to tell you the truth, because I thought if you knew it you might go away and not try to save him."

"You had better tell the whole truth to me now. Nothing you can now say will make it worse for Penreath, and it may be possible to help him. When did you first meet him?"

"Nearly three weeks before–it happened. I used to go out for long walks, when I could get away from grandmother, and this day I walked nearly as far as Leyland. He came walking along the sands a little while afterwards, and he looked at me as he passed. Presently he came back again, and stopped to ask me if there was a shorter way back to Durrington than by the coast road. I told him I didn't know, and he stopped to talk to me for a while. He told me he was in Norfolk for a holiday, and was spending the time in country rambles.

"I will tell you the whole truth. I returned to the headland next day in the hope that I might see him again. After I had been there a little while I saw him walking along the sands. He waved his hand when he saw me, as though we had been old friends, and that afternoon we stayed talking much longer. "I saw him nearly every afternoon after that—whenever I could get away I walked down to the headland, and he was always there. The spot where we used to meet was hidden from the road by some fir-trees, and I do not think we were ever seen by anybody. He told me all about himself, but I did not tell him anything about myself or my home. I knew he was a gentleman, and I thought if I told him that my father kept an inn he might not want to see me any more, and I could not bear that. I told him my Christian name, and he liked it, and used to call me by it, but I would not tell him my other name.

"The night that he came to the inn I met him in the afternoon at the headland as usual, and we stayed talking until it was time for me to go home. He was very troubled that day, and it grieved me to see him looking so white and ill. When I questioned him he told me that he had been slightly ill that morning, and that he was very much worried about money matters. I felt very unhappy to think that he was troubled about money, and when he saw that he said he was sorry he had told me.

"When I left him it was later than usual. I was supposed to look after my grandmother every afternoon, and when I went to the headland I usually got Ann to sit in her room until I returned. I was always careful to get back before my father came in from fishing on the marshes. He would have been very angry if he had returned and found me absent, and I should not have been able to get out again. It was nearly four that afternoon when I left the headland, and I walked very quick so as to be back in time. It was getting on towards dusk when I reached home.

"I went straight up to my grandmother's room, so that Ann could go down and get dinner for Mr. Glenthorpe, who usually came in about dark. I sat with grandmother till past six o'clock, and then, as Ann hadn't brought grandmother's tea, I went down to the kitchen to get it myself. Ann was very busy getting dinner, and she told me a young gentleman had arrived at the inn half an hour before, and he was going to dine upstairs with Mr. Glenthorpe, and stay for the night. I was surprised, for we rarely had visitors at the inn. I asked Ann some questions about him, but she could tell me very little. Charles, the waiter, came into the kitchen to get the things ready to take upstairs, and he told me that the visitor was young, good-looking, and seemed a gentleman.

"I got grandmother's tea ready, and was carrying it along the passage from the kitchen when I fancied I heard Mr. Penreath's voice in the bar parlour. I thought at first that I must be mistaken; then the door of the parlour opened, and Mr. Glenthorpe and Mr. Penreath came out. I was so surprised and frightened that I almost dropped the tray I was carrying. If they had looked down the side passage they would have seen me. But he and Mr. Glenthorpe turned the other way, and went upstairs. Then Charles came along carrying a dinner tray, and went upstairs also. I knew then that Mr. Penreath was the gentleman who was going to dine with Mr. Glenthorpe, and stay the night.

"I did not know what to do. I took grandmother's tea upstairs, and crept past the room where they were having dinner, because I did not want him to see me till I had made up my mind what to do. The door was shut, and they couldn't see me, though I could hear them talking inside. When I got to my grandmother's room I tried to think what was best to do. My first thought was that he had found out who I was. Then it seemed to me that he might have come by accident, in some way that I didn't understand, because why should he dine with Mr. Glenthorpe, and stay with him, if he had come to see me? Then I wondered if it were possible that he knew Mr. Glenthorpe, who was a gentleman like himself, and had come to ask him to help him. I had never told him anything about Mr. Glenthorpe or myself.

"I determined to try and see him that night to let him know that the inn was my home. If he had come to the inn by accident it was better that he should not meet me in front of my father, because in his surprise he might say that he had met me before. My father would have been very angry if he knew I had been meeting a stranger. So I went along the passage several times in the hope of seeing him as he came from dinner. But once my father was going into the room where they were having dinner, and he nearly saw me, so I dared not go again.

"A little after ten o'clock my grandmother began to get restless, as she always does when a storm is coming on, and I had to stay with her to keep her quiet. I can do more with her than anybody else when she is like that, and it is not safe to leave her. Sometimes my father goes and sits with her a while before he goes to bed, but this night he did not. She got very bad as the storm came on, and while it lasted I sat alongside of her holding her hand and soothing her. After about half an hour the rain ceased as suddenly as it had commenced, and grandmother fell asleep. I knew she was all right until the morning, so I left her for the night.

"As I turned to go to my room, I thought I saw a light in the other passage, and I went down to see what it was. I thought perhaps Mr. Penreath might be waiting up reading before going to bed.

"I crept along to the bend of the passage, and looked down it, thinking perhaps I might see him and speak to him. There was nobody in the passage, but the door of Mr. Glenthorpe's room was half open and a light was streaming through it.

"I do not know really what took me to Mr. Glenthorpe's room. I have tried to think it out clearly since, but I cannot. I know I was distressed and troubled about Mr. Penreath's presence at the inn, and I was afraid he would be cross and angry with me for not having told him the truth about myself. And before that, when I was walking home after meeting him that afternoon, I had been unhappy about his wanting money, and wished that I could do something to help him. These thoughts kept going through my head as I sat with grandmother during the storm.

"When I saw the door of Mr. Glenthorpe's room open, and the light burning, all these thoughts seemed to come back into my head together. I remembered how good and kind Mr. Glenthorpe had always been to me. I had heard my father tell Charles that morning that Mr. Glenthorpe had gone to the bank at Heathfield that day to draw out a large sum of money to buy Mr. Cranley's field.

"I think I had a confused idea that I would go and confide in Mr. Glenthorpe, and ask him to help Mr. Penreath. Perhaps I have not made myself very clear about this, but I do not remember very clearly myself, for I acted on a sudden impulse, and ran along the passage quickly, in case he should shut his door before I got there, because I knew if he did that I should not have the courage to knock. Through the half-open door I could see the inside of the room between the door and the window. It seemed to me to be empty. I gave a little tap at the door, but there was no reply. It was then I noticed that the bedroom window was wide open, and that a current of air was blowing into the room and causing the light behind the door to cast flickering shadows across the room.

"That struck me as strange. I knew Mr. Glenthorpe always used a reading lamp, and never a candle, and I knew that the reading lamp wouldn't cast shadows because of the lamp glass. I do not know what I feared, but I know a dreadful shiver of fear crept over me, and that some force stronger than myself seemed to compel me to step inside the room in spite of my fears."

18

"He was lying on the bed, quite dead. There was blood on his breast, and his hands were held out, as though he had tried to push off the man who had killed him. On the table, by the head of the bed, was a lighted candle, and it was the light of the candle which had cast the flickering shadows I had seen before entering the room. On the bed, near the pillow, was a match-box, and I remember picking it up and placing it in the candlestick– mechanically, for I am sure I did not know what I was doing, and I did not recall the act till afterwards. I have a clearer recollection of touching something with my foot, and stooping to pick it up. It was a knife–a white handled knife, with blood on the blade. And as I stood there, with it in my hand, there came to my mind, clear and distinct, the memory of having seen that knife on the dinner tray Charles had carried past me upstairs, as I stood in the passage near the kitchen, where I first discovered that Mr. Penreath was in the house. "I do not know how long I stood there, with the knife in my hand, looking at the body–perhaps it was not more than a moment. There seemed to be two individualities in me, one urging me to fly, the other keeping me rooted to the spot, petrified.

"Then I heard a sound downstairs. A wild panic came over me, and my head grew dizzy. The shadows in the corners of the room seemed full of mocking eyes, and I thought I heard stealthy steps creeping up the stairs. I dared not stay where I was, but I was too afraid to go out into the passage in the dark. Then my eyes fell on the candle, and I picked it up and was going to rush from the room, when I remembered that I had the knife in my hand.

"I did not know what to do with it. I wanted to shield him, but some feeling within me would not let me carry it away. I looked round the room for somewhere to hide it, and my eye fell on a picture against the wall, close to the door. Quick as thought I put the knife behind the picture as I ran from the room.

"There was nobody in the passage, and I gained my own room and locked the door. I think I must have fainted, or become unconscious, for I remember nothing more after throwing myself on my bed, and when I came to my senses the dawn was creeping in through my bedroom window. I was very cold, and dazed. I crept into bed without taking off my clothes, and fell asleep. When I awoke it was broad daylight, and as I lay in bed I heard the kitchen clock chime seven.

"I got up, and went into grandmother's room. A little while afterwards Ann came up with some tea, and she told me that Mr. Penreath had gone away early, without having any breakfast. She told me that she had found Mr. Glenthorpe's room empty, with the key in the outside of the door. She was afraid something had happened to him, so she had sent for Constable Queensmead. I did not tell her what I had seen in the night. I wanted to be alone, to think. I could not understand how Mr. Glenthorpe's body had disappeared from his room. I think I hoped that I would presently wake up and find that what I had seen during the night was some terrible dream. But Ann came up a little later and told me that Mr. Glenthorpe's body had been discovered in the pit on the rise, and that Mr. Ronald, as she called Mr. Penreath, was suspected of having murdered him.

"When she told me that I felt as though my blood turned to ice. I knew it was true—I knew that he had killed Mr. Glenthorpe because he wanted money—but I knew that in spite of all I wanted to shield and help him. I kept in my grandmother's room all day, determined to keep silence, and tell nobody about what I had seen during the night. The one thing that worried me was the knife which I had put behind the picture on the wall. I tried once to go into the room and get it, but the door was locked, and I dared not ask for the key.

"Then in the afternoon the police came from Durrington. I did not know who you were when you came with them into my grandmother's room, but as soon as I saw you I was afraid, though I tried hard not to let you see it. I knew you were cleverer than the others. But your eyes seemed to go right into mine, and search my soul. I asked my father afterwards who you were, and he said your name was Mr. Colwyn, and that you were a London detective. I had read about you; I knew that you were famous and clever, and after seeing you I felt that you would be sure to discover my secret, and put Mr. Penreath in prison.

"That night when I was downstairs, I heard you and the police officer talking in the room where you had dined, and I listened at the door. When I heard you say that you were not certain who committed the murder, I was very much surprised, because up till then I felt quite certain that you would think Mr. Penreath was guilty. I believed if you found the knife you would alter your opinion, Ann having told me that the police knew that Mr. Glenthorpe had been murdered with a knife which Mr. Penreath had used at dinner. The idea came into my head that if I could get the knife before you found it, you might go on thinking that somebody else had committed the crime, and perhaps persuade the police to think so as well.

"I made up my mind I would go into the room that night and get the knife. I knew that the door was locked, and that the police officer had placed the key on the mantelpiece in the bar parlour. During the evening I kept downstairs at the back of the passage waiting for an opportunity to get it. You both stayed there so long that I did not think I should get the chance.

"After you went upstairs to bed Mr. Galloway called Charles to get him some brandy. Charles came out from his room to get it. Mr. Galloway followed him into the bar. While he was there I slipped into the room and got the key, and left the key of my own room in its place. I did not think the police officer would notice the difference, but it was a risk I had to take. Then I ran up to my room.

"Although I had got the key I was for some time afraid to use it. I could not bear the thought of going into that room, and to get there I had to go past your door; I did not like that.

"Then I crept out along the passage as quietly as I could, carrying my shoes, for I had made up my mind that after I got the knife I would take it across the marshes to the breakwater and throw it into the sea. That was the one place where I felt sure you would not find it. I carried a candle in my hand, but I dared not light it until I got past your door, in case you were awake and saw the light. When I reached Mr. Glenthorpe's room I lit the candle and unlocked the door, turning the key as gently as I could. But it made a noise, and, as I stood listening, I thought I heard a movement in your room. I blew out the candle, stepped inside the room, took the key out, and locked the door on the inside.

"I do not know how long I stood there listening in the dark, but I know that I was not as frightened as I had expected to be—at first. I kept telling myself that Mr. Glenthorpe had always been kind to me while he was alive, and that he would not harm me now that he was dead. I did not look towards the bed, but kept close to the door, straining my ears to catch any sound in the passage outside. But after a while I began to get frightened in that dark room with the door locked, and dreadful thoughts came into my mind. I remembered a story I had read about a man who was locked up all night in a room with a dead body, and was found mad in the morning, and the position of the corpse had changed. It seemed to me as though Mr. Glenthorpe was sitting up in bed looking at me, but I dared not turn round to see. I knew that I must get out of the room or scream. I lit the candle, felt for the knife behind the picture, and opened the door. As soon as the candle was alight I felt braver, and I looked out of the door before going into the passage. I could see nothing–all seemed quiet–so I came out of the room and locked the door behind me and went downstairs.

"Once I was outside the house and could see the friendly stars all my fears vanished. I know the marshes so well that I can find my way across them at any time. And in my heart I had the feeling that I had been brave and helped him. When I had thrown the knife into the sea from the breakwater I felt almost lighthearted, and when I reached my room again I fell asleep as soon as I got into bed.

"Until you spoke to me the next day I had no idea that you had seen and followed me. But I knew it the moment you stopped me and said you wanted to speak to me. Then I realised you had watched me, and the story I told you to account for my visit to the room came into my head. I did not know whether you believed me or not, but I did not care much, because I knew you could not have seen what I threw into the sea. That secret was safe as long as I kept silence; and you couldn't make me speak against my will."

Peggy, as she concluded, glanced up wistfully to see how her companion received her story, but she could learn nothing from the detective's inscrutable face. Colwyn, on his part, was thinking rapidly. He believed that the innkeeper's daughter, yielding to the strain of a secret too heavy to be borne alone, had this time told him the truth, but, as he ran over the main points of her narrative in his mind, he could not see that it shed any additional light on the murder. The only new fact that she had revealed was that she and Penreath had been acquainted before. She had also, perhaps unconsciously, given away the fact that she and Penreath were in love with each other; at all events, her story proved that she was so deeply in love with Penreath that she had displayed unusual force of character in her efforts to shield him. But that knowledge did not carry them any further towards a solution of the mystery. It was with but a faint hope of eliciting anything of real value that he turned to her and said:

"There is one point of your story on which I am not quite clear. You said that in the morning, when you heard of the recovery of Mr. Glenthorpe's body from the pit, you knew that Mr. Penreath was the murderer. Why were you so sure of that? Was is because you picked up the knife with which the murder was committed? The knife was a clue—the police theory of course is that Penreath secreted the knife at the dinner table for the purpose of committing the murder—but, by itself, it was hardly a convincing clue. Was there something else that made you feel sure he was guilty of this crime?"

"Yes, there was something else," she repeated slowly.

"I thought as much. And that something else was the match-box—is that not so?"

"Yes, it was the match-box," she repeated again, this time almost in a whisper.

"What was there about the match-box that made you feel so certain?"

"Must I tell you that?" she said, looking at him helplessly.

"Of course you must tell me." Colwyn's face was stern. "As I told you before, nothing you can do or say can hurt him now, and the only hope of helping him is by telling the whole truth."

"It was his match-box. It had his monogram on it."

"You have brought it with you?"

For answer she took something from the bosom of her dress and laid it, with a heart-broken look, in Colwyn's hand. The article was a small match-box, with a regimental badge in enamel on one side, and on the other some initials in monogram. Colwyn examined it closely. "I see the initials are J.R.P.," he said. "How did you know they were his initials? You knew his name?"

"Yes. He used to light cigarettes with matches from that match-box when I was with him, and one day I asked him to show it to me. He did so, and I asked him what the initials were for, and he told me they stood for his own name—James Ronald Penreath. And then he told me much about himself and his family, and—and he said he cared for me, but he was not free."

She gave out the last few words in a low tone, and stood looking at him like a girl who had exposed the most sacred secret of her heart in order, to help her lover. But Colwyn was not looking at her. He had opened the match-box, and was shaking out the few matches which remained in the interior. They fell, half a dozen of them, into the palm of his hand. They were wax matches, with blue heads. A sudden light leapt into the detective's eyes as he saw them—a look so strange and angry that the girl, who was watching him, recoiled a little.

"What is it? What have you found?" she cried.

"It is a pity you did not tell me the truth in the first instance instead of deceiving me," he retorted harshly. "Listen to me. Does anyone at the inn know of your visit to me to-day? I do not suppose they do, but I want to make sure."

"Nobody. I told them I was going to Leyland to see the dressmaker."

"So much the better." Colwyn looked at his watch. "You have just time to catch the half-past one train back. You had better go at once. I will go to the inn some time this evening, but you must not let anyone know that I am coming, or that you have seen me to-day. Do you understand? Can I depend on you?"

"Yes," she replied. "I will do anything you tell me. But, oh, do tell me before I go whether you are going to save him."

"I cannot say that," he replied, in a gentler voice. "But I am going to try to help him. Go at once, or you will not catch the train."

19

Colwyn formed his plans on his way back to the hotel. He stopped at the office as he went in to lunch, and informed the lady clerk that he had changed his mind about leaving, and would keep on his room, but expected to be away in the country for two or three days. The lady clerk, who had mischievous eyes and wore her hair fluffed, asked the detective if he had been successful in finding the young lady who had called to see him. On Colwyn gravely informing her that he had, she smiled. It was obvious that she scented a romance in the guest's changed plans.

As the detective wished to attract as little attention as possible in the renewed investigations he was about to make, he decided not to take his car to Flegne. After lunch he packed a few necessaries in a handbag, and caught the afternoon train to Heathfield. Arriving at that wayside station, he asked the elderly functionary who acted as station-master, porter and station cleaner the nearest way across country to Flegne, and, receiving the most explicit instructions in a thick Norfolk dialect, set out with his handbag.

The road journey to Flegne was five miles. By the footpath across the fields it was something less than four, and Colwyn, walking briskly, reached the rise above the marshes in a little less than an hour. The village on the edge of the marshes looked grey and cheerless and deserted in the dull afternoon light, and the sighing wind brought from the North Sea the bitter foretaste of winter. The inn was cut off from the village by a new accession of marsh water which had thrust a slimy tongue across the road, forming a pool in which frogs were vociferously astir.

As Colwyn descended the rise the front door of the inn opened, and the gaunt figure of the innkeeper emerged, carrying some fishing lines in his hands. He paused beneath the inn signboard, the rusty swinging anchor, and looked up at the sky, which was lowering and black. As he did so, he turned, and saw Colwyn. He waited for him to approach, and left it to the visitor to speak first. He showed no surprise at Colwyn's appearance, but his bird-like face did not readily lend itself to the expression of human emotions. It would have been almost as easy for a toucan to display joy, grief, or surprise.

"Good afternoon, Benson," said the detective cheerfully. "Going to be rather wet for a fishing excursion, isn't it?"

"That's just what I can't make up my mind, sir," replied the other. "Clouds like these do not always mean rain in this part of the world. The clouds seem to gather over the marshes more, and sometimes they hang like this for days without rain. But I do not think I'll go fishing to-night. The rain in these parts goes through you in no time, and there's no shelter on the marshes."

"In that case you'll be able to attend to me."

"I'd do that in any case, sir," replied the other quickly.

"I think of spending a few days here before returning to London. I am interested in archæological research, and this part of the Norfolk coast is exceedingly rich in archæological and prehistoric remains, as, of course, you are well aware."

"Yes, sir. Many scientific gentlemen used to visit the place at one time. We had one who stayed at the inn for a short time last year–Dr. Gardiner, perhaps you have heard of him. He was very interested in the hut circles on the rise, and when he went back to London he wrote a book about them. Then there was poor Mr. Glenthorpe. He was never tired of talking of the ancient things which were under the earth hereabouts."

"Quite so. I should like to make a few investigations on my own account. That is why I have come over this afternoon. I have left my car and my luggage at Durrington, where I have been staying, thinking you might find it easier to put me up without them. I presume you can accommodate me, Benson?"

"Well, sir, you know the place is rough and I haven't much to offer you. But if you do not mind that—"

"Not in the least. You need not go to any trouble on my account."

"Then, sir, I shall be pleased to do what I can to make you comfortable. Will you step inside? This way, sir—I must ask Ann about your room before I can take you upstairs."

The innkeeper opened the door of the bar parlour, and asked Colwyn to excuse him while he consulted the servant. He returned in a few minutes with Ann lumbering in his wake. The stout countrywoman bobbed at the sight of the detective, and proceeded to explain in apologetic tones, with sundry catches of the breath and jelly-like movements of her fat frame, that she was sorry being caught unawares, and not expecting visitors, but the fact was that Mr. Colwyn couldn't have the room he slept in before, because she had given it a good turn out that day, and everything was upside down, to say nothing of it being as damp as damp could be. There was only poor Mr. Glenthorpe's room—of course, that wouldn't do—and the room next, which the poor young gentleman had slept in. Would Mr. Colwyn mind having that room? If he didn't mind, she could make it quite comfortable, and would have clean sheets aired in front of the kitchen fire in no time.

Colwyn felt that he had reason to congratulate himself that he had been asked to occupy the very room which he desired to examine closely. The lucky accident of turning out the other room would save him a midnight prowl from the one room to the other, with the possible risk of detection. He told Ann that the room Mr. Penreath had slept in would do very well, and assured her that she was not to bother on his account. But Ann was determined to worry, and her mind was no sooner relieved about the bedroom than she propounded the problem of dinner. She had been taken unawares in that direction also. There was nothing in the house but a little cold mutton, and some hare soup left over from the previous day. If she warmed up a plateful of soup–it was lovely soup, and had set into a perfect jelly–and made rissoles of the mutton, and sent them to table with some vegetables, with a pudding to follow; would *that* do? Colwyn replied smilingly that would do excellently, and Ann withdrew, promising to serve the meal within an hour.

Colwyn passed that time in the bar parlour. The innkeeper, of his own accord, brought in some of the famous smuggled brandy, and willingly accepted the detective's invitation to drink a glass of it. With an old-fashioned long-footed liqueur glass of the brown brandy in front of him, the innkeeper waxed more loquacious than Colwyn had yet found him, and related many strange tales of the old smuggling days of the inn, when cargoes of brandy were landed on the coast, and stowed away in the inn's subterranean passages almost under the noses of the excise officers. According to local history, the inn had been built into the hillside to afford better lurking-places, for those who were continually at variance with His Majesty's excise officers. There was one local worthy named Cranley, the lawless ancestor of the yeoman who had sold the piece of land to Mr. Glenthorpe, who was reported to be the most brazen smuggler in Norfolk, which was saying something, considering the greater portion of the coastal population were engaged in smuggling in those days.

Cranley was a local hero, with a hero's love for the brandy he smuggled so freely, and tradition declared of him that on one occasion he set light to some barns and hayricks in order to warn some of his smuggling companions who were "running a cargo" that a trap had been laid for them. The farmers who had suffered by the blaze had sought to carry Cranley before the justices, but he, with a few choice spirits, had barricaded himself in the inn, defying the countryside for months, subsisting on bread and brandy, and shooting from the circular windows on the south side of the house at the soldiers sent to take him. Local tradition varied as to the ultimate fate of Cranley and his desperate band.

According to some authorities, they escaped through the marshes and put to sea; but another version of the story declared that they had been captured and tried in the inn, and then ingloriously hanged, one after the other, from the stanchion outside the door from which the anchor suspended. This version added the touch that Cranley's last request was for a bumper of the famous old brandy he had lost his life for, and when it was given him he quaffed it to the bottom, dashed the cup in the hangman's face, and swung himself off into eternity. Confirmatory evidence of the siege of Cranley and his merry men was to be seen in the outside wall, which was dinted with bullet marks made by the King's troops as they tried to hit the smugglers, firing through the circular windows.

The innkeeper rambled on in this fashion until the entry of Charles with a table-cloth reminded him of the flight of time, and he withdrew with a halting apology for having sat there talking so long. The fat waiter saluted Colwyn with a grave bow, and proceeded to lay the cloth. When he had done this he left the room and returned with a bottle of claret, which he put down in front of the fire, and proceeded to warm the wine, keeping his hand on the bottle as he did so. Then he lifted the bottle and held it to the light before setting it carefully on the table.

"Your knowledge of wine is not of much use to you in Flegne, Charles," remarked Colwyn. "You do not belong to these parts, I fancy."

"No, sir. I'm a Londoner born and bred," replied the waiter, in his soft whisper.

"Why did you leave it? Londoners, as a rule, prefer their city to any other part of the world."

"I'd starve there now that my hearing is gone. London takes everything from you, but gives you nothing in return. I'm only too grateful to Mr. Benson for employing me here, considering the nature of my affliction. No London hotel would give me a job now. But though I do say it, sir, I think I make myself useful to Mr. Benson, and earn my keep and the few shillings he gives me. I save him all the trouble I can."

This was undoubtedly true, as Colwyn had observed during his former visit to the inn. The deaf waiter was, to all intents and purposes, the real manager of the inn, leaving the innkeeper free to pursue his solitary life while he attended to the bar and the cellar, helped Ann with the work, and waited on infrequent travellers. Doubtless the arrangement suited both, though it could not have been profitable to either, for there was little more than a bare living for one in such a place.

Looking up suddenly from his plate, Colwyn caught the waiter's black eyes fixed on him in a keen penetrating gaze. Meeting the detective's eyes, Charles instantly lowered his own. But for the latter action Colwyn would have thought nothing of the incident, for he was aware that Charles, on account of his deafness, had to watch the lips of people he was serving in order to read their lips. But if Charles had been merely watching for him to speak he would not have felt impelled to avert his gaze when detected. The sudden lowering of his eyes was the swift unconscious action of a man taken by surprise. The detective realised that Charles did not accept the reason he had given to account for his second visit to the inn. Charles evidently suspected that that reason masked some ulterior motive.

Colwyn finished his dinner and produced his cigar-case. Selecting a cigar, he lit it with a match from the box Peggy had given him that day.

"Have you ever seen this box before, Charles?" he said, placing the box on the table.

The waiter picked up the little silver and enamel box and examined it attentively.

"I have, sir," he said, handing it back. "It is Mr. Penreath's."

"How do you recognise it?"

"By the letters in enamel, sir. I noticed them that night at the dinner table, when I was holding Mr. Penreath's candlestick while he lit it with a match from that box."

"Did he put it back in his pocket after lighting the candle?"

"Yes, sir; into his vest pocket."

"It was picked up in Mr. Glenthorpe's room after the murder was committed. A strong clue, Charles! Many a man has been hanged on less."

"No doubt, sir."

The waiter, balancing a tray on his deformed arm, proceeded to clear the table. When he had completed his task he asked the detective if he needed him anymore, because if he did not it was time for him to go into the bar. On Colwyn saying that he needed nothing further he noiselessly withdrew, steadying the loaded tray with his sound hand.

Colwyn spent the evening sitting by the fire, smoking. It was fortunate he had plenty to think about, for the inn did not offer any resources in the way of reading to occupy the mind of the chance visitor to its roof. There were a few books in the recess by the fireplace, but they consisted of bound volumes of *The Norfolk Sporting Gazette* from 1860 to 1870, with an odd volume on *Fishing on the Broads* and an obsolete *Farmers' Annual*. The past occupants of the inn had evidently been keen sportsmen, for there were specimens of stuffed fowl and fish ranged in glass cases around the walls, and two old rusty fowling pieces and a fishing rod hung suspended near the ceiling.

Shortly after nine o'clock the innkeeper entered the room with a candlestick, which he placed on the table. He explained that it was his custom to go upstairs early, in order to sit with his mother for a little while before he retired. The poor soul looked for it, he said, and grew restless if he was late.

"Who is sitting with her at present?" inquired the detective.

"My daughter, sir. She always waits till I go up."

"You never leave her alone, then?"

"Only at night-time, sir. The doctor told me she could be safely left at night. She sleeps fairly well, considering, though when there's wild weather I always go in to her. The sound of the wind shrieking across the marshes from the sea excites her, and we get a lot of that sort of weather on the Norfolk coast, particularly in the winter months. I wish I could afford to have her better looked after, but I cannot, and that's the long and short of it."

"Things are pretty bad with you, Benson?"

"Very bad, indeed, sir. It keeps me awake at night, wondering where it's all going to end. However, I don't want to burden you with my troubles—I suppose we all have our own to bear. I merely came in to bring your candlestick, and to ask you if there is anything you want before I go to bed. Charles is gone to his room, but Ann is still up."

"Tell Ann she need not sit up on my account. I need nothing further, and I can find my way to my room. Is it ready yet?"

"Quite, sir. Ann has just been up there, putting on some fresh sheets. Perhaps you wouldn't mind turning off the gas at the meter as you go up—it is just underneath the stairs. If you would not mind the trouble Ann could then go to bed. We keep early hours here, as a rule. There is nothing to sit up for."

"I'll turn off the gas–I know where the meter is. How is it, Benson, that the gas is laid on in only two of the rooms upstairs–the rooms Mr. Glenthorpe used to occupy? It would have been an easy matter to lay it on to the adjoining rooms, once the pipes had been taken upstairs."

"That's quite true, sir, but the gas was taken upstairs on Mr. Glenthorpe's account, shortly after he came here. He thought he would like it, and he paid the bill for having it fixed. But after it was laid on he rarely used it. He said he found the gaslight trying for his eyes when he wanted to read in bed, so he got a reading lamp."

"And yet the gas tap was partly turned on in his room the morning after the murder," remarked Colwyn meditatively.

"Perhaps the murderer turned it on," suggested the innkeeper in a low tone.

But there was a slight tremor in his voice that did not escape the keen ears of the detective.

"That is possible, but the point was not cleared up at the trial; it probably never will be now," he replied, eyeing the innkeeper attentively. "And the incandescent burner was broken too. Have you had a new burner attached, Benson?"

"No, sir. The room has never been used since."

"It's a queer thing about that broken burner. That's another point in this case that was not cleared up at the trial. Who do you think broke it?"

"How should I know, sir?" His bird's eyes, in their troubled shadow, turned uneasily from the detective's glance.

"Nevertheless, you can hazard an opinion. Why not? The case is over and done with now, and Penreath–or Ronald, as he called himself–is condemned to death. So who do you think broke that burner, Benson?"

"Who else but the murderer, sir?"

"That's the police theory, I know, but I doubt whether
Penreath was tall enough to strike it with his head. It's
more than six feet from the ground." The detective threw
a critical glance over the innkeeper's figure as though he
were measuring his height with his eye. "You are well
over six feet, Benson—you might have done it."

It was a chance shot, but the effect was remarkable.
The innkeeper swung his small head on the top of his
long neck in the direction of the detective, with a strange
gesture, like a pinioned eagle twisting in a trap.

"What makes you say that!" he cried, and his voice
had a new and strident note. "I had nothing whatever to
do with it."

"What do you mean?" replied the detective sternly.
"What do you suppose I am suggesting?"

"I beg your pardon, sir," replied the other. "The fact is
I have not been myself for some time past."

His voice broke off in an odd tremor, and Colwyn
noticed that the long thin hand he stretched out, as
though to deprecate his previous violence, was shaking
violently.

"What's the matter with you, man?" The detective
eyed him keenly. "Your nerve has gone."

"I know it has, sir. What happened in this house a
fortnight ago upset me terribly, and I haven't got over it
yet. I have other troubles as well—private troubles. I've
had to sit up with mother a good deal lately."

"You'd better take a few doses of bromide," said the
detective brusquely. "A man with your nerves should not
live in a place like this. You had better go to bed now.
Good night."

"Good night, sir." The innkeeper hurried out of the
room without another word.

Colwyn sat by the fire for some time longer pondering
over this unexpected incident, until the kitchen clock
chiming eleven warned him to go to bed. He turned off
the gas at the meter underneath the stairs as Benson had

requested. When he reached the room in which Mr. Glenthorpe had been murdered, he paused outside the door, and turned the handle. The door was locked.

As he was about to enter the adjoining bedroom which had been allotted to him, a slender pencil of light pierced the darkness of the passage leading off the one in which he stood. As he watched the gleam grew brighter and broader; somebody was walking along the other passage. A moment later the innkeeper's daughter came into view, carrying a candle. She advanced quickly to where the detective was standing.

"I heard you coming upstairs," she explained, in a whisper. "I have been waiting and listening at my door. I wanted to see you, but it is difficult for me to do so without the others knowing. So I thought I would wait. I wanted to let you know that if you wish to see me at any time–if you need me to do anything–perhaps you would put a note under my door, and I could meet you down by the breakwater at any time you appoint. Nobody would see us there."

Colwyn nodded approvingly. Decidedly this girl was not lacking in resource and intelligence.

"I am so glad you are here," she went on earnestly. "I was afraid, after I left you to-day, that you might change your mind. I waited at one of the upstairs windows all the afternoon till I saw you coming. You will save him, won't you?"

She looked up at him with a faint smile, which, slight as it was, gave her face a new rare beauty.

"I will try," responded Colwyn, gravely. "Can you tell where the key of Mr. Glenthorpe's room is kept?"

"It hangs in the kitchen. Do you want it? I will get it for you. If Ann or Charles see me, they, will not think it as strange as if they saw you."

She was so eager to be of use to him that she did not wait for his reply, but ran quickly and noiselessly along the passage, and down the stairs. In a very brief space she returned with the key, which she placed in his hand. "Is there anything else I can do?" she asked.

"Nothing, except to tell me where you got the key. I want to put it back again without anybody knowing it has been used."

"It hangs on the kitchen dresser–the second hook. You cannot mistake it, because there is a padlock key and one of my father's fishing lines hanging on the same hook."

"Then that is all you can do. I will let you know if I want to see you at any time."

"Thank you. Good night!" She was gone without another word.

Colwyn stood at his door watching her until she disappeared into the passage which led to her own room. Then he turned into his bedroom and shut the door behind him.

He walked to the window and threw it open. The sea mist, driving over the silent marshes like a cloud, touched his face coldly as he stood there, meditating on the strange turn of events which had brought him back to the inn to pursue his investigations into the murder at the point where he had left them more than a fortnight before. In that brief period how much had happened! Penreath had been tried and sentenced to death for a crime which Colwyn now believed he had not committed. Chance–no, Destiny–by placing in his hand a significant clue, had directed his footsteps thither, and left it for his intelligence to atone for his past blunder before it was too late.

It was with a feeling that the hand of Destiny was upon him that Colwyn turned from the window and regarded the little room with keen curiosity. Its drab interior held a secret which was a challenge to his intelligence to discover. What had happened in that room the night Ronald slept there? He noted the articles of furniture one by one. Nothing seemed changed since he had last been in the room, the day after the murder was committed. There was a washstand near the window, a chest of drawers, a dressing table and a large wardrobe at the side of the bed. Colwyn looked at this last piece of furniture with the same interest he had felt when he saw it the first time. It was far too big and cumbrous a wardrobe for so small a room, about eight feet high and five feet in width, and it was placed in the most inconvenient part of the room, by the side of the bed, not far from the wall which abutted on the passage. He opened its double doors and looked within. The wardrobe was empty.

Colwyn made a methodical search of the room in the hope of discovering something which would throw light on the events of the night of the murder. Doubtless the room had not been occupied since Penreath had slept there, and he might have left something behind him—perhaps some forgotten scrap of paper which might help to throw light on this strange and sinister mystery. In the detection of crime seeming trifles often lead to important discoveries, as nobody was better aware than Colwyn. But though he searched the room with painstaking care, he found nothing.

It was while he was thus engaged that a faint rustle aroused his attention, and looking towards the corner of the room whence it proceeded, he saw a large rat crouching by the skirting-board watching him with malevolent eyes. Colwyn looked round for a weapon with which to hit it. The creature seemed to divine his intentions, for it scuttled squeaking across the room, and disappeared behind the wardrobe.

Colwyn approached the wardrobe and pushed it back. As he did so, he had a curious sensation which he could hardly define. It was as though an unseen presence had entered the room, and was silently watching him. His actions seemed not of his own volition; it was as though some force stronger than himself was urging him on. And, withal, he had the uncanny feeling that the whole incident of the rat and the wardrobe, and his share in it, was merely a repetition of something which had happened in the room before.

The wardrobe moved much more easily than he had expected, considering its weight and size. There was no rat behind it, but a hole under the skirting showed where the animal had made its escape. But it was the space where the wardrobe had stood that claimed Colwyn's attention. The reason why it had been placed in its previous position was made plain. The damp had penetrated the wall on that side, and had so rotted the wall paper that a large portion of it had fallen away.

In the bare portion of the wall thus revealed, about two feet square, was a wooden trap door, fastened by a button. Colwyn unfastened the button, and opened the door. A black hole gaped at him.

The light of the candle showed that the wall was hollow, and the trap opened into the hollow space. There was nothing unusual in such a door in an old house; Colwyn had seen similar doors in other houses built with the old-fashioned thick walls. It was the primitive ventilation of a past generation; the doors, when opened, permitted a free current of air to percolate through the building, and get to the foundations. But a further examination of the hole revealed something which Colwyn had never seen before—a corresponding door on the other side of the wall. The other door opened into the bedroom which had been occupied by Mr. Glenthorpe. Colwyn pushed it with his hand, but it did not yield. It was doubtless fastened with a button on the outside, like the other.

Colwyn, scrutinising the second door closely, noticed that the wood was worm-eaten and shrunken. For that reason it fitted but loosely into the aperture of the wall, and on the one side there was a wide crack which arrested Colwyn's attention. It ran the whole length of the door, along the top—that is, horizontally—and was, perhaps, a quarter of an inch wide. With the tightened nerves which presage an important discovery, Colwyn felt for his pocket knife, opened the largest blade, and thrust it into the crack. It penetrated up to the handle. He ran the knife along the whole length of the crack without difficulty. There was no doubt it opened into the next room.

Colwyn closed the trap-door carefully, and started to push the wardrobe back into its previous position. As he did so, his eye fell upon several tiny scraps of paper lying in the vacant space. He stooped, and picked them up. They were the torn fragments of a pocket-book leaf, which had been written upon. Colwyn endeavoured to place the fragments together and read the writing. But some of the pieces were missing, and he could only decipher two disjointed words–"Constance" and "forgive."

Slowly, almost mechanically, the detective felt for his pipe, lit it, and stood for a long time at the open window, gazing with set eyes into the brooding darkness, wrapped in profound thought, thinking of his discoveries and what they portended.

20

Colwyn was astir with the first glimmering of a grey dawn. He wanted to test the police theory that the murder was committed by climbing from one bedroom to the other, but he did not desire to be discovered in the experiment by any of the inmates of the inn. The window of his bedroom was so small that it was difficult to get through, and there was a drop of more than eight feet from the ledge to the hillside. After one or two attempts Colwyn got out feet foremost, and when half way through wriggled his body round until he was able to grasp the window-ledge and drop to the ground. The fall caused his heels to sink deeply into the clay of the hillside, which was moist and sticky after the rain.

Colwyn closely examined the impression his heels had made, and then walked along until he stood underneath the window of the next room. It was an easy matter to climb through this window, which was larger, and closer to the ground—five feet from the hillside, at the most. Colwyn sprang on to the ledge, and tried the window with his hand. It was unlocked. He pushed up the lower pane, and entered the room.

From the window he walked straight to the bedside, noting, as he walked, that his footsteps left on the carpet crumbs of the red earth from outside, similar to those which had been found in the room the morning after the murder. He next examined the broken incandescent burner in the chandelier in the middle of the room, and took careful measurements of the distances between the gas jet, the bedside and the door, observing, as he did so, that the gaslight was almost in a line with the foot of the bed. That was a point he had marked previously when Superintendent Galloway had suggested that the

incandescent burner was broken by the murderer striking
it with the corpse he was carrying. Colwyn had found it
difficult to accept that point of view at the time, but now,
in the light of recent discoveries, and the new theory of
the crime which was gradually taking shape in his mind,
it seemed almost incredible that the murderer, staggering
under the weight of his ghastly burden, should have
taken anything but the shortest track to the door.

After examining the bed with an attentive eye,
Colwyn next looked for the small door in the wall. It was
not apparent: the wall-paper appeared to cover the whole
of the wall on that side of the room in unbroken
continuity. But a closer inspection revealed a slight
fissure or crack, barely noticeable in the dark green wall-
paper, extending an inch or so beyond a small picture
suspended near the door of the room. When the picture
was taken down the crack was more apparent, for it ran
nearly the whole length of the space. The door had been
papered over when the room was last papered, which was
a long time ago, judging by the dingy condition of the
wall-paper, and the crack had been caused by the
shrinking of the woodwork of the door, as Colwyn had
noticed the previous night.

Colwyn let himself out of the room with the key Peggy
had given him, locked the door behind him, and took the
key down to the kitchen. It was still very early, and
nobody was stirring. Having hung the key on the hook of
the dresser, he returned to his room.

At breakfast time that morning Charles informed
him, in his husky whisper, that he had to go over to
Heathfield that day, to ascertain why the brewer had not
sent a consignment of beer, which was several days
overdue. Charles' chief regret was that for some hours his
guest would be left to the tender mercies of Ann, and he
let it be understood that he had the poorest opinion of
women as waitresses. But he promised to return in time
to minister to Colwyn's comforts at dinner. Somewhat

amused, Colwyn told the fat man not to hurry back on his account, as Ann could look after him very well.

As Colwyn was smoking a cigar in front of the inn after breakfast, he saw Charles setting out on his journey, and watched his short fat form toil up the rise and disappear on the other side. Immediately afterwards, the gaunt figure of the innkeeper emerged from the inn, prepared for a fishing excursion. He hesitated a moment on seeing Colwyn, then walked towards him and informed him that he was going to have a morning's fishing in a river stream a couple of miles away, having heard good accounts in the bar overnight of the fish there since the recent rain.

"Who will look after the inn, with both you and Charles away?" asked Colwyn, with a smile.

The innkeeper, carefully bestowing a fishing-line in the capacious side pocket of his faded tweed coat, replied that as the inn was out of beer, and not likely to have any that day, there was not much lost by leaving it. That seemed to exhaust the possibilities of the conversation, but the innkeeper lingered, looking at his guest as though he had something on his mind.

"I do not know if you care for fishing, sir," he remarked, after a rather lengthy pause. "If you do, I should be happy at any time to show you a little sport. The fishing is very good about this district—as good as anywhere in Norfolk."

Colwyn was quick to divine what was passing in the innkeeper's mind. He had been brooding over the incident in the bar parlour of the previous night, and hoped by this awkward courtesy to remove the impression of his overnight rudeness from his visitor's mind. As Colwyn was equally desirous of allaying his fears, he thanked him for his offer, and stood chatting with him for some moments. His pleasant and natural manner had the effect of putting the innkeeper at his ease, and there was an obvious air of relief in his bearing as he wished the detective good morning and departed on his fishing expedition.

Colwyn spent the morning in a solitary walk along the marshes, thinking over the events of the night and morning. He returned to the inn for an early lunch, which was served by Ann, who gossiped to him freely of the small events which had constituted the daily life of the village since his previous visit. The principal of these, it seemed, had been the reappearance, after a long period of inaction, of the White Lady of the Shrieking Pit—an apparition which haunted the hut circles on the rise. Colwyn, recalling that Duney and Backlos imagined they had encountered a spectre the night they saw Penreath on the edge of the wood, asked Ann who the "White Lady" was supposed to be. Ann was reticent at first. She admitted that she was a firm believer in the local tradition, which she had imbibed with her mother's milk, but it was held to be unlucky to talk about the White Lady. However, her feminine desire to impart information soon overcame her fears, and she launched forth into full particulars of the legend. It appeared that for generations past the deep pit on the rise in which Mr. Glenthorpe's body had been thrown had been the haunt of a spirit known as the White Lady, who, from time to time, issued from the depths of the pit, clad in a white trailing garment, to wander along the hut circles on the rise, shrieking and sobbing piteously. Whose ghost she was, and why she shrieked, Ann was unable to say. Her appearances were infrequent, with sometimes as long as a year between them, and the timely warning she gave of her coming by shrieking from the depths of the pit before making her appearance, enabled folk to keep indoors and avoid her when she was walking. As long as she wasn't seen by anybody, not much harm was done, but the sight of her was fatal to the beholder, who was sure to come to a swift and violent end.

Ann related divers accredited instances of calamity which had followed swiftly upon an encounter with the

White Lady, including that of her own sister's husband, who had seen her one night going home, and the very next day had been kicked by a horse and killed on the spot. Ann's grandmother, when a young girl, had heard her shrieking one night when she was going home, but had had the presence of mind to fall flat on her face until the shrieking had ceased, by which means she avoided seeing her, and had died comfortably in her bed at eighty-one in consequence.

Colwyn gathered from the countrywoman's story that the prevailing impression in the village was that Mr. Glenthorpe's murder was due to the interposition of the White Lady of the Shrieking Pit. The White Lady, after a long silence, had been heard to shriek once two nights before the murder, but the warning had not deterred Mr. Glenthorpe from taking his nightly walk on the rise, although Ann, out of her liking and respect for the old gentleman, had even ventured to forget her place and beg and implore him not to go. But he had laughed at her, and said if he met the White Lady he would stop and have a chat with her about her ancestors. Those were his very words, and they made her blood run cold at the time, though she little thought how soon he would be repenting of his foolhardiness in his coffin. If he had only listened to her he might have been alive that blessed day, for she hadn't the slightest doubt he met the White Lady that night in his walk, and his doom was brought about in consequence.

Ann concluded by solemnly urging Colwyn, as long as he remained at the inn, to keep indoors at night as he valued his life, for ever since the murder the White Lady had been particularly active, shrieking nearly every night, as though seeking another victim, and the whole village was frightened to stir out in consequence. Ann had reluctantly to admit that she had never actually heard her shrieking herself—she was a heavy sleeper at any time—but there were those who had, plenty of them.

Besides, hadn't he heard that Charles, while shutting up the inn the very night poor Mr. Glenthorpe's body had been taken away, had seen something white on the rise? On Colwyn replying that he had not heard this, Ann assured him the whole village believed that Charles had seen the White Lady, and regarded him as good as dead, and many were the speculations as to the manner in which his inevitable fate would fall.

The relation of the legend of the White Lady lasted to the conclusion of lunch, and then Colwyn sauntered outside with a cigar, in order to make another examination of the ground the murderer had covered in going to the pit. The body had been carried out the back way, across the green which separated the inn from the village, and up the rise to the pit. The green was now partly under water, and the track of the footprints leading to the rise had been obliterated by the heavy rains which had fallen since, but the soft surface retained the impression of Colwyn's footsteps with the same distinctness with which it had held, and afterwards revealed, the track of the man who had carried the corpse to the pit.

Colwyn examined the pit closely. The edges were wet and slippery, and in places the earth had been washed away. The sides, for some distance down, were lined with a thick growth of shrubs and birch. Colwyn knelt down on the edge and peered into the interior of the pit. He tested the strength of the climbing and creeping plants which twisted in snakelike growth in the interior. It seemed to him that it would be a comparatively easy matter to descend into the pit by their support, so far as they went. But how far did they go?

While he was thus occupied he heard the sound of footsteps crashing through the undergrowth of the little wood on the other side of the pit. A moment later a man, carrying a rabbit, and followed by a mongrel dog, came into view. It was Duney. He stared hard at Colwyn and then advanced towards him with a grin of recognition.

"Yow be lookin' to see how t'owd ma'aster was hulled dune th' pit?" he asked.

"I was wondering how far the pit ran straight down," replied Colwyn. "It seems to take a slight slope a little way down. Does it?" "I doan't know narthin' about th' pit, and I doan't want to," replied Mr. Duney, backing away with a slightly pale face. "Doan't yow meddle wi' un, ma'aster. It's a quare place, thissun."

"Why, what's the matter with it?" "Did you never hear that th' pit's haunted? Like enough nobody'd tell yow. Folk hereabowts aren't owerfond of talkin' of th' White Lady of th' Shrieking Pit, for fear it should bring un bad luck."

"I've been hearing a little about her to-day. Is she any relation of Black Shuck, the ghost dog you were telling me about?"

"It's no larfin' matter, ma'aster. You moind the day me and Billy Backlog come and towld yow about us seein' that chap on th' edge of yon wood that night? Well, just befower we seed un we heerd th' rummiest kind of noise— summat atween a moan and a shriek, comin' from this 'ere pit. I reckon, from what's happened to that chap Ronald since, that it wor the White Lady of th' Pit we heered. It's lucky for us we didn't see un."

"I remember at the time you mentioned something about it."

"Ay, she be a terr'ble bad sperrit," said Mr. Duney, wagging his head unctuously. "She comes out of this yare pit wheer t'owd man was chucked, and wanders about the wood and th' rise, a-yellin' somefin awful. It's nowt to hear her—we've all heerd her for that matter—but to see her is to meet a bloody and violent end within the month. That's why they call this 'ere pit 'the Shrieking Pit.' I'm thinkin' that owd Mr. Glenthorpe, who was allus fond of walkin' up this way at nights, met her one night, and that'll account for his own bloody end. And it's my belief that she appeared to the young chap who was hidin' in th'

woods the night we saw un. And look what's happened to
un! He's got to be hanged, which is a violent end, thow
p'r'aps not bloody."

"If that's the local belief, I wonder anybody went down
into the pit to recover Mr. Glenthorpe's body."

"Nobody wouldn't 'a' gone down but Herward. I
wouldn't 'a' gone down for untowd gowd, but Herward
comes from th' Broads, and don't know nartin' about this
part of the ma'shes. Besides, he ain't no Christian, down't
care for no ghosts nor sperrits. I've often heerd un say so."

"Is it true that the White Lady has been seen since
Mr. Glenthorpe was murdered?"

"She's been heered, shure enough. Billy Backlog, who
lives closest to the rise, was a-tellin' us in the *Anchor* bar
that she woke him up two nights arter th' murder, a-
yowlin' like an old tomcat, but Billy knew it worn't a cat–
it weer far more fearsome, wi gasps at th' end. The deaf
fat chap at Benson's arst him what time this might be.
Billy said he disremembered th' time–mebbe it wor ten or
a bit past. Then the fat chap said it wor just about that
time the same night, as he wor shuttin' up, he saw
somefin white float up to th' top of th' pit. He thowt at th'
time it might be mist, thow there weren't much mist on
th' ma'shes that night, but now he says 'es sure that it
wor the White Lady from the Shrieking Pit that he saw.
'Then Gawdamighty help yow, poor fat chap,' says Billy,
looking at him solemn-like. 'The hearin' of her is narthin',
it's th' seein' o' her that's the trouble.' The poor fat chap a'
been nigh skeered out o' his wits ever since, and nobody
in th' village wud go near th' pit a' nighttimes–no, not for
a fortin. I ain't sure as it's safe to be here even in
daytimes, thow I never heered of her comin' out in the
light." Mr. Duney turned resolutely away from the pit,
and called to his dog, who was sitting near the edge,
regarding his master with blinking eyes and lolling
tongue. "I'll be goin', in case that Queensmead sees me
from th' village. I cot this coney fair and square in th'

open, but it be hard to make Queensmead believe it. Well, I'll be goin'. Good mornin', ma'aster."

He trudged away across the rise, with his dog following at his heels. Colwyn was about to turn away also, when his eye was caught by a scrap of stained and discoloured paper lying near the edge of the pit, where the rain had washed away some of the earth. He stooped, and picked it up. It was a slip of white paper, about five inches long, and perhaps three inches in width, quite blank, but with a very apparent watermark, consisting of a number of parallel waving lines, close together, running across the surface. Although the watermark was an unusual one, it seemed strangely familiar to Colwyn, who tried to recall where he had seen it before. But memory is a tricky thing. Although Colwyn's memory instantly recognised the watermark on the paper, he could not, for the moment, recollect where he had seen it, though it seemed as familiar to him as the face of some old acquaintance whose name he had temporarily forgotten. Colwyn ultimately gave up the effort for the time being, and placed the piece of paper in his pocket-book, knowing that his memory would, sooner or later, perform unconsciously the task it refused to undertake when asked.

Colwyn spent the afternoon in another solitary walk, and darkness had set in before he returned to the village. As he reached the inn he glanced towards the hut circles, and was startled to see something white move slowly along by the edge of the Shrieking Pit and vanish in the wood. There was something so weird and ghostly in the spectacle that Colwyn was momentarily astounded by it. Then his eye fell on the sea mist which covered the marshes in a white shroud, and he smiled slightly. It was not the White Lady of the Shrieking Pit he had seen, but a spiral of mist, floating across the rise.

The sight brought back to his mind the stories he had heard that day, and when he was seated at dinner a little later he casually asked

Charles if he believed in ghosts. The fat man, with a sudden uplifting of his black eyes, as though to ascertain whether Colwyn was speaking seriously, replied that he did not.

"I'm surprised to hear of your scepticism, Charles, for I'm told that the apparition from the pit–the White Lady, as she is called–has favoured you with a special appearance," said Colwyn, in a bantering tone.

"I see what you mean now, sir. I didn't understand you at first. It was like this: some of the villagers were talking about this ghost in the bar a few nights back, and one or two of the villagers, who all firmly believed in it, declared that they had heard her wandering about the previous night, moaning and shrieking, as is supposed to be her custom. I, more by way of a joke than anything else, told them I had seen something white on the rise the previous night, when I was shutting up the inn. But the whole village has got it into their heads that I saw the White Lady, and they think because I've seen her I'm a doomed man. The country folk round about here are an ignorant and superstitious lot, sir."

"And did you actually see anything, Charles, the night you speak of?"

"I saw something, sir–something long and white–like a moving white pillar, if I may so express myself. While I looked it vanished into the woods."

"It was probably mist. I saw something similar this evening!"

"Very likely, sir. I do not think it was a ghost."

Colwyn did not pursue the subject further, though he was struck by the wide difference between Charles' account of the incident and that given to him by Duney at the pit that afternoon.

When Charles had cleared the table Colwyn sat smoking and thinking until late. After he was sure that the rest of the inmates of the inn had retired, he went to the kitchen and took the key of Mr. Glenthorpe's room from the hook of the dresser. When he reached his own bedroom, his first act was to push back the wardrobe and open the trap door he had discovered the previous night. He looked at his watch, and found that the hour was a little after eleven. He decided to wait for half an hour before carrying out the experiment he contemplated. By midnight he would be fairly safe from the fear of discovery. He lay down on his bed to pass the intervening time, but he was so tired that he fell asleep almost immediately.

He awakened with a start, and sat up, staring into the black darkness. For a moment or two he did not realise his surroundings, then the sound of stealthy footsteps passing his door brought him back to instant wakefulness. The footsteps halted—outside his door, it seemed to Colwyn. There followed the sound of a hand fumbling with a lock, followed by the shooting of a bolt and the creaking of a door. The truth flashed upon the detective; somebody was entering the next room. As he listened, there was the scrape of a match, and a moment later a narrow shaft of light streamed through the open wall-door into his room.

Colwyn got noiselessly off his bed and looked through the crack in the inner small door into the other room. The picture on the other side of the wall narrowed his range of vision, but through the inch or so of crack extending beyond the picture he was able to see clearly that portion of the adjoining bedroom in which the bed stood. Near the bed, examining with the light of a candle the contents of the writing table which stood alongside of it, was Benson, the innkeeper.

He was searching for something—rummaging through the drawers of the table, taking out papers and envelopes, and tearing them open with a furious desperate energy, pausing every now and again to look hurriedly over his shoulder, as though he expected to see some apparition start up from the shadowy corners. The search was apparently fruitless, for presently he crammed the papers back into the drawers with the same feverish haste, and, walking rapidly across the room, passed out of the view of the watcher on the other side, for the picture which hung on the inside wall prevented Colwyn seeing beyond the foot of the bed. Although the innkeeper could not now be seen, the sound of his stealthy quick movements, and the flickering lights cast by the candle he carried, suggested plainly enough that he was continuing his search in that portion of the room which was not visible through the crack.

In a few minutes he came back into Colwyn's range of vision, looking dusty and dishevelled, with drops of perspiration starting from his face. With a savage gesture, which was akin to despair, he wiped the perspiration from his face, and tossed back his long hair from his forehead. It was the first time Colwyn had seen his forehead uncovered, and a thrill ran through him as he noticed a deep bruise high upon the left temple. The next moment the innkeeper walked swiftly out of the room, and Colwyn heard him close the door softly behind him.

Colwyn waited awhile. When everything seemed quiet, he cautiously opened his door in the dark, and tried the door of the adjoining room. It was locked.

The innkeeper, then, had another key which fitted the murdered man's door. And what was he searching for? Money? The treasury notes which Mr. Glenthorpe had drawn out of the bank the day he was murdered, which had never been found? Money—notes!

By one of those hidden and unaccountable processes of the human brain, the association of ideas recalled to Colwyn's mind where he had previously seen the peculiar watermark of waving lines visible on the piece of paper he had picked up at the brink of the pit that afternoon: it was the Government watermark of the first issue of War Treasury notes.

Colwyn lit his bedroom candle, and examined the piece of paper in his pocket-book with a new and keen interest. There was no doubt about it, the mark on the dirty blank paper was undoubtedly the Treasury watermark. But how came such a mark, designed exclusively for the protection of the Treasury against bank-note forgeries, to appear on a dirty scrap of paper?

As he stood there, turning the bit of paper over and over, in his hand, puzzling over the problem, the solution flashed into his mind–a solution so simple, yet, withal, so remarkable, that he hesitated to believe it possible. But a further examination of the paper removed his doubts. Chance had placed in his hands another clue, and the most important he had yet discovered, to help him in the elucidation of the mystery of the murder of Roger Glenthorpe. But to verify that clue it would be necessary for him to descend the pit.

21

An orange crescent of a waning moon was sinking in a black sky as Colwyn let himself quietly out of the door and took his way up to the rise. But the darkness of the night was fading fast before the grey dawn of the coming day, and in the marshes below the birds were beginning to stir and call among the reeds.

Colwyn waited for the first light of dawn before attempting the descent of the pit. His plan was to climb down by the creepers as far as they went, and descend the remainder of the distance by the rope, which he would fasten to one of the shrubs growing in the interior. He realised that his chances of success depended on the slope of the pit and the depth to which the shrubs grew, but the attempt was well worth making. Assistance would have made the task much easier, but publicity was the thing Colwyn desired most to avoid at that stage of his investigations. There would be time enough to consider the question of seeking help if he failed in his individual effort.

He made his plans carefully before commencing the descent. He first tested a rope he had found in the lumber room of the inn; it was thin but strong and capable of bearing the weight of a heavier man than himself. The rope was not more than fifteen feet in length, but if the hardy climbing plants which lined the sides of the pit were capable of supporting him ten or twelve feet down, that length should be sufficient for his purpose. Having tested the rope and coiled it, he slipped it into the right-hand pocket of his coat with one end hanging out. Next he opened his knife, and placed it with a candle and a box of matches in his other pocket. Then turning on his electric torch, he lowered himself cautiously into the pit by the creepers which fringed the surface. There was no difficulty about the descent for the first eight or ten feet. Then the shrubs that had afforded foothold for his feet suddenly ceased, and the foot that he had thrust down for another perch touched nothing but the slippery side of the pit. Clinging firmly with his left hand to the network of vegetation which grew above his head, Colwyn flashed his electric torch into the blackness of the pit beneath him. One or two long tendrils of the climbing plants which grew higher up dangled like pendulous snakes, but the vegetable growth ceased at that point. Beneath him the naked sides of the pit gleamed sleek and wet in the rays of the torch.

Pulling himself up a little way to gain a securer footing, Colwyn took the coil of rope from his pocket, and selecting a strong withe which hung near him, sought to fasten the end of the rope to it. It took him some time to do this with the hand he had at liberty, but at length he accomplished it to his satisfaction, and then he allowed the coils of the rope to fall into the pit. He next essayed to test the strength of the support, by pulling at it. To his disappointment, his first vigorous tug snapped the withe to which the rope was attached. He tied the rope to a stronger growth, but with no better result: the growths seemed brittle, and incapable of bearing a great strain when tested separately. It was the twisted network of the withes and twigs which gave the climbing plants inside the pit sufficient toughness to support his weight. Taken singly, they had very little strength.

Colwyn reluctantly realised that it would be folly to endeavour to attempt the further descent of the pit by their frail support, and he decided to relinquish the attempt.

As he was about to ascend, the light of the torch brought into view that part of the pit to which he was clinging, and he noticed that the testing of the withes had torn away a portion of the leafy screen, revealing the black and slimy surface of the pit's side. Colwyn was amazed to see a small peg, with a fishing line attached to it, sticking in the bare earth thus exposed. Somebody had been down the pit and placed it there—recently, judging by the appearance of the peg, which was clean and newly cut. What was at the other end of the line, which dangled in the darkness of the pit? A better hiding place for anything valuable could not have been devised. The thin fishing line was indiscernible against the slimy side of the pit, and Colwyn realised that he would never have discovered it had it not been for the lucky accident which had exposed the peg to which the line was anchored. A place of concealment chosen at the expense of so much trouble and risk indicated something well worth concealing, and it was with a strong premonition of what was suspended down the pit that the detective, taking a firmer hold of the twining tendrils above his head, began to haul up the line. The weight at the end was slight; the line came up readily enough, foot after foot running through his hand, and then, finally, a small oblong packet, firmly fastened and knotted to the end of the line.

Colwyn examined the packet by the light of the torch. It was a man's pocket-book of black morocco leather, a large and serviceable article, thick and heavy. The detective did not need the information conveyed by the initials "R. G." stamped in silver lettering on one side, to enlighten him as to the owner of the pocket-book and what it contained.

Removing the peg from the earth, Colwyn was about to place the pocket-book and the line in his pocket, but on second thoughts he restored the peg to its former position, and endeavoured to untie the knots by which the pocket-book was fastened to the line. It was difficult to do this with one hand, but, by placing the pocket-book in his pocket, and picking at the knots one by one, he at length unfastened it from the line. He tied his own pocket-book to the end of the line, and dropped it back into the pit. He next replaced the greenery torn from the spot where the peg rested. When he had restored, as far as he could, the original appearance of the hiding place, he ascended swiftly to the surface.

The first act, on reaching the fresh air, was to examine the contents of the pocket-book. As he anticipated, it was crammed full of notes of the first Treasury issue. He did not take them out to count them; a rook, watching him curiously from the edge of the wood, warned him of the danger of human eyes.

Here, then, was the end of his investigations, and a discovery which would necessitate his departure from the inn sooner than he had anticipated. Nothing remained for him to do but to acquaint the authorities with the fresh facts he had brought to light, indicate the man to whom those facts pointed, and endeavour to see righted the monstrous act of injustice which had condemned an innocent man to the ignominy of a shameful death. The sooner that task was commenced the better. The law was swift to grasp and slow to release, and many were the formalities to be gone through before the conviction of a wrongly convicted man could be quashed, especially in a grave charge like murder. Only on the most convincing fresh evidence could the jury's verdict be upset, and none knew better than Colwyn that such evidence had not yet been obtained. But the additional facts discovered during his second visit to the inn, if not in themselves sufficient to upset the verdict against Penreath, nevertheless threw an entirely new light on the crime, which, if speedily followed up, would prove Penreath's innocence by revealing the actual murderer. The only question was whether the police would use the clues he was going to place in their hands in the manner he wished them to be used. If they didn't—but Colwyn refused to contemplate that possibility. His mind reverted to the chief constable of Norfolk. He felt he was on firm ground in believing that Mr. Cromering would act promptly once he was certain that there had been a miscarriage of justice in the Glenthorpe case.

It would be necessary to arrange his departure from the inn in such a manner as not to arouse suspicion, and also to have the pit watched in case any attempt was made to recover the money he had found that morning. Colwyn, after some consideration, decided to invoke the aid of Police Constable Queensmead. His brief association with Queensmead had convinced him that the village constable was discreet and intelligent.

It was still very early as he descended to the village and sought the constable's house. His knock at the door was not immediately answered, but after the lapse of a minute or two the door was unbolted, and the constable's face appeared. When he saw who his visitor was he asked to be excused while he put on some clothes. He was back speedily, and ushered Colwyn into the room in which he did his official business.

"Queensmead," said the detective earnestly, "I have to go to Norwich, and I want you to do something for me in my absence. I am going to tell you something in strict confidence. Fresh facts have come to light in the Glenthorpe case. You remember Mr. Glenthorpe's money, which was supposed to have been stolen by Penreath, but which was never recovered. I found it this morning down the pit where the body was thrown."

"How did you get down the pit?" asked Queensmead.

"I climbed down the creepers as far as they went. I had a rope for the rest of the descent, but it wasn't needed, for I found Mr. Glenthorpe's pocket-book suspended by a cord about ten feet down. Here it is."

Queensmead scrutinised the pocket-book and its contents, and on handing it back remarked:

"Do you think Penreath returned and concealed himself in the wood to recover these notes?"

Colwyn was struck by the penetration of this remark.

"No, quite the contrary," he replied. "Your deduction is drawn from an isolated fact. It has to be taken in conjunction with other fresh facts which have come to light–facts which put an entirely fresh complexion on the case, and tend to exculpate Penreath."

"I would rather not know what they are, then," replied Queensmead quietly. "It is better I should not know too much. You see, it might be awkward, in more ways than one, if things are turning out as you say. What is it you want me to do?"

"I want you to watch the pit on the rise while I am away, chiefly at night. It is of paramount importance that the man whom I believe to be the thief and murderer should not be allowed to escape in my absence. I do not think that he has any suspicions, so far, and it is practically certain nobody saw me descend the pit. But if he should, by any chance, go down to the pit for his money, and find it gone, he would know he had been discovered, and instantly seek safety in flight. That must be prevented."

"How?"

"You must arrest him."

"I do not see how that can be done," replied Queensmead. "I cannot take upon myself to arrest a man simply for descending the pit. It's not against the law."

"In order to get over that difficulty I left my own pocket-book tied to the cord in the pit," replied Colwyn. "It's a black leather one, like Mr. Glenthorpe's. If the thief goes down he is hardly likely to discover the difference till he gets to the surface. You can arrest him for the theft of my pocket-book, which contains a little money. You can make a formal entry of my complaint of my loss."

"Well, I've heard that you were a cool customer, Mr. Colwyn, and now I believe it," replied Queensmead, laughing outright. "Fancy thinking out a plan like that down in the pit! But as you've made the complaint it's my duty to enter it, and keep a look out for your lost pocket-book. I'll watch the pit, and if anybody goes down it I'll arrest him."

"If the attempt is made it will not be in daytime–it will be in the night, you may be sure of that. I want you to watch the pit at night. The life of an innocent man may depend on your vigilance. It will only be for two nights, or three at the most. I shall certainly return within three days."

"You may depend on me," replied the constable. "I will go to the pit as soon as it grows dark, and watch from the edge of the wood till daylight."

"Thank you," said Colwyn. "I felt sure you would do it when you knew what was at stake. I have an idea that your vigil will not be disturbed, but I want to be on the safe side. I suppose you are not afraid of the ghost?"

"You have heard of the White Lady of the Shrieking Pit?" said Queensmead, looking at the other curiously.

"I have heard of her, but I have not heard her, or seen her. Have you?"

"I cannot say I have, but I live at the wrong end of the village, and I never go out at night. But there are plenty of villagers, principally customers of the *Anchor*, who are prepared to take their Bible oath that they have heard her—if not seen her. The White Lady has terrorised the whole village—since the murder."

There was something in the tone of the last three words which attracted the detective's attention.

"There was not much talk of the ghost before the murder, then?" he asked.

"Very little. I have been stationed here for two years, and hardly knew of its existence. Of course, it's a deep-rooted local tradition, and every villager has heard the story in childhood, and most of them believe it. Many of them actually think they have heard moans and shrieks coming from the rise during this last week or so. It's a lonely sort of place, with very little to talk about; it doesn't take much to get a story like that going round."

"Then you think there is some connection between the reappearance of the ghost and the hiding of the money in the pit it is supposed to haunt?"

"It's not my business to draw inferences of that kind, sir. I leave that to my betters, if they think fit to do so. I am only the village constable."

"But you've already inferred that the legend has been spread round again by means of gossip at the *Anchor*. Was it started there?" "It was and it wasn't. A fool of a fellow named Backlog burst into the tap-room one night and said he had heard the White Lady shrieking, and Charles—that's the waiter—declared that he had seen something white the same night. That was the start of the business."

"So I have heard. But what has kept it going ever since?"

"Well, from what I hear—I never go to the inn myself, but a local policeman learns all the gossip in a small place like this—the subject is brought up in the bar-room every evening, either by the innkeeper or Charles, and discussed till closing time, when the silly villagers go home, huddled together like a flock of sheep, not daring to look round for fear of seeing the White Lady."

"Do Benson and Charles both believe in the ghost?"

"It seems as if they do." The constable's voice was noncommittal.

As Colwyn rose to go, Queensmead looked at him with a trace of hesitation in his manner.

"Perhaps you'd answer me a question, sir," he said in a low tone, as though afraid of being overheard. "That greenery that grows inside the pit, by which you climbed down, will it support a heavy weight?"

"It will hold a far heavier man than you, if you are thinking of making the descent," said Colwyn laughingly. "It's a case of unity is strength. The tendrils of the climbing plants are so twisted together that they are as tough as ropes."

"Thank you. What time will you reach here when you return?"

"Probably not before dusk, but certainly by then. In the meantime, of course, you will not breathe a word of this to anybody."

"I am not likely to do that. I shall keep a close watch on the pit till I see you again."

"That's right. Good day."

"Good day, sir."

It still wanted a few minutes to seven when Colwyn returned to the inn. The front door was as he had left it, closed, but unlocked. The house was silent: nobody was yet stirring. He locked the door after him, and proceeded to his room, pleased to think he had not been seen going or coming. His first act on reaching his room was to lock the door and count the money in the pocket-book. The money was all in single Treasury notes, with one five-pound note. The case contained nothing else except a faded newspaper clipping on Fossil Sponges. Colwyn replaced the notes, and put the case in an inside breast pocket. He next performed the best kind of toilet the primitive resources of the inn permitted, and occupied himself for an hour or so in completing his notes of his investigations.

While he was breakfasting he saw the innkeeper passing the half-open door, and he called him into the room and told him to let him have his bill without delay, as he was returning to Durrington that morning. The innkeeper made no comment on hearing his guest's intention, and Charles brought in the bill a little later. Colwyn, as he paid it, casually asked Charles if he happened to know the time of the morning trains from Heathfield.

"There's one to Durrington at eleven o'clock, sir," said the waiter, consulting a greasy time table. "There's one at 9:30, but it's a good long walk to the station, and you could not catch it because there's no way of getting there except by walking, as you know, sir."

"The eleven o'clock train will suit me," said Colwyn, consulting his watch.

"Shall I go and get your bag, sir?"

"No, thanks, I've not packed it yet."

Colwyn went upstairs shortly afterwards determined to pack his bag and leave the place as soon as possible. As he was about to enter his room he saw Peggy appear at the end of the passage. She looked at him with a timid, wistful smile, and made a step towards him, as though she would speak to him. Colwyn pretended not to see her, and hurried into his room and shut the door. How could he tell her what she had so innocently done in recalling him to the inn? How inform her what the cost of saving her lover would be to her? Somebody else must break the news to her, when it came to that. He packed his things quickly, anxious only to leave a place which had grown repugnant to him, and to drop the dissimulation which had become hateful. Never had he so acutely realised how little a man is master of his actions when entangled in the strange current of Destiny which men label Chance.

When he emerged from the room with his bag, Peggy was no longer visible. The innkeeper was standing in the passage as he went downstairs, and Colwyn nodded to him as he passed. He breathed easier in the fresh morning air, and set out briskly for the station.

He reached Heathfield an hour later, and found he had nearly half an hour to wait for his train. The first ten minutes of that time he utilised despatching two telegrams. One was to the chief constable of Norfolk, at Norwich, and the other to Mr. Oakham, in London. In the latter telegram he indicated that fresh discoveries had come to light in Penreath's case, and he asked the solicitor to go as soon as possible to Norwich where he would await him at his hotel.

22

Colwyn reached Durrington by midday, and proceeded to the hotel for his letters and lunch. After a cold meal served by a shivering waiter in the chilly dining room he went to the garage where he had left his car, and set out for Norwich. He arrived at the cathedral city late in the afternoon, and drove to the hotel where Mr. Oakham had stayed. While engaging a room, he told the clerk that he expected Mr. Oakham from London, and asked to be informed immediately he arrived. After making these arrangements the detective left the hotel and went to the city library, where he spent the next couple of hours making notes from legal statutes and the Criminal Appeal Act.

When he returned to the hotel for dinner the clerk informed him that Mr. Oakham had arrived a short time previously, and had requested that Mr. Colwyn would join him at dinner. Colwyn proceeded to the dining-room, and saw Mr. Oakham dining in solitary state at a large table, reading a London evening newspaper between the courses. He looked up as Colwyn approached, and rose and shook hands.

"This is an unexpected pleasure," said the detective. "I hardly thought you would get here before the morning."

"I had arranged to visit Norwich to-morrow, but in view of the urgent nature of your telegram I decided to catch the afternoon train instead," replied the solicitor. "Will you dine with me, Mr. Colwyn, and we can talk business afterwards."

Colwyn complied, and when the meal was finished, Mr. Oakham turned to him with an eagerness which he did not attempt to conceal, and said:

"Now for your news, Mr. Colwyn. But, first, where shall we talk?"

"As well here as anywhere. There is nobody within hearing."

The solicitor followed his glance round the almost empty dining-room, and nodded acquiescence. Drawing his chair a little nearer the detective, he begged him to begin.

"I have not very much to tell you—at present. But since the conviction of your client, James Ronald Penreath, I have been back to the inn where the murder was committed, and I have discovered fresh evidence which strengthens considerably my original belief that Penreath is an innocent man. But I have reached a stage in my investigations when I need your assistance in completing my task before I go to the authorities with my discoveries. It is hardly necessary for me to tell a man of your experience that it is one of the most difficult things in the world to upset a jury's verdict in a case of murder."

"What have you discovered?"

"This, for one thing." Colwyn produced the pocket-book, and displayed the contents on the table. "This is the murdered man's pocket-book, containing the missing notes which Penreath is supposed to have murdered him for. The prosecution dropped the charge of robbery, but the theft formed an important part of the Crown theory of the crime, as establishing motive."

"Where did you find this pocket-book?"

"Suspended by a piece of cord, half way down the pit where the body was flung."

"It's an interesting discovery," replied Mr. Oakham thoughtfully tapping his nose with his gold-rimmed eye-glasses as he stared at the black pocket-book on the white tablecloth. "Speaking personally, it is proof of what I have thought all along, that a Penreath of Twelvetrees would not commit a robbery. Therefore, on that line of reasoning, one could argue that as Penreath did not commit the robbery, and the Crown hold that the murder was committed for the money, Penreath must be innocent. But the Crown is more likely to hold that as Penreath threw the body in the pit, he concealed the money there afterwards, and was hiding in the wood to recover it when he was arrested. The real point is, Mr. Colwyn, can you prove that it was not Mr. Penreath who placed the money in the pit?"

"I believe I can prove, at all events, that it was not Penreath who threw the body into the pit."

"You can! Then who was it?"

"I am not prepared to answer that question at the moment. During my visit to the inn I made a number of other discoveries besides that of the pocket-book, which, though slight in themselves, all fit in with my present theory of the murder. But before disclosing them, I want to complete my investigations by testing my theory to the uttermost. It is just possible that I may be wrong, though I do not think so. When I have taken the additional step which completes my investigations, I will go to the chief constable, reconstruct the crime for him as I see it now, and ask him to take action."

"Then why have you sent for me?"

"To help me to complete my task. Part of my theory is that Penreath is deliberately keeping silent to shield someone else. The solicitor of a convicted man has access to him even when he is condemned to death. I want you to take me with you to see Penreath."

"For what purpose?"

"In order to get him to speak."

"It would be quite useless." The lawyer spoke in some agitation. "I have seen him twice since the verdict, and implored him to speak if he has anything to say, but he declared that he had nothing to say."

"Nevertheless, I shall succeed where you have failed. Penreath is an innocent man."

"Then why does he not speak out, even now—more so now than ever?"

"He has his reasons, and they seem sufficient to him to keep him silent even under the shadow of the gallows."

"And why do you think he will confide them to you, when he refuses to divulge them to his professional adviser?"

"He will not willingly reveal them to me. My hope of getting his story depends entirely upon my success in springing a surprise upon him. That is one of my reasons for not telling you more just now. The mere fact that you knew would hamper my handling a difficult situation. The slightest involuntary gesture or look might put him on his guard, and the opportunity would be lost. It is not absolutely essential that I should gain Penreath's statement before going to the police, but if his statement coincides with my theory of the crime it will strengthen my case considerably when I reconstruct the crime for the police."

"Your way of doing business strikes me as strange, Mr. Colwyn," said the solicitor stiffly. "As Mr. Penreath's professional adviser, surely I am entitled to your fullest confidence. You are asking me to behave in a very unprofessional way, and take a leap in the dark. There are proper ways of doing things. I will be frank with you. I have come to Norwich in order to urge Penreath for the last time to permit me to lodge an appeal against his conviction. That interview has been arranged to take place in the morning."

"Has he previously refused to appeal?"

"He has–twice."

"May I ask on what grounds you are seeking permission to appeal?"

"If he consents, my application to the Registrar would be made under Section Four of the Criminal Appeal Act," was the cautious reply.

"That means you are persisting in your original defence–that Penreath is guilty, but insane. Therefore your application for leave to appeal against the sentence on the ground of insanity only enables you to appeal to the Court to quash the sentence on the ground that Penreath is irresponsible for his acts. Even if you succeed in your appeal he will be kept in gaol as a criminal lunatic. In a word, you intend to persist in a defence which, as I told you before the trial, had very little chance of success. In my opinion it has no more chance of success before the Court of Appeal. You have not sufficient evidence for a successful defence on the grounds of insanity. The judge, in his summing up at the trial, was clearly of the opinion that Sir Henry Durwood was wrong in thinking Penreath insane, and he directed the jury accordingly.

"In my opinion the judge was right. I do not think Penreath is insane, or even subject to fits of impulsive insanity. If you ask my opinion, I think he is still suffering from the effects of shell shock, and, like many other brave men who have been similarly affected, he endeavoured to conceal the fact. I have come to the conclusion that Penreath's peculiar conduct at the Durrington hotel, on which Sir Henry based his theory of *furor epilepticus*, was nothing more than the combined effect of mental worry and an air raid shock on a previously shattered nervous system. Penreath is a sane man—as sane as you or I—and my late investigations at the scene of the murder have convinced me that he is an innocent man also. The question is, are you going to allow professional etiquette to stand in the way of proving his innocence?"

"But you have not shown me anything to convince me that he *is* an innocent man. Your statement comes as a great surprise to me, and you cannot expect that I should credit your bare assumption. It would be exceedingly difficult to believe without the most convincing proofs, which you have not brought forward. I prepared the case for the defence at the trial, and I only permitted that defence to be put forward because there was no other course—the evidence was so overwhelming, and

Penreath's obstinate silence in the face of it pointed so conclusively to his guilt."

"Nevertheless, you were wrong. The question is, are you going to help me undo that wrong?"

"You have not yet proved to me that it is a wrong," quibbled the solicitor.

"Mr. Oakham, let me make this quite clear to you," said the detective sternly. "I have sent for you out of courtesy, because, as I said before, I like to do things in a regular way. As you force me to speak plainly, there is another reason, which is that I did not wish to make you look small, or injure your professional reputation, by acting independently of you. It would be a bad advertisement for Oakham and Pendules if it got abroad–as it assuredly will if you persist in your attitude–that an innocent client of yours was almost sent to the gallows through your wrong defence at his trial. It is in your hands to prevent such a scandal from becoming public property. But if you are going to stand on professional etiquette it is just as well you should understand that I am quite prepared to act independently of you. I have sufficient influence to obtain an order from the governor of the gaol for an interview with the condemned man, and I shall do so. I have discovered sufficient additional evidence in this case to save Penreath, and I am going to save him, with or without your assistance. You have had your way–it was a wrong way. Now I am going to have my way. I only ask you to trust me for a few hours. After I have seen Penreath you are at liberty to accompany me to the chief constable, to whom I shall tell everything. That is my last word."

"I will do as you ask, Mr. Colwyn," replied the solicitor, after a short pause. "Not because I am apprehensive of the consequences, but because you have convinced me that it would be foolish and wrong on my part to place any obstacles in the way of establishing my client's innocence, even if it is only the smallest chance. You must forgive my hesitation. I am an old man, and your story has been such a shock that I am unable to realise it yet. But I will not stand on punctilio when it is a question of trying to save a Penreath of Twelvetrees from the gallows. I think I can arrange it with the governor of the gaol to permit you to accompany me when I see Penreath in the morning. That interview is to take place at twelve o'clock. We can go together from here to the gaol, if that will suit you."

"That will suit me excellently. And before that interview takes place I should be glad if you would tell me the facts of Penreath's engagement to Miss Willoughby."

"I really know very little about it," said Mr. Oakham, looking somewhat surprised at the question. "I have heard, though, that Penreath met Miss Willoughby in London before the war, and became engaged after a very brief acquaintance. Ill-natured people say that the girl's aunt threw her at Penreath's head. The aunt is a Mrs. Brewer, a wealthy manufacturer's widow, a pushing nobody—"

"I have met her."

"I had forgotten. Well, you know that type of woman, with an itch to get into Society. Perhaps she thought that the marriage of her niece to a Penreath of Twelvetrees would open doors for her. At any rate, I remember there was a great deal of tittle-tattle at the time to the effect that she manoeuvred desperately hard to bring about the engagement. On the other hand, there can be no harm in stating now that Ronald Penreath's father was almost equally keen on that match for monetary reasons. The Penreaths are far from wealthy. From that point of view the match seemed suitable enough—money on one side, and birth and breeding on the other. I am not sure that there was very much love in the case, or that the young people's feelings were deeply involved on either side. There is no reason why I should not mention these things now, for the match has been broken off. It was broken off shortly after Penreath's arrest."

"By the young lady?"

"By the aunt, in her presence. It happened the day after they went to Heathfield to identify Penreath. Mrs. Brewer was furious about the whole business as soon as she ascertained that it wasn't a mistake, as she had hoped at first, and that there was likely to be much unpleasant publicity over it. She said she would never be able to hold up her head in Society after the disgrace, and all that sort of thing. It all came about through my asking Miss Willoughby if she would like to see her lover while he was awaiting trial. The girl replied, coldly enough, that it would be time enough to see him after he had cleared himself of the dreadful charge hanging over his head. By the way she spoke she seemed to think herself a deeply injured person, as perhaps she was. Then the aunt had her say, and insisted that I must tell Penreath the engagement was broken off. I asked Miss Willoughby if that was her wish also, and she replied that it was. I told Penreath the following day, but I do not think that it worried him very much."

"I do not think it would," replied Colwyn with a smile.

23

Colwyn found Mr. Oakham awaiting him in the hotel lobby, a little before eleven the following morning, to inform him that the necessary arrangements had been made to enable him to be present at his interview with Penreath. Colwyn forbore to ask him on what pretext he had obtained the gaol governor's consent to his presence, but merely signified that he was ready. Mr. Oakham replied that they had better go at once, and asked the porter to call a taxi.

On arriving at the gaol they passed through the double entrance gates, Mr. Oakham turned to a door on the left just within the gates, and entered. The door opened into a plainly furnished office, with walls covered with prison regulations. Behind a counter, at a stand-up desk opposite the door, a tall burly man in a uniform of blue and silver was busily writing in a large ledger. Ranged in rows, on hooks alongside him, were bunches of immense keys, and as he turned to attend to Oakham and Colwyn another bunch of similar keys could be seen dangling at his side. Mr. Oakham explained the purpose of their visit, and produced the order for the interview. The functionary in blue and silver, who was the entrance gaoler, perused it attentively, and pushed over two forms for the solicitor and the detective to fill in. It was the last formality that the law insisted on—a grim form of visiting card whereon the visitor inscribes his name and business, which is sent to the condemned man, who must give his consent to the interview before it is granted.

When Mr. Oakham and Colwyn had filled in their forms the entrance gaoler took them and pulled a rope. Somewhere in a corridor a bell clanged, and a moment afterwards a gaoler opened a small door on the other side of the counter. The entrance gaoler gave him the forms, and he disappeared with them. There ensued a long period of waiting, and nearly half an hour elapsed before he reappeared again, accompanied by a warder. The blue and silver functionary silently lifted the flap of the counter, and beckoned Mr. Oakham and Colwyn to accompany the warder through the small door at the other end of the room.

They went through and the bell clanged once more as the door closed behind them. The warder took them along a corridor to a door at the farther end, and ushered them into a room—a large apartment, not unlike a board room, furnished with a table and chairs ranged on each side. It was the governor of the gaol's room, where the interview was to take place. Colwyn took one of the chairs at the table, Mr. Oakham took another, and silently they awaited the coming of the condemned man.

Another quarter of an hour elapsed before the door at the other end of the room opened, and Penreath appeared between two warders. They conducted him to the table, and placed a chair for him. With a quick glance at his visitors he sat down, and the warders seated themselves on each side of him. The warder who had brought the visitors in then nodded to Mr. Oakham, as an indication that the interview might begin.

In the brief glance that the young man cast at his visitors Colwyn observed both calmness of mind and self-possession. Although deep shadows under the eyes and the tenseness of the muscles round the mouth revealed sleepless nights and mental agony, Penreath's face showed no trace of insanity or the guilty consciousness of evil deeds, but had the serene expression of a man who had fought his battle and won it.

Mr. Oakham began the interview with him in a dry professional way, as though it were an interview between solicitor and client in the sanctity of a private room, with no hearers. And, indeed, the prison warders sitting there with the impassive faces of officialdom might have been articles of furniture, so remote were they from displaying the slightest interest in the private matters discussed between the two. No doubt they had been present at many similar scenes, and custom is a deadening factor. Mr. Oakham's object was to urge his client to consent to the lodgement of an appeal against the jury's verdict, and to that end he advanced a multitude of arguments and a variety of reasons. The young man listened patiently, but when the solicitor had concluded he shook his head with a gesture of finality which indicated an unalterable refusal.

"It's no use, Oakham," he said. "My mind is quite made up. I'm obliged to you for all the trouble you have taken in my case, but I cannot alter my decision. I shall go through with it–to the end."

"In that case it is no use my urging you further." Mr. Oakham spoke stiffly, and put his eye-glasses in his pocket with an air of vexation. "Mr. Colwyn has something to say to you on the subject. Perhaps you will listen to him. He believes he can help you."

"He helped to arrest me," said Penreath, with a slight indifferent look at the detective.

"But not to convict you," said Colwyn. "I had hoped to help you."

"What do you want of me?" Penreath's tone was cold.

"In the first place, I have to say that I believe you innocent."

The young man lifted his eyebrows slightly, as if to indicate that the other's opinion was a matter of indifference to him, but he remained silent.

"I have come to beg of you, even at this late hour, to break your silence, and give an account of your actions that night at the inn."

"You might have saved yourself the trouble of coming here. I have nothing whatever to say."

"That means that you continue in your refusal to speak. Will you answer one or two questions?"

"No."

"Will you not tell me why you kept silence about what you saw in Mr. Glenthorpe's room that night of the murder?"

"Man, how did you find that out?" Penreath's calm disappeared in a sudden fury of voice and look. "What do you know?"

"I know whom you are trying to shield," replied the detective, with his eyes fixed on Penreath's face. "You are wrong. She—"

"I beg of you to be silent! Do not mention names, for God's sake." Penreath's face had grown suddenly white.

"It is in your power to ensure my silence."

"How?"

"By speaking yourself."

"That I will never do."

"Then you compel me to go to the authorities and tell them what I have discovered. I will save you in spite of yourself."

"Do you think that I want to be saved–like that?"

Struggling desperately for self-control Penreath turned to Mr. Oakham. "Why did you bring Mr. Colwyn here?" he asked the solicitor fiercely. "To torture me?"

Before Mr. Oakham could reply Colwyn laughed aloud. A clear ringing laugh of unmistakable satisfaction. The laugh sounded strangely incongruous in such a place.

"Penreath," he said, "you've told me all that I came here to know. You're a splendid young Briton, but finesse is not your strong point. You've acted like a quixotic young idiot in this case, and got yourself into a nice muddle for nothing. The girl is as innocent as you are, and you are a pair of simpletons! Yes. I mean what I say," continued the detective, answering the young man's amazed look with a reassuring smile. "Do you think that I would want to save you at her expense? Now perhaps, when I have told you what happened that night, you will answer a few questions. Before you went to bed you sat down and wrote a letter on a leaf torn from your pocket-book. That letter was to Miss Willoughby, breaking off your engagement. After writing it you went to bed. At that time it was raining hard.

"You must have fallen asleep almost immediately, and slept for half an hour–perhaps a little more–for when you awoke the rain had ceased. You heard a slight noise in your room, and lit your candle to see what it was. There was a rat in the corner of the room. You got up to throw something at it, but as soon as you moved the rat darted across the room and disappeared behind the wardrobe at the side of the bed. You pushed back the wardrobe and—"

"For God's sake, say no more!" said Penreath. His face was grey, and he was staring at the detective with the eyes of a man who saw his heart's secret–the secret for which he was prepared to die–being dragged out into the light of day. "How did you learn all this?"

"That does not matter much just now. What you saw through the wall made you determine to leave the house as speedily as possible, and also caused you to destroy the letter you had written to Miss Willoughby.

"You were wrong in what you did. In the first place, you misinterpreted what you saw through the door in the wall. By thinking Peggy guilty and leaving the inn early in the morning, you not only wronged her grievously, but brought suspicion on yourself. Peggy's presence in the room was quite by accident. She had gone to ask Mr. Glenthorpe to assist you in your trouble, by lending you money, and, finding the door open, she impulsively went in and found him dead–murdered. And at the bedside she picked up the knife–the knife you had used at dinner–and this."

Colwyn produced Penreath's match-box from his pocket and laid it on the table in front of him.

"Because of the knife and this match-box she thought you guilty."

"I! Why I never left my room after I went into it," exclaimed Penreath. "I left the match-box in the room where I had dined with Mr. Glenthorpe.

When I awoke after falling asleep, and heard the noise in the room—just as you describe—I could not find my match-box when I wanted a match to light my candle, then I remembered that I had left it in the sitting-room on the mantelpiece. I happened to find a loose match in my vest pocket."

"Peggy came to see me at my hotel, after the trial, and told me all she knew," continued Colwyn. "It was well she did, for my second visit to the inn brought to light a number of facts which will enable me to establish your innocence."

"And what about the real murderer?" asked Penreath, in a hesitating voice, without looking at the detective.

"We will not go into that just now, unless you have anything to tell me that will throw further light on the events of the night." Colwyn shot a keen, questioning glance at the young man.

"I will answer any questions you wish to put to me. It is the least I can do after having made such a fool of myself. It was the shock of seeing Peggy in the room that robbed me of my judgment. I should have known her better, but you must remember that I had no idea she was in the house until I looked through the door in the wall which I had accidentally discovered, and saw her standing at the bedside, with the knife in her hand. I started to follow her home that day because I wished to know more about her. I lost my way in the mist. I met a man on the marshes who directed me to the village and the inn."

"When she heard your voice, and saw you going upstairs, she waited about in the hope of seeing you before she went to bed, as she wished to avoid meeting you in the presence of her father. When she saw Mr. Glenthorpe's door open she acted on a sudden impulse, and went in."

"I have been rightly punished for my stupidity and my folly," said Penreath. "I have wronged her beyond forgiveness."

"You really have not much to blame yourself for except your obstinate silence. That was really too quixotic, even if things had been as you imagined. No man is justified in sacrificing his life foolishly. And you had much to live for. You had your duty to do in life. Nobody knew that better than you—a soldier who had served his country gallantly and well. In fact, your silence has been to me one of the puzzles of this case, and even now it seems to me that you must have had a deeper motive than that of shielding the girl, because you could have asserted your innocence without implicating her."

"You are a very clever man, Colwyn," said the other slowly. "There was another reason for my silence."

"What was it?"

"I am supposed to be an epileptic. I happen to know a little of the course of that frightful disease, and it seemed to me that it was better to die—even at the hands of the hangman—than to live on to be a burden to my friends and relations, particularly when by dying I could shield the girl I loved. That is why I was glad when the plea put up for my defence failed. I preferred to die rather than live branded as a criminal lunatic. So, you see, it was not such a great sacrifice on my part, after all."

"What brought you back to the wood where you were arrested?"

"To see her. I do not know if I wanted to speak to her; but I wanted above all things to see her once again. When I left the inn that morning I had no idea that I might fall under suspicion for having committed the murder, but I was desperately unhappy after what I had seen the night before, and I didn't care what I did or where I went. Instead of walking back to Durrington I struck across the marshes in the opposite direction. I walked along all day, through a desolate area of marshes, meeting nobody except an old eel fisherman in the morning, and, later on, a labourer going home from his work. I was very tired when I saw the labourer, and I asked him to direct me to some place where I could obtain rest and refreshment. He pointed to a short cut across the marshes, which, he said, led to a hamlet with an inn. I went along the path he had pointed out, but I lost my way in the gathering darkness. After wandering about the marshes for some time I saw the light of a cottage window some distance off, and went there to inquire my way. The occupant, an old peasant woman, could not have heard anything about the murder, for she was very kind to me, and gave me tea and food. Afterwards I set out for the inn again, and when I reached the road I sat down by the side of it to rest awhile.

"While I was sitting there two men came along. They did not see me in the dark, and I heard them talking about the murder, and from what they said I knew that I was suspected, and that the whole country side was searching for me. It seemed incredible to me, and my first instinct was to fly. I sat there until the men's voices died away in the distance, then I turned off the road, and hurried across some fields, looking for a place to hide. After walking some distance I came to a large barn, standing by itself. The door was open, and I went in. I had no matches, but I felt some hay or straw on the floor. I lay down and pulled some over me, and fell fast asleep.

"I had only intended to rest in the barn for a while, but I was so tired that I slept all night. When I awoke it was broad daylight. I did not know where I was at first, but it all came back to me, and I started up in a fright, determined to leave the barn as quickly as possible, for I knew it was an unsafe hiding place, and likely to be searched at any time. But before I could get away I heard loud voices approaching, and I knew I should be seen. I looked hastily around for some place of concealment. It was just a big empty shed with one or two shelves covered with apples, and a lot of straw on the floor. In desperation, as the voices came nearer, I lay down on the floor again, and pulled straw over me till I was completely hidden from view.

"The door opened, and some men looked in. Through the straw that covered me I could see them quite distinctly–three fishermen and a farm labourer–though apparently they couldn't see me. From their conversation I gathered that they formed part of a search party looking for me, and had been told off to search the barn. This apparently they were not anxious to do, for they merely peeped in at the door, and one of them, in rather a relieved tone, said I wasn't in there, wherever I was. One of the fishermen replied that he expected that I was far enough off by that time. They stood at the door for a few moments, talking about the murder, and then they went away.

"I stayed in the barn all day, but nobody else came near me. When it was dark, I filled my pockets with apples from the shelves, and went out. I wandered about all night, and found myself close to a railway station at daybreak. I had been in that part of the country before, so I knew where I was–not far from Heathfield, with Flegne about three miles away across the fields. The country was nearly all open, and consequently unsafe. As I walked through a field I spied a little hut, almost hidden from view in a clump of trees. The door was open, and I could see it was empty. I went in, lay down, and fell fast asleep.

"When I awoke it was getting dusk. I was very stiff and cold, so I started out walking again to get myself warm. It was then, I remember well, that the longing came over me to see Peggy again. I cursed myself for my weakness, knowing what I knew–or thought I knew, God forgive me.

"I found myself making my way back to Flegne as fast as my legs would carry me–which wasn't very fast, because I was weak from want of food, and so footsore that I could hardly stumble along. But I got over the three miles somehow, and reached the wood, where I crawled into some undergrowth, and lay there all night, sometimes dozing, sometimes wide awake, and sometimes a bit light-headed, I think. It was there you found me next day, and I was glad you did. I was about finished when I saw you looking through the bushes and only too glad to come out. I didn't care what happened to me then. And now, I have told you all."

The young man, as he finished his story, buried his face in his hands, as though overcome by the recollection of the mental anguish he had been through, and what he had endured.

"Not quite all, I think," said Colwyn, after a pause.

"I have told you everything that counts," said Penreath, without looking up.

"You have not," replied the detective firmly. "You have not told me all you saw when you were looking through the door between the two rooms the night of the murder."

Penreath raised his head and regarded the other with startled eyes.

"What do you mean?" he said, in a whisper.

"I mean that you have kept back that you saw the body removed," he said grimly.

"Are you a man or a wizard?" cried Penreath fiercely. "God! how did you find that out?"

"By guess work, if you like," responded the other coolly. "Listen to me! There has been too much concealment about this case already, so let us have no more of it. It was because of what you saw afterwards that your suspicions were doubly fastened on the girl, is that not so? I thought as much," he continued, as the other nodded without speaking. "How long after Peggy left the room was it before the body was removed?"

"Not very long," replied Penreath. "After she went out of the room I sat on the bedside. I did not close the small door I had discovered, or replace the wardrobe. I was too overwhelmed. In a little while—perhaps ten minutes—I saw a light shine through the hole again. I went to it and looked through—God knows why—and I saw somebody walking stealthily into the room, carrying a candle. He went to the bedside and, with a groan, lifted the body on to his shoulders, and carried it out of the room. I crept to my door, and looked out and saw him descending the stairs. God in heaven, what a horror, what a horror!

"I waited to see no more. I shut the door in the wall, pulled the wardrobe back into its place and determined to leave the accursed inn as soon as it was daylight. In my cell at nights, when I hear the footsteps of the warder sounding along the corridor and dying away in the distance, it reminds me of how I stood at the door that night, listening to the sound of the footsteps stumbling down the staircase."

"You heard the footsteps distinctly, then?" said the detective.

"Distinctly and clearly. The staircase is a stone one, as you know."

"Did you put your boots out to be cleaned before you went to bed?"

"Yes."

"And were they there when you looked out of the door?"

"I do not remember. But I know they were there in the morning, dirty and covered with clay. I took them in, and was about to put them on, when the servant knocked at the door with a cup of morning tea. I answered the door with the boots in my hand. She offered to clean them for me, and was taking them away, but I called her back and said I would not wait for them. I was too anxious to get away from the place."

"Do you remember when you lost the rubber heel of one of them?"

"It must have been when I was walking the previous day. They were only put on the day before. I happened to mention to a bootmaker at Durrington that my left heel had become jarred with walking. He recommended me to try rubber heels to lessen the strain, and he put them on for me. I had never worn them before, and found them very uncomfortable when I was walking along the marshes. They seemed to hold and stick in the wet ground."

"And now there are one or two other points I want you to make clear. Why did you register in the name of James Ronald at the Durrington Hotel?"

"That was merely a whim. I was disgusted with London and society after my return from the front. Those who have been through this terrible war learn to see most things at their true worth, and the frivolity, the snobbishness, and the shams of London society at such a time sickened and disgusted me. They tried to lionise me in drawing rooms and make me talk for their entertainment. They put my photograph in the illustrated papers, and interviewed me, and all that kind of thing. What had I done! Nothing! Not a tithe of what thousands of better men are doing every day out there. So I went away from it all. I had no intention, when I went into the hotel, of not registering in my full name though. That came about in a peculiar way. It was the first registration form I had seen—it was the first hotel I had stayed at after nearly eighteen months at the front—and I put down my two christian names, James Ronald, in the wrong space, the space for the surname, which is the first column. I saw my error as I glanced over the form, but the girl, thinking I had filled it up, took it away from me. It then struck me that it was just as well to let it go; it would prevent my being worried by fools."

"And how came it that you ran so short of money that you had to leave the hotel?"

"I have practically nothing except what my father allows me, and which is paid quarterly through his bankers in London. I left London with a few pounds in my pocket, and thought no more about money until the hotel proprietor stopped me one morning and asked me politely to discharge my bill, as I was a stranger to him. It was then that I first realised the difference between a name like Penreath of Twelvetrees and plain James Ronald. I was furious, and told him he should have the money in two days, as soon as I could communicate with my London bankers. I wrote straight away, and asked them to send me some money. The money came, the morning I was turned out of the hotel; I saw the letter in the rack, addressed to J. R. Penreath, but what good was that to me? I could not claim it because I was booked in the name of James Ronald. I knew nobody in the place to whom I could apply. I had some thoughts of confiding in the hotel proprietor, but one look at his face was sufficient to put that out of the question.

"So I went in to breakfast, desperately angry at being treated so, and feeling more than a little ill. You know what happened at the breakfast table. I began to feel pretty seedy, and left my place to get to the fresh air, when that doctor–Sir Henry Durwood–jumped up and grabbed me. I tried to push him off, but he was too strong for me, and I found myself going. The next thing I knew was that I was lying in my bedroom, and hearing somebody talk. After you had left the room I determined to leave the hotel as quickly as possible. I packed a small handbag, and told the hotel-keeper on my way downstairs that he could keep my things until I paid my bill. Then I walked to Leyland Hoop, where I had an appointment with Peggy, as you know. I seem to have acted as a pretty considerable ass all round," said the young man, with a rueful smile. "But I had a bad gruelling from shell-shock. I wouldn't mention this, but it's really affected my head, you know, and I don't think I'm always quite such a fool as this story makes me appear to be."

"And your nerves were a bit rattled by the Zeppelin raid at Durrington, were they not?" said Colwyn sympathetically.

"You seem to know everything," said the young man, flushing. "I am ashamed to say that they were."

"You have no cause to be ashamed," replied Colwyn gently. "The bravest men suffer that way after shell-shock."

"It's not a thing a man likes to talk about," said Penreath, after a pause. "But if you have had experience of this kind of thing, will you tell me if you have ever seen a man completely recover–from shell-shock, I mean?"

"I should say you will be quite yourself again shortly. There cannot be very much the matter with your nerves to have stood the experience of the last few weeks. After we get you out of here, and you have had a good rest, you will be yourself again."

"And what about this other thing–this *furor epilepticus*, whatever it is?" asked Penreath, anxiously.

"As you didn't murder anybody, you haven't had the epileptic fury," replied Colwyn, laughing.

"But Sir Henry Durwood said at the trial that I was an epileptic," persisted the other.

"He was wrong about the *furor epilepticus*, so it is just as likely that he was wrong about the epilepsy. His theory was that you were going to attack somebody at the breakfast table of the hotel, and you have just told us that you had no intention of attacking anybody–that your only idea was to get out of the room. You are neither an epileptic nor insane, in my opinion, but at that time you were suffering from the after effects of shell-shock. Take my advice, and forget all about the trial and what you heard there, or, if you must think of it, remember the excellent certificate of sanity and clear-headedness which the doctors for the Crown gave you! When you get free I'll take you to half a dozen specialists who'll probably confirm the Crown point of view." Penreath laughed for the first time.

"You've made me feel like a new man," he said. "How can I thank you for all you have done?"

"The only way you can show your gratitude is by instructing Mr. Oakham to lodge an appeal for you–at once. Have you the necessary forms with you, Mr. Oakham?"

"I have," said the solicitor, finding voice after a long silence.

24

Mr. Oakham did not discuss what had taken place in the prison as he and Colwyn drove to the office of the chief constable after the interview. He sat silent in his corner of the taxi, his hands clasped before him, and gazing straight in front of him with the look of a man who sees nothing. From time to time his lips moved after the fashion of the old, when immersed in thought, and once he audibly murmured, "The poor lad; the poor lad." Colwyn forbore to speak to him. He realised that he had had a shock, and was best left to himself.

By the time the taxi reached the office of the chief constable Mr. Oakham showed symptoms of regaining his self-possession. He felt for his eye-glasses, polished them, placed them on his nose and glanced at his watch. It was in something like his usual tones that he asked Colwyn, as they alighted from the cab, whether he had an appointment with the chief constable.

"I wired to you both at the same time," replied the detective. "I asked him to keep this afternoon free," he explained with a smile.

A police constable in the outer office took in their names. He speedily returned with the message that the chief constable would be glad to see them, and would they step this way, please. Following in his wake, they were conducted along a passage and into a large comfortably furnished room, where Mr. Cromering was writing at a small table placed near a large fire. He looked up as the visitors entered, put down his pen, and came forward to greet them.

"I am pleased to see you again, Mr. Colwyn, and you also, Mr. Oakham.

Please draw your chairs near the fire gentlemen–
there's a decided nip in the air. I got your telegram, Mr.
Colwyn, and I am at your disposal, with plenty of time.
Your telegram rather surprised me. What has happened
in the Glenthorpe case?"

"Fresh facts have come to light–facts that tend to
prove the innocence of Penreath, who was accused and
convicted for the murder."

"Dear me! This is a very grave statement. What proofs
have you?"

"Sufficient to warrant further steps in the case. It is a
long story, but I think when you have heard it you will
feel justified in taking prompt action."

Before Mr. Cromering could reply, the police constable
who had shown in Colwyn and Mr. Oakham entered the
room and said that Superintendent Galloway, from
Durrington, was outside.

"Bring him in, Johnson," said Mr. Cromering. He
turned to Colwyn and added: "When I received your
telegram I telephoned to Galloway and asked him to be
here this afternoon. As he worked up the case against
Penreath, I thought it better that he should be present
and hear what you have to say. You have no objection, I
suppose?"

"On the contrary, I shall be very glad for Galloway to
hear what I have to say."

The police constable returned, ushering in
Superintendent Galloway, who looked rather surprised
when he saw his superior officer's visitors. He nodded
briefly to Colwyn, and looked inquiringly at the chief
constable.

"Mr. Colwyn has discovered some fresh facts in the
Glenthorpe murder, Galloway," explained Mr. Cromering.
"I sent for you in order that you might hear what they
are."

"What sort of facts?" asked Galloway, with a quick
glance at the detective.

"That is what Mr. Colwyn proposes to explain to us."

"I shall have to go back to the beginning of our investigations to do so–to the day when we motored from Durrington to Flegne," said the detective. "We went there with the strong presumption in our minds that Penreath was the criminal, because of suspicious facts previously known about him. He was short of money, he had concealed his right name when registering at the hotel, and his behaviour at the breakfast table the morning of his departure suggested an unbalanced temperament. It is a legal axiom that men's minds are influenced by facts previously known or believed, and we set out to investigate this case under the strong presumption that Penreath, and none other, was the murderer.

"The evidence we found during our visit to the inn fitted in with this theory, and inclined the police to shut out the possibility of any alternative theory because of the number of concurrent points which fitted in with the presumption that Penreath was the murderer. There was, first, the fact that the murderer had entered through the window. Penreath had been put to sleep in the room next the murdered man, in an unoccupied part of the inn, and could easily have got from one window to the other without being seen or heard. Next was the fact that the murder had been committed with a knife with a round end. Penreath had used such a knife when dining with Mr. Glenthorpe, and that knife was afterwards missing. Next, we have him hurriedly departing from the inn soon after daybreak, refusing to wait till his boots were cleaned, and paying his bill with a Treasury note.

"Then came the discovery of the footprints to the pit where the body had been thrown, and those footprints were incontestably made by Penreath's boots. The stolen notes suggested a strong motive in the case of a man badly in need of money, and the payment of his bill with a Treasury note of the first issue suggested–though not very strongly–that he had given the servant one of the stolen notes. These were the main points in the circumstantial evidence against Penreath. The stories of the landlord of the inn, the deaf waiter, and the servant supported that theory in varying degrees, and afforded an additional ground for the credibility of the belief that Penreath was the murderer. The final and most convincing proof–Penreath's silence under the accusation–does not come into the narrative of events at this point, because he had not been arrested.

"It was when we visited the murdered man's bedroom that the first doubts came to my mind as to the conclusiveness of the circumstantial evidence against Penreath. The theory was that Penreath, after murdering Mr. Glenthorpe, put the body on his shoulder, and carried it downstairs and up the rise to the pit. The murderer entered through the window–the bits of red mud adhering to the carpet prove that conclusively enough–but if Penreath was the murderer where had he got the umbrella with which he shielded himself from the storm? The fact that the murderer carried an umbrella is proved by the discovery of a small patch of umbrella silk which had got caught on a nail by the window. Again, why should a man, getting from one window to another, bother about using an umbrella for a journey of a few feet only? He would know that he could not use it when carrying the body to the pit, for that task would require both his hands. And what had Penreath done with the umbrella afterwards?

"The clue of the umbrella silk, and the pool of water near the window where the murderer placed the umbrella after getting into the room, definitely fixed the time of the murder between eleven and 11.30 p.m., because the violent rainstorm on that night ceased at the latter hour. If Penreath was the murderer, he waited until the storm ceased before removing the body. There were no footprints outside the window where the murderer got in, because they were obliterated by the rain. On the other hand, the footsteps to the pit where the body was thrown were clear and distinct, proving conclusively that no rain fell after the murderer left the house with his burden. It seemed to me unlikely that a man after committing a murder would coolly sit down beside his victim and wait for the rain to cease before disposing of the body. His natural instinct would be to hide the evidence of his crime as quickly as possible.

"These points, however, were of secondary importance, merely tending to shake slightly what lawyers term the probability of the case against Penreath. But a point of more importance was my discovery that the candle-grease dropped on the carpet was of two different kinds—wax and tallow—suggesting that two different persons were in the room on the night of the murder. Mr. Glenthorpe did not use a candle, but a reading lamp. Neither did Mr. Glenthorpe use the gas globe in the middle of the room. Yet that gas tap was turned on slightly when we examined the room, and the globe and the incandescent burner smashed. Who turned on the tap, and who smashed the globe? Penreath is not tall enough to have struck it with his head. Superintendent Galloway's theory was that it might have been done by the murderer when throwing the body of his victim over his shoulder.

"An ideal case of circumstantial evidence may be weakened, but not destroyed, by the destruction of one or more of the collateral facts which go to make it up. There are two kinds of circumstantial evidence. In one kind presumption of guilt depends on a series of links forming a chain. In the other, the circumstances are woven together like the strands of a rope. That is the ideal case of circumstantial evidence, because the rope still holds when some of the strands are severed. The case against Penreath struck me as resembling a chain, which is no stronger than its weakest link. The strongest link in the chain of circumstances against Penreath was the footprints leading to the pit. They had undoubtedly been made by his boots, but circumstances can lie as well as witnesses, and in both cases the most plausible sometimes prove the greatest liars. Take away the clue of the footprints, and the case against Penreath was snapped in the most vital link. The remaining circumstances in the case against him, though suspicious enough, were open to an alternative explanation. The footprints were the damning fact–the link on which the remaining links of the chain were hung.

"But the elimination of the clue of the footprints did not make the crime any easier of solution. From the moment I set foot in the room it struck me as a deep and baffling mystery, looking at it from the point of view of the police theory or from any other hypothesis. If Penreath had indeed committed the murder, who was the second visitor to the room? And if Penreath had not committed the murder, who had?

"That night, in my room, I sought to construct two alternative theories of the murder. In the first place, I examined the case thoroughly from the police point of view, with Penreath as the murderer. In view of what has come to light since the trial, there is no need to take up time with giving you my reasons for doubting whether Penreath had committed the crime. I explained those reasons to Superintendent Galloway at the time, pointing out, as he will doubtless remember, that the police theory struck me as illogical in some aspects, and far from convincing as a whole. There were too many elements of uncertainty in it, too much guess-work, too much jumping at conclusions. Take one point alone, on which I laid stress at the time. The police theory originally started from the point of Penreath's peculiar behaviour at the Durrington hotel, which, from their point of view, suggested homicidal mania. To my mind, there was no evidence to prove this, although that theory was actually put forth by the defence at Penreath's trial. I witnessed the scene at the breakfast table, and, in my opinion, Sir Henry Durwood acted hastily and wrongly in rushing forward and seizing Penreath. There was nothing in his behaviour that warranted it. He was a little excited, and nothing more, and from what I have heard since he had reason to be excited. Neither at the breakfast table nor in his room subsequently did his actions strike me as the actions of a man of insane, neurotic, or violent temperament. He was simply suffering from nerves. It is important to remember, in recalling the events which led up to this case, that Penreath was invalided out of the Army suffering from shell-shock, and that two nights before the scene at the hotel there was an air raid at Durrington. Shell-shock victims are always prejudicially affected by air raids.

"Even if the police theory had been correct on this point, it seemed inconceivable to me that a man affected with homicidal tendencies would have displayed such cold-blooded caution and cunning in carrying out a murder for gain, as the murderer at the *Golden Anchor* did. The Crown dropped this point at the trial. I merely mention it now in support of my contention that the case of circumstantial evidence against Penreath was by no means a strong one, because it originally depended, in part, on inferred facts which the premises did not warrant.

"Next, the discoveries made in the room where the murder was committed, and certain other indications found outside, did not fit in with the police case against Penreath. Superintendent Galloway's reconstruction of the crime, after he had seen the body and examined the inn premises, did not account for the existence of all the facts. There were circumstances and clues which were not consistent with the police theory of the murder. The probability of the inference that Penreath was the murderer was not increased by the discoveries we made. I am aware that absolute proof is not essential to conviction in a case of circumstantial evidence, but, on the other hand, to ignore facts which do not accord with a theory is to go to the other extreme, for by so doing you are in danger of excluding the possibility of any alternative theory.

"On the other hand, when I sought to account for the crime by any other hypothesis I found myself puzzled at every turn. The presence of two persons in the room was the baffling factor. The murderer had entered through the window in the storm, lighted the tallow candle which he brought with him, walked straight to the bed and committed the murder. Then he had waited till the rain ceased before carrying the body downstairs to the pit. But what about the second person–the person who had carried the wax candle and dropped spots of grease underneath the broken gas globe? Had he come in at a different time, and why? Why had he sought to light the gas, when he carried a candle? Why had he–as I subsequently ascertained–left the room and gone downstairs to turn on the gas at the meter?

"Eliminating Penreath for the time being, I tried next to fit in the clues I had discovered with two alternative theories. Had the murder been committed from outside by a villager, or by somebody in the inn? There were possibilities about the former theory which I pointed out to Superintendent Galloway, who subsequently investigated them, and declared that there was no ground for the theory that the murder had been committed from outside. The theory that the murder had been committed by somebody inside the inn turned my attention to the inmates of the inn. Excluding Penreath for the time being, there were five inmates inside the walls the night the murder was committed–the innkeeper, his daughter, his mother, the waiter, and Ann, the servant. The girl could hardly have committed the murder, and could certainly not have carried away the body. The old mad woman might have committed the murder if she could have got out of her room, but she could not have carried the body to the pit–neither could the servant. By this process of elimination there remained the landlord and the deaf waiter. "For a reason which it is not necessary to explain now, my thoughts turned to the waiter when I first saw the body of the murdered man. The possibility that he was the murderer was strengthened by the slight clue of the line in the clay which I found underneath the murdered man's bedroom window. That window is about five feet from the ground outside, and the waiter, who is short and stout, could not have climbed through the window without something to stand on. But the waiter could not possibly have carried the body to the pit. His right arm is malformed, and only a very strong man, with two strong arms, could have performed that feat.

"There remained the innkeeper. He was the only person on the inn premises that night, except Penreath, who could have carried the corpse downstairs and thrown it into the pit. Although thin, I should say he is a man of great physical strength. It is astonishing to think, in looking back over all the circumstances of this extraordinary case, that some suspicion was not diverted to him in the first instance. He was very hard-pressed for money, and he knew for days beforehand that Mr. Glenthorpe was going to draw £300 from the bank–a circumstance that Penreath could not possibly have known when he sought chance shelter at the inn that night. He was the only person in the place tall enough to have smashed the gas globe and incandescent burner in Mr. Glenthorpe's room by striking his head against it. He knew the run of the place and the way to the pit intimately–far better than a stranger like Penreath could. I was struck with that fact when we were examining the footprints. The undeviating course from the inn to the mouth of the pit suggested an intimate acquaintance with the way. The man who carried the body to the pit in the darkness knew every inch of the ground.

"It is easy to be wise after the event, but my thoughts and suspicions were centering more and more around the innkeeper when Penreath was arrested. His attitude altered the whole aspect of the case. His hesitating answers to me in the wood, his fatalistic acceptance of the charge against him, seemed to me equivalent to a confession of guilt, so I abandoned my investigations and returned to Durrington.

"I was wrong. It was a mistake for which I find it difficult to forgive myself. Penreath's hesitation, his silence—what were they in the balance of probabilities in such a strange deep crime as this murder? In view of the discoveries I had already made—discoveries which pointed to a most baffling mystery—I should not have allowed myself to be swerved from my course by Penreath's silence in the face of accusation, inexplicable though it appeared at the time. You know what happened subsequently. Penreath, persisting in his silence, was tried, convicted, and sentenced to death—because of that silence, which compelled the defence to rely on a defence of insanity which they could not sustain.

"I went back to the inn a second time, not of my own volition, but because of a story told me by the innkeeper's daughter, Peggy, at Durrington four days ago. The night before the inquest Peggy paid a visit to the room in which the murdered man lay. I did not see her go in, but I saw her come out. She went downstairs and hurried across the marshes and threw something into the sea from the top of the breakwater. The following day, after Penreath's arrest, I questioned her. She gave me an explanation which was hardly plausible, but Penreath's silence, coming after the accumulation of circumstances against him, had caused me to look at the case from a different angle, and I did not cross-examine her. The object of her visit to me after the trial was to admit that she had not told me the truth previously. Her amended story was obviously the true one. She and Penreath had met by chance on the seashore near Leyland Hoop two or three weeks before, and had met secretly afterward. The subsequent actions of these two foolish young people prove, convincingly enough, that they had fallen passionately in love with each other. Peggy, however, had never told Penreath her name or where she lived–because she knew her position was different from his, she says– and she could not understand how he came to be at the inn that night. Naturally, she was very much perturbed at his unexpected appearance. She waited for an opportunity to speak to him after hearing his voice, but was compelled to attend on her mad grandmother until it was very late.

"Before going to bed she went down the passage to see if by any chance he had not retired. There was a light in Mr. Glenthorpe's room, and, acting on a sudden girlish impulse, she ran along the passage to Mr. Glenthorpe's door, intending to confide her troubles in one who had always been very good and kind to her. The door was partly open, and as she got no reply to her knock, she entered. Mr. Glenthorpe was lying on his bed, murdered, and on the floor–at the side of the bed–she found the knife and this silver and enamel match-box. She hid the knife behind a picture on the wall. She did a very plucky thing the following night by going into the dead man's room and removing the knife in order to prevent the police finding it, for by that time she was aware that the knife formed an important piece of evidence in the case against her lover. It was the knife she threw into the sea, but she kept the match-box, which she recognised as Penreath's. When she came to me she did not intend to tell me anything about the match-box if she could help it. She was frank enough up to a point, but beyond that point she did not want to go.

"After Penreath's conviction she began, womanlike, to wonder if she had not been too hasty in assuming his guilt, and as the time slipped by and brought the day of his doom nearer she grew desperate, and as a last resource she came to me. It was a good thing she did so. For her story, though apparently making the case against Penreath blacker still, incidentally brought to light a clue which threw a new light on the case and decided me to

return to Flegne. That clue is contained in the match-
box."

25

Colwyn opened the silver and enamel box, and emptied the matches on the table.

"I showed this match-box to Charles on my return to the inn, and he told me that Penreath used it in the upstairs sitting-room the night he dined there with Mr. Glenthorpe. Therefore, it is a reasonable deduction to assume that he had no other matches in his possession the night of the murder.

"This fact is highly significant, because the matches in Penreath's silver box are, as you see, blue-headed wax matches, whereas the matches struck in Mr. Glenthorpe's room on the night of the murder were of an entirely different description—wooden matches with pink heads, of British manufacture—so-called war matches, with cork pine sticks. The sticks of these matches break rather easily unless they are held near the head. Two broken fragments of this description of match, with unlighted heads, were found in Mr. Glenthorpe's room the morning after the murder. Superintendent Galloway picked up one by the foot of the bed, and I picked up the other under the broken gas-globe. The recovery of Penreath's match-box in the murdered man's room suggested several things. In the first place, if he had no other matches in his possession except those in his silver and enamel box, he was neither the murderer nor the second person who visited the room that night. But if my deduction about the matches was correct, how was it that his match-box was found in the murdered man's room? The inference is that Penreath left his match-box in the dining room after lighting his candle before going to bed, and the murderer found it and took it into Mr. Glenthorpe's bedroom to point suspicion towards Penreath.

"This fact opened up a new possibility about the crime—the possibility that Penreath was the victim of a conspiracy. When we were examining the footprints which led to the pit, the possibility of somebody else having worn Penreath's boots occurred to me, because I have seen that trick worked before, but the servant's story suggested that Penreath did not put his boots outside his door to be cleaned, but came to the door with them in his hand in the morning. But Penreath told me this morning that he put out his boots overnight to be cleaned, but had taken them back into his room before Ann brought up his tea. The murderer, therefore, had ample opportunity to use them for his purpose of carrying the body to the pit and to put them back afterwards outside Penreath's door.

"But Peggy's belated admissions did more than suggest that Penreath was the victim of a sinister plot—they narrowed down the range of persons by whom it could have been contrived. The plotter was not only an inmate of the inn, but somebody who had seen the match box and knew that it belonged to Penreath.

"I returned to Flegne to resume the investigations I had broken off nearly three weeks before, and from that point my discoveries were very rapid, all tending to throw suspicion on Benson. The first indication was the outcome of a remark of mine about his height, and the broken gas light in Mr. Glenthorpe's bedroom. It was purely a chance shot, but it threw him into a pitiable state of excitement. I let him think, however, that it was nothing more than a chance remark. That night I was put to sleep in Penreath's room, and there I made two discoveries. The first was the existence of a small door, behind the wardrobe, opening on a corresponding door on the other side, which in its turn opens into Mr. Glenthorpe's room. Thus it would be possible for a person in the room Penreath occupied, discovering these doors as I did, to see into the next bedroom—under certain conditions. My second discovery was the outcome of my first discovery—I picked up underneath the wardrobe a fragment of an appealing letter which Penreath had commenced to write to his fiancée, and had subsequently torn up. It was a long time before I grasped the full significance of these two discoveries. Why should a man, after writing a letter of appeal to his fiancée, decide not to send it and destroy it? The most probable reason was that something had happened to cause him to change his mind. What could have happened to change the conditions so quickly? The hidden doors in the wall, which looked into the next room, supplied an answer to the question. Penreath had looked through, and seen–what? My first thought was that he had seen the murder committed, but that theory did not account for the destruction of the letter, and his silence when arrested, unless, indeed, the girl had committed the murder. The girl–Peggy! It came to me like a flash, the solution of the strangest aspect of this puzzling case–the reason why Penreath maintained his dogged silence under an accusation of murder.

"It came to me, the clue for which I had been groping, with the recollection of a phrase in the girl's story to me– her second story–in which she not only told me of her efforts to shield Penreath, but revealed frankly to me her relations with Penreath, innocent enough, but commenced in chance fashion, and continued by clandestine meetings in lonely spots. I remembered when she told me about it all that I was impressed by Penreath's absolute straightforwardness in his dealings with this girl. He was open and sincere with her throughout, gave her his real name, and told her much about himself: his family, his prospects, and even his financial embarrassment. He went further than that: he told her that he was engaged to be married, and that if he could get free he would marry her. A young man who talks in this strain is very much in love. The artless story of Peggy revealed that Penreath was as much in love with the girl as she was with him. 'If he could get free!' That was the phrase that gave me the key to the mystery. He had set out to get free by writing to Miss Willoughby, breaking off his engagement. Later he had torn up the letter because through the door in the wall he had seen Peggy standing by the bedside of the murdered man, and had come to the conclusion that she had murdered him.

"If you think it a little strange that Penreath should have jumped to this conclusion about the woman he loved, you must remember the circumstances were unusual. Peggy had surrounded herself with mystery; she refused to tell her lover where she lived, she would not even tell him her name. When he looked into the room he did not even know she was in the house, because she had kept out of his way during the previous evening, waiting for an opportunity to see him alone. Consequently he experienced a great shock at the sight of her, and the mystery with which she had always veiled her identity and movements recurred to him with a terrible and sinister significance as he saw her again under such damning conditions, standing by the bedside of the dead man with a knife in her hand.

"Penreath's subsequent actions—his destruction of the letter he had written to Miss Willoughby, his hurried departure from the inn, and his silence in the face of accusation—are all explained by the fact that he saw the girl Peggy in the next room, and believed that she had committed this terrible crime.

"I now come to the clues which point directly to Benson's complicity in the murder. I have already told you of his alarm at my chance remark about his height and the smashed gas globe. You also know that he was in need of money. The next point is rather a curious one. When Benson was telling us his story the day after the murder I observed that he kept smoothing his long hair down on his forehead. There was something in the action that suggested more than a mannerism. The night after I discovered the door in the wall, I left it open in order to watch the next room. During the night Benson entered and searched the dead man's chamber. I do not know what he was looking for–he did not find it, whatever it was–but during the search he grew hot, and threw back his hair from his forehead, revealing a freshly healed scar on his temple. The reason he had worn his hair low was explained: he wanted to hide from us the fact that it was he who had smashed the gas-globe in Mr. Glenthorpe's room, and had cut his head by the accident.

"But his visit to the dead man's room revealed more than the scar on his forehead. How did Benson get into the room? The room had been kept locked since the murder. That night I had taken the key from a hook on the kitchen dresser in order to examine the room when the inmates of the place had retired. Benson, therefore, had let himself in with another key. This was our first knowledge of another key. Hitherto we had believed that the only key was the one found in the outside of the door the morning after the murder. The police theory is partly based on that supposition. Benson's possession of a second key, and his silence concerning it, point strongly to his complicity in the crime. He knew that Mr. Glenthorpe was accustomed to lock his door and carry the key about with him, so he obtained another key in order to have access to the room whenever he desired. There would have been nothing in this if he had told his household about it. A second key would have been useful to the servant when she wanted to arrange Mr. Glenthorpe's room. But Benson kept the existence of the second key a close secret. He said nothing about it when we questioned him concerning the key in the door. An innocent man would have immediately informed us that there was a second key to the room. Benson kept silence because he had something to hide.

"I now come to the events of the next morning. My investigation of the rise and the pit during the afternoon had led to a discovery which subsequently suggested to my mind that the missing money had been hidden in the pit. I determined to try and descend it. I arose before daybreak, as I did not wish any of the inmates of the inn to see me. Before going to the pit I got out of the window and into the window of the next room, as Penreath is supposed to have done. That experiment brought to light another small point in Penreath's favour. The drop from the first window is an awkward one—more than eight feet—and my heels made a deep indentation in the soft red clay underneath the window. If Penreath had dropped from the window, even in his stocking feet, the marks of his heels ought to have been visible. There was not enough rain after the murder was committed to obliterate them entirely. There were no such marks under his window when we examined the ground the morning after the murder.

"I next proceeded to the rise and lowered myself down the pit by the creepers inside. About ten feet down the vegetable growth ceased, and the further descent was impossible without ropes. But at the limit of the distance to which a man can climb down unaided, I saw a peg sticking into the side of the pit, with a fishing line suspended from it. I drew up the line, and found attached to it the murdered man's pocket-book containing the £300 he had drawn out of the bank at Heathfield the day he was murdered.

"Let me now try to reconstruct the crime in the light of the fresh information we have gained. Benson was in desperate straits for money, and he knew that Mr. Glenthorpe had drawn £300 from the bank that morning, all in small notes, which could not be traced. The fact that he obtained a second key to the room suggests that he had been meditating the act for some time past. It will be found, I think, when all the facts are brought to light, that he obtained the second key when he learnt that Mr. Glenthorpe intended to take a large sum of money out of the bank. Penreath's chance arrival at the inn on the day that the money was drawn out, probably set him thinking of the possibility of murdering and robbing Mr.

Glenthorpe in circumstances that would divert suspicion to the stranger. Penreath unconsciously helped him by leaving his match-box in the room where he had dined with Mr. Glenthorpe. Benson found the match-box on looking into the room to see that everything was all right when his guests had retired, and determined to commit the murder that night, and leave it by the murdered man's bedside, as a clue to direct attention to Penreath. His next idea, to murder Mr. Glenthorpe with the knife which Penreath had used at dinner, probably occurred to him as he considered the possibilities of the match-box.

"It is difficult to decide why Benson chose to enter the room from the window instead of by the door when he had a second key of the room. He may have attempted to open the door with the key, and found that Mr. Glenthorpe had locked the door and left the key on the inside. Or he may have thought that as Penreath was sleeping in the next room, he ran too great a risk of discovery by entering from the door, and so decided to enter by the window. We must presume that Benson subsequently found Mr. Glenthorpe's key, either inside the door or under his pillow, and kept it. He entered the window, stabbed Mr. Glenthorpe, and placed the match-box and the knife at the side of the bed. His next act would be to search for the money. Finding it difficult to search by the light of the tallow candle, he decided to go downstairs and turn on the gas. "During his absence Peggy entered the room, saw the dead body, and picked up the knife and the match-box. Then she picked up the candlestick by the bed, and fled in terror. Benson, after turning on the gas at the meter, returned to find the room in darkness. Thinking that the wind had blown out the candle, he walked to the gas with the intention of lighting it. In doing so he knocked his head against the globe, cutting his forehead, and smashing the incandescent burner.

"Benson, when he found that the candlestick had disappeared must, in his fright, have rushed downstairs for another. He could not light the gas, because he had smashed the burner. In no other way can I account for the second lot of candle-grease that I found in the room underneath the gas-light, which made me believe at first that the room had been visited by two persons on the night of the murder. There *were* two persons, Benson and his daughter, but Peggy did not bring a candlestick into the room. It looks to me as though Benson, on returning with the second candle, attempted to light the gas with it and failed. That action would account for the gas tap being turned on, and the spilt grease directly underneath. He then searched the room till he found the pocket-book containing the money.

"The subsequent removal of the body to the pit strikes me as an afterthought. The complete plan was too diabolically ingenious and complete to have formed in the murderer's mind at the outset. The man who put the match-box and knife by the bedside of the murdered man in order to divert suspicion to Penreath had no thought, at that stage, of removing the body. That idea came afterwards, probably when he went upstairs the second time with the lighted candle, and saw Penreath's boots outside the door. I cannot help thinking that the clue of the footprints, which was such a damning point in the case against Penreath, was quite an accidental one so far as the murderer was concerned. The thought that the boots would leave footprints which would subsequently be identified as Penreath's was altogether too subtle to have occurred to a man like Benson. That is the touch of a master criminal—of a much higher order of criminal brain than Benson's.

"It is my belief that he originally intended to leave the murdered man in his room, thinking that the match-box and knife would point suspicion to Penreath. But after killing Mr. Glenthorpe he was overcome with the fear that his guilt would be discovered, in spite of his precautions to throw suspicions on another man, and he decided to throw the body into the pit in the hope that the crime would never be found out. The fact that he had entered the room in his stocking feet supports this theory, because he would be well aware that he would not be able to carry the body over several hundred yards of rough ground in his bare feet. He took Penreath's boots, which were close at hand, in preference to the danger and delay which he would have incurred in going to his own room, some distance away, for his own boots. Having put on the boots, he took the body on his shoulders and conveyed it to the pit.

"There are two or three points in this case which I am unable to clear up to my complete satisfaction. Why did Benson leave the key in the outside of the door? Was it merely one of those mistakes–those oversights–which all murderers are liable to commit, or did he do it deliberately, in the hope of conveying the impression that Mr. Glenthorpe had gone out and left the key in the outside of the door. In the next place, I cannot account for the mark of the box underneath the window. There is a third point–the direction of the wound in the murdered man's body, which gave me some ideas at the time that I am now compelled to dismiss as erroneous. But these are points that I hope will be cleared up by Benson's arrest, and confession, for I am convinced, by my observation of the man, that he will confess.

"There are one or two more points. Benson is an ardent fisherman, who spends all his spare time fishing on the marshes. The stolen pocket-book was suspended in the pit by a piece of fishing line. But I attach more importance to the second point, which is that since the murder has been committed the nightly conversation at the inn tap-room has centred around a local ghost, known as the White Lady of the Shrieking Pit, who is supposed from time immemorial to have haunted the pit where the body was thrown, and to bring death to anybody who encounters her at night. This spectre, which is profoundly believed in by the villagers, had not been seen for at least two years before the murder, but she made a reappearance a night or two after the crime, and is supposed to have been seen frequently ever since. It looks to me as though Benson set the story going again in order to keep the credulous villagers away from the pit where the money was concealed.

"This morning, in company with Mr. Oakham, I saw Penreath in the gaol, and by a ruse induced him to break his stubborn silence. His story, which it is not necessary for me to give you in detail, testifies to his innocence, and supports my own theory of the crime. He did not see the murder committed, but he saw the girl go into the room, and subsequently he saw her father enter and remove the body. It was the latter spectacle that robbed him of any lingering doubts he may have had of the girl's guilt, and forced him to the conclusion that she and her father were accomplices in the crime. But he loved her so much that he determined to keep silence and shield her."

26

"This is a remarkable story, Mr. Colwyn," said the chief constable, breaking the rather lengthy silence which followed the conclusion of the detective's reconstruction of the crime. "It has been quite entrancing to listen to your syllogistical skill. You would have made an excellent Crown Prosecutor." The chief constable's official mind could conceive no higher compliment. "Your statements seem almost too incredible for belief, but undoubtedly you have made out a case for the further investigation of this crime. What do you think, Galloway?"

"The question, to my mind, is what Mr. Colwyn's discoveries really represent," replied Galloway. "He has built up a very ingenious and plausible reconstruction, but let us discard mere theory, and stick to the facts. What do they amount to? Apart from Penreath's statement in the gaol that he saw the body carried down stairs—"

"You can leave that out of the question," said the detective curtly. "My reconstruction of the crime is independent of Penreath's testimony, which is open to the objection that it should have been made before."

"Exactly what I was going to point out," rejoined Galloway bluntly. "Well, then, let us examine the fresh facts. There are five as I see them. The recovery of Penreath's match-box, the discovery of the door between the two rooms, the wound on the innkeeper's forehead, the additional key, and the finding of the pocket-book in the pit. Exclude the idea of conspiracy, and the recovery of the match-box becomes an additional point against Penreath, because it strikes me as guess work to assume that he had no other matches in his possession except that particular box and the loose one he found in his vest pocket. Smokers frequently carry two or three boxes of matches. The discovery of the hidden door is interesting, but has no direct bearing on the crime. The wound on the innkeeper's head looks suspicious, but there is no proof that it was caused by his knocking his head against the gas globe in the murdered man's room on the night of the murder. As Mr. Colwyn himself has pointed out, there is not much in Benson having a second key of Glenthorpe's room. Many hotel-keepers and innkeepers keep duplicate keys of bedrooms. The significance of this discovery is that Benson kept silence about the existence of this key. Undoubtedly he should have told us about it, but I am not prepared to accept, offhand, that his silence was the silence of a guilty man. He may have kept silence regarding it through a foolish fear of directing suspicion to himself. That theory seems to me quite as probable as Mr. Colwyn's theory. There remains the recovery of the money in the pit. In considering that point I find it impossible to overlook that Penreath returned to the wood after making his escape. That suggests, to my mind, that he hid the money in the pit himself, and took the risk of returning in order to regain possession of it."

"You are worthier of the chief constable's compliment than I, my dear Galloway," said Colwyn genially. "Your gift of overcoming points which tell against you by ignoring them, and your careful avoidance of tell-tale inferences, would make you an ideal Crown Prosecutor."

"I don't believe in inferences in crime," replied Galloway, flushing under the detective's sarcasm. "I am a plain man, and I like to stick to facts."

"What was the whole of your case against Penreath but a series of inferences?" retorted Colwyn. "Circumstantial evidence, and the circumstances on which you depended in this case, were never fully established. Furthermore, your facts were not consistent with your original hypothesis, and had to be altered when the case went to trial. Now that I have discovered other facts and inferences which are consistent with another hypothesis, you strive to shut your eyes to them, or draw wrong conclusions from them. Your suggestion that Penreath must have hidden the money in the pit because he was arrested near it is a choice example of false deduction based on the wrong premise that Penreath hid the money there on the night of the murder. He could not have done so because he had no rope, and how was he, a stranger to the place, to know that the inside of the pit was covered with creeping plants of sufficient strength to bear a man's weight? The choice of the pit as a hiding place for the money argues an intimate local knowledge."

"You have not yet told us how you came to deduce that the money was in the pit," said Mr. Cromering, who had been examining the pocket-book and money.

"While I was examining the mouth of the pit the previous afternoon I found this piece of paper at the brink, trodden into the clay. Later on I recognised the peculiar watermark of waving lines as the Government watermark in the first issue of Treasury war notes. From that I deduced that the money was hidden in the pit. It was all in Treasury notes, as you see."

"I'm afraid I don't quite follow you now," said the chief constable, with a puzzled glance at the piece of dirty paper in his hand. "This piece of paper is not a Treasury note."

"Not now, perhaps, but it was once," said the detective with a smile. "It puzzled me at first. I could not account for the Treasury watermark, designed to prevent forgery of the notes, appearing on a piece of blank paper. Then it came to me. The first issue of Treasury notes were very badly printed. Ordinary black ink was used, which would disappear if the note was immersed in water. It was an official at Somerset House who told me this. He informed me that they had several cases of munition workers who, after being paid in Treasury notes, had put them into the pockets of their overalls, and forgotten about them until the overalls came back from the wash with every vestige of printing washed out from the notes, leaving nothing but the watermarks. It occurred to me that the same thing had happened in this case. The murderer, when about to descend to the pit to conceal the money, had accidentally dropped a note and trodden it underfoot, and it had lain out in the open exposed to heavy rains and dew until every scrap of printing was obliterated."

"By Jove, that's very clever, very clever indeed!" exclaimed Galloway. He picked up a magnifying glass which was lying on the table, and closely examined the dirty piece of white paper which Colwyn had found at the mouth of the pit. "It was once a Treasury note, sure enough—the watermark is unmistakable. You've scored a point there that I couldn't have made, and I'm man enough to own up to it. You see more deeply into things than I do, Mr. Colwyn. And I'm willing to admit that you've made some new and interesting discoveries about this case, though in my opinion you are inclined to read too much into them. But I certainly think they ought to be investigated further. If Penreath's statement to you this morning is true, Benson is the murderer, and there has been a miscarriage of justice. But what makes me doubt the truth of it is Penreath's refusal to speak before. I mistrust confessions made out at the last moment. And his explanation that he kept silence to save the girl strikes me as rather thin. It is too quixotic."

"There is more than that in it," replied Colwyn. "He had a double motive. Penreath heard Sir Henry Durwood depose at the trial that he believed him to be suffering from epilepsy."

"How does that constitute a second motive?"

"In this way. Penreath has a highly-strung, introspective temperament. He went to the front from a high sense of duty, but he was temperamentally unfit for the ghastly work of modern warfare, and broke down under the strain. Men like Penreath feel it keenly when they are discharged through shell-shock. They feel that the carefully hidden weaknesses of their temperaments have been dragged out into the light of day, and imagine they have been branded as cowards in the eyes of their fellow men. I suspect that the real reason why Penreath left London and sought refuge in Norfolk under another name was because he had been discharged from the Army through shell-shock. He wanted to get away from London and hide himself from those who knew him. To his wounded spirit the condolences of his friends would be akin to taunts and sneers. When Sir Henry Durwood questioned him he was careful to conceal the fact that he had been a victim of shell-shock. As a matter of fact, Penreath's behaviour in the breakfast room that morning was nothing more than the effects of the air raid on his disordered nerves, but he would sooner have died than admit that to strangers. After listening to the evidence for the defence at the trial, he came to the conclusion that he was an epileptic as well as a neurasthenic. He might well believe that life held little for him in these circumstances, and that conviction would strengthen him in his determination to sacrifice his life as a thing of little value for the girl he loved."

"If that is true he must be a very manly young fellow," said the chief constable.

"Supposing it is true, what is to be done?" asked Galloway, earnestly. "Penreath has been tried and convicted for the murder."

"The conviction will be upset on appeal," replied the detective decisively.

"But I do not see that carries us much further forward as regards Benson," persisted Galloway. "If he is the murderer, as you say, he will clear out as soon as he hears that Penreath is appealing."

"He will not be able to clear out if you arrest him."

"On what grounds? I cannot arrest him for a murder for which another man has been sentenced to death."

"True. But you can arrest him as accessory after the fact, on the ground that he carried the body downstairs and threw it into the pit."

"And suppose he denies having done so? Look here, Mr. Colwyn, I want to help you all I can, but if I have made one mistake, I do not want to make a second one. Frankly, I do not know what to think of your story. It may be true, or it may not. But speaking from a police point of view, we have mighty little to go on if we arrest Benson. If he likes to bluff us we may find ourselves in an awkward position. Nobody saw him commit the murder."

"I realise the truth of what you say because I thought it all over before coming to see you," replied Colwyn. "If Benson denies the truth of the points I have discovered against him, or gives them a different interpretation, it may be difficult to prove them. But he will not–he will confess all he knows."

"What makes you think so?"

"Because his nerve has gone. If I had confronted him that night when I saw him in the room I would have got the whole truth from him."

"Why did you not do so?"

"Because I had not the power to detain him. I am merely a private detective, and can neither arrest a man nor threaten him with arrest. That is why I have come to you. You, with the powers of the law behind you, can frighten Benson into a confession much more effectually than I could."

"I don't half like it," grumbled Galloway. "There's a risk about it—"

"It's a risk that must be taken, nevertheless." It was Mr. Cromering who intervened in the discussion between the two, and he spoke with unusual decision. "I agree with Mr. Colwyn that this is the best course to pursue. I will go with you and take full responsibility, Galloway."

"There is no need for that," said Galloway quickly. "I am quite willing to go."

"I will accompany you and Mr. Colwyn. It has been a remarkable case throughout, and I want to see the end–if this is the end. I feel keenly interested in this young man's fate."

"I should like to go also, but an engagement prevents me," said Mr. Oakham. "I am quite content to leave Penreath's interests in Mr. Colwyn's capable hands." He rose as he spoke, and held out his hand to the detective. "We have all been in error, but you have saved us from having an irreparable wrong on our consciences. I cannot forgive myself for my blindness. Perhaps you will acquaint me with the result of your visit when you return. I shall be anxious to know."

"I will not fail to do so," replied Colwyn, grasping the solicitor's hand. "We had better catch the five o'clock train to Heathfield and walk across to Flegne," he added, turning to the others. "It will be as quick as motoring across, and the sound of the car might put Benson on his guard. We want to take him unawares."

"He'll have got wind of something already if he finds the pocket-book gone," said Galloway. "He may have bolted while we have been talking over things here."

"I've seen to that," replied the detective. "I tied my own pocket-book to the fishing line in the pit, and left Queensmead watching the pit. If Benson tries to escape with my pocket-book Queensmead will arrest him for robbery. I've made a complaint of the loss."

"You haven't left much to chance," replied Galloway, with a grim smile.

27

It was characteristic of Mr. Cromering to beguile the long walk in the dark from Heathfield Station by discussing Colwyn's theory that Benson had circulated the reappearance of the White Lady of the Shrieking Pit in order to keep the villagers away from the place where the stolen money was hidden. Mr. Cromering had been much impressed–he said so–with the logical skill and masterly deductive powers by which Colwyn had reconstructed the hidden events of the night of the murder, like an Owen reconstructing the extinct moa from a single bone, but he was loath to accept that part of the theory which seemed to throw doubt on the authenticity of a famous venerable Norfolk legend which had at least two hundred years of tradition behind it.

Mr. Cromering, without going so far as to affirm his personal belief in the story, declared that there were several instances extant of enlightened and educated people who had seen the ghost, and had suffered an untimely end in consequence. He cited the case of a visiting magistrate, who had been visiting in the district some twenty years ago, and knew nothing about the legend. He was riding through Flegne one night, and heard dismal shrieks from the wood on the rise. Thinking somebody was in need of help, he dismounted from his horse, and went up to the rise to investigate. As he neared the pit the White Lady appeared from the pit and looked at him with inexpressibly sad eyes, drew her hand thrice across her throat, and disappeared again in the pit. The magistrate was greatly startled at what he had seen, and related the experience to his host when he got home. The latter did not tell him of the tragic significance which was attached to the apparition, but the magistrate cut his throat three days after his return to London. "Surely, *that* was more than a mere coincidence?" concluded Mr. Cromering.

"I do not wish to undermine the local belief in the White Lady of the Shrieking Pit," said Colwyn, with a smile which the darkness hid. "All I say is that her frequent reappearances since the money was hidden in the pit were exceedingly useful for the man who hid the money. I can assure you that none of the villagers would go near the pit for twice the amount. There are plenty of them who will go to their graves convinced that they have heard her nightly shrieks since the murder was committed."

"It is difficult to believe that they are all mistaken," said Mr. Cromering slowly.

"I do not think they are mistaken—at least, not all of them. Some have probably heard shrieks."

"Then how do you account for the shrieks?" asked the chief constable eagerly.

"I think they have heard Benson's mother shrieking in her paroxysms of madness."

"By Jove, that's a shrewd notion!" chuckled Superintendent Galloway. "You don't miss much, Mr. Colwyn. Whether you're right or not, there's not the slightest doubt that the whole village is in terror of the ghost, and avoids the Shrieking Pit like a pestilence. I was talking to a Flegne farmer the other day, and he assured me, with a pale face, that he had heard the White Lady shrieking three nights running, and when his men went to the inn after dark they walked half a mile out of their way to avoid passing near the pit. He told me also that the general belief among the villagers is that Mr. Glenthorpe saw the White Lady a night or so before he was murdered."

"I heard that story also," responded Colwyn. "He was in the habit of walking up to the rise after dark. He appears to have been keenly interested in his scientific work."

"He was absorbed in it to the exclusion of everything else," said the chief constable, with a sigh. "His death is a great loss to British science, and Norfolk research in particular. I was very much interested in that newspaper clipping which was found in his pocket-book with the money. It was a London review on a brochure he had published on sponge spicules he had found in a flint at Flegne, and was his last contribution to science, published two days before he was struck down. What a loss!"

Their conversation had brought them to the top of the rise. Beneath them lay the little hamlet on the edge of the marshes, wrapped in a white blanket of mist. Colwyn asked his companions to remain where they were, while he went to see if Queensmead was on the watch. He walked quickly across the hut circles until he reached the pit. There his keen eyes detected a dark figure standing motionless in the shadow of the wood.

"Is that you, Queensmead?" he said, in a low voice.

"Yes, Mr. Colwyn." The figure advanced out of the shadow.

"Is everything all right?"

"Quite all right, sir. I've watched from this spot from dark till dawn since you've been away, and there's not been a soul near the pit. I've not been disturbed—not even by the White Lady."

"You have done excellently. The chief constable and Superintendent Galloway have come over with me, and we are going to the inn now. You had better keep watch here for half an hour longer, so as to be on the safe side. If anybody comes to the pit during that time you must detain him, and call for assistance. I will come and relieve you myself."

"Very good, sir, you can depend on me," said Queensmead quietly, as he returned to his post.

Colwyn rejoined his companions, and told them what had passed.

"I want to be on the safe side in case Benson tries to bolt when he sees us," he explained. "He's hardly likely to go without making an effort to get the money. Now, let us go to the inn."

"One moment," said the chief constable. "How do you propose to proceed when we get there?"

"Get Benson by himself and frighten him into a confession," was the terse reply. "I want your authority to threaten him with arrest. In fact, I should prefer that you or Superintendent Galloway undertook to do that. It would come with more force."

"Let it be Galloway," responded the chief constable. "You will act just as if I were not present, Galloway, and it is my wish that you do whatever Mr. Colwyn asks you."

"Thank you," replied the detective. "Let us go, now. There is no time to be lost. Somebody may have seen me speaking to Queensmead."

They descended the rise and, reaching the flat, discerned the gaunt walls of the old inn looming spectrally from the mist. A light glimmered in the bar, and loud voices were heard within. Colwyn felt for the door. It was shut and fastened. He knocked sharply; the voices within ceased as though by magic, and presently there was the sound of somebody coming along the passage. Then the door was opened, and the white face of Charles appeared in the doorway, framed in the yellow light of a candle which he held above his head as he peered forth into the mist. His black eyes roved from Colwyn to the forms behind him.

"I'm sorry you were kept waiting, sir," he said, in his strange whisper, which seemed to have a tremor in it. "But the customers will have the door locked at night now. They are frightened of this ghost–this White Lady– she's been heard shrieking—"

"Never mind that now," replied Colwyn. He had determined how to act, and stepped quickly inside. "Where's Benson?"

"He's sitting upstairs with his mother, sir. Shall I tell him you want him?"

"No. I will go myself. Take these gentlemen into the bar parlour, and return to the bar."

Colwyn made his way upstairs in the dark. He passed the rooms where Mr. Glenthorpe had been murdered and Penreath had slept, and the room from which he had watched Peggy's nocturnal visit to the death chamber. That wing of the inn was as empty and silent as it had been the night of the murder, but a lighted candle, placed on an old hall stand which Colwyn remembered having seen that night in the lumber room, flickered in the wavering shadows—a futile human effort to ward off the lurking terrors of darkness by the friendly feeble companionship of a light which could be extinguished even more quickly than a life.

Colwyn took the candle to light him down the second passage to the mad woman's room. As he reached it, the door opened, and Peggy stepped forth. She recoiled at the sight of the detective.

"You!" she breathed. "Oh, why—"

"I have come to see your father," said Colwyn. It went to his heart to see the entreaty in her eyes, the pitiful droop of her lips and the thinness of her face.

The door was opened widely, and the innkeeper appeared on the threshold beside his daughter. Behind him, Colwyn could see the old mad woman in her bed in the corner of the room, mumbling to herself and fondling her doll. The innkeeper fastened his bird-like eyes on the detective's face.

"What are you doing here?" he said, and there was no mistaking the note of terror in his voice. "What is it you want?"

"I want to speak to you downstairs," said the detective.

The innkeeper looked swiftly to the right and left with the instinct of a trapped animal seeking an avenue of escape. Then his eyes returned to the detective's face with the resigned glance of a man who had made up his mind.

"I will come down with you," he said. "Peggy, you must look after your grandmother till I return."

The girl went back into the room and shut the door behind her, without a word or a glance. Once more Colwyn felt admiration for her as a rare type of womanhood. Truly, she had self-control, this girl.

He and the innkeeper took their way along the passages and descended the stairs without exchanging a word. When they got to the foot of the stairs Benson half hesitated, and turned to Colwyn as if for direction. The latter nodded towards the door of the bar parlour, and motioned the innkeeper to enter. Following closely behind, he saw the innkeeper start with surprise at the sight of the two inmates of the room. Mr. Cromering was seated at the table, but Superintendent Galloway was standing up with his back to the fireplace. There was a moment's tense silence before the latter spoke.

"We have sent for you to ask you a few questions, Benson."

"I was under the impression–that is, I was led to believe–that it was Mr. Colwyn who wanted to see me."

"Never mind what you thought," retorted Galloway impatiently. "You know perfectly well what has brought us here. I'm going to ask you some questions about the murder which was committed in this inn less than three weeks ago."

"I know nothing about it, sir, beyond what I told you before."

"You will be well advised, in your own interests, not to lie, Benson. Why did you not tell us you had a second key to Mr. Glenthorpe's room?"

There was a perceptible pause before the reply came.

"I didn't think it mattered, sir."

"Then you admit you have a second key?"

"Yes, sir."

"Very well." Superintendent Galloway took out a pocket-book and made a note of the reply. "Now, where did you conceal the money?"

"What money, sir?"

"Don't equivocate, man!" Superintendent Galloway produced the pocket-book Colwyn had recovered from the pit, and held it at arm's length in front of the innkeeper. "I mean the £300 in Treasury notes in this pocket-book, which Mr. Glenthorpe drew from the bank, and which you took from his room the night he was murdered."

"I know nothing about it."

To Colwyn at least it seemed that the expression on the innkeeper's face as he glanced at the pocket-book might have been mistaken by an unprejudiced observer for genuine surprise.

"I suppose you never saw it before, eh?" sneered Galloway.

"I never did."

"Nor hid it in the pit?"

"No, sir."

Galloway paused in his questioning in secret perplexity. Benson's answers to his last three questions were given so firmly and unhesitatingly that some of his former doubts of Colwyn's theory returned to him with redoubled force. But it was in his most truculent and overbearing manner that he next remarked:

"Do you also deny that you carried Mr. Glenthorpe's body from his room and threw it down the pit?"

The spasm of sudden terror which contorted the innkeeper's face was a revelation to the three men who were watching him closely.

"I don't know anything about it," he quavered weakly.

"That won't go down, Benson!" Galloway was quick to follow up his stroke, shaking his head fiercely, like a dog worrying a rat. "You were seen carrying the body downstairs, the night of the murder. You might as well own up to it, first as last. Lies will not help you. We know too much for you to wriggle out of it. And never mind smoothing your hair down like that. We know all about that scar on your forehead, and how you got it."

A wooden clock, standing on the mantelpiece, measured off half a minute in heavy ticks. Then the innkeeper, in a voice which was little more than a whisper, spoke:

"It is true. I carried the body downstairs."

"Why did you not tell us this before?"

"It would not have made any difference."

"What!" Superintendent Galloway's indignation and amazement threatened to choke his utterance. "You keep silence till an innocent man is almost hanged for your misdeeds, and now have the brazen effrontery to say it makes no difference."

"Is Mr. Penreath innocent?"

"Nobody should know that better than you."

"Then who murdered Mr. Glenthorpe?"

"Let us have no more of this fooling, Benson." Superintendent Galloway's voice was very stern. "You have already admitted that you carried Mr. Glenthorpe's body downstairs."

"Oh!" The wretched man cried out wildly, like one who sees an engulfing wave too late. "I see what you mean—you think I murdered him. But I did not—I did not! Before God I am innocent." His voice rang out loudly.

"We don't want to listen to this talk," interrupted Galloway roughly. "You are under arrest, Benson, for complicity in this murder, and the less you say the better for yourself."

"But I tell you I am innocent." The innkeeper brought his skeleton hands together in a gesture which was almost tragic in its despair. "I carried the body downstairs, but I did not murder him. Let me explain. Let me tell you—"

"My advice to you is to keep silence, man. Keep your story for the trial," replied the police official. "You'd better get ready to go to Heathfield with me. I'll go upstairs with you, and give you five minutes to get ready."

"Let him tell his story before you take him away, Galloway," said Colwyn, who had been keenly watching the innkeeper's face during the dialogue between him and his accuser. "I want to hear it."

"I do not see what good it will do," grumbled Superintendent Galloway. "However, as you want to hear it, let him go ahead. But let me first warn you, Benson, that anything you say now may be used in evidence against you afterwards."

"I do not care for that–I am not afraid of the truth being known," replied the innkeeper. He turned from the uncompromising face of the police officer to Colwyn, as though he divined in him a more unprejudiced listener. "I did not murder Mr. Glenthorpe, but I went to his room with the intention of robbing him the night he was murdered," he commenced. "I was in desperate straits for money. The brewer had threatened to turn me out of the inn because I couldn't pay my way. I knew Mr. Glenthorpe had taken money out of the bank that morning, and in an evil moment temptation overcame me, and I determined to rob him. I told myself that he was a wealthy man and would never feel the loss of the money, but if I was turned out of the inn my daughter and my old mother would starve.

"My plan was to go to his room after everybody was asleep, let myself in with my key, and secure the pocketbook containing the money. I knew that Mr. Glenthorpe was a sound sleeper, and I was aware that he generally locked his door and slept with the key under his pillow.

"I went to my room early that night, and waited a long time before making the attempt. It came on to rain about eleven o'clock, and I waited some time longer before leaving my room. I walked in my stocking feet, so as to make no sound, and I carried a candle, but it was not lighted. When I got to the door I stood and listened awhile outside, thinking I might judge by Mr. Glenthorpe's breathing whether he was asleep, but I could hear nothing. I unlocked the door quietly, and felt my way towards the bed in the dark, hoping to find his coat and the money in it without running the risk of striking a light.

"But I could not lay my hands on the coat in the dark, so I struck a match to light the candle. I had made up my mind that if Mr. Glenthorpe should wake up and see me at his bedside I would tell him the truth and ask him to lend me some money.

"By the light of the candle I saw Mr. Glenthorpe lying on his back, with his arms thrown out from his body. He was uncovered, and the bed-clothes were lying in a tumbled heap at the foot of the bed. I stood looking at him for a minute, not knowing what to do. I did not realise at the time that he was dead, because the wind blowing in at the open window caused the candle to flicker, and I could not see very clearly. I thought he must be in a fit, and I wondered what I could do to help him. As the candle still kept flickering in the wind, I picked up the candlestick and walked to the gas-jet in the centre of the room, turned on the tap and tried to light it with the candle. It would not light, and then I remembered that I had told Ann to turn it off at the meter before going to bed. I walked back to the bedside, put the candle down on the table, and had a closer look at Mr. Glenthorpe. As he was still in the same attitude I put my hand on his heart to see if it was beating. I felt something warm and wet, and when I drew back my hand I saw that it was covered with blood.

"When I realised that he was dead—murdered—I lost my nerve and rushed from the room, leaving the candle burning at the bedside. My one thought was to get downstairs and wash the blood off my hand. It was not until I had reached the kitchen that I remembered that I had left the candle burning upstairs. I considered whether I should return for it at once or wash my hands first. I decided on the latter course, and went into the kitchen.

"I had just lit a candle, when I heard a door open behind me, and, turning round, I saw Charles coming out of his room in his shirt and trousers, with a candle in his hand. He said he had seen the light under his door, and wondering who had come into the kitchen had got up to see. Then his face changed when he saw my hands, and he asked me how the blood came to be on them.

"I tried to put him off at first by telling him I had knocked my hand upstairs. He didn't say any more, but stood there watching me wash my hands, and when I had finished he said that if I was going upstairs he would come with me, as he remembered he had left his corkscrew in Mr. Glenthorpe's sitting room, and would want it in the morning.

"I could see that he suspected me, and that if he went upstairs he would see the light burning in Mr. Glenthorpe's bedroom, and might go in. So, in desperation, I confessed to him that I had gone into Mr. Glenthorpe's room, and found him dead. I asked Charles what I should do. He heard me very quietly, but when he learnt that I had left my candle burning in Mr. Glenthorpe's room he said the first thing was to go and get that, and then we could discuss what had better be done.

"I realised that was good advice, and went upstairs to get the candlestick. But when I got to the door I was amazed to find the room in darkness. The door was on the jar, just as I remembered leaving it, but there was not a glimmer of light. I was in a terrible fright, but as I stood there in the dark, listening intently, the sound of the wind roaring round the house reminded me how the candle had flickered in the wind while I was in the room before, and I concluded that it must have blown out the light. So I went into the room, feeling my way along the walls with my hands. When I got near the bed I struck a match and looked for the candlestick. But it was gone.

"Then I knew somebody had been in the room, and I made my way downstairs again as fast as I could, and told Charles, and asked him what he thought of it. Charles said it was clear that the murderer, whoever he was, had revisited the room since I had been there, and finding the candle, had carried it off with him. I asked Charles for what purpose? Charles turned it over in his mind for a moment, and then said that it seemed to him that he might have done it to secure himself, in case he was caught, by being able to prove that somebody else had been in Mr. Glenthorpe's room that night.

"I saw the force of that and was greatly alarmed, and asked Charles what he thought I had better do. Charles, after thinking it over for a while, said in my own interests I would be well advised if I carried the body away and concealed it somewhere where it was not likely to be found. He pointed out that if the facts came to light it would be very awkward for me. On my own admission I had gone into Mr. Glenthorpe's room in the middle of the night, and had come away leaving him dead in bed, with his blood on my hands, and my bedroom candlestick alight at his bedside. Charles pointed out that these facts were sure to come to light if the body was left where it was, but if the body was removed and safely hidden, it might be thought that Mr. Glenthorpe had simply disappeared.

"I was struck by the force of these arguments, and we next discussed where the body should be hidden. We both thought of the pit, but I didn't like that idea at first because I thought the police would be sure to search the pit when they learnt of Mr. Glenthorpe's disappearance, because his excavations were near the pit. Charles, on the other hand, thought it was the safest place—much safer than the sea, which was sure to cast up the body. He said it would never occur to the police to search the pit, until the body had lain there so long that it would be impossible to say how he came by his death. Perhaps it would never be searched, in which case the body would never be recovered.

"We decided on the pit, and Charles said he would keep watch downstairs while I went up and got the body. But first I went and opened the back door and went to the side of the inn to see if anybody was about. The rain had ceased, it was a dark and stormy night, and everybody long since gone to bed. The rough stones outside cut my feet, and recalled to my mind that I was without boots. I knew I could not carry the body all the way up the rise without boots, and I was about to go to my room to get them when I remembered that I had seen Penreath's boots outside his bedroom door. I decided to wear them and avoid the risk of going back to my room for my own boots. I have a small foot, and I had no doubt that they would fit me.

"Charles suggested that I should go into the room in the dark, so as to lessen the risk of being seen, and light the candle when I got inside. I took the candle, but I said I would turn on the gas at the meter, in case the wind blew out the candle. I will keep nothing back now. The real reason was that I wanted the better light to make quite sure if the money was gone. I thought perhaps the murderer might have overlooked it, and I hoped to find it because I needed it so badly. When I got upstairs I stopped outside Mr. Penreath's room, picked up his boots, and put them on. I went into the room in the dark, intending to strike a match, and light the gas, and search for the money. I miscalculated the distance, and bumped into the gas globe in the dark, cutting my head badly. When I struck a match I found that I couldn't light the gas because the incandescent burner had been broken by the blow, so I lit the candle.

"I shuddered at the ordeal of carrying the body downstairs, and only nerved myself to the task by reflecting on the risk to myself if I allowed it to remain where it was. As I stood by the bedside, I noticed Mr. Glenthorpe's key of the room lying by the pillow, and I picked it up and put it in my pocket. I then lifted the body on my shoulders, carried it downstairs, steadying it with one hand, and carrying the candle in the other. Charles was waiting for me at the bottom of the stairs, and he took the candle from me and lighted me to the back door.

"A late moon was just beginning to show above the horizon when I got outside, and by its light I had no difficulty in finding my way up the rise and to the pit. It was a terrible task, and I was glad when I had accomplished it. I returned to the back door, where Charles was awaiting me. We then fastened the back door, and he went to his room off the kitchen, and I went upstairs to my room. As I passed Mr. Glenthorpe's room I saw the door was open, and I pulled it quickly to, but I forgot to take out the key I had left in the door when I first entered the room.

"I remembered the key in the morning when Ann told me Mr. Glenthorpe's room was empty, but I dared not remove it then because I knew Ann must have seen it. And later on, when you were questioning me about the key in the door, I was afraid to tell you about the second key, because I knew you would question me.

"When I learnt from Ann that Mr. Penreath had left early in the morning, and wouldn't stay for breakfast, I felt sure it was he who had committed the murder. It was a little later that Charles took me aside in the bar and told me that he had walked up to the rise early that morning to see if everything was all right, and that I had left traces of my footprints across the clay to the mouth of the pit. I was very much upset when I heard this, for I knew the body was sure to be found. But Charles said that, as things turned out, it was a very lucky accident.

"Charles said there was no doubt Mr. Penreath was the murderer. He had not only cleared out, but the knife he had used at dinner had disappeared. Charles said he had not missed the knife the night before, but he had discovered the loss when counting the cutlery that morning. If the police found out that it was his boots which made the prints leading to the pit it would only be another point against him, and as he was sure to be hanged in any case the best thing I could do was to go and inform Constable Queensmead of Mr. Glenthorpe's disappearance and Mr. Penreath's departure, but to keep silence about my own share in carrying the body to the pit. Even if the murderer denied removing the body nobody would believe him. I thought the advice good, and I followed it. I don't know whether I could have kept it up if I had been cross-questioned, but from first to last nobody seemed to have the least suspicion of me. The only time I was really afraid was when one of you gentlemen asked me about the key in the outside of the door, but you passed it over and went on to something else.

"And now you know the whole truth. But I should like to say that I kept silence about carrying the body away because I didn't think I was injuring anybody. I believed Mr. Penreath to be guilty. Now you tell me he is innocent. If I had had any idea of that I would have told the truth at once, even though you had hanged me for it."

28

"You're a nice scoundrel, Benson," said Superintendent Galloway, nodding his head at the innkeeper with a kind of ferocious banter. "You're really a first-class villain, upon my soul! But this precious story with which you've tried to bamboozle us is not complete. Would it be putting too much strain on your inventive faculties to ask you, while you are about it, to give us your version of how the money which was stolen from Mr. Glenthorpe came to be hidden in the pit in which you flung his body?"

"But I didn't know the money was hidden in the pit," said the wretched man, glancing uneasily at the pocket-book, which was still lying on the table. "I never saw the money, though I've confessed to you that I would have taken it if I had seen it. That's the truth, sir—every word I've told you to-night is true! Charles will bear me out."

"I've no doubt he will. I'll have something to say to that scoundrel later on. There's a pair of you. I've no doubt he caught you in the act of carrying away the body of your victim, and that you bribed him to keep silence. You planned together to let an innocent man go to the gallows in order to save your own skin. Now, my man—"

"Wait a moment, Galloway."

It was Colwyn who spoke. The innkeeper's story had been to him like a finger of light in a murky depth, revealing unseen and unimagined abominations, but supplying him with those missing pieces of the puzzle for which he had long and vainly searched. During the brief colloquy between Galloway and the innkeeper his brain had been busy fitting together the whole intricate design of knavery.

"I want to ask a question," he continued, in answer to the other's glance of inquiry. "What time was it you went to Mr. Glenthorpe's room–the first time I mean, Benson. Can you fix it definitely?"

"Yes, sir. I kept looking at my watch in my room, waiting for the time to pass. It was twenty past eleven the last time I looked, and I left my room about five minutes later."

"Was it raining then?"

"Yes, sir, but not so hard as previously, and it stopped altogether before I entered the room, though the wind was blowing."

"That is as I thought. Benson's story is true, Galloway."

"What!" The police officer's vociferous exclamation was in striking contrast to the detective's quiet tones. "How do you make that out?"

"He couldn't have committed the murder. Mr. Glenthorpe was killed during the storm, between eleven and half-past. Benson says he didn't enter the room till nearly half-past eleven."

"If that's all you're going on—"

"It isn't." There was a trace of irritation in the detective's voice. "But Benson's story fills in the gaps of my reconstruction in a remarkable way–so completely, that he couldn't have invented it to save his life, because he does not know all we know. In this extraordinarily complicated case the times are everything. My original theory was right. There were two persons in the room the night of the murder–three, really, but Peggy doesn't affect the reconstruction one way or the other. The murderer, who carried an umbrella to shield himself from the rain, entered the room about twenty past eleven. He murdered Mr. Glenthorpe, took the money, and escaped the same way he entered–by the window. Benson entered by the door at half-past eleven, certainly not later, and after standing at the bedside for two or three minutes, rushed downstairs, as he related, leaving his candle burning at

the bedside. During his absence downstairs his daughter
entered the room. Benson returned for the candle and
found it gone. Had he returned a minute or two earlier he
would have seen his daughter carrying it away, because
in her story to me she said she thought she heard
somebody creeping up the stairs as she left the room. I
thought at the time that she imagined this, but now I
have very little doubt that it was her father she heard,
going upstairs again to get the candle. Finally, Benson,
after planning it with Charles, removed the body to the
pit some time after midnight."

"This is mere guess-work. Let us stick to facts. On
Benson's own confession he entered the room nefariously
and removed the dead man's body."

"Yes, but it was a dead body when he got there—just
dead. Mr. Glenthorpe was alive and well not ten minutes
before."

"Oh, come, Mr. Colwyn, this is going too far,"
Galloway expostulated. "Again, I say, let us have no
guess-work."

"This is not guess-work. There can be no doubt that
the murderer left the room by the window just before
Benson entered it by the door."

"How do you know that?" asked Galloway.

"*Because he was watching Benson from the window.*"
Galloway looked startled.

"You go too deep for me," he said. "Was it Penreath
who got out of the window?"

"No, Penreath, like Benson, was the victim of a deep
and subtle villain."

"Then who was it?"

Before Colwyn could reply a shriek rang out—a single
hoarse and horrible cry, which went reverberating and
echoing over the marshes, rising to a piercing intensity at
its highest note, and then ceasing suddenly. In the hush
that ensued the chief constable looked nervously at
Colwyn.

"It came from the rise," he said in a voice barely raised above a whisper. "Do you think—"

Colwyn read the unspoken thought in his mind.

"I'll go and see what it was," he said briefly.

He opened the door and went out. In the passage he encountered Ann shaking and trembling, with a face blanched with terror.

"It came from the pit, sir–the Shrieking Pit," she whispered. "It's the White Lady. Don't leave me, I'm like to drop. God a' mercy, what's that?" she cried, finding her voice in a fresh access of terror as a heavy knock smote the door. "For God's sake, don't 'ee go, sir, don't 'ee go, as you value your life. It's the White Lady at the door, come to take her toll again from this unhappy house. You be mad to face her, sir–it's certain death."

But Colwyn loosened himself quickly from her detaining grasp, and strode to the door. As he passed the bar he caught a glimpse of a ring of cowering frightened faces within, huddled together like sheep, and staring with saucer eyes. The mist spanned the doorway like a sheet.

"Who's there?" he cried.

"It's me, sir." Constable Queensmead stepped out of the mist into the passage, looking white and shaken. "Something's happened up at the pit. While I was watching from the corner of the wood I saw somebody appear out of the mist and come creeping up the rise towards the pit. I waited till he got to the brink, and when he made to climb down, I knew he was the man you were after, so I went over to the pit. He had disappeared inside, but I could hear the creepers rustling as he went down. After a bit, I heard him coming up again, tugging and straining at the creepers, and gasping for breath. When he was fairly out, I turned my torch on him and told him to stand still. It is difficult to say exactly how it happened, sir, but when he saw he was trapped he made a kind of spring backwards, slipped on the wet clay, lost his balance, and fell back into the pit. I sprang forward and tried to save him, but it was too late. He caught at the creepers as he fell, hung for a second, then fell back with a loud cry."

"Who was it, Queensmead?"

"Charles, the waiter, sir."

"We must get him out at once," said Colwyn. "We shall need a rope and some men. Can you get some ropes, Queensmead? There's some men in the bar—we'll get them to help.

"I don't think they're likely to come, sir. They're all too frightened of the Shrieking Pit, and the ghost."

"I'll go and talk to them. Meanwhile, you go and get ropes." Colwyn returned to the bar parlour and, after explaining to Mr. Cromering and Galloway what had happened, went into the bar.

"Men," said Colwyn, "Charles has fallen into the pit on the rise, and I need the help of some of you to get him out. Queensmead has gone for ropes. Who will come with me?"

There was no response. The villagers looked at each other in silence, and moved uneasily. Then a man in jersey and sea-boots spoke:

"None of us dare go up to th' pit, ma'aster."

"Why not?"

"Life be sweet, ma'aster. It be a suddint and bloody end to meet th' White Lady of th' pit. Luke what's happened to Charles, who went out of this bar not ten minutes agone! Who knows who she may take next?"

"Very well, then stay where you are. You are a lot of cowards," said Colwyn, turning away.

The faces of the men showed that the epithet rankled, as Colwyn intended that it should. There was a brief pause, and then another fisherman stepped forward and said:

"I'm a Norfolk man, and nobbut agoin' to say I'm afeered. I'll go wi' yow, ma'aster."

"If yower game, Tom, I'll go too," said another.

By the time Queensmead returned with the ropes there was no lack of willing helpers, and the party immediately set forth. When they arrived at the pit Colwyn said that it would be best for two men to descend by separate ropes, so as to be able to carry Charles to the surface in a blanket if he were injured, and not killed. Colwyn had brought a blanket from the inn for the purpose.

"I'll go down, for one," said the seaman who had acted as spokesman in the bar. "I'm used to tying knots and slinging a hammock, so maybe I can make it a bit easier for the poor chap if he's not killed outright."

"And I'll go with you," said Colwyn.

Mr. Cromering drew the detective aside.

"My good friend," he said, "do you think it is wise for you to descend? This man Charles, if he is still alive, may be actuated by feelings of revenge towards you, and seek to do you an injury."

"I am not afraid of that," returned Colwyn. "I laid the trap for him, and it is my duty to go down and bring him up."

Colwyn left the chief constable and returned to the pit. The next moment he and the seaman commenced the descent. They carried electric torches, and took with them a blanket and a third rope. They were carefully lowered until the torches they carried twinkled more faintly, and finally vanished in the gloom. A little while afterwards the strain on the ropes slackened. The rescuers had reached the bottom of the pit. A period of waiting ensued for those on top, until a jerk of the ropes indicated the signal for drawing up again. The men on the surface pulled steadily. Soon the torches were once more visible down the pit, and then the lanterns on the surface revealed Colwyn and the fisherman, supporting between them a limp bundle wrapped in the blanket, and tied to the third rope. As they reached the air they were helped out, and the burden they carried was laid on the ground near the mouth of the pit. The blanket fell away, exposing the face of Charles, waxen and still in the rays of the light which fell upon it.

"Dead?" whispered Mr. Cromering.

"Dying," returned Colwyn. "His back is broken."

The dying man unclosed his eyelids, and his dark eyes, keen and brilliant as ever, roved restlessly over the group who were standing around him. They rested on Colwyn, and he lifted a feeble hand and beckoned to him. The detective knelt beside him, and rested his head on his arm. The white lips formed one word:

"Closer."

Colwyn bent his head nearer, and those standing by could see the dying man whispering into the detective's ear. He spoke with an effort for some minutes, and hurriedly, like one who knew that his time was short. Then he stopped suddenly, and his head fell back grotesquely, like a broken doll's. Colwyn felt his heart, and rose to his feet.

"He is dead," he said.

29

"There are several things that I do not understand," said Superintendent Galloway to Colwyn a little later. "How were you able to decide so quickly that Benson had told the truth when he declared that he had not committed the murder, after he had made the damning admission that he had removed the body?"

"Partly because it was extremely unlikely that Benson could have invented a story which fitted so nicely with the facts. The slightest mistake in his times would have proved him to be a liar. But I had more than that to go upon. I said this afternoon that my reconstruction was not wholly satisfactory, because there were several loose ends in it. At that time I believed he was the murderer, and I was anxious to frighten the truth out of him in order to see where my reconstruction was at fault. His story proved that my original conception of the crime was the correct one, and my mistake was in departing from it, and ignoring some of my original clues in order to square the new facts with a fresh theory. I should never have lost sight of my first conviction that there were two persons in Mr. Glenthorpe's room the night he was murdered.

"When Benson told his story I asked myself, Could Charles' conduct be dictated by the desire to have a hold over Benson—with a view to blackmail later on? But he was not likely to risk his own neck by becoming an accomplice in the concealment of the murdered man's body! Charles, if he were innocent himself, must have thought that Benson was the murderer. It was impossible that he could have come to any other conclusion. He discovers a man washing blood off his hands at midnight, and this man admits to him that he has just come from a room which he had no right to enter, and found a dead man there. Why had Charles believed—or pretended to believe—Benson's story?

"It came to me suddenly, with the recollection of the line under the murdered man's window—one of the clues which I had discarded—and the whole of this baffling sinister mystery became clear in my mind. The murder was committed by Charles, who got out of the window by which he had entered just before Benson came into the room. Charles saw a light in the room he had left, and returned to the window to investigate. Crouching outside the window, he saw Benson in the room, examining the body, and it came into his mind as he watched that his employer had conceived the same idea as himself—had seized on the presence of a stranger staying at the inn in order to rob Mr. Glenthorpe, hoping that the crime would be attributed to the man who slept in the next room. Charles was quick to see how Benson's presence in the room might be turned to his own advantage. Charles had taken precautions, in committing the murder, to leave clues in the room which should direct suspicion to Penreath, but the innkeeper's visit to the room suggested to him an even better plan for securing his own safety. When Benson left the room Charles got through the window again, and followed him downstairs.

"Charles' story, told to me when he was dying, filled in the gaps which I have omitted. He said that he watched the whole of Benson's movements from the window. He saw him searching for the money, saw him feel the body, and saw the blood on his hands. When Benson turned to leave the room he forgot the candle, and it was then that the idea of following him leapt into Charles' mind. He divined that Benson would go downstairs and wash the blood off his hands. Charles' idea was to go after him and surprise him in the act. He followed him swiftly, and was never more than a few feet behind. While Benson was striking a match and lighting the kitchen candle Charles slipped into his own room, lit his own candle, and then emerged from his door as though he had been disturbed in his sleep. The rest of his plan was easily carried out through the fears of Benson, who agreed, in his own interests, to conceal the body of the man whom the other had murdered.

"The clue by which Penreath was virtually convicted—the track of bootmarks to the pit—was an accidental one so far as Charles was concerned. It is strange to think that Chance, which removed the clues Charles deliberately placed in the room, should have achieved Charles' aim by directing suspicion to Penreath in a different, yet more convincing manner.

"The murderer's revelation clears up those points which I was unable to settle this afternoon. He entered Mr. Glenthorpe's room during the heaviest part of the storm. He carried a box, under his arm, because he was too short to get into the window without something to stand on, he shielded himself from the rain with an umbrella, which got caught on the nail by the window, and he lit a tallow candle which he had brought from the bar.

"Another clue, which I originally discovered and laid aside, is also explained. The wound in Mr. Glenthorpe's body struck me as an unusual one. You heard Sir Henry Durwood say, in answer to my questions, that the blow was a slanting one, struck from the left side, entering almost parallel with the ribs, yet piercing the heart on the right side. The manner in which Mr. Glenthorpe's arms were thrown out, his legs drawn up, proved that he was lying on his back when murdered. For that reason, the direction of the blow suggested Charles as the murderer."

"I am afraid I do not follow you there," said Mr. Cromering.

"Charles had a malformed right hand; his left hand was his only serviceable one. The blow that killed Mr. Glenthorpe struck me at the time as a left-handed blow.

The natural direction of a right-handed blow, with the body in such a position, would be from right to left—not from left to right. But, after considering this point carefully, I came to the conclusion that the blow might have been struck by a right-handed man. I was wrong."

"I do not think you have much cause to blame yourself," said the chief constable. "You were right in your original conception of the crime, and right in your later reconstruction in every particular except—"

"Except that I picked the wrong man," said Colwyn, with a slightly bitter laugh. "My consolation is that Benson's confession brought the truth to light, as I expected it would."

"It took you to see the truth," said Galloway. "I should never have picked it. I suppose there has never been a case like it."

"There is nothing new—not even in the annals of crime," returned Colwyn. "But this was certainly a baffling and unusual case. The murderer was such a deep and subtle scoundrel that I feel a respect for his intelligence, perverted though it was. His master stroke was the disposal of the body. That shielded him from suspicion as completely as an alibi. I put aside my first suspicion of him largely because I realised that it was impossible for a man with a deformed arm to carry away the body. Such a sardonic situation as a murderer persuading another man that he was likely to be suspected of the murder unless he removed the body was one that never occurred to me. That, at all events, is something new in my experience."

"It is a wonder that Charles, with his deformed arm, was able to go down the pit and conceal the money," said the chief constable.

"He did not go down very far. It is not a difficult matter to climb down the creepers inside with the support of one hand, and he was able to use the other sufficiently to thrust the small peg into the soft earth. He first hid the money in the breakwater wall, being too careful and clever to hide it in the pit until after the inquest. When he had concealed it in the pit he revived the story of the White Lady of the Shrieking Pit so as to keep the credulous villagers away from the spot. He need not have taken that precaution, because the hiding place was an excellent one, and it was only by chance that I discovered the money when I descended the pit. But he left nothing to chance. The use of the umbrella on the night of the murder proves that. Murderers do not usually carry umbrellas, but he did, because he feared that if his clothes got wet they might be seen in his room the following day, and direct suspicion to him. He chose to commit the crime when the storm was at its height because he thought he was safest from the likelihood of discovery then.

"The callous scoundrel told me with his last breath that he was waiting until Penreath was safely hanged before disappearing with the money. When he opened the door to us to-night, he knew that he was at the end of his tether, and he decided to try to bolt. He realised that Benson would tell the truth when he was questioned and, although the innkeeper's story did not implicate him directly, he did our common intelligence the justice to believe that, through his dupe's confession, we should arrive at the truth."

THE END

Now from the Resurrected Press

The Hampstead Mystery

High Court Justice Sir Horace Fewbanks found shot dead in his Hampstead home, a butler with a criminal past, a scorned lover and a hint of scandal. These are the elements of the *Hampstead Mystery* that Detective Inspector Chippenfield of Scotland Yard must unravel with the assistance of the ambitious Detective Rolfe. But will he be able to sort out the tangled threads of this case and arrest the culprit before he is upstaged by the celebrated gentleman detective Crewe. Follow the details of this amazing case at it plays out across Hampstead, London and Scotland until it reaches a stunning conclusion in the courts of the Old Bailey.

The Hampstead Mystery
by John R. Watson & Arthur J. Rees
RPM -101

Visit www.resurrectedpress.com to order now.

Other Resurrected Press Mysteries

From the pen of R. Austin Freeman

Dr. John Thorndyke - Lecturer on Medical Jurisprudence and Forensic Medicine. Before Bones, before CSI, before Quincy, M.E – there was Dr. John Thorndyke solving the most baffling cases of Edwardian London using the latest tools of medical science. Read about his cases in:

The Eye of Osiris
John Bellingham, noted Egyptologist has vanished not once but twice in the same day. Now Dr, Thorndyke must unravel the tangled claims on his estate, solve the riddle of the missing man and find the "Eye of Osiris".

The Mystery of 31 New Inn
When Dr. Jervis is whisked away in a coach with no windows to an unknown location to treat a man in a coma from undivulged causes it is Dr. Thorndyke who must come up with the solution.

The Red Thumb Mark
The first of Dr. Thorndyke's cases finds him trying to prove the innocence of a young man accused of being a diamond thief despite the fact that his finger print was found at the scene of the crime.

John Thorndyke's Cases
More cases of medical mysteries as told by his trusted assistant Jervis, M.D. Eight stories of crime and deduction in Edwardian London.

Visit www.resurrectedpress.com

Other Resurrected Press Mysteries

Mysteries on a Train

Before the Orient Express there was:

The Rome Express by Arthur Griffiths
A man is found dead in his first class sleeping compartment on the express from Rome to Paris. Who was his murderer? The Countess? The English General? His brother the clergy man? The maid who has disappeared? Is the French justice system up to solving the crime? Read about it in The Rome Express.

The Passenger from Calais by Arthur Griffiths
Colonel Basil Annesley finds he is the only passenger on the train from Calais to Lucerne. That is until a mysterious woman shows up at the last minute to book a compartment. Who is after her? What is her secret? Is she a criminal or a victim? Read about it in The Passenger from Calais

Visit us at www.resurrectedpress.com

The Fictional Detective
by Greg Fowlkes

Who killed Ezekial O. Handler?

A beautiful dame, a hard-boiled private eye – and a dead body.

It started like any other case. When a famous writer dies in a mysterious car crash, private detective Frank Slade is called in to find answers, but all he finds is more questions. Who killed Ezekial Handler? Who is Janet Nielsen and why is she so interested in finding out? Who is leaving the neatly typed clues? And as Slade tries to find answers to these questions he starts to wonder if the ultimate answer will threaten his very existence.

Read about it in
The Fictional Detective

Visit www.thefictionaldetective.com

About Resurrected Press

A division of Intrepid Ink, LLC, Resurrected Press is dedicated to bringing high quality, vintage books back into publication. See our entire catalogue and find out more at www.ResurrectedPress.com.

About Intrepid Ink, LLC

Intrepid Ink, LLC provides full publishing services to authors of fiction and non-fiction books, eBooks and websites. From editing to formatting, from publishing to marketing, Intrepid Ink gets your creative works into the hands of the people who want to read them. Find out more at www.IntrepidInk.com.

www.ingramcontent.com/pod-product-compliance
Lightning Source LLC
Chambersburg PA
CBHW071051250626
47159CB00002B/444